HOLDING THE REINS

HOLDING THE REINS

A Silver Pines Novel

PAISLEY HOPE

DELL BOOKS

NEW YORK

2024 Dell Trade Paperback Edition

Copyright © 2024 by Paisley Hope

Excerpt from *Training the Heart* by Paisley Hope copyright 2024 © Paisley Hope

Published in the United States by Dell, an imprint of Random House, a division of Penguin Random House LLC, New York.

DELL and the D colophon are registered trademarks of Penguin Random House LLC.

Originally self-published in the United States by the author and subsequently in the United Kingdom by Century, an imprint of Cornerstone. Cornerstone is a part of the Penguin Random House group of companies in 2024.

This book contains an excerpt from the forthcoming book *Training the Heart* by Paisley Hope. This excerpt has been set for this edition only and may not reflect the final content of the forthcoming edition.

ISBN 978-0-593-97711-8
Ebook ISBN 978-1-738-02945-7

Printed in the United States of America on acid-free paper

randomhousebooks.com

2 4 6 8 9 7 5 3 1

To all my babes who know they can be strong, modern women, yet still shamelessly drop to their knees like the good fucking girls they are the moment their cowboys tell them to.

A Note from the Author

This book is intended for people age eighteen plus. It includes, but is not limited to, open-door sexual content, minor breath play, alcohol consumption, talk of a cheating and manipulative ex, death of family members through dream sequence/ flashbacks, talk of therapy, trauma, and dealing with tragedy. Please proceed with this knowledge. I trust you know what you're comfortable with.

HOLDING THE REINS

CHAPTER ONE
CeCe

"Oh, my dear! You dropped your hair curler thingy! Dear!"

I stop dead in my tracks and look down at the suitcase I'm struggling to haul behind me. The back pocket is unzipped just enough, and Mrs. Danforth—my best friend's grandmother—is calling to me in her sing-song voice, holding my teal blue vibrator in the air as she chases me down through the Car Depot lobby.

My face instantly heats and turns a fine shade of pink as I move quickly to meet her, keeping my gaze on the spotless marble floor so I don't have to meet the eyes of way too many people I've known since childhood.

I consider crawling under the big white reception desk and hiding there until they close the place at five. This is the last thing I need today—my flight was delayed, and I cried like a baby on the plane because I left my Kindle at my condo... correction, my old condo. I just want to get home, change into my pajamas and unpack, but something tells me I won't be able to do that. Because even though it's my first night home, it's

Sunday, so I know I'll be lured to The Horse and Barrel with Olivia and Ginger.

I snatch the vibrator quickly from her weathered hands as she leans in and gives me a wink and a grin.

"Was I sly, dear?" she whispers.

My mouth falls open. *Fuck my life.* She knows what it is.

"Nothing to be ashamed of, honey. A girl's gotta do what a girl's gotta do," she says as she pats my arm.

Can Jesus choose this moment to come back? I could really use an apocalypse right about now.

"T-Thank you, Granny Dan," I mutter, stuffing my Saturday nights into my bag and making sure the damn thing is zipped tight.

"Be sure to say hi to your mama, CeCe." She waves.

I bulldoze my way to the door, hoping Ginger is waiting on the other side to drive me the last leg of my trip home.

Unfortunately for me, she isn't, so I sit on the bench outside the car rental depot and marvel at my luck. Home for five minutes and I already have one embarrassing moment under my belt. Off to a great start. I accept my fate and toss my sunglasses on, praying Granny Dan keeps her mouth shut.

It's a typical early July afternoon in Laurel Creek, Kentucky. The sun is still high above Sugarland Mountain in the distance, and shoppers are milling about down the town's one and only main street.

I can smell baked goods from Spicer's Sweets, our resident trendy coffee shop, and see the local patrons carrying bags from our upscale home décor boutique, Jennings Mercantile. It's all very quaint and *Anytown, USA* like.

I take a deep breath of fresh mountain air and check my phone to see if Ginger has messaged me to indicate why she's late, not that I should be surprised she is. Ginger Danforth always flows to her own routine. I'm just putting my phone back in my purse when I hear the tell-tale announcement loud and clear that Ginger has arrived in the downtown core. Dolly Parton blaring full blast from the rolled down windows of her white VW Bug that is currently careening around the corner of Main Street.

I stand and wave her down on the side of the road, and she pulls up, almost onto the curb. My best friend has never been known for her driving skills.

"Get in, quick," she says as she pops the trunk and looks around like she needs to get the hell out of dodge, and fast.

"Did you do something illegal again? Cole can only get you out of trouble so many times," I grumble.

I put my suitcase in her trunk, and make my way to the passenger side of the door.

"You have it backwards, babe. Having Cole arrest me would be a reason *to* break the law. That man can put me in handcuffs any day of the week."

I swat at her for the lewd comment about my older brother who just happens to be the Deputy Sheriff and then smile before reaching over to give her a big squeeze.

"Ew... and hi."

She grins at me and pushes her sunglasses back up.

"Alright, buckle up, baby. We need to get out of here before anyone else in town sees that pretty teal heat you're packing in your suitcase.

I groan and put my head in my hands.

"Did your Granny text you the moment I walked out the damn door?"

She looks at me like I must be crazy.

"No, she called me, why do you think I was late? I had to pull over and laugh for five straight minutes." Ginger winks and mortification washes over me.

Note to self: you're home now, where everyone will know everything you do before you even think of doing it.

Ten minutes later, we make our way under the arches of Silver Pines, my family's full-service equestrian ranch, and a bitter-sweet mixture of peace and grief settles into my bones with the view of our ranch logo. The half a mile long, white fenced drive always looks the same, no matter what. It's my haven, my safe space; and even with Dad no longer here, it's still my only true home and the closest I'll ever feel to him again. I haven't been home since he died in January and the grief is no less crushing now than it was then. The old, massive white farmhouse, the 'big house,' comes into view in the distance.

"So, have you heard from the good-for-nothing prick again?" Ginger asks, doing her best to distract me.

"Not in the last hour," I say and sigh. "He's just malfunctioning because I was the one who left him. How dare I. The great Andrew Waterfield couldn't keep his fiancée? What will Page Six say?"

Ginger snorts. "He should've thought about that before he stuck his overzealous dick in every woman under thirty in Seattle."

"I think he got the message that I'm gone for good. I wrapped my ring up in the thong I found in his jacket pocket and left it in the middle of the kitchen table." I start laughing and Ginger's mouth falls open.

"You bad ass bitch, you." Ginger shakes her head with a smile that tells me she's impressed.

"I should've seen it before this winter. The late nights, the trips away, the elite club of assistants always accompanying him and his colleagues everywhere."

"People tend to trust the man they're engaged to; this is not on you."

I nod and turn to let the sun hit my face through the window.

In my defense, Andrew is a rich, gorgeous, manipulative asshole that swept me off my feet my freshman year at Washington University. I wanted to believe in true love, so much so that I let it blind me. It took me over seven years, and my dad's dying words to help me see the light. Finally, I went with my gut and got the hell out of Seattle and the toxic cloud that hung over us. I'm only twenty-five; I spent my crazy, wild years playing the aristocratic, soon-to-be wifey, and now, I just want to see my family, have fun, hopefully find a job and breathe.

As we pull up to the house and the gravel crunches under Ginger's tires, a million memories and images flash through my mind. Grief is the oddest thing—it hits you hard in the moments you'd least expect. Cream soda in the pantry my dad used to love to drink on a hot summer day over ice, the old rake leaning against the house that created the most incredible leaf jumps in the fall when I was young, the tree swing where he pushed me on countless hot afternoons. Grief swells in my chest, overwhelming me. I half expect to see him bound through the front door, but I know in my head he never will again.

"I'm home, Dad," I whisper.

Ginger squeezes my hand beside me. "He knows, babe."

CHAPTER TWO
CeCe

"Hell, baby, I feel like I haven't seen you in a month of Sundays," my mother, Jolene—aka, Mama Jo—calls to me through the kitchen.

She prances into the living room like a breath of fresh air, chasing my somber mood away instantly. Skinny jeans, bare feet, Farrah Fawcett hair tied back with a pink scarf and a Brooks & Dunn t-shirt hanging off her shoulder.

"Let me look at you." She smiles as she leaps into my arms.

Wade, my oldest and grumpiest brother pushes his way through the front door with our old golden retriever, Harley. Harley nuzzles up against me like I'm his favorite human. I'm officially covered in fur and slobber but he's the cutest dog alive, so I'll forgive him as I rustle behind his ears.

"CeCe Rae," Wade greets in his gruff, settled voice, tugging on my ponytail, always adding in my middle name.

"Sergeant," I retort naturally.

He has a lot on his shoulders—our entire ranch for one, but it hits me so much more now than it ever did before. He looks exactly like my dad and just seeing his face reminds me that my dad is still here.

I let go of Harley and give Wade a big squeeze. He tenses a little as he always does. He's not the touchy-feely type, but I know his heart is somewhere under that tough exterior.

"I'll get your bags; Mama has you set up in Stardust." He mentions one of the five tiny help cabins, each named after Willie Nelson albums on our ranch. Spirit, Stardust, Blue Eyes, Legend and Bluegrass.

"I got you new linens and it's all clean and fresh for you, darlin'. I even stocked it with food."

"Thank you, Mama," I say as she tucks an errant strand of hair behind my ear, keeping her hands at the side of my face to look at me.

Jolene Ashby is still beautiful, and vibrant at fifty-eight and she never takes shit from anyone. She's a true free spirit. I strive to be more like her every day.

"You look like you've been crying, baby."

I make the universal sound for "yeah-huh."

"So, how many times has that good-for-nothing bastard called you?"

I laugh at her assessment of my ex-fiancé, and sit down on the edge of the living room sofa. She looks at me expectantly, hands on her hips, but I don't answer her, I just sigh in response because at this moment I'm not ready to talk about Andrew with everyone.

"Can I just have tonight? I promise I'll fill you in tomorrow, all the details. I just want to breathe in the fresh air, unpack, and hide in my cabin with a book."

Ginger creeps in from the shadows of the kitchen at the back of the house like my stay home plan summoned her.

"Oh, no you won't." Her boots make a quick tapping sound on the floor as she comes into the living room with a glass of Mama Jo's sweet tea. "I already told everyone you're home, we're not missing Sangria Sunday. You can sleep tomorrow, no time for wallowing."

"Who's everyone?" I groan.

She flashes me a gorgeous, perfect smile, her pretty caramel eyes dance with mischief and her deep brown natural curls frame her face. She's always been one of the prettiest girls I've ever seen in real life.

"The girls, of course. It is ladies' night after all." She grabs my wrist.

"Now let's get some dinner into you and get ready. You are going to look like the single hottie you are."

I look at my mom for help but she raises her hands like she wants nothing to do with it.

"Beats staying home alone with your vibrator." She giggles.

"Mother!" I yell as she and Ginger double over in laughter.

This goddamn town.

Two hours later, Mama Jo and Ginger's wardrobe consultation service has put together an outfit I would never, *ever* wear in public at any other time. But, as they so eloquently put it, "the whole town knows I have a personal stash of sex toys now, so I may as well own it."

There are more clothes spread out than this space can handle. My cabin is small, almost like a little apartment, but this one is my favorite because it has a big picture window over the kitchen sink, that looks out to one of the large horse corals on our property. And in the distance, you can see Sugarland Mountain in all her glory.

Mama has it set up like I've lived here forever—complete

with decorative candles, throw pillows, and magazines on the living room coffee table. It only has one bedroom and one bathroom with dark cabin walls, but it's perfect for me to start over in.

Back in the old days on our ranch, we had multiple horse trainers live on site, especially during my dad's derby years. For the last ten years, we've had Wade leading the pack, so two of these cabins usually sit empty now that Cole lives in town with my favorite girl—my seven-year-old niece, Mabel.

I look myself over in the full length mirror that we moved to the living room for this makeshift fashion show.

I grunt and groan as I ask myself if I'm actually going to wear this: a dark jean mini skirt I keep pulling down to try to get it to at least meet my mid-thigh, and a red, lacy camisole of Ginger's my breasts barely fit into.

I was blessed and cursed as an early bloomer but I've at least grown into my curves now. I adjust the layers of necklaces and big gold hoop earrings that Ginger added. She's also styled my long hair into a mass of muted blonde waves and curls. I've never had so much hairspray in it, even at my prom.

"It just needs something," Ginger says as she chews her bottom lip. "Take those sandals off," she commands, raising one French manicured finger in the air.

"I don't have any other shoes unpacked—"

"Don't mess with my creativity, just take them off."

She pulls her ivory colored Lucchese boots off her feet and tosses them to me. We've been sharing shoes since seventh grade.

"Yes," she says. "Put these on first." She tosses me a pair of high ivory socks from the middle of my bed.

"You want me to wear your babies?" I question. She rarely parts with these beloved boots.

"Yes, you need them tonight more than I do."

9

I do as she says, popping them on and turning to see the finished product.

"Yes! Just like Dolly baby, if Dolly had smaller tits." She winks and I toss a pillow at her from the couch.

"Just like Dolly," I mutter as I look at my reflection in the mirror. Ginger kisses Mama Jo on the cheek and turns to me.

"Alright, get ready for some sangria and unsavory decisions!" She tosses on my sandals, locks arms with me, and pulls me out the door.

The sun is just thinking about setting as we get in the car and wave to my mom—she's still standing on the front porch of my cabin.

"Bye, Mama," I call out the window.

"Have fun, girls! Break some hearts, not the law."

I giggle, shaking my head at her as we start the car and Jason Aldean croons through the sound system.

I'm so far from Seattle, and for the first time since I made the decision to leave Andrew, I feel totally, completely free.

The Horse and Barrel is alive with women from all over town, and a few brave men that don't want to miss out on their after-dinner beer. Sangria Sundays have been a ritual in Laurel Creek for as long as I remember. It's a night just for the girls, the best country music plays through the vintage sound system; we dance, gossip, and enjoy cheap drinks, especially the house made sangria. Everyone in town knows you don't seek good customer service from a woman on Mondays in Laurel Creek. Chances are, they're probably still a little hungover.

The crowd isn't disappointing tonight. The place is

packed and my girls and I are sandwiched into the corner of the only rustic cowboy bar Laurel Creek has to offer. It's been a couple of years since I've been inside but I can't see much of a difference—aside from some new pine floors. I look around and take in the antique tin signs that adorn the entire back wall over the stage where house bands play on Friday and Saturdays. Jack Daniels bottles have been hollowed out and made into wall sconces over the dark rustic wood walls. Cozy booths have dim chandeliers hanging over them, and in the middle of the wide open space is a large dance floor. The entire east wall is a bar complete with neon lights and our town mascot, Archibald the Tiger, gracing the center as a large neon Tiger shrine.

"Someone remind me why the hell the giant Tiger is hanging there again? It freaks me out, it's like it's looking at me," Avery Pope, the newest and youngest addition to our crew asks. I've just met her but she's sweet and funny. Ginger tells me she moved here two months ago from Lexington to teach figure skating at the town sports facility. I've heard all about her. Apparently, she drinks my girls under the table and I can see why as she gulps down what's left in her glass.

"Well, he's a hero," I say. We all love to tell this story and I'm an official expert after writing a paper on him in eighth grade.

"When the traveling circus used to come to town—"

"In like, the 1800's," Ginger pipes up.

"Yes, 1889," I correct. "Archibald chased another tiger that got loose from the circus—a younger tiger, some even say a cub. The cub was on the train tracks and Archibald sensed the train was coming so he chased the other tiger out of the way and was hit by the train himself. He sacrificed his life to save the cub, it's our town legend. There's a statue of him near Cave Run Park."

"Aww..." Avery says.

"You know that's all bullshit right?" a deep and even voice says from beside me. One I know well.

I brace myself and turn to meet the face I know is waiting for me.

"Is not," I argue, one eyebrow raised.

"It's true. Turns out Archibald was just a selfish asshole that always tried to escape from the circus, probably because they treated those animals horrifically." A corded, inked forearm places a handful of napkins on the center of the table and I note the number ten, in Roman numerals incorporated into honeysuckle vines that disappear up into his rolled up flannel sleeve.

"Anyway, he got away one night and was all by his lonesome when the train hit him. The whole 'saving a cub' story was made up to make him appear like a hero. Good press. But none of it was actually true."

Ginger and I gasp.

"How dare you?" Olivia Sutton, my other best friend and final portion to our lifelong trio pipes up.

"You get away from our table with those lies, and stop tarnishing our town lore Nash Carter!" She wags a finger at him.

He chuckles at Olivia before he responds.

"Alright, well I was bringing you this, just to welcome Rae home, but I guess I'll just give it to another table then?" Nash holds up a fresh pitcher of the best sangria in three counties, grinning at us and goddammit, if he isn't the most devastating specimen of a man I've ever seen. He always has been, but his looks are even more perfect than I remember and the worst part is, he *knows* it. He uses it to his benefit and I, for one, have had enough of men like that to last me a lifetime.

"No, no, no," Ginger says, "ashing him a wide smile. "No need to rush off, I'm sure we can work something out. I guess there could be two sides to every story. We'll consider your version of Archibald's history. Thanks for bringing us a refill... on the house, Nashby?" She winks and pats his forearm, calling him by a blend of his first name and my last name. He's like my parent's fourth child and has been since he was a teenager.

He nods and puts it on the table.

"My pleasure, ladies. Enjoy. Avery, see you tomorrow."

She smiles at him and nods, fresh-faced. "Sure thing."

I look her over—long dark hair, a skater's figure, petite but strong, tan skin and olive eyes. She is beautiful and young and doesn't know yet that he'll probably just use her until he's had his fill. He's definitely banging her, I decide.

Nash puts a hand on my shoulder and leans down before he speaks. "Good to see you, Rae," he says in his deep tenor, his eyes momentarily connecting with mine, as he gives me a gentle squeeze that makes me feel sort of melty all over.

I watch him over my shoulder as he walks away, trying to make sense of what is going on. Nash 'The Rocket' Carter— record breaking, slap shot scoring, Stanley cup winning, Laurel Creek fan favorite hockey star and my brother Wade's best friend—now works as a *server* at the Horse and Barrel?

"I know what you're thinking." Olivia leans across the table. Her copper hair falls around her shoulders as she does, and her glossy pink lips turn up into a grin.

"He has been helping Rocco Pressley since he retired and moved back here in April. Rocco just can't do it anymore, but he can't let it go either. Nash doesn't even get paid. He just apparently can't sit still."

"I didn't hear that," I say nonchalantly as I let myself take in the sight of Nash on the other side of the bar. He's offen-sively gorgeous. I'll admit it. Everything about him is ominous and big. At 6'4, he towers over me by more than a foot. He's the rugged type with dark wavy hair, close-cut stubble and a wide jaw. He looks like he should be leaning back in a wooden chair, drawing off a cigar in his flannel and Wranglers. His stacked, muscular form has always been so perfect. Ever since the days of playing hockey with my brothers in the driveway or shoveling hay, shirtless at eighteen on our ranch as I watched him from my bedroom window. Although, it seems his NHL years have honed his body to almost godlike chiseled proportions, judging by the way his upper arms are testing the limits of his flannel right now. I notice he's added even more ink to his skin since I saw him briefly in January at my dad's funeral. Vines creep out of his shirt collar and trail up the side of his neck now. Nash's eyes meet mine across the room for a split second before I look away. They've always sucked me in, deep cobalt and intense. They render me a bumbling idiot any time they focus on me.

There's no doubt that Nash Carter is insanely gorgeous, but he's always been a cocky, older brother type that treated me like a pain-in-the-ass kid and tormented me for as long as I can remember—at least until I left for college. He was always showing up at our house with a different girl on any given day, making out with them on our living room sofa when my parents weren't home, with absolutely no regard for me keeping my lunch down. More memories flood my mind of him eating all the snacks in our house, tailgating with my brothers before football games, pulling my hair, knocking my hat off my head, and helping my brothers prank me to their hearts' content.

It's been a long time, but as I watch him exude the same confidence and charisma talking to the bar patrons, while adjusting his Dallas Stars baseball hat, I just know he's still the same.

Nash Carter is a full-of-himself, womanizing superstar, and he's the type of man I just ran half way across the country from.

CHAPTER THREE
Nash

The last thing I ever expected to see midway through my typical Sunday night was that flash of honey-colored hair. No one has hair like hers, it's not even blonde, it's like the color of the sun itself. But here she is. CeCe Rae Ashby, all grown up and in the shortest, tightest mini skirt this bar has ever seen. A skirt that's making me consider dragging her ass out the back door and tying a jacket around her waist because not only did I notice her, so did all the other men in this place.

Thankfully, on ladies' night, the men are few and far between, so I can handle them if any of them get out of line with her.

I picture how her face looked in January, the last time I saw her, as I slice lemons and limes behind the bar. She was so heartbroken and pale then. Puffy, tear-filled eyes, long, black wool dress and her hair in a tight bun. Her dad's funeral. I could only stay in town for one night because I had the All-Star Weekend starting in Nashville the next day. But I had to be there for the family when Wyatt died, at least for the bulk of it.

Every damn one of them has always been there for me, even CeCe.

Aside from that day, it's been at least five years since I've really seen her, but it doesn't matter how much time passes, I fall right back into protective mode—just like when she was younger. It took all three of us boys to watch out for her when she became a teenager. She's still just one of those girls who never understands her own beauty and that makes her all the more enticing to every man in this room. And for reasons I don't understand, I can't seem to take my eyes off of her tonight, either.

The last thing I need on a busy ladies' night is to play CeCe's bodyguard, but if she's here, it's bound to happen, so I suppose I'll be adding that to my list of jobs.

I glance up at the large, framed photo of half the town in this very pub with The Stanley Cup that I brought home three years ago. The locals love having a hometown hockey player, but it means I always have to be on my game. Sometimes it's exhausting but I try not to complain, if all I have to do is sign a few autographs and offer cheap drinks to keep this downtown core alive, I'll do it. This town has always been good to me, and watching it thrive gives me a tiny bit of peace—something I don't get a lot of.

I keep myself busy slinging whiskeys and mixing sangria pitchers as CeCe sashays her tipsy little self out to the dance floor an hour later with Olivia and Ginger—Charlie's *Not Angels*, that's what the Ashby boys and I used to call them after bailing them out of every situation imaginable. Drunken party pick-ups when they were in high school, covering for them when they smoked pot and almost burned the damn house down making pancakes. These girls were a full-time job. I wonder, as I wipe the bar down, why CeCe is even here. Last I'd heard, she was engaged to some hot shot lawyer in Seattle.

I can't help but grin as I watch her. She looks as far away from Seattle as possible right now, with three glasses of sangria under her non-existent belt, and Morgan Wallen on the sound system. Out there on that dance floor, she's all southern and all Kentucky. I restock the glasses at the bar as Shania Twain's "Man! I Feel Like a Woman" comes on and the crowd goes crazy. It's their damn anthem.

Visions of CeCe in braces and a long braid dancing in the Ashby living room to Shania's Rock This Country tour flash through my mind. I can't help but smirk at the memory, she'd just get into a rhythm and then crash into something clumsily and cuss.

"You feeling social tonight?" Asher, the weekend bartender, asks, knowing this is out of the ordinary. He came from New York to run Laurel Creek's Fire Department and he's been working here since before I came home and jumped in. I couldn't say why the hell he moonlights on his weekends off, but he's quiet, always sober and scary-as-fuck looking so it helps to keep things in line around here when he is tending bar. I grin at him. Normally, I come out and check on things periodically, but I mostly work in Rocco's office, which is starting to feel like my office, on Sunday nights. Of course, he's one of those men that notices everything, probably why he's a good firefighter.

"Yeah, just keeping an eye on Wade and Cole Ashby's little sister."

I nod in her direction and Asher looks toward the girls.

"So that's CeCe Ashby, is it?" He looks her over in a non-threatening way but it irks me just the same. I can't get a read on the guy, even after four months of working with him, as hard as I try. "Well, I hate to tell you this but every man in here is keeping an eye on her. Nothing like a pretty, new smile to get the attention of drunken men."

I grit my teeth and look her way. I ponder the drag-her-outside-and-toss-a-coat-on-her option as I avert my eyes, trying not to notice how her waist curves to the small of her back and the way her long, thick hair meets it. She certainly doesn't look clumsy now as she sways to the music. Times have changed.

Just as I'm about to go back to the office so I can stop myself from feeling like a depraved pervert, all hell breaks loose in the crowd and our resident *Not Angels* are at the center of it, forcing me right out to the dance floor.

"You're lucky I don't smack that sleazy little smirk right off your face, Gemma." I hear CeCe yell as I approach, her southern drawl is back in full force. Kentucky fire rises in her emerald eyes, as Olivia holds her back.

"What kind of a mother tells her daughter she's coming to see her then gives up her only night to hang out in *a pub?*" she barks out.

"Says the girl in the booth next to me sucking back her second pitcher," Gemma scoffs.

Gemma is a real treat and Cole's ex-wife. She's basically dumped Mabel on Cole full-time for the last two years while she revisits her youth. Having these two together a few pitchers deep is bad fucking news.

"I don't have an amazing daughter I could be spending time with, but *you* do."

"Come on, honey, she's not worth it." Ginger leans in to CeCe's ear.

"Let her wallow in her self-pity and shattered dreams. She's a worthless little slut anyway, cheating on Cole with half the damn town." Ginger puts a hand on Gemma's shoulder. "Isn't that right, darlin'?" Ginger smirks sweetly just before Gemma lunges at her.

Fuck me.

It's a flurry of nails and long hair flying as I cut right into the middle and pull Ginger and CeCe off Gemma, while Victor, my bouncer, holds Olivia back.

"I'm gonna have to call the cops on you girls. Jesus, it's your first night back, Rae, and you're already getting yourself into shit."

"Please call Cole, let's get his fine, grumpy ass down here." Ginger giggles as I roll my eyes.

"She started it." CeCe points at Gemma, and I grin. Fierce protector of her brother and the damage his first and only wife did to him.

"What are you even doing here, CeCe Rae? Your hot lawyer realized he out-classed you?" Gemma slurs, her hand on her hip.

CeCe lunges back at her. I take matters into my own hands this time and toss CeCe right over my shoulder, as I nod to Victor and Asher to get Gemma and her crew out of here. I cover CeCe's backside with my hand so no one can see up her skirt. Looks like I have to drag her ass out of here after all.

"Nash Everett Carter, you put me down right now. I'm gonna beat that tramp's ass for what she said about Cole."

"Settle down, slugger, you're gonna do no such thing." I chuckle as I push through my office door and drop her onto the leather chair in front of my desk. Her hair tumbles over her shoulders and her chest is heaving with alcohol-induced fury.

"A couple glasses of sangria and you turn right back into a wild child, Rae?" I ask, folding my arms across my chest.

"She hurt Cole, she hurt Mabel. You should kick her out of your bar."

I lean down so I can look into her eyes and try to calm her down. I grip both her wrists on the arms of the chair.

"Already done, but you're gonna have to get used to seeing her if you're home for longer than this weekend. She works at the hair salon and she's here every Sunday. She's usually peaceful," I add.

CeCe looks up at me, her eyes are filled with something I can't place. "I'm home to stay."

Ginger and Olivia bust in, laughing uncontrollably.

"Just like old times, Nashby." Ginger pats me on the shoulder.

I shake my head at her. This little shit disturber was always the one that started everything and CeCe was always her wingwoman, her back up, and caught in the crossfire.

"If you call causing all sorts of trouble 'old times' then yeah, just like old times..."

"Always, it's the only way to live honey," she retorts.

With my hands on my hips, I look up and huff out a sigh before turning back to Cece, still sitting in the chair.

"Can you go back out there and keep the peace, Rocky?"

She narrows her eyes at me.

"As long as the trash has been taken out, yes." She stands and fixes herself up as she leans into me. The scent of strawberries and fresh clean shampoo washes over me.

"Be a good boy and send us another one of those on the house pitchers... okay, darlin'?" She pats a perfectly manicured hand on my cheek and it sends an unexpected current straight to my dick.

Cole and Wade's little sister, Cole and Wade's little sister, I repeat in my head. Apparently, my dick doesn't realize that's a hard fucking no.

"I'll be sure to get right on it, ladies," I say sarcastically, removing her hand from my face and ushering them out of my office and back into the crowd.

I make my way back over to the bar shaking my head. Never a dull moment with the *Not Angels.*

"Send that table another pitcher but half the wine and brandy." I pat Asher on the back and he nods.

"Sure thing, boss."

My eyes follow CeCe back out to the dance floor. The way she's moving to "Vice" by Miranda Lambert has me standing behind the bar like an old creep watching her.

Fucking Christ. Home to stay?

I'm gonna need to get a little more desensitized to CeCe Ashby. She's looking like a whirlwind of things right now but the two that stand out the most are really fucking beautiful and really fucking off limits.

CHAPTER FOUR
CeCe

"So he was too busy? For Christmas?" My dad's face is kind but his brow is furrowed, like the weight of my happiness sits on his shoulders.

"Yes, he's got two clients that are settling right now, and he had to stay behind to meet with them."

"And no plans to set an actual wedding date? I was hoping to walk my daughter down the aisle before I check out."

"Dad."

"Sorry, baby, but I know my time is limited and I want to know—no, I need—to know you're happy. You're the most important thing in the world to me. I worry you're not getting what you deserve, which is all the happiness your heart can hold."

I pat his hand across the sofa.

"Andrew loves me."

"But does he love you enough? A man should be there for you no matter what, so long as the creek don't rise."

I laugh at his age-old saying.

"And I'm sorry, baby, but a few clients settling isn't exactly a natural disaster, if that's even what's really going on."

I let the tears slide down my cheeks as I nod. How does my

dad always know? I haven't been happy in months. I have a strong feeling Andrew is sleeping around on me. And when I get home, I'm going to be paying extra attention to him to see if I'm right, but I can't say anything now. The last thing I want to do is cause my sweet dad stress, especially now.

"Promise me something, CeCe Rae." *I look up at his hallow face, a ghost of the face he used to have, a ghost of the man that he used to be. Cancer has ruined him, but experimental treatment this Thanksgiving has given us this last Christmas with him and for that, I'm so grateful.*

I choke back a sob and wipe my tears.

"Anything," *I say.*

"Just don't settle, baby. Find a man that will move heaven and earth for you. A man that knows your worth. You should be his entire heart, always."

"I promise," *I say as I squeeze his hand.*

"Cecilia Rae Ashby, get your shit kickin' ass up!"

My eyes fly open, expecting to see the ceiling of my Seattle bedroom. The moment they open, pain floods my head.

"Ow..." I groan.

"Yeah, I guess so. Jesus Christ, CeCe. Home less than twenty-four-hours and so far you've managed to shock the whole town with your... lady gear"—*Oh God*—"almost get yourself kicked out of the Horse and Barrel, *and* get into a fight with the mother of my child. What are you gonna do today? Set town hall on fire? Push Grady Thompson into traffic on his way to Spicer's Sweets for his morning coffee? I can't always save your ass, you know. It's about time you grow up some."

"Cole... stop shouting at me... my head," I whine as I open one eye to see my pissed-off-as-fuck older brother, the middle child in our family, standing over me. Large and in charge, hands on his hips like he's about to scold me the way he would Mabel if she misbehaved.

"You're scary like this," I mutter as I bury my head in the pillow.

"Good. Maybe you'll learn to behave next time. You ain't sleeping in on my watch, get up."

I groan again.

"Hear you drank the Horse and Barrel out of sangria last night with your band of merry mates."

Dammit, Nash. I'm too hungover for this.

"Water. I need water," I mutter.

"I'm here to hang your curtains and get you settled. I put water and Tylenol on your bedside table. Get up and clean this place up, God's sakes, girl."

"Thank you, Cole."

"You're welcome, asshole." His dark eyes soften. "Glad you're home though," he grunts and I smile into my pillow. I'm the only person on earth besides Mabel that he can't stay angry at.

I chug down the water and Tylenol and lay back in my bed, listening to Cole crash around. After thirty minutes passes, it no longer hurts to open my eyeballs.

I get up reluctantly, tossing on my fluffy fleece robe over my pajamas.

Cole is already hard at work leveling my book shelf when I saunter out to the kitchen rubbing my eyes.

"I sure hope you're planning to unpack and clean up today, it looks like a cyclone went through here."

I look around my living room at the ten different outfits from the night before strewn across my couch.

"You know, I'm not a child. Nash didn't have to tattle tale on me."

"He's just looking out for you is all, CeCe," Cole retorts.

Sure.

24

Cole scrubs his face with his hand. "He said he had to cut you all off last night."

"Nash Carter isn't exactly a saint. I had like, five glasses. It's the sugar that makes me feel bad. I can't help it if he makes the sweetest sangria in three counties."

"Sure... must have been the sugar," Cole chuckles.

"Whatever, Nash judging me about having a good time is like the pot calling the kettle black."

"He wasn't judging you. He was worried about you. He didn't know you and Andrew broke up. He wanted me to know so I could make sure you were okay this morning. He's changed, CeCe. You'd be surprised."

I snort back my laughter and mouth "okay" to him.

"I'll believe it when I see it." I toss my hair into a ponytail.

"I'm going to the big house for breakfast so I can withstand your yelling. I'll be back before you're done with that shelf." I rub my head.

"Need something to soak up all that alcohol?" Cole smirks at me, showing me his dimples and contagious smile.

"Shut up, it was one night."

"Let's hope so, the last thing I need is Gemma saying my little sister beat her ass at our next mediation.

"Sorry. She just said some things, I'm not gonna let her talk about you like that."

"What did she say?" His curiosity is piqued now.

"That you were good for a piece of ass, but that all you cared about was Mabel and would never be able to truly make a woman happy."

His eyebrows relax at my words and his wide, dimpled grin forms as he speaks.

"If that's all she's got, I'm okay with it. I got the prize, I've got Mabes." He walks over and puts a hand on my shoulder.

"No more bar fights, got it?"

I nod like a child.

"Okay, I promise. And Ginger says hi." I grin.

"Fucking Ginger. You ever notice the only time you get in shit, you're with her? Maybe go out with someone different and take it easy on Sangria Sunday, yeah?"

"Thanks for the advice. I'll forget about the time you came home in your boxers and bare feet after Jason Handler's wedding," I joke.

"That was ten years ago, let me live it down." I hear him call as I breeze through the cabin door.

The big house is fairly quiet when I enter, I can faintly hear a John Prine song coming from the kitchen. It's there that I find my mother with yoga pants on and her hair in a long blonde ponytail, similar to mine.

"Morning, Mama Jo," I croak.

"Morning, baby." She turns to glance at me over her shoulder. "Oof... you look like wine and unwise choices."

I grunt in response.

"I'm making bacon and eggs, figured you'd need it after last night."

I pour myself a cup of steaming coffee.

"Please."

I sit down at the kitchen island just as my phone starts to ring. I put my head in my hands. Andrew's second call of the day and it's only nine a.m. I silence it and sip my coffee.

"You might as well face him, or he's never going to go away. You can't avoid him forever. Just tell him what a good for nothing prick he is," my mom says as she fries the bacon.

My phone lights up silently again before I can ever answer her.

"Fine!" I give in, as I stand with my phone. "I'll take it on the porch."

"Take Harley with you, put him on the leash or he'll run

26

halfway to the northside field, and don't be long; this will all be ready in fifteen minutes or so."

The words don't leave her mouth before Harley is at my side looking up at me expectantly. I hook his leash into his collar as I answer Andrew, tucking the phone between my cheek and my shoulder.

"Andrew," I say as I walk the dog towards the door.

"You can't avoid me forever, Cecilia. You've made your point. It's time to come home."

The warm, early July sun hits my face as I make my way onto the wide covered front porch juggling Harley and my coffee.

"I'm not coming back Andrew. It's over between us." I keep my voice calm and even.

"The hell you aren't. We have a life here, friends, we're engaged, for Christ's sake."

I'm just about to lose my shit when Harley's leash wraps around my ankle and I go ass-over-tea-kettle in my pajamas. My phone and my coffee both go flying, mercifully most of the scalding liquid hits the grass and not me.

"Harley!" I yell as he untangles himself from my hold and takes off across the yard. I go to sit up but I'm dizzy. *Did I hit my head? Yep, definitely did.*

"Fucks sake, Rae, are you alright?" Nash's deep, familiar voice is hurried as he skids in beside me. Strong arms take hold from under me and pull me to a seated position.

"Did you hit your head?" I feel his hand gently press against my skull searching for damage. His large fingers feel good and warm.

"I think so, not too hard though..." I mutter, wondering where the hell Nash Carter came from on my front lawn at nine a.m.

"Cecilia?" I hear Andrew's muffled yelling from my phone in the grass.

Nash picks up the phone, his face sullen and his jaw tense as his eyes stay on mine.

A tattered cowboy hat, jeans and tack on the grass tells me he's here helping Wade with the horses this morning.

"She'll have to call you back, buddy," he bites out, and then he hangs up the phone on Andrew.

Goddamn, cowboy Nash is fucking hot.

CHAPTER FIVE
Nash

I was on my way back from cleaning tack in the west barn when she came into my sightline. I knew she was going down before she even made it down the front steps into the yard. Trying to juggle the dog leash, her phone and a coffee in her sock feet? Recipe for disaster.

As if looking after CeCe last night wasn't already a full-time job, the universe thinks I should do it again today. As last night wore on, more men started coming into the bar and the more men that came in, the more men I had to intercept as they made their way over to talk to her.

Because she was drinking—and because she's like my family—it's my job to protect her and make sure some sleazebag doesn't pick her up. At least, that's what I kept telling myself.

I tried to go back to get some paperwork done, but that lasted all of twenty minutes before I was back out to watch CeCe, and watch her I did. I watched her as she danced in my periphery, as she laughed and sang to Ginger, her arms up over her head as she moved. How she commanded all the attention in the room. The way her hips swayed under her tight little skirt made me wonder how her hips move in other scenarios, how they'd look with my hands gripping them pulling her down into my lap.

CeCe Ashby is almost eight years younger than me, but she's all woman now. That clumsy, semi-awkward girl she used to be is long fucking gone.

When I heard her on the phone just now, declaring her freedom, I hung back near the barn so I could let her finish her conversation. I didn't mean to eavesdrop, I just lost myself for a minute or two in the simple vision of her. The way the light hit her long ponytail in the morning sun and the smooth, sleek style she's wearing now is a far cry from last night's mass of waves and curls that hung down her back. Drunk CeCe was my long lost best friend and when the bar closed, she hugged me goodbye, those waves trailing down my arms. The strawberry scent of her hair hung onto my clothes until I got home, where I proceeded to remind myself I really need to get laid if I'm thinking about CeCe like this.

"Where on earth did you come from?" she asks as she focuses on my face.

"Cleaning tack for Mama Jo." She still looks confused so I elaborate. "I help Wade three times a week now."

"Oh... so because hockey is over, you think you're a cowboy?" She laughs, flashing me a perfect smile as she tugs the front of my cowboy hat. I let go of her and stand, holding out a hand to help her up.

"Part-time cowboy, at least," I retort.

"I guess I should be thanking you for helping Wade," she replies, looking around her familiar surroundings that I'm sure feel just a little emptier since Wyatt passed. I can see it in her eyes as she takes in the mountain behind her.

"It's kind of weird here now. I really wish I would've come home more before he got sick. I was so... involved with my own things," she blurts out.

I nod, because I know exactly how she feels. So was I. I didn't get back nearly as much as I should've for the man that saved my life, for all intents and purposes, until he was sick and unable to fish or ride or even sit on the porch and drink bourbon just shooting the shit like we used to.

Silence fills the space between us for a beat, filled with years of family connection and memories.

"Alright, guess I gotta go find this quarterback of a mutt now," she says, rubbing the back of her skull and wincing.

"You okay?" I ask.

She doesn't look okay. She looks dizzy.

"Yeah, I think so..." she says, as she teeters to her left.

"I think I'll just go with you." I decide, grabbing hold of her arm. "If you did give yourself a concussion, I don't need you going down all alone in the field."

"You don't have to come, it's not your problem I can't handle my crazy dog."

"I'm coming, just go get some damn shoes," I command.

She must have a concussion because miraculously, she listens and comes back out the door in record time, her socks long gone. She's wearing flip flops and holds a fresh mug of coffee. We begin to wander the long drive that passes the cabins in search of Harley.

"Life support this morning," she muses holding her mug up.

"Sounds about right, you were a handful last night. Come to think of it you've been a handful for me since you rolled back into this town."

"What do you mean? Aside from almost hitting Gemma—which I don't regret by the way because she's a colossal bitch that never deserved Cole."

I nod because I don't disagree.

"I didn't cause you any trouble for the rest of the night."

31

"You just had me out on the dance floor having to stop almost every man in the place from hitting on you."

"What do you mean? I had a chance for a one-nighter and you blocked me?" She giggles like it's the most natural thing in the world.

I don't find it funny.

"You were in no shape to make that decision, and that's the last thing you need, judging by the phone call I just overheard."

She stops in her tracks and turns to face me.

"A: Don't eavesdrop, it's rude. And B: I'm not looking for a husband but it's just... I need to meet new people. I didn't have a good relationship with Andrew and Ginger says—"

I scoff, interrupting her, "I'm going to stop you right there. Ginger Danforth is the last person you should be taking relationship advice from." I look down at her, her eyes have that fiery look in them like she's gonna sock me one.

"Who said anything about a relationship? I don't want a relationship, just someone to have fun with, maybe, I don't know. Ginger said it might do me some good and it's none of your damn business what I do anyway, Nash. *You're* the last person that should be offering me relationship advice. I mean, have you ever even had one?"

I shake my head. *Fuck, no.* "No, but the last thing you need around this gossipy little town is more rumors flying. Look how fast everyone knew that you couldn't leave home without a damn vibrator stuffed in your luggage."

Yeah, that was a fun visual to try to mentally block when I heard it last night.

"Good Lord, is there some kind of direct phone line to every resident in this place that gives daily updates on people's embarrassing moments and personal lives? Also, don't make me your problem just because you own the bar. It's none of your concern what I do, I'll be just fine."

I turn and grip both her shoulders. She's a stubborn little brat, I'll give her that.

"CeCe, you've been like my family for the better part of my life." Just saying those words to her feels wrong with all the things I've been picturing since last night, but I continue on anyway, dropping my hands from her body. Even that proximity in this morning heat feels like too much. "I'll always look out for you, whether you want me to or not."

"What are you two nattering on about?" Cole pushes the screen door open and comes out onto the front deck of Stardust with none other than the escape artist himself. Harley sprints to greet us.

"Lose something, CeCe Rae?" Cole asks. "You have coffee on your shirt, by the way. Still drunk?"

CeCe sticks out her tongue and flips him the bird as she grabs Harley's collar.

I laugh because despite being annoying, she's adorable as fuck.

"You coming in to show me where you want the rest of these shelves or what? I've been waiting on you; I don't have all day," he says to her.

Cole can be a grumpy motherfucker lately, for good reason.

"Yeah, I just got sidetracked, I'm gonna take Harley back and grab a quick, to-go breakfast from Mama. I'll be right back," she says.

"You coming in?" Cole nods in my direction.

I look at CeCe and shake my head. "Nah, gotta get to work and restock the bar, some crazy ass group of girls drank us out of house and home last night."

CeCe scoffs and heads off toward the big house.

"Bye bye, Nash, see ya never," she yells behind her without even turning around.

"Actually, see you tonight?" Cole asks. "Mama Jo says bring the Betty."

"Wouldn't miss it," I say, and I mean it because suddenly Monday night dinners at the Ashby's just got a hell of a lot more interesting.

CHAPTER SIX
CeCe

I watch Sandy Elliot, my mom's oldest and sweetest friend make her way over to Ginger, Olivia and me with our lunches as I pop my sunglasses on my face to shield my eyes from the afternoon sun. We're sitting on the patio at Sage and Salt, a cozy little breakfast and lunch hot spot on Laurel Creek's main drive that Sandy and her sister co-own.

"Thank you, Sandy. You're a saint." I smile up at her as she sets my lunch in front of me.

"Brought you some fries too, on the house. Figured you girls could use some grease, heard you almost roughed Gemma up last night and drank our resident hockey star out of house and home."

"Ugh, don't remind me," Ginger grumbles, her chin resting on her palm. Her wild mane surrounds her and she is wearing the biggest sunglasses I've ever seen. She looks like a modern version of Audrey Hepburn.

I laugh as I take in her scowl. She's always the most hungover and the most complain-y of all of us.

Sandy looks around and leans into us. "Not saying she wouldn't have deserved it." She winks and I smile back at her.

"Sorry I missed it, I'll make sure I'm there this Sunday, I'll bring Mama Jo, we'll raise the roof," she says with a smile, pushing up her imaginary roof with her hands.

"Lord have mercy on this town," Jack Pearlman, our resident seventy-year-old bluegrass busker, says from the table behind us as we all giggle at him.

"Hush your mouth and eat your burger, Jack, or I'll have to rethink your marriage proposal," Sandy says before sliding up to him and dropping a smooch on the top of his head.

I smile at their comforting, small town banter and start in on my chicken salad, scrolling through my phone as Ginger and Olivia prattle on about the women in the pub last night. Who's seeing whom, who's pregnant, who has money problems. The gossip never ends and I'm only half focusing as I read through the slim pickings in the town job ads.

My degree in Business Admin is over-qualified for most of these—Clerk at Lianne's Clothing Boutique. Interior design consultant at Jennings. I get to the very last page and see an ad for an Accounting Admin at the newly revamped Olympia Sports and Rec Center. I read through the fine print and realize I'm actually very qualified for this. The woman's name to contact is familiar: Sherri Lynn Johnson. She used to work at the post office, we didn't know her well but I remember my mom always calling her Sonny whenever she picked up packages or was mailing out. I quickly ready my resume and send it off to her email. The ad is at least 60 days old so that tells me they haven't had any luck finding anyone.

"Earth to CeCe."

I look up to see Olivia's expectant face, her dusting of freckles on the bridge of her nose glimmers as she grins.

"What? Sorry. I need a job; I was just searching through our dismal choices," I say.

"The one and *only* thing Andrew was good for, earning

enough money for you to do whatever you wanted, career wise." Ginger says, and she isn't wrong. I've been doing charity work for the last two years with a women's shelter full-time and working as a tax consultant for Andrew's firm part-time for little money because I could. There was never a need for me to earn a large income with Andrew pulling in six figures. I was free to pursue anything I was passionate about with Andrew, but now it's time to get serious and truth be told, I really am looking forward to it. If nothing pans out, I might even start my own business.

"You could always work with me? Even part-time I could use some help." Olivia owns a very popular lingerie boutique on the other side of town near the beach at Cave Run Lake. In the summer, they bring in brand name swimsuits and sell a lot to the tourists taking in the lake and Sugarland Mountain recreation.

"You know I love you and appreciate it, Liv, but I need to do something in my field or I'm going to feel like all that money my parents spent on my degree was a waste."

Ginger nonchalantly sucks back the rest of her sweet tea. "I need more Advil, and a mini nap before I teach my afternoon class," she groans.

How this woman makes it through a typical Monday as a high school English teacher during the regular school year, I'll never know. Thankfully for her, in the summer she only has one class a day, a refresher for any kids that need it.

I haven't even paid my lunch bill yet when I get a response from Sherri-Lynn asking when I'm available to interview.

I answer her back with "anytime" and she returns the message almost immediately asking me to come in around three today.

That gives me two hours to formally print out my resume

and credentials and make myself one hundred percent human after last night.

I smile to myself as I say goodbye to the girls and head to my dad's old Silverado. I may know nothing about sports and rec but I know a lot about business and finance and they seem desperate. This day is looking up.

CHAPTER SEVEN
Nash

"We just need to involve the community." Harry Martin has been the head coach for the high school hockey team for over thirty years. He was even my coach, and right now, he looks his sixty-four-years and then some as he continues. "The team committee appreciates your offer, Nash, but we don't want a hand out. We want this to be a grassroots type of thing. It will mean more to the families and the kids. People feel better about taking if it comes from the community. We can use Olympia as a sponsor but we need upwards of twenty-five thousand to fund the teams, the equipment, and everything else that goes along with having five different divisions for one year."

I nod. I get it and I hate to throw money around—this town isn't the kind of place that is impressed by that—but I want to help. The Laurel Creek Lightning is drowning financially and there are so many good little hockey players here and in the surrounding counties. I've been seeing it all summer through our camps. Olympia Sports Center or something like it, has been a lifelong dream of mine.

"When I was ten, I won a spot in a hockey camp in Michigan for two weeks and it's what led me to my future. If I hadn't had the opportunity to play when I got home, I never would've made it to the college rink or the NHL. These kids need sports and the opportunities they present. It's something I'm passionate about. I know there is pride involved. We'll come up with a way before fall to fund the program and using this ice will be on us," I say to him.

I didn't buy the old arena last year and put it through a huge renovation to create this space for nothing. I knew my NHL career was coming to an end and I needed to be busy. I don't do well if I'm alone with my thoughts. Wyatt always said idle hands do the devil's work, and in my case, he was always bang on. I knew I'd need this outlet.

The renos finished just in time for my season to end and I was able to flow effortlessly from the Stars to Facility Director and Trainer here. Yes, I have three jobs. Like I said, I can't sit still.

"Maybe we can sell raffle tickets? Or have an auction?" Sonny suggests from his right.

She's been a Godsend since we opened—scheduling all the camps, calling parents, taking payments, waivers, bills. You name it, she does it. All the things I'm not good at. But it's become quite apparent that she needs some help. She's semi-retired and is only supposed to be here part-time. Neither of us could have predicted the need this area has for organized sports and camps. Just with running our skating, hockey and figure skating programs, we're stretched to the max. I nod in response to her.

"That's a good start, we'd have to run some numbers," Harry answers.

Sonny smiles then looks up at me and taps her wristwatch.

"My interview should be here any second, pop your head in in twenty, if you can."

"Sounds good," I say, then I get back to going over suppliers for equipment with Harry, hoping this interview is better than her last. We really need the help.

CHAPTER EIGHT
CeCe

I pull up to Olympia Sports Center fifteen minutes early and I'm genuinely impressed with what I see. This isn't the old, run down arena I used to skate in with my friends when I was a kid. This is state of the art and double the size it used to be. It looks fresh and clean and the large parking lot is near full.

Kids and parents are coming and going as I park. Granted, I didn't have any time to actually research what this place even does anymore, but I can see they're doing it well, especially since it's July, not exactly ice skating season.

When I come up to the large entryway, there is a massive set of stairs in front of me that never used to be there, leading up to a second story that also never used to be there. A ticket window—I'm assuming is for game nights for the house league and competitive hockey teams—is to my right and beyond that, I see two full size ice rinks behind the stairs. The one to the left has glass windows that overlook the ice and a long line of stools for viewing. There are kids on the ice now, mostly girls but a few boys too, that look to be about seven or eight, and Avery is on the ice with them. They are all wearing figure skates. I wave to her through the glass and she gives me a puzzled look as she smiles, probably wondering what I'm doing here.

"Little Cecilia Rae Ashby, all grown up!" Sherri Lynn says as she approaches.

I turn to greet her and smile. She looks the same as when I was young, just older, somewhere in her mid-sixties, her hair is a neat grayish blonde bob and she wears big rimmed glasses with leopard frames. She looks like the fun Grandma.

"Yes, it is. Ms. Sherri, how are you?"

"Please, call me Sonny," she says as she gives me a big squeeze.

"Okay, Sonny."

"We're a pretty relaxed group around here."

"My new friend works here, so I've heard. Avery Pope?"

"Yes, she's a doll. Boss says we're lucky to have her, she skated with the 2018 Olympic team you know."

I nod, impressed with my new friend. I did not know that.

"Come on down to my office, and we'll have a chat."

She shows me all the immediate changes that have been made to the arena as we wander slowly to her office. There are parents drinking milkshakes and watching their kids' classes. One is just finishing up as we go through the waiting area so the space fills with loud, happy kids as we duck inside her office.

"So, how're your Mama and brothers?" Sonny asks. Small town interview at its finest.

"They're all good. We're all adjusting to life now," I say honestly.

"And why are you here? Last time I saw Mama Jo, she said you had some lawyer fiancé and you were staying out west."

I laugh and tuck a piece of hair behind my ear. It's like I'm having a friendly coffee visit instead of a job interview.

"Well things weren't what they seemed and I made the decision to end it and come back home."

"So he was a jackass, is what you're sayin'?"

I laugh in spite of myself, because that's exactly what Andrew is.

"Pretty much."

"Well, your resume looks incredible. Handling the finances for the Seattle and Grommet Women's Shelter is a big feat. I think we'll seem like small potatoes compared to that, but we'll keep you busy. I haven't had near the time I've wanted to spend on our books and Boss simply doesn't have the time."

I nod taking it all in as she explains their programs, their summer camps, the way they lend out the rink for a dollar to the community to house hockey tournaments. I'm liking the sound of it more and more and when she mentions the pay, I'm in. It's more than generous and I feel elated as she pretty much offers me the job on the spot.

"You may have a lot to go over with us. Like I said, Boss isn't the least bit handy when it comes to the business side, old Mrs. Cutter is his accountant for his other business and she simply won't take on any more work." She winks. "He just brings the talent."

"And what talent is that? Is he a trainer?"

She looks at me and shrugs.

"Well, it's Nash Carter, honey. Didn't you know that? He's the owner, I'm sure you were close with him when y'all we young, weren't you?"

"I-what? He helps Rocco at the bar—" I begin to say but I'm interrupted.

"Twice in one day... you following me around, Rae?" I hear from behind me as I turn to see Nash, leaning against the door frame fully suited up to skate, helmet in his hand. Hockey gear clads his body and a heavy, navy jersey with white writing that says Olympia across his chest and Coach on his sleeve.

The view of him like this takes up all the air in the room, especially from my lungs. There is no scenario where he doesn't look overwhelmingly good and it pisses me off, because I really wanted this job.

CHAPTER NINE
Nash

CeCe scoffs at me and rolls her eyes.

"You couldn't be so lucky."

But I am, because here she is.

This could just work out perfectly. Partly because I know that CeCe is ridiculously smart when it comes to business and finance, and also because the annoyed look she's wearing fuels me to try to get her to stay even more.

"This—I feel like... this may be a conflict of interest, Sonny." She looks over at me and I notice the effort she put in to be professional. She looks dressed for a high-end firm in a big city. "You own this place *and* work at the bar? I didn't realize... although, I don't know how I didn't, who else would do this or have the time or money?" CeCe mutters, almost more to herself than me. Her pretty emerald eyes ping-pong between Sonny and me.

"He's a great boss, kind of a hard ass on the details... but great," Sonny says, trying to convince CeCe to give me a chance like she's being asked to work for Dracula himself. Sonny shrugs. "If you can get him to keep the music at a reasonable level all day while you're trying to work, I'd say he's damn near perfect." She shoots me a little smirk and I chuckle.

CeCe stands up. "Thank you so much for the opportunity, but I just feel like this won't work out."

She tries to leave but I easily block her from getting around me. I've known this woman over half my life and have no idea what it is that I've done to piss her off, but I'm not letting her get away that easily.

"CeCe," I say, looking down at her. With my skates on, I'm towering over her tiny frame.

She looks up at me and blinks expectantly.

"What, Nash? I just don't think I could work for you."

Now I'm just offended. I try to recall all my interactions with her in a matter of ten seconds. She glares up at me through thick lashes, waiting for me to move.

I don't. I double down. I don't take no for an answer when I want something.

"I disagree. It would work perfectly. You haven't even given it some fair thought. You're definitely qualified, I can already trust you, and you know the town. How about this—I have a short power skating class to get started. Let Sonny show you around the facility, meet the instructors, show you where your office would be and what you'd be working on and then, I'll meet with you afterwards and if you still say no, I'll respect that."

She won't say no. I'm placing all my bets on the fact that the pretty office destined to be hers that looks over the ice and all the good we're doing for the kids around here will pull her back in. If I remember correctly, CeCe has a big heart for kids and loves a challenge. Our accounting is definitely a challenge at the moment.

Sonny can tempt her with all we offer and then, after my class, I'll close the deal. More money, better hours, whatever she wants. We need her, and not just because she looks fucking incredible in the little black pencil skirt and silky white blouse she's wearing. We need her for her skills. How good she looks is just a bonus that I'm sure Wade or Cole would squarely punch me in the dick for just noticing.

She eyes me up as if to see if I'm being straight with her, calculating the opportunity over her sudden, unfair disdain for me.

"Okay," she says.

"Good, I'll see you soon." I smile at her as I say it, and nod to Sonny to handle this, she nods back. I head to my class, looking forward to seeing CeCe afterwards a little more than I care to admit.

Forty minutes later, I'm off the ice, leaving Chris, one of my trainers, in charge for the last ten minutes of class so I can catch a quick shower. I'm not going to woo my prospective new administrator if I smell like my hockey bag.

I find CeCe in her new office when I'm done. Yes, I'm going to will it into existence. It's *her* office. I'll manifest it and all that hippy shit, just like Mama Jo always tells me to.

She sits across from Sonny, wearing thin, gold-rimmed glasses as she looks over paperwork.

"Have you seen enough yet?" I ask her casually, leaning against the door frame.

She looks up from a mess of paperwork.

"You really need a lot of help here. This is way too much for one person, you've been running poor Sonny ragged and this is all highly unorganized. It's raising my anxiety just looking at it," she says accusingly.

"I know, you're right, and I feel just terrible about it, that's why we need you *so* desperately," I plead.

Sonny gets up from the seat across from CeCe and pats me on the shoulder as she breezes by me.

48

"Way to lay it on thick, Boss. I trust you can finish this? I have registration at 4:15."

I nod and turn a smirk back to CeCe.

"Poor thing, she hasn't even had a lunch break today. She just can't stop or things fall behind." She rolls her eyes at me, and even that is hypnotizing to watch.

Hypnotizing? What the fuck is the matter with me? Sex. I need to have sex.

"Oh shut up, Nash. I'm not going to let you pull on my heartstrings. Do you really think this will work? You kind of grate on my nerves, in case you haven't noticed."

"Yeah, I can plainly see that... but what I don't get is why?" I ask.

I want her to work here—no, I need her—so we need to hash this out and I'm never one to beat around the bush.

CeCe grunts the cutest little sound; her pretty face is in a tormented scowl as if it's obvious why she has a problem with me. Yet, I'm still clueless. Aside from picking on her with the boys a zillion years ago, I can't think of a single thing. I've always respected her and even watched out for her.

"Cause... it's just... you've always tormented me, my whole life. Every time I turned around, you were picking on me. You told Michael Merriweather I had mono so he wouldn't ask me to the junior prom," CeCe says as she holds up her thumb like she's about to count off the many reasons.

I snicker because yes, I did that. I was home to visit when CeCe was fifteen and Cole heard Michael was bragging that he was going to take CeCe's v-card, but Wyatt strictly forbade Wade and me—who were grown ass men of twenty-three—from knocking out a seventeen-year-old, so we had to get creative to stop that date from happening.

She's still rambling reasons as to why I annoy her so I let her finish.

"And lastly, Avery is a really nice girl and if you treat her the way you treated every girl you dated in high school and college, I'm gonna have a bone to pick with you. Be nice to her or find someone else to romp with."

Whoa. What the fuck?

I move closer to her. I have one shot here to make her understand so I just go for it.

"First, Avery is my *employee only*. I would never get involved with an employee, ever. It's my cardinal rule. We're really lucky to have her. Secondly, I was a dumb kid when I picked on you with your brothers. I never meant anything by it and if I offended you I apologize. Thirdly, I'm not the same person I was back then."

"So you don't sleep around with women for sport anymore?"

It's at this moment I notice the look in her eyes—a look that has absolutely nothing to do with me, it's about the person I used to be that reminds her of the person that just hurt her.

She's not wrong, I used to sleep with women. A lot of them. When you play hockey, women are everywhere—puck bunnies at every turn. But that was a different time in my life. The man CeCe remembers has left the building.

I heard from Wade what a piece of shit this Andrew is, and I'm nothing like him. He filled me in while we set up for the four-level riding class this morning and it made me clench my fists at my sides to imagine someone ever hurting CeCe Rae.

"I'm not like you think, at least not anymore. I get why you'd remember me that way."

She scoffs at me. "Yeah... you had a no-longer-than-three-times rule."

Again, she's not wrong, but now I just want to fuck with her and her smug little attitude.

"I have to say, CeCe, I never pegged you for the judgy

type." I cross my arms over my chest, doing my best to look insulted.

She looks up at me, trying to appear very non-judgy and failing. She pulls her plush bottom lip between her teeth and thinks for a second before answering.

"I'm not judgy, Nash. It's just, people rarely change."

"Maybe not, but people do grow up, CeCe. You haven't lived here, in what? Seven, eight years?"

Something in her eyes softens. She paces the space, picking up a stack of invoices and carrying them to *her* new desk. She stands there for a second tapping her baby pink nails on it.

"You really do need me here; this is the most unorganized accounting system I've ever seen."

I smile wide at her. I can taste the victory.

"I know I do. Sonny is amazing, but she's old school. We need to streamline this place. I don't want anything slipping through the cracks, but I haven't been able to find any more qualified help. Is the pay fair for you?" I ask.

I know it is—it's twenty percent a year higher than the going rate.

She nods in response. "Yes, it is."

"Your hours are yours to choose, whatever works for you. I'm sure you want to spend some time with Mama Jo. Cole told me it's important to you, now that you're home. You can work remotely whenever you want. The choice is yours."

Her eyes narrow, like she doesn't believe me.

"You smiling at me like that is making me nervous. When did you get so nice and accommodating? What's the catch?" she asks as she twirls a piece of her hair between her fingers.

"I'm not nice and accommodating, I'm a hard-ass, remember?"

She smirks in spite of herself.

"Does that mean you're in?" I ask.

She stops twirling her hair and eyes me up.

"I'm gonna need an office supply budget, and an updated version of Quicken."

"Done," I say instantly.

"And I'm gonna need Mondays off."

I smirk. "Shocker."

Her arms fold under her perky tits and form a little shelf for them.

"Now, who's judgy? I want to help Mama prepare Monday dinners and pick Mabes up from school."

"Fair enough. Domestic Mondays," I say. I don't press her. I've almost got her.

"Alright, a trial basis. But don't you make me regret it, Nash. I mean it."

I smile even wider. "Hell yes, girl," I hoot out.

I move across the room, scooping her body up into a hug without thinking. What I'm not prepared for is my body's reaction to hers. CeCe melts into me like I have the perfect place carved out just for her. That sweet strawberry scent fills my nostrils and I breathe it in as her tiny palms against my chest cause the hairs on the back of my neck to rise.

"Do you hug all your employees?" she asks as I notice how soft and pliable she is in my arms.

"Sorry," I mutter, releasing her. "I'm just so happy to have the help we need here is all." I clear my throat. *Smooth.*

"Alright, well... rule number one, when we're here, I expect you to be professional." CeCe wags a finger at me and all I see is the hot accountant scolding me.

God dammit, Nash.

"I'll start Wednesday. I want to take tomorrow to get fully settled and I need some new clothes."

"What you are wearing now is just... fine," I manage to eke

out like a fifteen year old with a school boy crush. *Again, real fucking smooth.*

She looks down to her outfit.

"I left a lot of my stuff in Seattle. This is really all I have." The look in her eyes makes me want to gut punch this Andrew once again but instead of saying something stupid I nod.

"We're gonna make this work, CeCe. You'll see."

She nods as she walks by me, tossing her purse over her shoulder and she winks at me.

"See you Wednesday then, if the creek don't rise."

Hearing her utter Wyatt's signature saying sucker punches me in the chest so hard that I forget to tell her she'll be seeing me a lot sooner than that.

CHAPTER TEN
Nash

"You sleeping any better, son?"

"Somedays," I answer Wyatt as he lays a five-numbered run on the table. Tile Rummy is our thing, we've been doing it every time I come home since he got sick, and for years before that.

"Still no good at bullshitting, I see."

I blow out a raspberry. "Guess not."

"You taking the voodoo shit Jo gave you?" he asks, mentioning the melatonin and chamomile in my kitchen cupboard.

"Yeah. It hasn't helped much, but don't tell her that. I'll take it anyway." I smirk.

"Smart boy. Your secret is safe with me. I value the time I have left—I'd never tell Jo she was wrong about anything."

I chuckle but I hate hearing about the little time he has left. He's so young. Only sixty. This is so unfair.

"Maybe that's what you need. Your own kind of Jo. You're thirty-two, maybe it's time you find someone to start a life with? Someone to fill your time, some babies to tire you out. Maybe *then you'll sleep better." Wyatt winces in pain as he stretches his arm across the table to lay another run down.*

"You alright?" I brace myself to stand and help him but he waves me off.

"Fine, just damn nerves catch fire every so often."

I nod. I hate cancer. Hate isn't even a word strong enough for the way I feel about it. It's taken the strongest man I know and reduced him to skin and bones. I admire him so goddamn much. Wyatt never complains, he takes everything in stride and even now, when he's in his last days, he's still worried about me.

"That life just isn't for me," I say.

"Horseshit, that life is for everyone when you find the right person, you kids are the best thing that ever happened to me."

My chest tightens and I lay a run out on the table. A good one.

"Fucker, you just holding that back like you were waiting on a special occasion to lay it?"

"Yeah, the occasion of beating your old ass again, three tiles left." I point at my tray and smirk.

Wyatt grimaces. He hates to lose but he'd hate it even more if I went easy on him. A beat of silence passes between us.

"I can't even look after myself, I could never look after someone else or kids. It's just not in the cards for me. I'm happy with the career I've had so far, and when it's over I'll be back here. Come April, we'll fish, work on my boat, and you can help me find a homestead. That's all I need. Just a little land, some room to breathe. Some peace."

Wyatt's eyes glimmer still as he smiles. "I don't have that kind of time."

The bridge of my nose stings. I know he's right but I can't face it. Not again.

"Let's see how this experimental treatment goes after Thanksgiving, I've heard great things."

"Boy, I'm gonna cut the shit sandwich for a minute," he blurts and I chuckle.

"Y'always do."

Wyatt startles me by grabbing my forearm.

"Just be here for them, all of them. You're stronger than you think, Nash. You know what this is like—to lose someone. A parent. They don't. Use your pain and help them through when I'm gone. Especially the girls. My girls are gonna need you."

"You're talking nonsense but I'll humor you, old fella."

"Good." He nods "Now put some effort in for the rest of the game, it's no fun if you don't challenge me here..." he says, laying out a six-tile run.

"Two tiles left." He grins.

I sober myself up from the memories that still flood my thoughts daily, and grab the brown Betty Cobbler from our local bakery off the front seat, and toss my keys in my truck console.

Monday night dinners at the Ashby's are legendary. Like, I've been here every Monday since I was fifteen years old, aside from my years in the NHL and even then, I would always call on Mondays. No one invites you, no time is confirmed, we all just show up because Jo always said that even if your Monday is shitty, you've always got a good old-fashioned family dinner to look forward to.

I come through the front door to the sounds of Johnny and June rolling out from the kitchen and Mabel's laughter. It's like coming home. Mama Jo has been a true mother to me since I lost everything and for that, I could never repay her, as much as I constantly try. She didn't even question her role, she and Wyatt both just stepped right in and took over. Now, she's the only one left. There isn't a single thing on this planet I wouldn't do for her, especially now that Wyatt is gone.

"Hey, baby." Jo beams at me from the kitchen island, her hands working to roll out homemade biscuits.

Cole and Mabel are the first ones here. Mabel is pretty much the coolest kid in the world. She's right beside Jo in her matching red apron, helping her roll and spread flour.

"Mama Jo," I say as I kiss her on the top of her head.

"Able Mabel," I greet Mabel, high-fiving her. She laughs as I realize my hand is now covered in flour.

"Thanks for that, little bud." I say wiping my hand on a dish towel.

Cole tosses a piece of biscuit dough at me.

"Poor fella, wouldn't want to mess up your Matthew McConaughey-like appearance. You got your Lincoln parked outside?"

I sneak behind Mama Jo and flip him the bird on the way to the bar area for the standard drink of Monday night. Wyatt's favorite bourbon. It's the only time I ever have a drink. Once a week, for Wyatt.

"A dollar in the swear boot, Uncle Nash!" Mabel pipes up, pointing to her baby cowboy boot we stuff money into when we cuss in front of her.

"You got eyes in the back of your head? And I didn't say it, I mimed it, it shouldn't count."

"It does!" she squeals. I'm single-handedly making her rich, but I don't mind one bit.

I stuff a five in the boot that's already half full, and it's only Monday.

"That'll pay me up for the next couple." I smirk at her.

"Never have kids," Cole mutters, shaking his head as Wade comes through the back door.

"Mama, fam," he greets.

"Sergeant," we all say at almost the same time, which earns a laugh from Mabel.

"Hi, Uncle Wade."

"Hi, baby." He kisses her head. Even the Sergeant's icy heart melts for Mabel.

Harley scrambles for the front door, anticipating people before we even hear them.

"I get what you're saying, Papa, but we gotta come up with another way to say it," CeCe says as she swings open the front door.

"Auntie!" Mabel calls as she drops what she's doing and bounds up to CeCe who is still coming through the front foyer with Jo's dad, Papa Dean. He's still spry at seventy-eight, always mischievous and always trying new hobbies. Tonight, he's carrying his old acoustic guitar with him.

Mabel squeals and lunges into CeCe's arms before CeCe can even put down her purse and keys.

"My darlin', ohhh... let me hug you. Look at you, FaceTime doesn't show me how grown you are. Did you bring your kit to give me a mani? My nails are just awful." She holds a perfectly manicured hand out for Mabel to view.

"Yeah, I brought some pretty colors. You always wear pink. How about blue?"

CeCe smiles and squeezes Mabel's chin in her palm.

"You read my mind darlin', I've been wanting blue for a while. After dinner?"

Mabel beams up at her and nods, then skips to the kitchen.

"Can I watch Rosana Pansino on Nana's computer in the den?" she asks Cole.

"Yes, baby. No headphones, use the speakers," he directs and she nods, taking off into the other room.

"You gonna play us a song on that guitar, Pop?" Cole chuckles, knocking back a swallow of bourbon.

"I just picked him up from his guitar class at the senior center, his lesson got moved to today." CeCe stops, looking up at me like she's making the mental realization that I'm here. Of course I'd be here. Where else would I be?

"Y'all want to hear what my teacher said to me? I think she has the hots for me. She's a youngin' too, only seventy." He grins.

"Papa..." CeCe warns.

Cole smiles wide, even Wade's interest is piqued as he looks up from pouring his drink.

"I'm invested," Cole says. "Did she ask you on a date, old fella?"

Papa Dean sets down his guitar and shrugs.

"She said she wants to help me work on my fingering. She said I work a tight finger and I need to loosen it up."

Wade snickers and Cole breaks out in a grin.

"Well that's good, Pop. You just gotta practice your fingering then," Cole says, laughter rumbling from his chest.

"I mean, don't we all?" Wade asks in a shrug.

Mama Jo looks horrified and we all crack up laughing. All of us but CeCe.

"Children," she says.

Dean continues, "I'm trying my best. I broke the damn G-string while I was fingering a tight major tonight."

"Jesus, Papa," CeCe says, but her face breaks out into a wide grin before burying her head in her hands as the rest of us give into our laughter.

Dean just smirks like the old shit disturber he is, knowing exactly what all of this sounds like and adds, "Did you boys know if you finger the A just right, it produces a higher note?"

"Dad!" Mama Jo belts out at him, swatting him with a dish towel as the three of us boys double over.

I can't wait to be old, you get away with everything.

"Good thing Mabes left the room," she scolds Cole.

"How do you expect to raise a lady with this kind of behavior around her?"

"And y'all are just encouraging him," CeCe says, pouring herself her bourbon.

I take in the sight of her, such a sharp contrast to the professional businesswoman from earlier. Now she's in her cut-off jean shorts, the kind that end just at that perfect spot beyond the curve of her plump ass, a white Blondie tour t-shirt with a wide cut out neck so it hangs off her bare shoulder. I remember her obsession with vintage t-shirts and realize she must still have them all, she had so many back in her teen years, from all different eras of music. When was the last time Blondie actually went on tour? She's padding around the kitchen in her bare feet. Her thick hair is pulled back into a smooth high ponytail and her face is free of any makeup. I decide this is how I like her best. Natural. Fresh and so goddamn young looking it reminds me who she is as I try to sober myself up.

I clear my throat and Cole swats me.

"You alright?"

I look at him. Did he just see me ogling CeCe like some old pervert?

I nod and decide I need to talk. Now.

"Well, I can't top that story, Papa Dean... but CeCe and I have some interesting news from our day for y'all," I pipe up, everyone looks at me expectantly, especially CeCe.

"Olympia has a new administrator and accounting manager." I nod toward CeCe.

Mama Jo looks between CeCe and me.

"Wade finally took on the job?" she asks, without missing a beat, a smirk on her face.

"Reluctantly," Wade retorts. "But I told him no sexual harassment, I have to endure enough of that from him in the barn."

"Aww, bud. You're not my type." I grin.

Mama Jo looks at CeCe with a knowing smile but speaks to me.

"Funny, CeCe never mentioned it all afternoon while she was home with me, but I think that's just fabulous. He needs the help in that shit show of an office." Her eyes move to mine. "No offense, you got a pretty face, boy, but you're not the best with accounting."

"Thanks?" I say, wondering if I was just insulted or complimented. Jo has a way of doing that better than anyone.

"I was gonna tell you, Mama. I was just getting used to the idea myself and making sure I wasn't gonna quit before I even started," CeCe says, her eyes on mine. I smirk. Bullshit. She ain't quitting.

Cole gets up and pats her on the shoulder.

"I'd need to get used to it if I had to work for this fucker too. At least we know he'll never bang the women in his office." Cole chuckles and then adds, "CeCe is... well, CeCe. And let's be real, he could never handle Sonny."

Wade chuckles. "Ain't that the truth."

Jo hands me the cutlery.

"Well, set the table, big boss man."

I nod and head into the dining room, glad none of them can actually read my thoughts as I go.

CHAPTER ELEVEN
CeCe

E very time I turn around today, Nash is there. I've only been employed by him for four hours but I'm already questioning my sanity. I want to believe everything he said, that he's not who he used to be, that this can work... because I need this job. All I can think about is starting over and keeping myself busy.

Andrew is calling and texting me nonstop, trying to put thoughts into my head that don't belong.

It seems like such an uphill climb to start fresh and this job is number one on my list of things I need to help me. It's the first wrung in the ladder. The pay and circumstance is great; Sonny says Nash pays everyone well above fair wage just to keep his staff happy. It also seems like a challenge on account of how much disarray their accounting system is in. The accounting is the last and only part of the business I see that needs help. The rest—the areas Nash excels in—seems to be working fantastic.

I was both impressed and surprised when Sonny took me on the tour of Olympia. The reimagined space is perfection. State of the art rink effects, new Zambonis, updated locker and change rooms, the entire floor in the back half is covered in rubber mats so skaters can get easily to restroom facilities and changing rooms without taking their skates off. The spectator area is actually comfortable and warm—something I've never seen at a hockey rink before.

Nash had a new concession area added that allows for different food trucks to pull up outside to a pass-through window into the building so Olympia can host feature nights with local businesses.

Sonny says he is big on supporting the community now. She told me all about the charity nights they offer, where the money made from the Lightning games is all donated to local charities in need, a gesture that helps make me believe maybe Nash has grown up to be someone other just than an older, still self-centered man version of the teenage and college boy I knew. I had an idea of him, an illusion and he is shattering it every time I see him and he does something kind or thoughtful.

I chew on my bottom lip as I help Mama get dinner ready.

I think I want him to still be the Nash I used to know. The cocky, womanizing superstar. Without that, I have no choice but to notice how goddamn gorgeous he is in any setting. Just the scent of him draws me in—like fresh sandalwood and spice. It was so manly and warm when he hugged me today. It's like walking inside from the cold to a warm blanket and a mug of tea. Comforting. Homey. And I hate it. The last thing I need is to be drooling over him, especially when he's like a part of my family. Being away over these last years forced me to forget just how ingrained he is in our family lore and history.

"You're quiet, baby... just taking it all in?" Mama asks me while we mash potatoes and she pulls her meatloaf out of the oven.

"Just adjusting."

"I think it's great, you working for Nash. He really needs the help."

"I know, I had a quick look today. It's just a lot, having all these people around all the time. I'm not used to it."

I look out to the dining room where Nash stands. I nod in his direction.

"He always here since he's been home?"

Mama Jo thinks carefully as she slices the meatloaf and puts it on the serving plate.

"He's here as much as I need him to be, and he's here even when I don't know I need him. He misses your daddy something fierce. Whenever he was on a break from playing hockey, he was here. Losing your daddy was hard on him, as hard as it was on the rest of us. He could've gone a different way in life after all that trauma, but he chose the right path. He's good for this town. The people really love him," she says, like he's a politician running for office.

"Yeah, he's a real crowd pleaser," I snicker, remembering him chatting with patrons in the bar last night, all boyish grins and deep bronze haired charisma.

I glance into the dining room to see Nash standing at the table in his perfectly fitted jeans, and a black t-shirt that showcases his toned, inked arms which are folded across his muscular chest while he talks to Wade. His wavy dark hair is peeking out ever so slightly and he's wearing his signature Dallas Stars, Stanley Cup-winning baseball hat backwards.

My depraved pussy doesn't stand a chance. She's a whore for a backward baseball hat—especially on this devastating looking hockey star turned part-time cowboy. He locks eyes with mine across the room, it anchors me where I stand. Nash doesn't look away, he owns it and grins then takes a sip of his bourbon, never breaking the stare.

"Let's eat!" Mama calls, breaking my trance as Mabel and Cole venture in from the den.

"Smells good as always, Mama," Cole says, giving her shoulder a squeeze.

We sit down at the table like it's where we all just belong, leaving my dad's chair at the head forever empty.

"To Pa." Wade raises his glass of bourbon and the rest of us follow suit.

"To Pa," we say in unison, before we tap the bottom of our glasses on the table and drink.

"I'll tell you one thing, that cheeky bugger is disgusted you're wearing that Yankees shirt at his table." Papa Dean nods to Cole.

"Hey, Pa respected our differences," Cole retorts.

"He *grew* to respect them," I say. "When you told him you were a Yankees fan, he almost made you sleep in the garage."

"I believe his words were 'where did I go wrong?'" Wade chimes in.

"Shut up, y'all," Cole mutters as we all chuckle over ancient history.

Grief floods my chest in a fresh wave as I remember that he'll never sit with us and hound Cole again.

CHAPTER TWELVE
CeCe

"We're gonna have to talk about it sooner than later, is all I know." Wade is gruff and speaks matter-of-factly. He's in deep discussion with Mama and Cole about our need to hire a new horse trainer, as we eat the cobbler Nash brought from Spicer's.

Our resident horse trainer is adopting twins and needs to take an extended maternity leave. Replacing her will be a bitch, partly because Wade isn't exactly an easy man to work for.

"How long will Sam be gone?" I ask.

"A year at least," Wade answers as he rubs his forehead.

Samantha has been with our family since I left for college.

"With Sam gone, I won't be able to keep up and we have four horses that need to retire. We need someone that can train the new horses and train jumpers, and y'all keep telling me to make another derby run."

Mama Jo nods, and Wade continues.

"Starting wages aren't what they used to be, I think we'll have to offer more to get the best. We want to attract someone who has a lot of experience. I don't want to spend months training someone fresh."

"Much as I hate to admit it, he's right," Cole pipes up in between bites.

I look over to spy Mabel feeding Harley from the table. She looks up at me but I just wink at her. That tricky dog knows where the money is.

"What are we talking here?" Mama asks.

"Maybe a fifteen percent increase, twenty? It's a temporary position so we have to make it more enticing," Wade replies.

Mama thinks for a moment, and then looks to Nash of all people, with the quickest of glances. He locks eyes with her across the table for only a fleeting moment and I swear I see him nod.

"Alright, get it done—we only have a couple months before she leaves," Mama commands.

"Will do," Wade retorts in his usual terse tone. "I'd like to have the new person work with Sam until she leaves and have them ready. She also might face an early birth, since it's twins. I just want to be ready, that's all."

I narrow my eyes and look at Nash, he looks back at me but looks away quickly.

Something is up, my Spidey senses are tingling. *What the hell have I missed around here?* I'm making it my mission to find out why my Mama is looking at Nash Carter before making a financial decision.

In true Ashby fashion, Mama and I sit in the living room after dinner listening to Papa Dean snooze while we get manicures from Mabel and all the boys clean up the kitchen. I can see the three of them in there talking while Cole washes, Nash dries and Wade sweeps the kitchen floor.

"I know this must seem foreign after so long, but you're in the right place, baby. Andrew turned out to be no good," Mama says with a wink as she turns to look at Mabel. "And we're almost even numbered with the boys now that Auntie is home."

Mabel giggles. "Is that why we didn't have to watch baseball at dinner tonight?" Mabel asks.

"If it is, I'm glad I could help save you from that." I grin at her while she paints my nails the most hideous shade of blue imaginable.

I look over at my Mama.

"Speaking of help, what sorts of things has Nash been helping you with since Daddy..." Just saying the words gives me a shooting pain in my chest.

Mama looks away and shrugs. I'm definitely right—something is up.

"Same thing he's always helped with, he comes three times a week and works with Wade in the stables. We're short staffed, people aren't taking jobs in ranching as much anymore."

I frown at her. If they're having any trouble, I'd like to know.

"Don't worry about the ranch. We have it under control here. You just focus on *your* new job. I'm excited for you and this fresh start."

She changes the subject as I narrow my eyes at her, but I decide to let it go for now. I'll get to the bottom of the odd way she's acting soon enough. I have nothing but time and I'm exhausted tonight. I'm dreaming about my bed and a new book.

"I need to go shopping tomorrow if you want to come along, most of my stuff is still in Seattle. I'm going to have to deal with that sooner than later."

"Have you heard from the horse's ass?"

"Nana Jo, put a dollar in," Mabel pipes up, hiking her thumb over her shoulder without even looking up from painting nails. She never misses a beat.

"Y'all are funding her college." I giggle. Mabel eyes me and grins. Little old soul, she is.

"Yes, Andrew is a pain right now, he calls me every few

hours. I've only answered three times. Once, I hung up on him —that was out of my control. The other two times I pretended to lose service part way through the call. As soon as he starts telling me to come home, I'm out." Or asking me why strange men are speaking for me. He accused Nash of being a new boyfriend. As if he has the right to question me, after years of being unfaithful to me.

"He just doesn't get that I'm serious, or he thinks I'm having a little temper tantrum and that I'll come back to him eventually. He has no faith that I will make it on my own. I should've seen all the red flags."

"Coulda-shoulda-woulda," Mama says, waving off my worry. "You can't go back, only forward. You're here now, that's all that matters. Daddy would be proud, he never really liked him."

I smile. "I know."

"He was a good judge of character, your daddy."

"The best," I reply.

I watch Nash carefully from hooded eyes as he cleans. Corded forearms and veins ripple as he works, proceeding to wipe the counters in even straight swipes, ringing the cloth out and starting the process over again. He's too neat. Something tells me he has a messy side somewhere. I wonder briefly if he tucks in his bedsheets and a slight grin plays on my lips.

Mabel finishes up my nails. I hold a hand out to admire them. Aside from the color, they don't look half bad.

"Beautiful, Mabey-Baby." I kiss her forehead.

"I'm gonna have a beauty salon one day," she quips.

"I bet you will," Nash says to her as he enters the den, finished with his chores.

The doorbell rings and startles me.

I look at Mama Jo as if she were expecting someone.

"Well, answer it. My nails are wet," she says, helpless.

As I get closer I see the telltale UPS uniform through the glass. *That was quick.*

"Package for Cecilia Ashby?" He smiles a friendly smile at me as I open the door.

"That's me."

"Sign here, please."

I do as he asks and muster the strength to lift the heavy box into the entryway. How I got it from the car into the UPS drop off on Friday, I'll never know.

"Delivery?" Nash says from behind me, lifting the box from me with ease into his powerful arms. His fingers brush mine as he does, a current surges through my skin with the contact.

"Shania t-shirts?" he asks, judging its weight.

"My laptop and my favorite romance novels."

He nods in response. "I'll walk it down to Stardust for you, when you're ready."

I begin to protest but then realize I can't carry it the quarter mile walk, and I do work for him now so I should play nice.

"Thank you. I'm ready to go anytime, I'm exhausted, to be honest."

He nods. "I'll let the boys know I'm heading out. I have an early morning here tomorrow with Wade, before heading to the Center."

"Are you next, Uncle Nash? Stars green again?" Mabel calls from the den.

I grin, picturing Nash Carter, his massive rugged hands propped up on the coffee table getting his finger nails painted by my seven-year-old niece. He shakes his head at me, a warning not to make fun of him.

"Not this time, bud. But I'll take a raincheck," he calls to her, a smile lighting up his face.

I hug Mama Jo and Mabel.

"See ya, Rae. Try not to get into any tussles on the walk home." I hear from Cole in the kitchen.

"Ha-ha," I call back to Cole.

"I'll keep her in check," Nash jokes as I roll my eyes at them. *It was one time.*

I lead Nash out the door. He totes my box of worldly goods like it weighs nothing, as we walk the gravel road.

The only sound in the air is the crickets. I follow the glow of the fireflies as we walk. This ranch really comes alive in the summer.

"So, what about the rest of your stuff? Seven years? Eight? You must have a lot there still," he says.

"I do. I'll have to get it at some point. Andrew will have to sell our condo, I'll have to either go back for my stuff or send for it, I don't know yet. The idea of seeing him again stresses me out."

Nash nods from beside me, and even though it's dark, I swear I see his jaw tense.

"How did it get to be that way? If just the thought of being around him causes you stress, how did you live there?"

"I don't know, I think I mentally blocked the misery out, if that makes sense."

Nash chuckles. "Much more than you know."

I sense more in his words but I don't pry, I just continue on. "I mean, I should've known. There were signs he was unfaithful, he would always have his phone on Do Not Disturb, he'd take it everywhere he went." I scoff because hindsight tells me I saw the signs I just ignored them. "He'd even take it to the shower, like—*in* the shower."

Nash huffs out a breath.

"You should be glad you've never had a relationship. It rips you apart from the inside out when it ends."

"Precisely," he retorts. "Or you lose it all when you least expect it."

I nod. He's had a rough go. I don't push on the subject and we walk for a few seconds in silence before he speaks again.

"What pushed you to the point of no return, if you don't mind me asking."

I sigh, as weird as it is to be telling this to Nash, it feels good to say it nonetheless, now that it's done.

"When I was home at Christmas last year, my dad was real lucid one morning. We had coffee in the den, well it was his makeshift bedroom then."

Nash nods. "I remember; I was here in January for a few days before he passed."

My eyes snap to him.

"I didn't know that," I say. Apparently, this is a theme, I don't know a lot about what Nash has done over the last few years.

"Yeah, I came back whenever I could... especially at the end. It was like losing my dad all over again; only this time I had the chance to say goodbye. I wasn't letting go of that for a second."

A few seconds of silence sits between us and I feel the need to say something.

"Dad really loved you."

He nods, but doesn't look at me. "He was the best, never be another like him," he says so quietly that it's almost a whisper.

I look straight ahead and fight the tears threatening to spill. I clear my throat. "Anyway, he told me a man should be there for me. He said someone that loved me wouldn't make me travel home alone for Christmas, especially when my dad was so sick. And then he insinuated that maybe Andrew was being unfaithful to me. I realized in that moment if it was that obvious to my dad from across the country, that all the excuses I was making for him was just me lying to myself."

"So you found out for sure there was another woman after that?"

"Women," I correct.

Nash turns his face to me, looking both surprised, and if I didn't know any better, just downright angry.

"Son of a bitch..." he mutters.

"Tell me about it." I smirk because there's nothing I can do but laugh at this point.

"I started watching what he did more carefully, looked at his credit card charges, saw lunches and dinners for two that didn't include me, charges to lingerie stores when I hadn't received anything from him..."

"Jesus, CeCe."

The old steps of Stardust creek under our feet as we climb them. Inside, I direct Nash to my newly set up computer desk in front of the kitchen window as I turn on the lamp in the entryway. He sets the box down and I go to the kitchen to get something to open it with. I turn the light over the stove on and it offers us a soft glow in the dark room.

"The real kicker was when I took his coats to the dry cleaners in May like I do every year. When I picked them up, the clerk handed me a little garment bag with a glittery pink thong inside. She said it was in the inside pocket, assuming it was mine. I hadn't thought to check it. I knew in that moment with certainty. Those were the most humiliating days I've ever lived through but I knew what I had to do. I just kept hearing my dad's voice. I still dream about it sometimes, and it makes me feel like he's proud of my decision and it seems silly, but maybe he's visiting me in my dreams to tell me."

I'm rambling at this point and then remember who I'm talking to. In another life, I assume Nash was like Andrew.

"More story than you bargained for, sorry." I laugh awkwardly as I cut into the box. I turn to him to find his eyes raking over me, as if he's deep in thought.

"No woman ever deserves to be cheated on, used, or degraded. I'm damn glad you listened to your dad and followed your gut instincts."

I eye him up as I start pulling books out of the box.

"I haven't really been fair to you, Nash. I guess I was seeing you as the old you—more like Andrew."

He blows out a raspberry and looks horrified when I look up at him.

"You think I'd treat a woman like that?" he asks.

I shrug, trying to be careful with my words so I don't insult my new boss. Sometimes I wish I had a filter between my brain and my mouth. I turn away and avoid his searing blue eyes, fumbling to backtrack.

"Well... I... not the cheating part, but you always had a different girl, every day of the week. I read things when you played hockey. That model you dated, she said you were sleeping with Cory Kane's wife."

Nash takes his hat off and sets it down on my sofa as he runs a hand through his hair before moving to the window. Sugarland mountain is still ominous even in the dark out the window.

"I don't give a fuck what anyone in the media thinks about me. That model I dated that you're talking about—Kelsey. We were never serious and I never cheated on her. I've dated a lot of women, casually, yes... but I would never cheat on someone. Not ever. Every woman I've ever been with knew where I stood. I don't date. I don't do relationships. Kelsey just thought she'd be the one to change me. It became real apparent to me that she was more concerned with her social media followers than me after only a few weeks. We were long through when

74

she said those things about me to *TMZ* and none of them were true."

He moves away from the window and comes closer to me. It's odd to be alone with Nash like this.

"Cory knows it, I know it, and his wife knows it. I'm actually still very close with them, I talk to Cory at least once a week. Hell, that's where I celebrated Christmas last year and I just went to their son's birthday party in June. Rumors are par for the course. Kelsey was looking for her fifteen minutes of fame, and she got it. She seemed genuine when I met her."

He moves closer and his hands slide to my shoulders and grip me tightly as he looks down at me, his sapphire pools just boring into my eyes and I can tell instantly that he's being honest.

"Make no mistake, what Andrew did to you was wrong, and you deserve so much fucking better, Rae."

I'm not prepared for the magnetism that is Nash one foot from me, staring down at me with his navy eyes. I don't have the will to do anything but stare back up at him. This proximity, his words, his hands on my body. Hell, even his delicious scent is commanding every ounce of my attention. He tucks a piece of hair behind my ear and that simple action alone is like striking a match against my skin.

His gaze travels to my mouth. I watch his throat bob as he swallows. Am I seriously thinking about what it would feel like to have Nash Carter's lips on mine? *God, they're nice lips.* The vision of us melting together instantly sends heat to my core. My pulse quickens in a way that it hasn't for a man in so long, and I can feel every single piece of clothing I'm wearing touching my skin. Our breathing syncs as his thumb slides errantly under the neckline of my t-shirt and traces my shoulder gently.

"I'll say this, the fact that he even chose to *look* at another woman tells me he is either insane or the stupidest mother fucker alive."

It's too much, his eyes, these words, his thumbs tracing my skin. It's intoxicating.

Kiss me. My pussy screams.

We both jump when we hear a knock on the door.

Nash's hands slide down my arms and he clears his throat, backing away from me.

"Sorry, CeCe. I left my hat and sunglasses here earlier," Cole's voice calls from the door.

I sober up and look around for them, my body still on fire from Nash's rough hands sliding down my arms only seconds before.

I find Cole's things on my coffee table and hand them to him.

"You heading out?" Nash asks Cole.

"Yep, right now," Cole says, oblivious to the tension in the room that was just roasting me alive.

"Cool, I'll walk with you to my truck." Nash turns back to me. "I'll see ya, Rae," he says, returning his hat to his head as he leaves.

"See ya," I mutter as the door closes and I ask myself what the fuck just happened.

CHAPTER THIRTEEN
Nash

"I appreciate your help with the new trainer's salary, you know. It's not charity. When things start turning around here, we're going to pay you back," Wade says to me from across the stall.

I nod. "It's no trouble, I'll say the same thing to you that I told Mama Jo—don't sweat it. We're family, I don't think twice about it."

He nods so I continue. I've been meaning to touch base with him for a few weeks on this.

"Have you given any more thought to trying to qualify for the derby next year? Good way to earn some decent cash if you place. Now that I'm home, I'd help you any way I can around here when you have to go to qualifiers and I'd be happy to help with any costs."

Wade grunts, his brows furrowing like they do when he's uncomfortable.

"I hate taking money from you, Nash."

"It's everyone's money. I wouldn't even have *any* money if it weren't for your mom and dad. There's no better place to invest it than this family."

Also, I'd never say this to him, but I have so much of it I don't even know what to do with it. The Stars paid me millions of dollars a year for the nine years I played with them and I invested it right at every turn. Derby costs mean nothing to me.

"I appreciate it, we'll see what kind of trainer we end up with and what his or her experience is. And thanks, brother. I mean it," Wade says with a grin.

It's seven am already and we're picking hooves. We've been at the daily chores for almost two hours now and I've had no sleep.

"You seem a little keyed up today, you alright, man?" Wade asks as I drop my second hoof nipper in ten minutes.

"Fine," I bite out.

All I can think about is your little sister's soft warm skin under my fingers, and it's really fucking with my head.

"Just tired, I have a lot on the go today."

"And you only have one day until CeCe takes over your office with Post-It Notes and planners and all the weird shit she does when she's trying to control everything. But thanks for giving her this job, she needs the distraction."

"I need her too, I'm grateful for it."

"I swear if I see that fucker Andrew around here, you're gonna have to hold me back." He starts into a story about Andrew answering his phone in the middle of CeCe's college graduation, talking loudly before leaving the room in the middle of a slideshow.

I half listen to him, but I have my own problems today. Like trying to figure out why I couldn't help myself last night, why I grabbed CeCe like that. I wanted to kiss her. Not only did I want to kiss her, I wanted to bury myself so deeply in her that she'd forget another man ever hurt her... and oh yeah, if I ever see this Andrew character, I'll be cracking his fucking skull. Wade's going to be the one to hold *me* back.

I sigh as Wade finishes his story, trying to push CeCe from my mind.

"You have my help if he ever comes to town," I say, which makes Wade snicker.

A moment of silence passes.

"Sure is nice having both you and CeCe Rae home, though. After dad, it was too quiet here. Just funny you both end up back here the same summer. Between us, I'm so damn happy she got the guts to leave him."

"She told me a little about him last night when I walked her home. I can't see the CeCe I knew letting someone treat her like that."

"Andrew is a sly dog. Charming, shiny and manipulative as fuck. Dad couldn't stand him."

I'm not surprised but still glad to hear it, Wyatt was always a very smart man.

"I remember one time, Dad said he'd pay good money for us to rough him up a little like we did Steven Connolly. Remember when he told the football team he got to second base with CeCe? You and Cole gave him a good knock. Almost made him piss his pants," he says to me, chuckling at the memory.

Sure fucking do remember.

"She was in ninth grade and he was in twelfth! I remember sitting on your porch with her while she cried to us about it. She couldn't understand why he broke up with her."

"She always chose the wrong guys," I say to him, probably a little more aggressively than I should.

"None of us has the greatest track record choosing our love interests," Wade says under his breath.

Wade and his wife Janelle split up a year ago. She was a frigid bitch who only cared about appearances. I never understood what he saw in her, other than the fact that she was his college sweetheart. He was way too loyal and hung onto her, even when their relationship was one sided. Now she's living in his house, using his alimony to get her boobs done and going through some sort of mid-thirties crisis, and hooking up with every available man in town.

"I've determined that we all just try to live up to the way Mom and Dad were, but that kind of love just doesn't exist anymore. People are too selfish. Who knows, maybe we're all just destined to be alone."

"Nah, you just need to meet the right person," I say, sounding a lot more wishy-washy than I normally do.

Wade's laughter booms in the quiet barn. "Listen to you, all philosophical. A relationship hypocrite is what you are. I'll tell you what, I'll settle down when you do," he laughs and so do I. We both know I have no desire to settle down or get attached to anyone, not when I know that in a single breath, you can lose it all.

"Well, hopefully CeCe can find someone better than her last choice. Everyone has to try to learn from their mistakes. But I'll tell you one thing, it's good to know you have her back, with the three of us around, he'll never want to show his face around these parts," Wade says.

"It'll be a resurgence of The Good, The Bad, and The Ugly," I laugh as I say it, wiping my brow, remembering our trio's famous name whenever we were shit-kicking or getting into trouble.

"We'd have to convince Mr. Law Daddy Sheriff to rejoin though, which may not be easy," I add.

Wade thinks for a second.

"Nah... we've got Mabes now, she'd kick more shit than any of us."

"You ain't lying," I say back as we finish the rest of our morning work in silence.

The big house kitchen is quiet and sunny as I pour myself a coffee to attempt to wake myself up two hours later. This morning is kicking my ass and I still have a full day of training and meetings at the Center ahead of me.

Jo has gone to take Mabel to school, while Cole works a double and Wade is already onto his next task—training with Sam.

I grab a freshly made scone and have a seat at the kitchen table, taking in the view of Sugarland Mountain behind the house with my steaming brew. I just need five minutes to get my head clear. But I don't get it. The front door opens, and a groggy CeCe comes through it, rubbing her eyes, unaware yet that I'm here.

The ten seconds that I see her when she doesn't see me, feels too intimate. I should say something, but I don't. I can't bring myself to. She is wearing pink silk pajama shorts that flow over her tanned, silky thighs like water. Just the thought of sliding my hands up under them makes my cock begin to swell in my jeans. Her matching silky tank trails over her perfect tits, stopping just at her waist, exposing the tiniest sliver of her skin. And just because the universe is testing me, she has no bra on so the outline of her pebbled nipples are on full display. Her hair is a mess and falling over her shoulders in long, wavy cascades. Morning CeCe is on a whole other level. She's a goddamn experience. The only place she'd look better like this is wrapped up in my bedsheets under me while she screams my

—

"Jesus Christ, Nash." She jumps as she registers my presence. Normally, I'd stand but right now, I simply can't so I just sip my coffee and try to act like I don't have a semi-wood under the kitchen table.

"I didn't realize it was you," I say. "Thought you were Wade coming in after me."

She yawns and covers her chest with her short little robe, but it's too late—the image she just offered me is already burned into my brain for eternity.

"I don't have a coffee maker yet, so you get me instead."

She stands on her tiptoes, reaching for the top shelf. My gaze follows her hand to see the mug she's after and there's not a chance in hell she's reaching it on her own. I'm finally able to stand, so I get up and move toward her until I'm directly behind her.

"You're not reaching that, shortcake," I say as I grab the mug down for her and set it on the counter in front of her. I'm almost wrapped around her at this angle, and I'm liking the idea of caging her in a little too much.

It goes against everything in me, but I back up.

"Sit," I tell her. She looks at me with a 'don't tell me what to do' face. I cock my head to the side.

"Since you weren't dressed for company," I say to her. "I'll get your coffee for you."

She wraps her robe around herself even tighter, she knows I'm right. What I don't say is I haven't gotten laid in well over a year and her ass in those shorts is too fucking much for me right now.

"Well, I didn't expect some part-time cowboy to be sitting in *my* kitchen."

"Darlin', this is everyone's kitchen."

"I'm trying to get used to that again," she says as she does what I command and sits at the table.

"Still two cream and one sugar?" I ask her.

"Surprised you remember. Yes, thanks."

There really isn't much I don't remember about CeCe. I place the steaming Kentucky Derby mug in front of her. I can picture Wyatt sitting at his very table drinking from it on any given morning.

"I'll never forget that day. You?" I ask as I return to my seat.

"How could I forget?" she replies and it makes me smile.

"I remember that whole spring like it was yesterday," I say as I sip my coffee across from her.

She tosses her wild hair into a messy bun of sorts as she gets lost in the memory.

"I've never seen my dad so invested in a horse. I remember him taking you boys with him to everything. All the derby pre-race events, Arkansas, so many at Keeneland."

A beat of silence passes.

"You know he never confirmed it, but I know..." I say, admitting something to her that I've never admitted to anyone. "He knew. He knew I needed it. Something to invest my time in, something to distract me from my reality."

CeCe takes a sip of her coffee but says nothing. Tears fill her eyes and one spills over. I reach over without thinking and wipe it from her face. She freezes with the contact I just didn't have control over. *Be there for them when I'm gone. Especially the girls.*

"Sometimes, life just isn't fair. Taking him from us that quickly was definitely one of those times, but he was the best there ever was, we were all lucky to have him as long as we did." I say it all the time, but somehow in this moment, it seems more significant.

A smile pushes through her tears.

"I still have my hat." She laughs and I smile back, remembering that hideous looking purple fascinator.

"You looked like you were going to a royal wedding in that wild thing," I say as I chuckle.

"And I've never seen all you boys so fancy like in all my life. Y'all looked so uncomfortable all day."

I laugh even harder too, because her clear, bell laugh is contagious, always has been. She holds the mug up.

"Rising River," she says, looking down where that old horse's name is etched beside the year 2006—the year after my entire life changed forever.

"You still visit him?" CeCe asks.

"He's the horse I ride most days," I say back, honestly. I still can't believe he kept him all these years but that horse was Wyatt's biggest professional accomplishment and he couldn't bear to give him up. "That horse lives better than all of us." I chuckle

"Sure does." She grins.

He's been living the retired life as a riding horse for thirteen years, and he could possibly live another ten with the right care. He reminds me every time I ride him that I can overcome anything, and the lengths Wyatt Ashby went to for me. He kept my head above water and it's because of him that I am the man I am today. Fuck, I miss him more than my own parents sometimes.

I swallow my coffee and ignore the knotted feeling in my chest as CeCe and I stare out the back windows for a few moments, just remembering her dad in our own ways. Nothing more is said, it's just a comfortable peace as we drain our mugs.

"Wipe your paws, Harley." Mama Jo comes in the front door, breaking the easy, comfortable silence between us.

She looks back and forth between us as she enters the kitchen.

"Rising River, daddy's favorite," she says, kissing CeCe on the head.

I stand up and clear my throat because this is too heavy for me. Air. I need air. I need a minute away from CeCe's face.

Most of all I need to put a halt on this little crush or whatever this is and get back to my regular frame of mind. CeCe Ashby is off-limits and always will be, no matter how fucking good she looks in those shorts, and no matter how much history lies between us.

CHAPTER FOURTEEN
CeCe

LIV

We're celebrating.

> I don't need to go out to celebrate my new job.

GINGER

Who says this is about you? I ran into Cole today and he didn't scowl at me. AND he said hello. I'm breaking through. One step closer to his handcuffs on my bed posts.

LIV

Holy shit, plan the wedding!

> Both first and Second: Eww. Third: We can't go out again, I just recovered from Sunday, and I have to start work tomorrow.

GINGER

We're going out. We'll be good tonight. I have a nine am class tomorrow. One drink.

> I'm trying to keep a professional boundary because my new boss is always helping out at the only pub in town.

GINGER

You know what I say to that?

LIV

The whole town knows what you say to that.

GINGER

Save a horse. Your new boss is hot AF.

LIV

There it is. Do you go through even one day without saying that?

GINGER

I try not to, have you seen the cowboys in this town?

Yeah, stop grossing me out, two of them are my brothers

GINGER

That sounds like a you problem.

LIV

So... 8?

This is peer pressure

GINGER

CeCe

What?

GINGER

Dress like you want a pay raise and there's only one way to get it

LIV

Dress like you're about to get written up and you know just the way to change the boss's mind

I hate you guys

Why do I listen to them? *Why?*

As I walk in the Horse and Barrel, I'm exhausted. After my heartfelt conversation with Nash this morning I've discovered it's a lot harder to ignore how perfect this man's appearance is when he's this earthy rustic version of himself that I've never witnessed before. It only makes him hotter. Especially when I walked into that kitchen and saw him in full cowboy glory again. I thought Nash, the ice hockey player was hot? He doesn't hold a candle to Nash, the part-time cowboy. There is just something about a rugged man in a pair of jeans and cowboy boots, and his tattered cowboy hat ready to shade his face from the sun. Cowboy Nash is in his element. I'm going to need to use my now 'town famous' vibrator in the very near future to get that Cowboy Nash image out of my brain.

"Have I mentioned I hate you guys?" I ask as I approach our table.

It's much busier tonight with the after work mid-week crowd and my girls are crammed into a little corner booth while a good chunk of the bar dances to Zach Bryan's "Revival."

"You love us, and you listened—you look hot," Ginger says.

I look down at my strapless floral sundress and my worn jean jacket. A simple look but I did pair it with a new pair of red strappy sandals that I got at Olivia's shop today and cherry red lipstick.

"Hot enough that I'd stay late to work with you and I wouldn't tell my wife." Olivia smirks.

"God damn, you guys," I start to say. "I've known him my whole life, it's not like that."

Both of them laugh at me like there's a secret I'm not in on.

"You can't see the way he's looking at you right now. If I

didn't know any better, I'd say it's *exactly* like that," Olivia quips.

"I'd say he's looking at you like he wants to give you a promotion," Ginger says, looking over my shoulder.

Olivia cranes her neck to see him again and I die a little inside thinking Nash will notice that they're talking about him.

"Yep, he is definitely over there plotting out his next performance review and he knows *exactly* which tasks he's going to judge you on." Olivia giggles.

Then they both start to giggle. They think they're hilarious and I can't help but laugh with them after a minute of this.

"Oh shit, hot boss man is coming over here and he has sustenance," Ginger says.

Olivia straightens herself up and clears her throat. I look over my shoulder to see Nash in fact making his way over to us, with what looks like three margaritas.

"Not Angels," he greets as I breathe in his spicy, clean scent.

"Nashby," Ginger retorts.

I look up at him and his eyes meet mine.

"I don't want any trouble tonight; this is a classy place, you know." He looks right at me, wearing a shit eating grin on his face.

"One time," I say, not being able to hold back. "One time *and* she deserved it," I add.

"Simmer down, little Southpaw." Nash chuckles at me and it makes me want to smack the smug look he's wearing off his face.

"Three house margs on me." He passes them out to us then he looks down at me and smirks. "Be good tonight, CeCe Rae." His voice hits a lower octave as he tweaks my chin and my mind goes completely blank.

"You too..." I reply awkwardly, and then internally face-punch myself as he gives me a face that says, '*okay then.*' As soon as he's turned his back to us, Ginger and Olivia die laughing.

"Why can't I just act normal around this man? The way I have my whole life," I groan as I put my head down into my folded arms on the table.

"Because for the first time, you're not seeing him as the pompous heartbreaker you thought he was. You're seeing him for who he actually is." Ginger offers.

"Admit that you like it," Olivia adds.

"Shit," I offer. I know they're right.

"However, the second-hand embarrassment I have for you right now is off the charts. *You too?*" Olivia repeats my words as Ginger dies laughing.

"Have I mentioned I hate you guys?" I say again as I knock back almost half of my delicious margarita in one sip, made by my even more delicious bartender.

$$\infty$$

The alarm buzzes way too early. I open one eye and hope I'm dreaming. I'm not. I reach over and hit snooze.

Ten minutes later, I realize I have to get up. I'm extremely nervous, semi-attracted to my new boss and somewhere in between margaritas last night, I realized I forgot to buy myself a coffee maker. I tried to find an extra one in the big house when I got home, but after crashing around too much I gave up so I have to rush if I'm going to make it to Spicer's Sweets before I head into Olympia Sports. A good coffee to start my day is simply a *need*. I want to get a jump start on my office organization, and I told Nash when I left that I'd be in by eight-thirty.

I know he's already here on the ranch. I'm pretty sure he never stops moving. The man is a machine. Here until eight, and then in the office by nine. I let myself think about him while I get ready. He is everywhere all the time and it makes me wonder if he ever sleeps.

I select an outfit I think will do for my first day, but everything that can go wrong while I get ready, does.

My hair falls flat, I poke myself in the eye with my mascara wand, and I spill toothpaste on my blouse, forcing me to change at the last minute. I glance at my clock and realize the inevitable. I'm going to have to wait until I get to my office to have a coffee. I grumble. I didn't earn the nickname zombie girl in college for nothing. I'm useless before coffee.

I rush to put my shoes on and head out the front door. I almost lose my footing coming through it in my new sandals, I'm distracted by a large steaming to-go cup sitting on my porch rail from Spicer's. 2C 1S written on the top, Rae written on the side by the barista.

I don't see him when I look around, but I know it's from Nash. It has to be. Cole is working and Wade is already running a trail class. I take a deep breath and pick up the cup, breathing in that sweet elixir of the gods. A smile moves across my face as I head to my car. Nash Carter had my back this morning, and just like that, my whole morning feels a little bit brighter.

CHAPTER FIFTEEN
Nash

I wish I could see her face as she steps out onto the porch and gets her coffee, but I'm trying not to appear like the stage five stalker I'm quickly becoming. CeCe probably doesn't realize I was in earshot to hear her tell her *Not Angels* that she forgot to buy a coffee maker last night, but I was, and anything I can do to help make this transition easier for her is my new mission.

Because I need her for the Center—at least that's what I keep telling myself. Over and over and fucking over. She's good for the business. Regardless of whatever this little crush is, I'm determined to treat her the way I always have and stop eye fucking her every chance I get. She's Wade and Cole's sister, and my employee, that's where it ends.

I scrub my face with my hand as I head through the barn to my truck with my own coffee from Spicer's. It's only eight-fifteen but I'm already behind. I have to get home, shower and I have a full morning of training ahead of me. It dawns on me just what I need to take my mind off CeCe—I need a good distraction. I buckle my seatbelt and start my truck as I call Cole.

Two hours later, I'm on the ice with a very energetic group of third grade skaters, running a skills class. I can't figure out if I'm wearing them out or if they're wearing me out as Chris and I play games with them and get them flowing into a backward skate.

We move through passing and shooting drills and begin the last part of our class. The fastest kid to get through all the drills gets to pick the last activity.

"I pick... a 95'er," Sherri-Lynn's grandson, Micah, says, pumping his little fists. He won the race and wants me to put on a show and knock one into the net at full speed—a 95'er.

The whole class cheers.

"Okay, well go ahead and give them one, Micah," I joke and he starts giggling, the whole class following suit.

"You give us one, Coach!" Micah pleads.

"Alright. But then you all have to give your best slap shot after I do. Agreed?"

They nod enthusiastically and start tapping their sticks on the ice, chanting, "Slap shot!

Chris joins in and taps his stick on the ice. He's a great hockey player, still plays for the 18U Lightning, and has a good chance to get drafted next year. Even better than that, he's a great kid and loves to help.

"Alright, to the boards!" I call and point to the other side of the rink.

They all hustle over to the boards and wait expectantly for me to tear off a slap shot. Chris uses his phone to change the song on our system to "Thunderstruck" by ACDC and the kids go crazy.

I cock my head to the side. "Really?"

"Gotta set the tone, boss," he chuckles.

I give them some theatrics and pretend to play the guitar on my stick as they all laugh, seeing their little toothy grins makes all of this worth it.

I skate down to the end of the rink with a dramatically determined look on my face, as if I question my ability. I turn around for one split second and then I'm flying. I get two-thirds up the ice in less than three seconds flat, and fire the shot as I come to a stop, with ice flying from my blades. It lands smack in the back of the net, top shelf.

My mini crowd goes wild. The reader on the net says 98.4.

I cheer with them, giving a little celebratory stick pump before I turn to lead them to the net to take their own shots as a flash of CeCe's golden hair catches my eye from behind the glass of her office, then disappears from my sightline.

"Settling in?" I ask, peeking into CeCe's office. A curtain of long, thick hair is tossed over her shoulder as CeCe meets my eyes. It's almost lunch time and I'm through with my morning training and showered, again. I have jobs that require multiple showers a day, every day. Now, I'm dressed for the afternoon and ready for the business side of things. She flashes me an earth shattering smile that almost makes me forget my own name as I remind myself, *good for business, not my cock.*

"Yes, a little easier than I expected after an early delivery of the best coffee in town."

"The only coffee in town."

"Semantics," CeCe says as she tucks her hair behind her ear and pulls her glasses off. "Thank you."

"It was nothing. I just wanted you to have the best start. We need you here."

"I'll say," she says. "I've got a good start on sorting all this paperwork. We need to start a file room, somewhere we can store these documents, and we also need to have them digitally filed."

"How do we do that?"

"We send them out, there are companies that do it, I can look into it if you want? Then you keep the hard copies in a file room. An *organized* one," she says.

"Yes, please."

She nods.

"I don't have your phone number anymore," I say to her as I walk over to her and hold out my hand. "Your phone, please?"

CeCe looks at me with one eyebrow raised, but unlocks it anyway and hands it to me. I enter my number in and hand it back to her.

"No need to look skeptical, it's just a number," I say to her.

"I never know with you, Nash. Remember when I got my own phone line to my bedroom and you and Wade called it and pranked me for three straight days? Every time I answered, you guys would tell me I won concert tickets, or ask me if I wanted to do a survey. So annoying."

I'm chuckling now but I wave her off. "Just a number, CeCe."

Sonny knocks on the door frame. "Harry is here. He's hoping we have a plan to raise him a lot of money. Do we?"

"Harry Martin?" CeCe asks. "Your old hockey coach?"

I am shocked she remembers, but I nod. "Yeah, we're trying to raise money for all divisions of the Lightning this fall, but he has some pretty strict ways he wants to see us do it, he wants it to be a community thing." She looks down and chews her plump bottom lip.

I don't know why I didn't think of it before, but I ask now, "Do you want to sit in?"

"That's a great idea," Sonny says. "You're a part of the team now, we'd love your perspective."

"Sure," CeCe replies. "I helped raise money for the women's shelter in Seattle over the last two winters so I have some experience with this sort of thing."

We move to the boardroom. Harry and his new assistant, Kevin, are already seated. They rise as we come in and I make introductions to CeCe. Harry remembers her instantly. Kevin shakes my hand. "It's a pleasure Mr. Carter, I'm a big fan," he says as I nod.

"Thanks, call me Nash," I offer back.

"I remember you watching these boys play hockey when you were young. Your dad and your family's ranch was always a big sponsor for us. He was a great man. I was sorry to hear he passed on," Harry tells CeCe as he shakes her hand.

She smiles at him but I don't miss her wince as he says it.

Kevin, looks her over. He's younger, maybe even younger than her and he's like a little lovesick puppy panting for her the moment she makes eye contact with him. She shakes his hand and turns to sit while I watch his eyes trail her ass in her gray sweater dress that accentuates every curve. I mentally rescind my offer for him to call me Nash and run through my afternoon tasks in my mind.

1. *Implement new dress code.*
2. *Better yet, implement baggy office uniforms, neck to ankles.*
3. *Don't kill Kevin.*

CHAPTER SIXTEEN
Nash

We spend the next hour brainstorming. The funds we need to raise just keep going up, and finally we go over all the approximate numbers.

"So, I've run the numbers and I just don't think there is any way to raise this kind of money with something simple like we originally thought," Sonny says. "We need something bigger, and the summer is going to fly by. We could capitalize on something related to fall?"

"I really hope we can find a way to involve the entire community, make it more grassroots like we used to do in the seventies and eighties. We ran car washes, bake sales, concerts, everyone got involved for the kids. I realize money doesn't stretch as far anymore, but that's what I'm hoping for," Harry says.

"I have an idea, maybe," CeCe talks for the first time, raising one slender finger in the air and everyone's eyes focuses on her at the end of the table. She's got her glasses on again and her hair is drifting behind her shoulders. A pencil sits neatly between her fingers. She taps the end of it while she thinks.

"It's a pretty big endeavor for this town, but I think we can do it if we get all the right people involved. When I lived in Seattle with my... former partner," she begins. "We used to travel to Palm Springs every winter for business. Every Thursday night in Palm Springs, they shut down Palm Canyon Drive and host a night market. Vendors line the streets, there are twinkling lights, food trucks, and local artisan items. The whole community comes out for it, and it attracts people from all over. If we plan it right, we could do something like that?"

"A night market?" Sonny asks

"Not just a night market, I think it could be an all-day event, into the night," CeCe says.

"A community festival," I say, loving the idea already.

"Yes, exactly. We could advertise it to Lexington, and, sorry in advance, Nash, but we should use your celebrity status." She grins, knowing I hate that. "Make it like a sort of Hometown Hockey fundraiser. If we could get permits for it, we could use the Center and the parking lot. Bouncy castles for the kids, etcetera. Like a mini fair, almost—charge a few dollars to ride the little rides. Have some other NHL'ers come in, sign autographs, auction off signed jerseys, maybe have some synthetic ice, parents could donate to have their kids take shots on net, or play with an NHL'er, whatever we can come up with. We have time to plan it."

"How long do you think we'd need?" I ask.

CeCe shrugs. "It's only the second week in July, I'd say if we plan it for the end of August that gives lots of time. Most of the local artisans always have items on hand and if we market it right to social media and local radio stations."

"I love it," Harry says, completely won over.

"What a fantastic idea," Lovesick Kevin chimes in.

"It definitely involves the community and keeps it grassroots..." Sonny pauses, giggling.

"But it allows the boss to cheat and bring in some heavy

hitters to raise *a lot* of money," CeCe adds as she winks at Sonny.

"You have quite the addition to your team here Nash," Harry says.

"I'm happy to help," CeCe says as she gives them a winning smile that I'm pretty sure has Kevin bricked up under the table.

CeCe spends the next thirty minutes jotting down points in her bible of a day planner/notebook and by the end of it, we have an entire plan formatted.

"Okay, well this is a great start." Harry turns to Kevin. "Let's let them get to planning."

Kevin nods, adding, "We'll help however we can. I say we meet weekly to touch base?"

"Sounds great. We'll pick the date based on what the township says and get back to you," CeCe says to him, as I make mental notes of everything that will have to be done.

We'll keep it as grassroots as we can, but I also want to sneak in as much as I can to give every team in each division what they need for the season.

CeCe stands and shakes their hands. She's a natural and I think for the tenth time today how lucky we are that she's here. I'm going to do everything in my power to keep her. Including forcing myself to ignore the way Kevin is looking at her and the way she's smiling back at him.

I walk the two men out and feel my phone buzzing in my pocket. Two texts wait for me—one from Cole with the contact number I asked for, the other from an unknown number.

UNKNOWN

> I made you copies of the notes I jotted down. When you have time, come grab them. By the way, nice slap shot this morning. Way to go for the peanut butter.

I grin like a fifteen year old, realizing it's CeCe texting me and chuckle, remembering the stupid saying Cole used to chant every time he scored a goal at the top of the net. *Top shelf, baby, where the peanut butter is kept.*

> Watching me play? Just like old times, huh?

RAE

> Kind of hard not to watch when you hear the little crowd roaring below your office window.

> If you want, I can have the sound pumped into your office too. Get the full experience?

RAE

> Sounds like a dream but that's a hard pass, I have a feeling I wouldn't get my work done.

I decide the number Cole just sent me can wait and head up to CeCe's office.

We spend the next hour going over all her ideas and lay out a full-size draft of the community festival, complete with vendors she plans on asking. Sonny joins us after a short while and the three of us come up with the name *Sunset Festival*, since it will hopefully happen the last weekend in August, just after school has started and people are getting ready for fall.

CeCe has already contacted the municipality and is waiting on a call back. She has a list of ten places to call for synthetic ice, bouncy castles, carnival game rentals. I find myself struggling to keep up with the way her beautiful mind works. She is actually brilliant and has a mind for planning. Her phone rings as we're talking about a list of old NHL buddies I can call and email and she excuses herself.

I look down at my phone and realize it's already three-thirty.

"She is incredible. We can't lose her," Sonny says echoing my thoughts.

"Tell me about it," I say, watching her pace outside the glass of her office on the phone. I wonder who she's talking to as I watch the way her hips—

"If you want to keep her around, maybe stop looking at her like that," Sonny offers.

"Sorry?" I say, feigning innocence. *Am I that obvious?*

"It's just, sorry to say, boss, but you have a track record and I would hate to see you act on those 'hearts in place of eyeballs' in your head and break her heart." She wiggles a finger back and forth between my eyes across the table "We'll never find anyone around here as good as her."

"I'm crushed you think so little of me," I joke with Sonny.

"I don't think little of you. I just don't want to see you give into whatever this is"—she waves a hand over me—"and we're left without her. In other words, to be blunt—just keep it in your pants, kid."

"Jesus Christ, Sonny." I rub my forehead but I don't deny her.

She raises her hands in truce. "I'm just sayin', is all."

"Just saying what?" CeCe asks, coming back into her office.

"Just Sonny being Sonny," I retort, shooting Sonny a side eye.

"I have to go soon, if that's okay?" CeCe asks. "I'm going to pick up Mabel for Cole."

"Of course," I answer. "You set your own hours, remember?"

"Right," she says, her bottom lip between her teeth again, but when her emerald eyes meet mine she smiles. "This was a good day." She says it like she's surprised.

I smile smugly, leaning back in my chair. "Told ya. I can't believe you doubted me." My grin grows and she rolls her eyes.

Sonny gets up and gives her a squeeze.

"You did great today, darlin', and you should give that Kevin a call. He's cute." She looks at me as she says it. The idea of CeCe going anywhere with Kevin has my blood boiling in two seconds flat.

"Yeah, he's nice but I'm not looking to date anyone right now. *At all*," she says back.

'Who said anything about dating?" Sonny winks at her and CeCe laughs.

A barrage of cuss words fly through my head at my beloved little Sonny.

"Now, that's more my style right now," she says back to Sonny and I inadvertently scoff, loudly. I instantly regret it. Both women look at me with disgust at the sound I just made.

CeCe starts laughing and puts her hands on her hips.

"Oh, I know you of all people aren't slut shaming me, Nash Carter." *This woman's mouth.*

Sonny roars with laughter.

"Not at all." I clear my throat, back peddling. "Just wouldn't be wise to get involved with anyone we'll be working with on this event. It has to go smoothly."

"Oh yeah, I guess so. You're right," CeCe says. "Your 'cardinal rule.'" She uses air quotes then she pats me on the shoulder and heads over to her desk.

"Yep," I bite out while Sonny snickers.

I stand and say goodbye to both of them. Just feeling the need to get the fuck out of here, I make a beeline for my own office. Only two things on my mind. Use that phone number Cole gave me real soon, and make sure every goddamn man in this town is helping us with our Sunset Festival so they're off limits to CeCe.

CHAPTER SEVENTEEN
Nash

I miraculously manage to keep my hands to myself over the next three weeks, or "keep it in my pants," as Sonny advised. And although it's not without incredible effort, deep down I know she's right.

CeCe has charmed not only the township but all the local businesses too. She has thirty-seven local artisans from town and the surrounding counties coming to sell their wares so far, and they've agreed to donate a large portion of the proceeds to the Lightning.

Spending every day with CeCe is the worst kind of torture for me. The kind I both can't stand and race to be a part of every damn day. If it isn't enough that she comes in every morning looking like a cross between the hot accountant and the fresh faced college girl, her brain is the most attractive thing about her. Her ideas are smart and thought out. She's managed to organize a file room for all the paperwork, she's sent it out to have it digitized, and she's got our accounting system well on its way to law and order. All in under a month.

When CeCe is around, everything is just a little brighter. A little more exciting. She's like bringing sunshine into the office.

I'm pretty sure Sonny is going to ask to adopt her—they have become the best of friends and have dubbed themselves *Thelma and Louise*. They bring each other books and baked goods, for Christ's sake. Sonny doesn't have much since her husband died and seeing CeCe laugh with her every day and show an interest in her grandkids is the sweetest fucking thing I've witnessed as they work day in and day out on the Sunset Festival.

We'll be blocking off all of Main and part of Decker Lane for the festival. Wade and Cole have even offered to help in any way they can, and Silver Pines is donating a horseback lesson package to be auctioned off.

A lot of my active and retired—but still very famous—NHL buddies are coming out of the woodwork during the offseason to sign autographs and do meet and greets. Cory Kane, for one, still plays with the Nashville Predators and is a big draw. He's going to help me run the shootout competition. I have synthetic ice coming in, because Kentucky in late August is still steamy as hell. A host of activities will happen in the Center parking lot as well, and we may even have enough for a team. CeCe had the idea to put on a game of Pros vs Townies, incorporating the police department, fire department, anyone that lives in Laurel Creek and wants to take us on.

I hop out of my truck and head inside. I have no camps running this week, and Chris is handling classes for me so I can spend the week getting all the details set in stone with CeCe and Sonny.

CeCe is giving up her usual Monday off today, and we're meeting with the municipality to go over zoning rules and to fill our permit documentation. I'd be lying if I said I wasn't looking forward to it way more than I should.

I find myself wondering what she'll wear or how her hair will be styled as I make my way through the parking lot like a love-sick teenager. I'm over scolding myself. It would be impossible for any man not to be attracted to CeCe Ashby, is what I settle with. It makes me feel a little better about picturing her sliding off those silky little blouses she wears that hug those perfect tits, when I'm fisting myself in the shower almost nightly after spending my days with her. I imagine it's her full, cherry lips wrapped around me—not my own hand—or her moaning my name as I drive into her, gripping her hair as I take her from behind. After almost a month with her, I have several fantasies saved up to choose from.

The scene is already bustling at Olympia when I breeze through the doors. Avery's training the figure skating group on rink one, Chris and a helper are running power skating on rink two and happy kids are milling about. There are days when this dream feels even more fulfilling than my NHL dream. Like I'm giving back to my childhood self and making my parents proud. There were times when I know they struggled, and if there was a place like this to help them, it would've meant the world. The familiar pang of guilt settles in my soul that always creeps in when I think about everything they did so I could play hockey. Essentially, they even died for it.

CeCe has her head resting on her folded arms on her desk when I come in, the coffee I left her on her porch rail this morning is beside her, and Sonny sits across from her.

"Uh-oh, here's the hard ass," Sonny quips as she giggles.

"Not one word this morning, Nash Carter," CeCe groans, her voice muffled as I chuckle.

"Have one too many sangrias last night, Rae?"

Fucking right she did. She danced all night with her *Not Angels* and Avery while I kept tabs on her fan club of men that are slowly starting to pile into lady's night every week.

She raises her pretty little head and looks at me. She's dressed casual today, as most women in town are on Mondays.

Laurel Creek, Kentucky; the only place in the continental US that needs a casual *Monday*.

Her long wavy hair is pulled back into a high ponytail and she's wearing Birkenstocks and a sleeveless navy sundress that falls to her ankles.

"I don't want to hear one word until my Advil kicks in."

I chuckle and turn to leave when Sonny speaks.

"Maybe you should reschedule with Kevin," she says to CeCe.

I freeze. *Kevin?* I turn back around.

"Kevin and Harry are coming?" I ask.

Sonny shakes her head. "Just Kevin, he wanted to go over the list of needs with CeCe this afternoon."

Did he now?

"Yeah maybe, let's make it for Wednesday," CeCe says, and I make a mental note to be in that meeting with her. Look at Kevin go, sliding in where he can. I can't say I blame him, but it won't be happening. Not on my watch.

"I'll sit in, too. I-uh, have some items to go over with him," I say. A total lie, but CeCe thinks nothing of it and nods.

"I need twenty minutes, Nash. And hey, please don't have a Shania cover girl in all night and plan a Monday meeting again."

"Noted." I chuckle as I wander to my office and wait for my hot little accountant to be ready.

RAE

Ok, I'm semi-human. What time should we leave?

Now is good. Don't forget those sunglasses. It's a scorcher already. Light bad. Dark good.

RAE

> Sunglasses and Advil. I think that is from a song I used to listen to in college. It shouldn't still be my life at twenty-five.

> Straighten up, wild one. Your boss is coming down the hall.

RAE

> Ugh. He's such a hard-ass.

I grin as I peek my head around the corner just as she pops her sunglasses on her head like I told her to.

"I'll drive; you might still be over the limit." I grimace.

She sticks her tongue out at me as she walks by and my dick takes it to heart.

"Let's go, hangover enabler," she mutters.

The air is, in fact, scorching hot outside as we ride into town with the windows down. CeCe's clean, strawberry scent fills my truck and her hair blows around in the summer breeze. My appreciation for summer has spiked immensely in the last month. Things like fishing, barbeque and boating used to be my highlights of Kentucky's warmest months. Not now. Now, I appreciate summer most because CeCe wears sleeveless tanks and sundresses in the summer and her shoulders are a fucking masterpiece. It actually makes me sad that come winter, they'll be in hiding.

I listen as she hums along with the radio while we drive. It would take nothing for me to reach across the seat, pull that dress up and run my hand up her thighs to her—

CeCe clears her throat, cutting into my thoughts of how her thighs would feel under my hand. I look at her with a fleeting glance. "Thank you for the extra-large this morning," she says.

Title of your sex tape. I smirk inwardly.

"Figured you needed the extra-large today," I retort out loud. *Title number two.*

"I did. I've been thinking about this," she says, turning her emerald eyes to me. "Do you ever sleep?"

My eyes focus on the road as her personal question hits home.

"Not much," I say honestly.

"Between the Center, the ranch and the bar, I've done the math." *Of course she has.* "You can't get more than three or four hours a night, if you're lucky. That's not good for you."

I shrug, but she's about right.

"I just don't sleep. When I try to sleep, things... come back to me. I get a few hours, but I'm usually up long before the sun."

"Oh." She nods.

"Have you ever tried talking to someone about it?"

I smirk because she has no idea the lengths I've gone to. Her question doesn't pry, it's like she's just curious.

"I've tried everything. Three different therapists, hypnosis, melatonin, every natural remedy you can think of that your Mama could dig up. It's much better now than it was the first ten years after. I can sleep on and off now, but some nights and moments are just worse than others." I shrug.

She reaches over and startles me by placing her tiny hand over mine and squeezes gently. Her hand is warm and soft on my skin. Heat races up my forearm with her touch.

"If you're struggling, you're living. You have to hold some

peace in that, and I can be a good friend for listening if you ever want to talk about it."

I pull my hand away, because I'm not used to people touching me when I haven't planned for it.

"Here we are," I say as we pull up to Town Hall.

CeCe replaces her hand back in her lap and nods as I mentally kick myself for shutting her down.

CHAPTER EIGHTEEN
CeCe

Maybe I shouldn't have said anything, but after spending these last weeks with Nash I'm starting to actually care about him and his well-being. I know what he went through and knowing he is everywhere all the time tells me he doesn't take time for himself and possibly works himself away from his demons.

He eats like he's still in NHL training and never stops going physically, but that can't be enough. It's natural I worry—I'm used to seeing him everywhere now—at our dinner table on Monday nights, at the bar when I'm out with the girls and almost every day at the Center. It's no longer uncomfortable like it was in the beginning. It's now *comforting,* and somewhere over the last few weeks, I've come to look forward to seeing him.

As much as I hate crushing on someone I will never have, I look forward to coming to work and that makes my days easier. It's easier to put up with Andrew's constant voicemails and emails when I've come home from an otherwise good day. It's also slow torture because he is just too gorgeous in any setting.

Business Nash, Backwards ball-cap-wearing bar Nash,

Cowboy Nash, Hockey Nash—they're all starring characters in my Saturday night imaginary reels. It's not just his looks, it's the way he brings Sonny her morning donut every single day, and the way he pays for the kid's camp fees when their parents can't afford it—I've uncovered a lot of that while I've been going over the books. It's when I come outside the mornings that he's at the ranch, to find Spicer's coffee on the porch rail, always steaming hot, always perfect. We never really talk about it much but it's always there and I appreciate the way he's making me feel as welcome as possible to his team.

It's giving me hope that we can be friends going forward. Real friends. Which is why I offered a listening ear to him, but I should've known he wouldn't accept it.

Somewhere under there, he's still the same elusive, closed off Nash and that will probably never change.

We meet with the Mayor's assistant, Leslie and spend the next hour going over rules with her. I take notes as she flirts with an oblivious Nash. Everything he says is "so smart" and "such a great idea" that she "never thought of."

My stomach growls as I shake Leslie's hand to say goodbye. I'm pretty sure she has drool on her chin as she shakes Nash's.

"Sage and Salt?" he asks, as we walk toward Main.

"Absolutely," I reply as we pass his truck and opt to walk the short distance.

My hometown is so pretty and I'm getting all the homey feelings again as we take in the summer tourists and shoppers. We cross over the tiny bridge in the harbor and select a patio table to have our lunch at.

"Hey, honey!" Sandy calls as we sit.

"Rocket," she addresses Nash. "The usual?"

"You know it," Nash says in return.

"And for you, CeCe?" She turns to me expectantly.

111

"The breakfast croissant and home fries. And an orange juice, please," I say. No menus required.

"Breakfast after too many sangrias," she chuckles.

"That Shania cover was great last night," she says to Nash. "We need to get her here again."

"She came from Louisville," Nash says.

"What a welcome home for you," she says to me, nudging my shoulder.

I look at her with confusion. "For me?" I ask.

Nash clears his throat and asks, "Can I get a green protein smoothie with mine Sandy?"

"Sure thing, hun." She winks and heads off.

I eye Nash and he avoids me for as long as he can.

"What?" he asks.

"What did she mean *for me*?"

"I don't know; everyone knows you like Shania." He shrugs.

"How often do you have cover musicians in?"

He looks at me, bullshit in his brilliant blue eyes. "From time to time."

"How long have you had her booked for?"

"A while," he retorts.

"If I didn't know any better I'd think you were championing my Monday hangover by bringing my close to favorite country singer into your bar on cheap drink night."

Nash chuckles and leans back in his seat, relaxing his legs, turning his Stars baseball hat backwards, little tendrils of his wavy dark hair poke out from under it. He steals my breath as he folds his arms over his chest and stares right through me. I decide looking at him is more fun that giving him a hard time for the time being.

"Yeah, that's it, you got me. Hungover CeCe is such a joy that I brought Shania *Twin* into the pub just to experience this delightful treat this morning."

I laugh and throw my napkin at him as a young waitress I've never seen comes out with our drinks. She places my orange juice in front of me without a second glance, and gives Nash an award winning smile as she offers him his smoothie.

"Your breakfast is coming right up, Mr. Carter," she says, and turns right in front of him offering him a perfect view of her very toned behind. Surprisingly, he's a perfect gentleman and doesn't even look. Even *I* looked, her ass is that perfect.

I scoff as she saunters away.

"Does that happen to you all the time?" I ask.

Nash looks at me as he takes the straw between his plush lips.

I wish I was the straw.

"What?"

"Women—they throw themselves at you," I say, and then add, "*Mr. Carter,*" mimicking her sultry voice.

"I have no idea what you're talking about." He feigns innocence as he shifts in his seat.

"She might even be younger than me," I observe, then instantly regret saying anything as I take in Nash's smirk across from me.

"First off, Rae, if I didn't know any better, I'd say you sound a little annoyed, even jealous maybe."

"Ha." I make the most embarrassing sounding laugh—it's a cackle really which makes it obvious that he's right. Nash grins at me.

"Two, you're one to talk, it's become my full-time job on Sunday nights to relieve you of the drunken men in the bar as they work up the nerve to hit on you. And don't even get me started on Kevin."

"Oh, please." I giggle at his ridiculous description. "Kevin is just friendly."

"You don't see him stare at your ass," he fires back.

I shrug. "Well, I guess it's settled then."

"What's settled?" He chuckles

"We're both just too hot for our own good," I say, just as Flirty McShows-her-ass comes back with our orders.

"Enjoy, Mr. Carter," she says, ignoring me completely, proving my point.

I gesture to her while she's still in earshot by hiking my thumb over my shoulder and mouthing "see what I mean," which makes Nash laugh harder as he shakes his head at me.

CHAPTER NINETEEN
Nash

After we spend an hour at Sage and Salt going over everything we have for the Sunset Festival, I find myself not wanting to leave CeCe with Sonny at the office to go meet with Rocco and the supplier at the Horse and Barrel.

It's quiet when I arrive. Mondays always are. It's the only day of the week we're closed and I work at the bar going through our inventory list and giving the place a good wipe down before the delivery is due to arrive.

Something shimmery catches my eye from the area the *Not Angels* were sitting last night. I make my way over to the booth and pick up the glittery gold infinity shaped charm necklace off the seat. I recognize it at once as CeCe's. She was wearing it last night with her white dress and red sandals. I bring it to my nose like an obsessed stalker and breathe in the strawberry scent that still lingers there.

Since when in my life have I ever remembered a woman's outfit? I ask myself, just as my delivery driver pulls up to the door. I put her necklace in my pocket and head out to help him unload.

By the time I get back to the office at four, I notice her car is gone.

> Couldn't hack it the rest of the day? Had to sneak out early?

RAE

> Don't tell my boss. Such a hard-ass.

I chuckle.

> Secret's safe with me, Rae.

I push down my disappointment that she's gone already and count how many hours I have left before I can see her face again.

It's a full out dance party at the ranch when I come through the front door for Monday dinner with a Spicer's cake in my hands for Mama Jo.

CeCe and Mabel have the stereo blasting in the living room as the evening sun streams in the big picture window, and they are dancing up a storm to Miranda Lambert's "Geraldine." They've got a little dance routine going as I pass by them.

"Evening, Mr. Carter," CeCe sing-songs as I wander past her. Something about the way she emphasizes Mr. Carter makes my dick twitch. It's not just her tone but also the formal address. Everything she does is fucking sexy as hell.

"Mr. Carter?" Wade grunts as I enter the kitchen.

"Work joke," I say quickly.

He nods as he swirls his bourbon before taking a sip.

"It's going well for you, having CeCe Rae around?"

I nod. "Yeah, she's been a big help."

There is nothing going on but I feel like he can read my "hearts for eyeballs" as Sonny puts it, a mile away.

"Good, I'm glad she's with you. Watch over her, Andrew hasn't given her an easy time, Mama says. He won't agree to sell, won't agree to ship her belongings. Keeps telling her she has to come back to Seattle if she wants them. He's a real piece of work. I have half a mind to run him up the creek if I see him, and CeCe tends to bury herself in work when she's trying to avoid something."

My jaw tenses as I turn to watch her laugh and spin around the living room with Mabel. Her hair is loose and wavy down to her waist, her jean shorts and tank sit perfectly around her curves but it's her smile—it's a sucker punch to the gut. It lights up my whole fucking day that smile.

This Andrew must be a special kind of stupid. What kind of a moron lets her go?

"I'll be right there with you, brother," I say as he hands me a glass of bourbon and we clink glasses before taking a big swallow.

In fact, if I ever see Andrew, I won't just be with the Ashby boys to beat him down, I'll be *first* in line.

"What's good, boys?" Cole says, pulling his sheriff hat off and placing it on his chair at the kitchen table as he comes into the kitchen.

He pulls the bottle of bourbon from the counter and pours himself a glass. Mama Jo has joined the dance party in the living room now.

The oven starts beeping as Jo changes the song on her phone for the girls.

"Cole, take the lasagna out and toss in the bread. You boys can serve us girls tonight."

CeCe and Mabel cheer as they start dancing to "That Don't Impress Me Much," CeCe's Shania favorite.

I look at the boys and we chuckle. As always, no one argues with Jo, so Wade pulls out the loaf of bread and makings of a salad, and I make a quick garlic butter to spread on it, as Dean squeezes into the kitchen past the girls. "You fellas making dinner tonight on account of this?" he says hiking his thumb over his shoulder.

"Yep, Pop," Wade says. He hands him the cutlery. "Make yourself useful, you can set the table."

"What's wrong with you, you're younger than me," Dean jokes, taking the cutlery from him as he pours his own bourbon.

"Can't. I'm tossing the salad." Wade shakes his head as soon as the words leave his mouth while he mixes the salad.

"Yeah, Wade's the best at tossing salad. Maybe even the best in the whole county." Cole chuckles as he pops a crouton into his mouth.

"You know, come to think of it, I have heard around town that he tosses a mean salad," I say.

Papa Dean winks, waving his handful of cutlery at Wade. "That only comes with lots of practice like my fingering."

"Damn you, fuckers," Wade mutters as I clap him on the back and start buttering the bread.

"Two dollars in my boot, Uncle Wade," Mabel yells over the music and I laugh.

"Her hearing becomes supersonic for cuss words," Wade mumbles as he tosses two bills in the boot.

"Mama Jo!" CeCe protests as the opening strings to "Cecilia" by Simon & Garfunkel begin to play. They always do this to her every chance they get, and although she protests, she always dances to her namesake.

I put the bread in the oven to crisp, then lean against the door frame and watch the girls make fools out of themselves while I knock back the rest of my bourbon. I just may need a second tonight.

No matter how many times I tell myself not to let her in, CeCe Ashby is getting under my skin. Wade's words ring in my mind. *Watch out for her.* He trusts me to care for her the way *he* would. I can't let him or Wyatt down for a crush, okay, a semi-obsession at this point. I make a mental note to use the phone number Cole passed onto me a few weeks ago, and soon, just to help clear my head. This family is the only one I have. But as I watch the free-spirited blonde that has all my attention lately dance and sing to the lyrics,

You're breaking my heart,
I'm down on my knees,
I'm begging you please to come home...

I know it's gonna be a tough fight. She's just creeping into the crevices of my otherwise closed off soul and lighting it up like the fucking fourth of July. She looks up at me watching her, wearing what I'm sure is the world's goofiest grin on my face and she smiles wide, tips her head back and laughs. It's the prettiest fucking thing I've ever seen.

"Dinner, Pistol Annies!" Cole calls to the out of breath dance team in the living room, fifteen minutes later. They shuffle in, and as CeCe passes by me still breathing heavy after her pre-dinner workout. I grab her wrist.

"You left this last night in the bar, must have fallen off you."

I pull her infinity necklace out of my pocket and it dangles between my finger and thumb. She holds her palm out and I drop it in, curling her fingers around it. The size difference between our hands is staggering. Her hand molds underneath mine so perfectly it momentarily stuns me.

She smiles up at me. "I was so worried I lost it. My dad gave me this two Christmases ago." She leans in. "He's with me for eternity," she whispers, I assume quoting his words.

"He is, you know," I say back, looking deeper into her eyes than warranted.

She looks around and nods. "He's everywhere I look here. It's comforting."

"Sure is," I say as she smiles at me again.

She pinches my t-shirt, her nails grazing my torso through my shirt and I threaten to brick up with the simple contact.

"Come on, Mr. Carter, pour me a bourbon, sir." She nods toward the kitchen as she moves in front of me.

I do my best not to watch her perfect ass sway under her shorts but I fail, miserably.

I am so fucked.

CHAPTER TWENTY
CeCe

I stare at my reflection in the mirror on Wednesday night. I can't believe I'm doing this. I can't believe he showed up here unannounced. Andrew's words were hurried and curt when he called to say he was in town this afternoon.

"What choice did you leave me with? You don't answer my calls. It's been weeks. Enough is enough. You can't avoid me forever, Cecilia. I'm ready to settle this. Meet me for coffee... it's just coffee."

I push his pleads out of my mind as I smooth my hair.

Andrew doesn't take no for an answer, that's one thing I know for sure. So avoiding him like I've been doing the last month is pointless and I do need to get this over with, so Spicer's Sweets, it is. It's the only option. I'm not going to the Horse and Barrel bar with Andrew, that is for damn sure, and the only other place in town to meet is our resident upscale restaurant, Dolcettos Steakhouse and Pasta Bar.

This most certainly isn't a date, *just* coffee. I sigh and take in my appearance. As basic as I can be, just like Ginger said. *Basic bitch mode.* Jeans, black t-shirt, sandals. I grab my purse and head out to my truck just as it starts to rain. An omen for my night ahead, I'm sure of it.

Spicer's Sweets is quiet at dinner time mid-week. At least that is working in my favor. Andrew looks like a fish out of water in this town. His wavy blond hair is perfectly styled, and he's wearing Tom Ford head to toe. He looks like he belongs on my Pinterest page, and not the rustic town coffee shop in Laurel Creek, Kentucky.

Melissa White, a girl I went to school with, is seated in a dimly lit booth and she recognizes me. She smiles and nods and I nod back.

So much for me doing this on the down low.

Within the next hour, everyone I know will know that I had coffee with a 'gorgeous city type' and my family will all know Andrew is here.

He comes to me the moment I walk through the door, my hair is damp from the rain. He pulls me to his chest, and I freeze.

Touching him feels foreign. I can't believe just over a month ago this man was my fiancé. I strive to remember the last time he tried to hug me, or kiss me. I can't recall.

I pull back from him.

"CeCe. I miss you," he breathes out, looking down at me.

"Ironic. You didn't miss me while you were busy fucking everything that walked," I retort quietly, giving him a 'bless your heart' type of smile.

"That's not how I want to start this night, Cecilia," he says back, fiddling with his keys.

"Andrew... let's just get a coffee and sit down." I sigh, gesturing to the counter.

"No, no, I'll get us a coffee, you sit. Chai latte?" he asks and I internally laugh. Andrew offering to do something for me?

"Sure, I'll be over there." I gesture to the open booths that line the dark brick wall of Spicer's. I sit and take a deep breath as he gets in line. I wonder how I could've been so attracted to him. On the outside, he is good looking in a Ken doll sort of way, but he's so preppy, so polished, and just expensive looking all around.

Either my tastes have changed or I'm just seeing way too much of my rugged, hyper masculine boss—a whole different type of gorgeous. Lately, I've been dreaming of a light stubble that would scrape lightly along my skin. Flannels and boots— real boots not fancy Gucci boots you're not allowed to scuff. I've also been dreaming of rough, warm, calloused hands— hands that know hard work and spend their days gripping a hockey stick tightly while coaching.

A beautiful sight I've grown accustomed to rewarding myself with when I need a break from my computer screen. I watch Nash on the ice every day, almost like a scene from *You*, staying just out of sight behind the curtain over the glass in my office. He's so damn good with all the kids and they clearly look up to him. This morning, he was teaching one of the kids how to pass through the legs to trick his teammate and the errant thought that he would one day help to make beautiful, cheeky little babies crossed my mind before I scolded myself for ogling him instead of working on the fall budget. Between all these endearing qualities—and watching him in his element skating at warp speed and firing off goals without even really trying while scrimmaging with the teen camp—my Saturday night vision roster is already almost full again for this week and it's only Wednesday.

I turn my attention back to Andrew as he pays with no real friendly demeanor in his eyes. He says thank you to the server as if she's lucky to make his coffee. No warmth, no kindness. Without even realizing it, I'm comparing him to Nash again who would take the time to tip her and tell her to say hi to her parents for him.

I realize at this moment that I really haven't been in love with Andrew in a really long time, if I ever was at all. What my eighteen-year-old self wanted and craved is entirely different than what my twenty-five-year-old self wants and craves.

I would never have been happy with him. This epiphany is about to make this conversation go a lot easier.

"Here we go," he says, setting my steaming mug down.

"Thanks."

Andrew sits and pulls a wet nap out of his wallet. He wipes the worn and rustic wood table down in disgust.

"It won't kill you." I roll my eyes. "Jesus, Andrew."

"What? They should be wiping this table down every time someone uses it. That's how germs spread." Imagined visions of him banging his last three secretaries come to mind. Not too worried about germs then, now was he?

"I'm going to get right down to it, CeCe. We have a life in Seattle. You can't just run from it. I know I haven't been... fair to you."

I laugh. I actually laugh loud enough for Melissa White to turn and look at me from across the coffee shop.

"Andrew," I whisper. "Fair? Seriously? Have you *ever* been faithful to me?"

His eyes grow wide because I'm sure he doesn't expect me to stand up to him.

"Like ever?" I add.

"Cecilia, my job is very stressful. I shouldn't have gone behind your back. I'll try to be on my best behavior when you come home."

"You'll try? You'll *try?*" He's out of his mind.

"No one is monogamous, you're naive if you think any men

in my business don't make mistakes or have little indiscretions from time to time."

I roll my eyes at his lame attempt to justify his actions.

"Andrew. You don't get it. That's not good enough for me."

"We have a life. We have friends. I have tickets for the Bancroft Charity Gala in two weeks, what will I say when you aren't there with me?"

So that's it.

"So I'm leaving you after almost eight years, ending our engagement, and you're worried about what *people will think?*"

His lifeless pale blue eyes stare straight through mine like he really can't understand why I'm making this choice to leave him as he sips his coffee.

"Well, yes of course. We have an image; don't you care about that at all? What will Rachel and Lenora think and what did you tell the women at the shelter? Do they all know you've moved back here permanently to Hillbilly Haven to work where? At the Dollar General?"

Rage seeps into my bones at his rude assumption of my life here and the people in this town, not to mention that he is quite obviously playing it off like I'm on a trip and not permanently living here to the people we know in Seattle. I'm having an out of body experience looking at my old life from the outside at the moment, and I can't believe what I put up with.

"Fuck you, Andrew," I whisper-yell. "We're done. I'm not coming back and I don't give a shit what those women think, they were never my friends and Amy at the shelter knows everything. Now, I'll ask you only once to stop being so ignorant about my family and this town or this meeting is over. You said you wanted to settle this, let's settle it. We have to sell the condo and I need the rest of my personal belongings."

He is seething. His ego can't take the rejection. Andrew is used to a world where everyone bends over backwards for him and the fact that I'm pushing back leaves him frothing at the mouth. I can see it in his eyes as he speaks.

"So you're going to stay here, Cecilia? And *actually* work at the Dollar General? There's nowhere for you to even apply your degree here. They barely even have a grocery store." He scoffs in disgust. "You're going to give up everything I've given you... for this?" He waves his hands outward to showcase the coffee shop I've always loved.

I have so many memories here I can't even count them and he has no idea. He's never tried to learn about my life before him, my past. He knows nothing about me really, only that I am a good trophy to keep at his side and smile at his colleagues when he needs me to.

I lean back in my seat, done. Awakened. I deserve so much better than this.

Come at me, asshole.

"Yes, Andrew, that's exactly what I'm going to do," I say calmly, ignoring his insults. "Now, I've been looking at comparable sales on Zillow. I think we could get a million-five for the condo." My voice is quiet and even, to show him he can't upset me, but he isn't listening.

If I know the look he's wearing, he is about to become mean.

He leans back in his seat and folds his arms across his chest, a vile chuckle escapes him and I've never hated him more.

"You know, ever since your dad died, you've turned into a real frigid cunt."

I gasp at his words and then, I see red.

The couple across from us stop talking and turn to look at us. I'm pretty sure the man staring at me works at the pharmacy and knows my mom. I lean forward but I don't give a shit if they can hear me.

"Never, *ever* talk about my father again." I can feel tears stinging my eyes but I fiercely push them down. I need to remain strong here and I won't give Andrew the satisfaction. "We're done, Andrew. If I need a lawyer, I'll get one but don't call me or text me again. We can email correspondence to avoid arguments. We'll sell the condo and go on our separate paths. If you don't call a realtor in the next week, I will."

I try to stand but he grabs my arm and I notice something in his eyes I've never seen before. Fear. He's afraid. He treated me like dirt and used me for *at least* the last five years, but he is afraid for his own reputation so much that he's willing to spend his life in a loveless marriage with me. Lucky for him, I'm smarter than he is.

"Let go of my arm."

"Cecilia. Please..." he pleads. "Just give me another chance."

"Andrew, that ship has long sailed," I scoff and snatch my arm away, throwing a twenty-dollar bill on the table to tip the place. Hopefully, they won't gossip too much about the scene we're creating.

I turn on my heel and leave without another word but he rises and follows me.

I push through the doors into the misty July rain and wish I could've found a closer parking spot. I begin walking and checking for traffic as he trails behind me.

"You could've talked to me, you know, instead of just leaving. How was I supposed to know you were unhappy?"

I spin around to face him once I reach the other side of the street.

"So, I should've begged you to stop cheating on me? It's my fault? Got it." I tip my head back and actually laugh because he's so pathetic I feel sorry for him.

"You're so self-centered, Andrew. I never cheated on you. I was always faithful. You simply didn't deserve me."

I turn to leave but once again he grabs my arm, only this time he pulls me toward him, hard.

"Cecilia, you're not leaving me in the middle of the fucking road. You're coming home and we're going to work this out. We owe this relationship that. I'll never give up on you," he yells.

I open my mouth to protest that he's squeezing my arm too tight when air whooshes by me, and before I know what's even happening, there's an eerie cracking sound and Andrew is on his ass on the sidewalk.

"Touch her again and I'll fucking bury you."

Nash's voice sends a shiver up my spine. I turn to see where he came from and recognize Shelby Christie, my former cheer coach standing under Dolcetto's awning, her mouth hanging open with shock at what just happened.

I realize that they must have been on a date as I see Andrew try to stand and Nash grip his perfectly pressed shirt collar, like he's about to hit him again.

"Nash!" I yell.

He turns to face me and the fury I see behind his eyes startles me.

"He cannot put his hands on you, CeCe."

"Who the fuck are *you*? This is between me and my fiancée," Andrew whines, holding a hanky to his profusely bleeding nose.

I smirk from behind Nash. Andrew with a broken nose in court next week is a funny thought to me.

"*Who the fuck am I?*" Nash's voice is calm but so deep and scary I wouldn't want to be Andrew. He clips Andrew on the chin again, hard, as he reels backward with Nash still firmly gripping his shirt, holding him up.

"*Who the fuck am I?*" he repeats, louder this time.

"I'm Nash fucking Carter and I'm about to spill every one of your teeth onto this sidewalk if you call CeCe your fiancée again." He's holding Andrew so tightly by the collar, he's cutting off his air supply. "She isn't anyone's fiancée, and she was clearly done talking to you. So, *Drew,* take a look at my face. Memorize it. There will never be a day you see CeCe without me beside her again. Now, if you want to walk away in one piece tonight, you're going to apologize."

Goddamn. Yes, Mr. Carter.

This time, Andrew is smart enough to know now that Nash isn't messing around.

"I'm sorry, CeCe. I shouldn't have... grabbed you," he bites out, panicked.

Nash looks at me, almost like he's asking for my approval. I nod once and Nash lets go, dropping Andrew to his ass again. Andrew tries to stand but looks woozy.

"Good, dipshit. Now apologize for not knowing how to treat a woman. For not understanding what you had when you had it," he barks out. Andrew looks up at him, probably wondering how Nash knows so much about our relationship.

"I-I'm sorry, CeCe," Andrew says from below me on the sidewalk. His hands are moving to cover his face in fear that Nash might hit him again.

"Now, get out of my town and don't ever fucking come back," Nash growls at him as he pushes him away, then he turns his back to Andrew with zero vulnerability. Not a fear in the world that Andrew might retaliate.

This whole scene just got bumped up to the top of my Saturday night roster.

Andrew scrambles. "Nice company you keep, Cecilia." He points at Nash. "And you're going to hear from my lawyer, pal," he yells from the safety of the other side of the street.

"Looking forward to it, *Drew,*" Nash calls back, not even giving him a glance.

"Are you alright?" he asks me. His whole demeanor has

shifted 180-degrees in all of two seconds flat. Both his hands are on my arms which are now covered in goosebumps from standing out in the misty rain. His thumbs run over my forearms.

"Nash, can you unlock the doors?" Shelby yells as she makes her way over to his truck. He moves to unlock it immediately.

"Shit. I'm so sorry, Shelby. I'll be right there," he mutters than looks down at me. "Shit..." He runs a hand through his hair. "I...we had dinner," he says as he flexes his bloody knuckled hand, assessing any damage.

I put my hand on his arm and look up at him.

"What are you doing, Nash?" I ask. "I mean, thank you, at least he's gone now and probably won't come back, but you're clearly on a date. A date that's probably now ruined."

He goes to say something but I cut him off.

"Take her home. I'm going to get out of these wet clothes. I'll just see you tomorrow." I start walking to the safety of my truck.

"CeCe," Nash says from behind me.

I turn to face him expectantly.

He looks tormented, like he's carefully planning what to say. But, "I'm sorry he hurt you," is all he musters out.

I nod and head to my truck while Nash goes back to his date like I told him to.

CHAPTER TWENTY-ONE
Nash

'm sorry he hurt you? What the fuck is wrong with me?

I turn and walk back to my truck. I can't even believe Shelby is still standing here after the worst date she's probably ever been on. I'm surprised she didn't just start walking home.

Even before I saw that flash of her hair out the window of Dolcettos, it was a bland night, but the moment I saw that piece of shit put his hands on CeCe, I was out the door, red lining my vision as I made my way to where they were on the sidewalk.

Everything else that happened, I'm going to admit I had zero control over but I meant every word. I don't care what I have to do, CeCe will never face Andrew alone again.

I get into my truck and turn to look at Shelby.

"I wish I could rewind this night for you. I'm so sorry."

She grins and pats my hand. "Dinner was nice and you weren't terrible company."

Shelby is a pretty girl of thirty-three, recently divorced and she teaches fourth grade at the elementary school. Wade and I went to school with her.

Cole's been trying to set me up with her forever, so he was

pretty excited when I asked for her number. She is friends with Gemma, and Cole says he has no idea why, she's too nice to be friends with his ex. Tonight, she's been nothing but funny, sweet, and gracious through my beast-like theatrics with CeCe. I should like her, I should be ready to go back to her place and do what I intended at the start of this night—which was have a good time, and hopefully push CeCe Ashby from my mind, even temporarily. But somewhere between appetizers and the main course, I just felt *guilty,* like sleeping with her would be wrong. She called me right out on it during dinner and I decided to just be honest with her.

"You seem like your head isn't in this date, Nash, although I'm not complaining. I'll never turn down dinner at Dolcetto's." She smiles at me and I notice how pretty her smile is, but it doesn't take me out at the knees the way another blonde's does.

"You're right, maybe I shouldn't have asked you. I have a lot on my mind. I apologize for that. You're not getting me at my best."

"Or you can admit another woman is eating at you," she notes.

"That obvious?" I ask.

"I'm a good listener, no strings attached," she says, and I smirk because it isn't the no strings attached I had in mind but I'm grateful she's a good sport nonetheless.

"Ugh... you're right, I have a woman on my mind that won't vacate no matter how hard I try. It's really fucking annoying." I chuckle.

Shelby laughs and pops a bite of pasta into her mouth. *"Those are the worst kind."*

"I thought maybe if I came out with you and had a good time, I would prove to myself it was nothing and we'd make a connection. But turns out, I'm not really being honest with myself, or you. I'm sorry. You are great."

"Nash, how long have we known each other?" Shelby asks as she sips her wine.

"A long time," I say. *"Since middle school?"*

She nods. *"Exactly. Don't sweat it. I'm just happy to do something different other than watch the Food Network and grade papers. A friendly dinner is fun so it's all good."*

"So the woman you can't get out of your head, that was her?" Shelby asks now as we're closing the distance between the restaurant and her house.

I turn and face her; the only sound is the wipers going on my truck windshield. "Yes."

"I don't understand, CeCe Ashby was always a nice girl, last I'd heard she wasn't married, so what's the problem?"

Of course, she knows who CeCe is.

"It's complicated in so many ways. She works for me. I'm like part of her family, her brothers and I are close, and she's a lot younger than me. I'm pretty sure the boys would rightly kick my ass for even thinking like this."

Shelby giggles and is clearly thinking for a moment as I pull into her driveway.

"You only have so many trips around the sun, Nash, you never know when your opportunity to do something will disappear. Take that from me. By the way she was looking at you, I'd say these feelings aren't one-sided."

Unbuckling her seatbelt, she smiles again. "I had a nice time though, regardless. I guess I'll see ya around, hun. Thanks for dinner." She winks, exiting my truck as I say goodnight.

Nash from five years ago would be cuffing himself up the side of the head right now for letting a nice, pretty woman like Shelby walk away, but Nash from right now can think of one thing and one thing only.

CHAPTER TWENTY-TWO
CeCe

I step out of the longest, hottest shower of my life contemplating the fury in Nash's eyes as he gripped Andrew. That and the look on his date's face when he left her at the restaurant door. I'm glad we never ended up kissing that night in the kitchen right after I got home from Seattle. I wonder what it would be like, multiple times a day, to kiss Nash. I've even had moments over the last month where I thought maybe he felt something for me, but seeing him out with Shelby tells me I was way off base.

My love life is complex enough at the moment. No matter how good he looks, no matter how good he *is*, and no matter how much peace I feel the moment I hear his voice in any room, Nash is off limits. It would be just my luck that the man I'm fantasizing about is the man I shouldn't want and the man I can't have.

Incessant pounding on my cabin door is ringing through the space before I even get myself fully dried off.

"Baby, I know you're in there. Let me in."

I wrap my robe around me so I'm decent and pad out into

the living room and turn the porch light on. I swing the door open to find my mother in her cheetah pajamas, just fuming.

"That little prick thinks he can come into this town and disrespect *my* family?"

"Mama—"

"Why didn't you tell me he was here? Why did you go see him, CeCe Rae? He is never going to be what you need."

"Mama!" I yell this time to get her attention. "I know."

That calms her down a little as Wade comes through the door behind her.

"What in Sam Hill is going on in here?" His gruff voice echoes through my small space. "I could hear you yelling at CeCe from Legend," he says to my mother.

I throw my hands up. "Can't a girl just get a shower and go to bed?" I ask. It's only eight-thirty but I've just had enough.

"Andrew is here and he called CeCe a C-U-Next-Tuesday at Spicer's," Mama tells him.

"How do you know that already?" I ask in horror.

"Bertie called me." She mentions Spicer's night manager and I realize my bribe wasn't enough to stop the gossip.

"He *what*?" Rage takes over Wade's face and I groan, putting my head in my hands. "Where is that fucker? Is he at the Motorside?" He mentions the only hotel in town.

"He's probably gone and if you want to beat his ass, you'll have to get in line. Nash already gave him a shit kickin'," I say as they both turn to face me.

"Nash hit Andrew? Nash was with you?" Wade asks.

"No. He was on a date, I think. He must have seen Andrew grab my arm and he—"

"He *grabbed* you?" Wade is about to go feral.

"Too much testosterone for one night," I say. "It's handled, Wade. He knows I'm not going back to Seattle. Nash told him to get out of *his* town." I laugh and this makes my mother break into the cheekiest little grin.

"That boy has been kicking ass for you your whole life. It doesn't surprise me he was there."

"Right place, right time. I'll be thanking him tomorrow," Wade says.

A thought occurs to me.

"Wait, what do you mean he's been kicking ass for me my whole life?" I ask.

Wade chuckles. "It's ancient history now, I guess. But pretty much every guy that ever looked at you the wrong way, or said anything about you even remotely unflattering, Nash was always the first one in line to lay a beat down."

I gulp. "What?"

Mama uses her hand to cup my face.

"You deserve so much better than Andrew, baby. I'm glad Nash was there."

"Who did Nash beat up?" I ask Wade, looking at him over my mom's shoulder with her hands still on my face. I'm not letting Mama change the subject.

Wade chuckles. "Michael Merriweather, he said he was gonna take your v-card at junior prom."

Mama cuffs him in the shoulder.

"Steven Connolly, Jason Westman, Paul Stevenson," he continues.

"So everyone I *ever* tried to date?" I ask in horror.

"No, just everyone that ever talked shit about you to anyone," Wade says.

My mind is racing.

"Anyway, I'm not surprised he hit Andrew, and I'm not mad about it either. He's had it coming. Pa is slow clapping from the grave, I'll be shaking Nash's hand for that one."

I sit on the couch and try to register that Nash has been

going behind my back participating in his own personal defend CeCe fight club for my entire adolescence. But why? My brain is fried.

"I want to go to bed. I love you both, y'all don't have to go home but you have to leave now," I say quietly and thankfully, neither of them argue.

"Okay, baby," Mama says, kissing on the top of my head.

"Put tonight behind you. Tomorrow is a new day and you're already off to a great start here. You just keep at it."

I nod. "Thanks, Mama. I love you."

"Not as much as I love you," she says

"Night, Wade."

"Night, CeCe Rae. Don't be too hard on Nash when you see him tomorrow, he's always had your back. Like me and Cole."

I nod. Is that what I should see when I look at Nash? An extension of Wade and Cole?

They mercifully leave me in the quiet of my tiny space. I lean back onto my sofa, huffing.

"Never a dull moment," I mutter as I think back over the events of the night in my mind.

I will admit I did enjoy seeing Andrew groveling for forgiveness though. It makes me smirk all the way back into the bathroom while I dry my hair into a long, straight sheet down my back. I change into my favorite silk pajama set, dreaming of a hot tea and a rom-com to escape the drama my life has turned into. I don't even get the kettle filled before I hear another knock at the door.

What goddamn family member is here to get in my business now? Cole? Papa Dean? I move to the door, ready to say I'm just fine. Until I swing the door open to find none other than Nash Carter standing under my porch lights.

CHAPTER TWENTY-THREE
CeCe

I fold my arms over my chest to cover my breasts as the cool night breeze hits me.

"What are you doing here?" I ask, looking over his shoulder to see if his date is still in his truck.

"I just... I had to come and check on you." He runs a hand through his hair and looks up. "Can I just come in?"

"Where is your date?"

"I took her home and it was hardly a date." His jaw tenses as he stares at me expectantly.

I cock my head to the side. "Nash, I'm gonna ask you again, what are you doing here?"

"I needed to know, I had to see that you were okay."

"I'm fine."

He sighs. "Let me in, Rae. I just want to talk."

I analyze him for a minute, and then I swing the door open wide and he steps into my tiny entryway, taking up all the available space with his large, solid frame.

His hair is damp but still manages to look perfect and his slim fitting sky blue dress shirt is just wet enough to cling to his powerful form. A jealousy I can't stop—or understand—ripples through me unexpectedly at the idea of him dressing like this to take another woman on a date and impress her. It's irrational, but I digress and just accept it. It is what it is and I'm going to have to get used to it. It was only going to be so long before Nash took someone out.

"I'm sure Andrew will be half way to Seattle by now. He won't come here, so if you're looking for him you're wasting your time," I say as I turn to head to my kitchen.

"No, I'm here to see you. I didn't... I'm sorry I hit him but he is a real piece of shit, Rae. If he ever calls you and wants to see you here again, you tell me and I'll go with you."

I scoff as I finish filling the kettle. "Okay, I didn't realize I was opening the door to Caveman Nash."

He rolls his eyes.

"I won't be seeing Andrew again anytime soon. I'm going to do everything by email, and thank you, but I don't need a bodyguard, Nash, and FYI"—I turn to face him—"I didn't need a bodyguard all through high school either."

His jaw goes slack as he realizes someone has spilled the tea to me.

"What gave you the right to decide who I could and could not date back then?" I ask.

Nash says nothing, just stares at me like he doesn't know what to say.

"That's right, your secret's out. I know about Michael and Jason and Paul and Steven and whoever else you felt the need to knock around. This is why no one asked me out after eleventh grade, isn't it? They all thought you'd come after them."

He closes his mouth and runs a hand through his hair again. I watch the muscles in his upper arm seriously challenge the confines of his shirt and I take in the ink that peeks out from his shirt collar. The Kentucky vines that run up the side of his neck pulse with his flexed jaw. I want to wrap myself in them and live there.

"Wade or Cole?" he asks.

"Wade," I say honestly, forcing myself to pull my eyes from his body to his face.

He huffs out a breath, frustration etching across his face. "I just feel... protective of you, CeCe. I always have. I'm not going to apologize for that."

"But I'm not your responsibility." I turn away from him and place the kettle on the stove and continue, "You don't have to worry about me. I have two brothers already. The way I see it, you ruined a perfectly good date coming here."

He scoffs from behind me.

"I don't know how she is as a person now, but I've heard that Shelby is lots of fun in bed. So I actually feel sorry for you that you took her home, you're probably missing out on a real fun time—"

Nash grunts and then he's moving toward me, I spin around to face him but he's in front of me already and gripping both of my wrists at my side—hard.

"I took her home because the whole time I was with her, all I could fucking think about was *you*."

I say nothing, I just breathe in tiny uneven breaths. His Adam's apple bobs as he restrains himself, still gripping my wrists, and his spicy sandalwood scent warms me.

"Do you have any fucking idea how hard it is to see your face no matter who I'm looking at?"

He moves even closer to me; our bodies are almost touching. "Do you know how I torture myself? Telling myself not to think about you? Reminding myself who you are and why I shouldn't?"

He turns his face away from me and I see his jaw tense even further as he grits his teeth. His eyes turn back to mine, his pupils blown out, dark and endless. I breathe for the first time in what feels like minutes as his eyes trail to my mouth. I dart my tongue out to wet my lips without thinking. A low rumble rises from his chest.

"Fuck it—" he growls as his hands grip my face and he presses his lips to mine. He pulls back after a few seconds and stares at me, almost in disbelief, before the flood gates open and his mouth is crashing down on mine. It isn't gentle or soft, it's demanding and consuming.

A moan escapes me but Nash swallows it. He kisses me so deeply that I lose myself with every sweep of his tongue. It's chaotic and calculated, slow but frenzied. I'm utterly helpless as shivers echo down my spine.

My thighs squeeze together as my core heats, Nash's mouth plunders mine like he's starved for me, like my lips offer him his only salvation. His large, rough hands roam over my body as I fist his shirt, they move through my hair, over my shoulders, down my back to my waist, under the silk of my shirt, so warm on my skin. He's overwhelming and not enough all at the same time. I want more.

I whimper as his mouth moves down my neck, tracing a line from my ear to my collarbone. His kisses aren't caresses, they're open mouthed and hungry, he mixes them with little nips and bites that sting my skin before he licks over them and soothes the pain. His hands hold me to him, pressing his hips into mine. My entire being is preening for him. I'm trying to fight it, I'm trying to tell myself no, that this is wrong, this is *Nash,* I know we shouldn't do this but my body's saying yes, *screaming* yes. Weeks of being with him everywhere, every day finally implode and I can't do a damn thing to stop it, nor do I want to.

He pulls back from me startling me and his eyes rake over my face. "I fucking want you, Rae. I need you, *now,* and I never need anyone, ever."

"I do too," I moan as he kisses the corner of my lips.

"What if...what if it's just once?" I whisper, and he kisses me again then pulls his face back to look at me, a million questions in his eyes. "Just sex, I mean, just tonight. I mean... If you're going to break your cardinal rule, you may as well go all the way."

He smiles into my lips, then kisses my jaw. "I think"—Another kiss—"I'm breaking every rule I've ever had with you right now."

My eyes roll as his lips trail my neck.

"B-but no feelings. Just sex," I say breathless.

"I don't get feelings; just sex I can handle," he bites out.

"So, it's a deal?" I ask.

He groans again and crushes himself to me so powerfully, I feel his cock pressing into my abdomen. His hands come under my shorts as another low growl erupts from his chest. "These fucking shorts." He lifts me onto the counter. "They should be illegal."

I wrap my legs around him as he grips my thighs, then look down to see where I'm rocking into his cock shamelessly from my countertop seat. Desperate for him, I squeeze my thighs around him even tighter.

"*Fuck,* CeCe," he whispers, and I love it. I love that he wants me just as badly as I want him.

He palms my breasts as my nipples beg for his touch. He knows what I need before I even finish thinking it. My tank top comes down roughly to expose me to him, his thumbs find my pebbled nipples as he pulls his face back from mine and just looks at me. The pad of his thumb traces my cheekbone.

"You're so fucking beautiful, Rae," he says as he drinks me in.

He wastes no more time, moving his mouth to each of my breasts. I let my head fall backward and moan softly while he tethers between sucking and pinching my nipples. A deeper, delicious heat coils in my core. I've never wanted a man's hands on my body like this in my entire life. All those years with Andrew and never once did I want him like this. The ripples of Nash's muscled form under my fingertips feel just like I imagined. Hard and warm. So strong. It registers with me that I not only *want* Nash Carter, I'd sell my soul for him right now. His mouth returns to mine and his kisses become languid and slow, scorching through me as he slides his hands down towards the apex of my thighs.

"Tell me something, Rae... how wet will I find you, if I slide my fingers into these panties right now?" he asks into my lips.

"S-so wet," I stutter as his middle finger slides down over my shorts. Two layers of fabric still divide his skin from mine, but I know he can feel how wet I am through both of them.

"Mmm..." he groans into my lips, and I feel it vibrate through my entire being.

"Look at you, Rae. Such a good girl, already so fucking wet for me." His deep voice reaches an even lower octave as the pad of his finger circles my clit expertly.

I'm afraid I may come before he even slides his hand into my panties with the combination of his touch and words. My breathing is erratic and uneven. No one has ever talked to me like this—so forward, so direct, and fuck, if I don't love every damn word.

"Nash..." I whine as I rock against his finger.

"Fuck, I love hearing my name on your lips. I can't wait to hear you scream it." He pushes my shorts and panties to the side and slides one large finger into my pussy. I shudder around him. I've never been so wet but my walls clench around him as he moves in and out of me while his thumb stays over my clit in tight little circles hurling me at record speed toward my climax.

"So fucking *tight*, Rae." He marvels as he adds another finger and I gasp.

"I've never... come like this before," I pant out. "But I... Nash... I think I'm going to."

Nash smirks at me. "Of course you're going to." He pulls me closer, pushing even deeper into me. "You mean to tell me you've *never* come over a man's fingers before?"

I shake my head no as I try to control my breathing. I've only come during sex and it wasn't all the time. Andrew cared mostly about himself. Nash kisses my lips, never slowing down his fingers. I've been missing this? *This* is what it's supposed to feel like?

"I'm gonna take care of you so well, Rae. All I think about is touching you, tasting you, burying myself in you," he confesses as he continues to expertly work my pussy like he wrote the all-knowing playbook for making vaginas happy.

Nash slides me forward even further and plunges a third finger into me, curving them in such a way that I've never felt before, he holds me with his other hand at my hip securely, moving in and out of me and hitting a spot inside me that threatens to shatter me from the inside out every time he comes in contact with it with his thick digits. I'm dripping down his hand and he gives me no time to process what I'm feeling. But it's so good... too good.

Only a few moments pass as my moaning grows louder, and I feel like I'm falling, spiraling, losing control as Nash fucks my pussy expertly with his fingers and circles my clit with my arousal and his thumb, timing all of it to my bucking hips the same way he kisses, perfectly calculated and perfectly chaotic.

I feel like I may die, lose control of my bladder, or even both at the same time as he moves his fingers into me one more time so deeply, then pulls them out as stars explode behind my eyelids. Electricity centers from every corner of my being, every nerve, every cell. He's still circling my clit and I'm coming. Everywhere. What feels like an eternity passes as I come down from the dimension he just sent me to, whimpering into his chest as I rest my head on it.

"Look what a beautiful mess you made, Rae... so fucking pretty," he says as I open my eyes and see both his hand and my floor soaked. He pulls his fingers up to his mouth and sucks them clean. It's the most attractive thing I've ever seen a man do.

"So fucking sweet," he mutters. "I can't wait for you to come on my tongue."

I'm so sensitive still, I try to return my breath to normal as he continues to give me no reprieve, using my arousal to skim over my slick entrance.

"Did I just...?" I can't say the word, as my cheeks heat. I'm so embarrassed. I've never thought coming like that was possible for me. The feeling was unlike anything I could ever describe. The most earth-shattering orgasm I've ever felt.

"Yes, you did. I told you I'd take care of you and I'm nowhere near done with you yet." He lifts me off the counter and his lips find mine effortlessly as he carries me to my bedroom, never breaking the kiss.

His cock is rock hard and feels huge, still pressing into me as he lays me down on my bed and hovers over me, kissing me slowly, like he's taking his sweet time. Staring down at me in the dim orange glow of my bedroom, he pulls my shorts and my soaked panties off and tosses them aside, lazily trailing his tongue down my body as he lifts me up just enough to pull my tank top off. I lay naked in the center of my bed. His eyes ravage me like this, but I don't even feel self-conscious. I want him to look.

"Fuck, you're so incredibly perfect,"

I say nothing, just kiss him in response.

"I have another rule of my own," he says.

I nod. "Okay?"

"I'm always in control," he growls.

"Well then, better make it count," I say as he trails his tongue down my throat.

He chuckles into my skin. "You just imagine how many times you want to come and I guarantee, I'll make you come more than that." His words alone cause heat to flood my core again.

Lips crush against mine as he holds himself between my legs controlled, moving against me. His piercing blue eyes are too much, his wavy hair over his forehead. He's so beautiful it hurts.

I search for friction against his hardened cock through his clothes as he undoes his shirt one button at a time. My mouth turns as dry as the Mojave desert when he pulls it off. He's all abs and strong inked arms around me. On his chest is a large anchor and ornate cross wrapped in greenery with ancient writing, my mind can't take it all in at once. Just as I'm getting used to that view, he stands, pulls his jeans off and kicks them aside, returning to the bed over me. Nash Carter almost naked is sensory overload. He's a god and it hits me that in this moment, he's all *mine*.

"Why do you have to be that perfect under these clothes?" I blurt without thinking.

Nash starts to laugh and whispers into my ear, "You're asking me that? You're a fucking work of art."

He's so strong, so powerful it turns me to putty in his hands. To say I want everything he's about to give me is the understatement of the century.

CHAPTER TWENTY-FOUR
Nash

I stare down at her, her chest rising with her breath, her beautiful, perfect tits on display in front of me and her sweet pink nipples hardened to points begging for my mouth. She's even more incredible than I pictured in my mind so many nights since she's been home; CeCe is living, breathing perfection. She bites her bottom lip and it sends a jolt of lust to my already rock-hard cock. Her silky-smooth skin under my hands sets me on fire and the taste of her skin? *Fuck*. It's like a drug. She's all sugary and sweet. I'm an addict stepping up for his fix.

I move down her body with my mouth. I'm dying to taste her. I'm the first man to make her come over his fingers—*me*. Knowing that just fuels this depraved desire I've developed for her. I didn't know what she was capable of, but I knew if she had never come like that before, there was a chance even she didn't know what her body could do—and I was right. Not only was I right, she fucking soaked me and it was the hottest thing I've ever seen.

I slide two fingers over her still soaking wet bare lips as she quivers beneath me. I trail my tongue down her body as she shivers and moans, each adorable sound throws little cherry bombs into the pool of fire I am for her.

"Will I be the first man to have you come on his tongue too?"

"Y-yes," she stammers, and I grin wide. I fucking love it and I want to give it all to her.

"Such a fucking crime," I say as I center myself between her legs. "That no one has ever taken the time to give this perfect little cunt all the attention it deserves. You are perfect, you know." I kiss her softly on her clit, her back arches. "Absolute perfection, CeCe."

I have no idea how I'm the lucky bastard that gets to give CeCe these first experiences, but I know I'm going to fucking ruin every other man's chance of comparing to me. I move a finger in and out of her tight, wet heat slowly. The mad desire to forget about a condom overtakes me. Something I've never wanted to do in my life but to feel CeCe wrapped around me, just her skin on mine as I sink into her, would no doubt be like heaven on earth.

"Nash?" she moans my name like a question.

"Yes, Rae?" I ask

"Make me come again?" she begs. I fucking almost blow in my boxers from her words alone. I let my hands roam every place I can, not wanting to miss any part of her.

"I'm going to give you what you need, CeCe. I'll help you get rid of that ache..." I push a second finger into her and she gasps at the feeling.

"Please...?" she moans, and I smile at her innocence, at her not wanting to ask directly for my tongue. It's okay, I'll do all the talking for both of us.

"Spread these thighs for me, Rae..." I say as I lick a firm trail over her slit with the flat of my tongue, her back arches right off the bed as her legs open to accommodate me.

Fucking delicious.

"Yes..." she almost yells into the silence of her room.

"What do you want, tell me baby."

"Please? Your tongue," she begs, and that's all I need to hear as I take in this feast before me. I breathe her in, the sweetness of her overwhelms me.

"Such a fucking crime," I repeat as I bury my face between her legs and lap up every drop of her glistening cunt like a starved man at his last meal.

I suck her clit into my mouth and revel in the way she moves her body under me. The sounds she's making have me so desperate for friction, I'm ready to start pushing my cock into the mattress below me like a horny teenager.

"Oh my God, Nash," CeCe breathes as I hook my arm around her leg, tossing it over my shoulder and pull her even closer to me. Her hands move to my hair and pull tightly. It's just enough pain that it sends me reeling. I fuck my tongue in and out of her tight little pussy and keep my fingers on her clit as she starts trembling under me and then cries out, pushing her hips into my face as she rides my tongue and comes again as I do in fact, grind my hips into the mattress below me.

I could suffocate like this. I could die right here, right now, and I wouldn't have one regret. I'd be happy to bid this world farewell between CeCe Ashby's thighs. I continue licking and sucking her clean until her breathing comes down and she whispers, "I've never... I... that was—"

"Incredible," I finish for her as I move to her face and kiss her lips.

"Taste how sweet you are, CeCe." She licks her lips and kisses me back as I whisper, "You're fucking delectable."

As I kiss her deeply on the lips, she grinds against my thigh still looking for friction.

"So greedy," I chuckle. "You want my cock now, baby?" I

ask as I use my thumb to spread her slippery arousal down her slit. My dick throbs in my boxers.

"Yes," she breathes. She's as desperate as I am, and that realization ignites me.

"Just how long have you been waiting for my cock?" I ask.

CeCe doesn't let even a beat of time pass. "Since the fucking moment I saw you, my first night home," she admits.

"Atta girl, way to be honest." I kiss her lips and grin. "I'm gonna wreck you."

She looks up at me, a challenge in her eyes, and it stuns me.

"So stop fucking around then, and wreck me. Condom... bedside table." *Fuck, this woman.* I raise an eyebrow and stand, pulling open her drawer and reaching into her surprisingly large stash of condoms. Two things happen simultaneously. 1. I realize these could be used with someone else and it causes a deep seeded rage to fill my chest. 2. I spot her secret vibrator.

I smirk. CeCe is wilder than anyone would ever guess, and something about that drives me fucking crazy for her.

"Not a word," she says as she realizes what I see.

"Never be embarrassed with me. Got it?" I say, looking her dead in the eye.

She simply nods as I pull my boxers down, all innocent smiles until the moment she sees my cock. Then she jolts right up on the bed, sober as fuck in one second flat.

"No... uh-uh, you *are* going to wreck me." She's shaking her head as she speaks. "You won't fit that battering ram inside me."

I look down at my dick, desperate to fuck. Okay, he is big and he is a little scary right now. So fucking hard and pointing straight at her. Her eyes are as wide as saucers.

I chuckle and move to the bed again, hovering over her. I kiss her lips gently, twice. If she's used to that vibrator, I can understand her worry. It's half my size.

"I assure you, baby, I will."

150

She shakes her head. "No, you're too big."

I take each nipple into my mouth and suck gently, flicking my tongue over her as her eyes roll and she pants. My fingers slide to her pussy and I give her clit a little pinch. She yelps and begins kissing me back, hot and urgent, running her hands over my body. I grasp her tiny palm and press it to my cock, pre-cum leaks from the tip for her. She moans into my mouth.

"Do you trust me, CeCe?" I ask

She continues kissing me in response, her kisses are so warm and so sweet. Her soft tongue moving against mine, matching me, is so fucking intoxicating.

"Yes I do," she answers as I let go of her hand, but she keeps it pressed to the base of my cock as I roll the condom on, getting accustomed to the idea of me inside her.

"We'll make it fit, baby. I promise, and it will feel good," I say to her.

CeCe nods. Her emerald eyes are so full of passion and something that looks a lot like trust.

"I need to hear the words though, Rae. I need to hear you say you want me right now."

Her plush lips turn up at me in a smile. It does something to me that has nothing to do with my dick, twisting my chest into knots when she says, "I want you, Nash."

I nod and kiss her again, guiding my cock to her center, sliding over it to ready her as she moans and reaches up around my shoulders. She moves her hips up and the first inch of me slips into her, we both suck in a breath and look at each other. For a few frozen moments, our breathing synchronizes and slowly, I push into her more, halting our breath again. I allow myself to breathe and use my middle finger to circle her clit, begging her tight channel to stretch and accommodate me. She moans and all my will leaves me. I push into her further and her walls practically strangle my cock. The feeling virtually stuns me.

"I'm gonna need you to take a breath, baby, relax just a little," I grunt as I kiss her shoulders and her collarbone gently trying to calm her.

She does what I ask. I hear her inhale.

"You're taking me so well, Rae... just keep breathing."

A beat passes and her breathing slows as I feel her body start to welcome me.

"Nash, give me all of you, now," she commands, her voice is husky and fucking sexier than I've ever heard it.

"I just don't want to hurt you."

She shakes her head.

"We've only got one night. Don't hold back. I'll recover tomorrow." CeCe kisses me, breathing deeply as I sink all the way in, letting her swallow me up into her warm rapture. I push further still until I'm buried in her to the hilt. There is no friction on account of how wet she is but she's like a vice around my cock. She cries out as I pull out then bottom out inside her again. Her back comes off the bed.

"*Fucking Christ,* Rae, you feel so goddamn good." I say, my breath ragged now as she moans my name in response.

I'm dying.

Dying a slow death from the feeling of CeCe Ashby wrapped around my cock. *Death by perfect pussy.* Someone better write it on my headstone.

"Too full..." she manages to say.

Fucking right, she's too full but it's unparalleled. She's molded to me in a way I've never felt in my life. Every single part of her fits with me perfectly, we're like a goddamn lock and key.

Her eyes are full of fire as I look down at her.

"Fuck me like you mean it now, Nash."

Have I said? *This fucking woman.*

I kiss her lips. "Better hold on, baby."

She slides her fingers through my hair as I kiss her, and then I start moving. There's no way I'm not hurting her but she takes my full depth like the little warrior she is. I push every thought from my mind and let my body completely take over. I fuck her for every moment I've thought of her like this. Every moment she's been home when I've thought of nothing else, but she just feels *too fucking good*. So instead, I picture every single unsexy thing I can think of—the team locker room, sandwiches, the entire Stars roster, cleaning the barn—anything to just make the moments last longer. Every part of me is feral for her. The headboard rocks against the wall as I push her body up the bed further with every deep thrust. I feel her pussy clamping down around me and I know she's close to coming again, drawing my release forward every time I move inside her.

CeCe's moans are loud and uncontrolled, and we're both covered in a layer of sweat as I somehow find the will to slow my pace down, to settle into the rhythm of stalling her orgasm, staying buried in her for a beat or two longer than I should before I drag myself out. I grip her thigh tightly in a bruising hold, taking a few moments to just enjoy her, to kiss her lips, to just ingrain this feeling into my mind for eternity. I never want it to end. Her hair all around her, her plump, full lips swollen from kissing me, her watering eyes as I fill her. Nails dig into me as she closes in on her high, clawing down my arms as she moans and whimpers illegible words. I'm sure she's drawing blood from my shoulders and that pain heightens all the pleasure I'm feeling, taking it to a level I've never experienced before.

"If you come, I come," I say.

She whines and then moans my name. "Then come with me, Nash."

And it does me in. Her whole body spasms around me and pulls my release from me as my vision goes static and I spill into the condom with a force like no other. I move and jerk inside her, as I kiss her, letting her pull forth every last drop I have.

"You're fucking paradise, Cecilia," I whisper as I kiss her, knowing there's not a fucking chance that just one night of her will ever be enough.

CHAPTER TWENTY-FIVE
CeCe

I am going into panic mode because Nash Carter is inside of me. Nash, who I've known most of my life and always sort of kind of drooled over from afar, especially lately. Nash—who I work for and the man who doesn't date, but sleeps with women for sport—just gave me the most mind blowing sexual experience of my life. My poor pussy is so abused, yet so desperately in love with Nash Carter's cock.

I lie here looking up at the ceiling, just trying to memorize this feeling of fullness. It's worth all the regret I'm probably going to have to face tomorrow. *Just sex.* One night to get it out of our systems.

"Your freight train of a cock just assaulted me," I whisper into his shoulder.

"You asked for it, Rae," he replies, smirking over me.

He is the most stunning specimen of a man I've ever seen, even in this dim light.

He pulls out of me finally, leaving me feeling hollow. We both breathe out a moan when he does. Nash makes quick work of getting rid of the condom and then flops down on the bed beside me and for a short time, we just let our breathing return to normal.

"So... I don't have one-night stands. Like, ever. What happens now? Do you leave?" I ask awkwardly.

Nash rolls over and props himself up on his elbow. He looks amused and grins at me, his strong inked arm supports his head as he reaches across and brushes my hair from my sweaty forehead, tucking it behind my ear.

"CeCe, I'm not leaving. The night's not over yet," he says as he kisses my forehead.

I eye him suspiciously, but secretly love the idea of him staying here.

"Let's get you cleaned up," he says, pulling me to my feet.

Lightheadedness takes over my body as I grip him to steady myself.

"You okay?" he asks

The fuzziness leaves my head as I get used to standing.

"Yes." I look up at him and he's smirking at me with the world's most satisfied look on his face.

"Why are you looking at me like that?" I ask. "Is it because you just fucked me into a dizzy stupor with your ginormous dick?"

He nods, satisfied with my description. "Yup," he answers simply, popping the P.

"Yes, it is just my luck you have the world's most perfect cock, blah, blah, blah," I say as we make our way to the bathroom.

He nuzzles into the back of my neck.

"Tonight, it is," he says, slapping my ass.

He's still beaming as he turns the shower on. Thankfully, the one thing in this little cabin that is built for two is the shower. It's the entire length of the six-foot back wall with glass doors and white subway tile. Cole redid it two years ago, just as he redid the rest of the cabins.

Cole. Wade.

"My brothers can never know about this," I blurt.

Nash turns to face me as he tests the water with his hand. Not one ounce of self-consciousness permeates from him. He's completely confident in his skin. And he should be.

Fuck, he's incredible. No one should look that good. It should be illegal. It's literally killing my brain cells.

"I'm willing to respect whatever wishes you have, CeCe. I'm a grown-ass man, so I don't feel the need to hide that this happened but if that is what you want, I'll go along with it."

"It's only one night," I say. "Surely we can keep it to ourselves and not make it weird."

He nods and holds the shower door open for me. I do what he wants and get in, letting the water run over me.

"How long has it been for you?" I ask, as he rubs my vanilla body wash over my shoulders.

"Since my last shower?" He chuckles.

"Since your last... woman." I laugh.

"A while," he answers.

I turn around. "Really?"

"Like a couple weeks?" I joke.

He sighs. "Nineteen months," he replies as he turns my body around and grabs the shampoo.

"*Nineteen months?*"

"Yes."

"Why?"

Nash scoffs at me from behind me. "I'm not a manwhore, contrary to what you think. I mean... yeah, I maybe was when I was younger, but I just haven't met anyone. My knee was all fucked up for a while last year, I had to abruptly plan my retirement because of it, and then I came home and I've just been so involved in the Center and helping with the bar. I haven't had time; no one has interested me."

He says nothing more as he scrubs my hair clean, massaging strawberry shampoo into my skull with the pads of his fingers. My shoulders relax and I take a deep breath.

He leans down to my ear. "Feel good?"

"Yes," I give. "So good. So, is this the full package Nash Carter one-night stand?"

He rinses my hair clean and reaches around me for the conditioner.

"I've never washed a woman's hair before," he says.

My eyes fly open.

"So what you're saying is, when it comes to your one-night stand packages, I pulled the golden ticket?"

He chuckles. "Something like that, Rae."

I think for a minute while he runs his fingers through my conditioner covered hair, working out the knots.

"Honest question time," I say.

"Shoot."

"Was that what you were going to do tonight? Hook up with Shelby?"

"Yes," he admits, and I feel my heart drop into my feet.

But I know this about him. This shouldn't surprise me.

"But I wasn't... feeling it. I told her I couldn't stop thinking about you. Then I saw you out there and the date was all but over."

I skim my hand over my squeaky-clean hair and turn around to face him as he begins to wash himself. Water trails his muscled torso like even it can't help but cling to him. *Soap suds...body...glistening.* God, I'm already dying for his touch again.

"How long for you?" he asks, interrupting my pornographic daydream.

I half snort the answer. "I don't even remember. The past year, I've never felt safe with Andrew. I mean, I've been on the pill since college but I knew he was being unfaithful. I had myself checked out to make sure I was clean when I proved he was cheating on me—after my dad died—and then I started making my plan to come home." I look down. "I don't want to talk about Andrew while I'm in the shower with you, do you?"

"Fuck no." He scoops me up and kisses me on the lips. "I only have six and a half hours left, and I want to make you come at least three more times tonight."

"Is that so? I have to work tomorrow, you know."

He runs his nose along my neck and follows it with his tongue. Every thought I have leaves my mind.

"You can't call in sick. Your boss is too strict."

"Ugh, he's such a hard ass," I say just as the water starts to run cold over us and I shudder.

"Hot water still doesn't last long here," he observes the obvious, shutting it off and wrapping us both in towels.

"Old cabin problems," I say as I dry my hair and body with the towel as best I can.

He follows me back to my bedroom.

"Just as well, we need your disgustingly large stash of condoms."

"Shut up." I swat at him.

"At least I know where to send the whole county if the stores run out," he snickers, wrapping his towel low around his waist and running a hand through his hair, pushing it back off his face.

Innate desire rushes over me with this view. I walk to him and stand before him. Looking up at him, I reach my hand up and press it to his face. His large jaw is too big for my small hand but he turns his face to it and kisses my palm. I reach between my breasts and unhook my towel. It drops to the wood

159

floor. I stand naked before him and wait as he registers the vision in front of him. He trails a finger over my shoulder.

"Where do you want me, Mr. Carter?" I smirk.

"You're so fucking sexy, Rae," he rasps.

I use my free hand to press my palm to his already hard-ened cock through the slip in the towel and he groans as he devours me with his lips and pulls my body to his as if my touch has lit a fire in him. Nash snatches his towel off between us, and suddenly we're a clash of warm, naked skin. Droplets of water still trickle down my back, he smears them into my skin as he kisses me, his tongue searching every corner of my mouth. He pulls my bottom lip into his teeth and bites it, enough to make me moan with a mixture of pleasure and pain.

"On your knees is where I want you. I want to see these pretty lips around my cock, CeCe."

My brain tells me to protest his controlling tone, but my traitorous pussy forces me to do exactly as he wants. He takes his cock into his hand and strokes himself a few times before tapping it on my lips. This sight alone, combined with his clean warm skin on my lips makes my mouth water.

"Open up, stick out your tongue, and show me where you want my cock," he commands, and I do. What even is feminism when I'm naked with Nash Carter? Just his filthy words alone have such an effect on me. They're like foreplay on their own.

He drops his cock on my tongue, and I take over immedi-ately. I lick a hot trail from his base all the way to his tip then attempt to take him as deeply as possible into my throat.

He's much too big, but he's about to find out I simply don't have a gag reflex. Never have. He hits the back of my throat and I open wider and look up at him through my lashes.

He sucks in a breath and mutters, "Fuck, CeCe, *fuck*."

As I pull him in, almost swallowing him down, tears well

up in my eyes as he continues fucking my mouth, gripping my hair tightly at the roots.

"You feel So. Fucking. Good." He looks down at me like this and I maintain my eye contact with him. I've never seen him look so out of control and I love it. It's a sight I wish I could see over and over. Chest heaving, eyes rolling back. Perfection. He lets me continue on like this, moving in and out of my mouth, hitting the back of my throat with every thrust as his large hands weave through my damp hair. My air comes in little bursts around him as I try to breathe through my nose.

He groans a long carnal sound as he finds the will to pull himself from my mouth, pinching my swollen bottom lip between his thumb and forefinger.

"You take my cock so well, but I don't want to come like this. *Fuck—*" He stares down at me as if he's considering thrusting back into my mouth. "That might have been the hardest thing I've ever had to do," he says as he pulls me up to him by my arms. He sucks my bottom lip into his mouth and then kisses it. "This mouth was made for me."

"No gag reflex," I admit.

"Like I said, made for me," he rasps hungrily into my ear and then he's kissing me, running his hands over my body, squeezing and kneading my thighs, my ass, my waist. He's everywhere all at once. He turns me around and presses his rock hard cock into the small of my back, my cool damp hair still between us as he cups my breasts and slides his other hand down to my soaking core.

"Mmm, this pussy, so fucking ready for me..."

"Yes..." I manage to breathe out as he continues his gentle assault of my clit, bringing me almost to the point of coming, then stopping when he senses I'm close.

"I want to feel you fall apart on my cock." His voice is gravel and I can almost feel his smirk against my skin as he pushes my body down onto the bed so I'm on all fours before him. His hands glide over my back, pushing my face down into the pillows, gripping the back of my neck, he pulls my ass up so I'm on full display, but there is nothing vulgar or demeaning about his actions, he simply takes what he wants with a surety I've never experienced from a man before. He kneels behind me on the bed and runs his hands from my upper back down to the globes of my ass, sliding them outward as he grips my hips and presses my backside into his erection.

"Your body is fucking perfection," Nash whispers to me again as he slides his cock against my slick entrance.

I move my body against his, grinding shamelessly, searching for friction. The ache I feel for him pushes any other thought from my brain. I revel in the feel of his skin against mine.

He reaches into my drawer beside us and produces a condom faster than I can fathom and tears it open with his teeth, rolling it over his cock expertly with one hand as I watch him over my shoulder.

He's pressed back up against me now.

"This isn't going to be gentle," is his only warning before he's thrusting into me, as deep as possible, gripping my hair. "*Fuck*," Nash groans a long drawn out form of the word as my mouth falls open but no sound comes out because I'm so intensely full and gripping him as tight as humanely possible.

This angle, this is something I can't handle. He is hitting that spot inside me. So deep.

"I really, really need you to try to breathe, Rae." His words are shaky as he stays fully seated inside me but doesn't move. Gentle fingers trace my spine in an attempt to get me to relax.

"Okay," I say as I try to breathe.

I blow out a long shaky breath as he uses my hips to slowly push me forward then pull me back down onto him again until I'm once again full to the hilt. I have no strength to do anything but let him use my body for his pleasure. He's not moving at all. He's simply using my body to do the work for him and the way it feels is indescribable.

"This tight little cunt"—he grunts as he drags me almost all the way off his cock and then pulls me back down by my hips— "Was fucking made for me." Nash drives into me again, meeting my hips with force before I'm ready and I feel like I'm about to orgasm all over him.

"You're going to come already..." he states, gratification and something else in his voice. Surprise?

"It's your words... I can't—" I start to explain but I can't finish my sentence or even string a thought together, it's too much as he thrusts into me and hits that spot again. Over and over he moves in and out of me. It's methodical and rough. I'm trying to hold it together but I'm about to lose it, only he senses when I'm going to and never lets me, like he is completely in tune with my body. Gripping my ass, he spreads me wide as he fucks in and out of me, I watch him staring down at where we connect over my shoulder.

"Such a pretty pussy, such a good girl, taking my cock like it was made for you. Fucking beautiful." I settle with the fact that Nash could probably ask me to do just about anything and I'd do it if it meant he would call me his good girl afterwards. He moves expertly in deep thrusts and slow withdrawals, almost all the way before consuming me again. A state of steady euphoria washes over me.

He grips a large fistful of my hair and pulls my body back up to his, pressing his front to my back, then slides his large hand over my throat to my jaw, turning my face so he can kiss me as he presses a finger to my clit. I'm instantly a goner.

I'm shattering. Broken moans and whimpers leave my body as his lips absorb them. I spasm around him and do just what he wants.

"That's it, CeCe. Come. Come all over my cock," he growls as he continues thrusting into me. "Take exactly what you want from me."

I do just that. My walls clench around his length, coaxing his release from him.

His legs tense behind me as a hand grips my hips in a tight hold. Somehow, he grows even more inside me then jerks and groans my name with inaudible cuss words as he fills the condom. Moments pass like this, there's no sense of time before he collapses onto me, resting his head on my back, his breathing heavy.

"Fuck...I'm pretty sure you just wrecked *me*," Nash mutters, then kisses under my shoulder blade.

CHAPTER TWENTY-SIX
Nash

The feel of warm, sweet-scented skin and soft hair on my arm is foreign as I open my eyes and take in the view of CeCe's room. The log cabin walls are a stark contrast to the antique white bedroom furniture, white duvet and white curtains. The only other colors in the room are the light gray and pink throw pillows and CeCe's golden hair. The sun is streaming in, which means the night is technically over. I glance over at her. She's out cold so I adjust myself to lie on my side and just watch her sleep. Her arms are tucked under her head and her hair is splayed everywhere. We're both still naked.

I have no idea what time we fell asleep, but I do know for the first time in a long, long time—maybe ever—I actually slept without any bad dreams. I still woke up at 3:13 but instead of terror, I felt a sort of peace. CeCe's hand was on my chest, so I took her again just because I could and she didn't stop me, she let me in like it was the most natural thing on earth. Now, her breathing is silent and I take this time to appreciate her beauty like this. The smallest details I may never see like this again. The tiny freckle she has over her lip, her dark lashes fluttering as she dreams, her silky skin in the morning sun, her tiny heart shaped, rose gold earrings that sit in her cute little earlobes. Her *earlobes*. When the hell have I ever admired a woman's earlobes before?

I just lie here, amazed that this universe can create something so perfect. It's overwhelming that she exists, and that she's lying here beside me. She stirs and opens one stunning green eye, reminding me that all good things come to an end. It's just as well the night is technically over. I cannot get attached to CeCe and I know it.

"Good morning." I brush her hair off her forehead as I say it, unable to stop myself from touching her.

Her perfect little mouth forms an O as she yawns and stretches beside me.

"I'm pretty sure you fucked my pussy into oblivion last night," she remarks, and I chuckle. What comes out of her mouth never ceases to surprise me.

"You challenged me with only one night, what did you expect?" I ask.

She opens both her eyes. "You know it's customary when you abuse someone's vagina with your unnaturally large dick to make them coffee in the morning."

With that, she turns over like there's no doubt in the world that I'll do what she wants. As crazy as it may seem, I'm already standing up and pulling on my boxers because what's slowly becoming apparent to me is what CeCe Ashby wants from me, she gets.

I fumble around her kitchen looking for filters and ground coffee for this monstrosity of a coffee maker she purchased the week after she got here. After reading the manual and grinding the beans, I think I have it figured out. I add her cream and sugar once it's brewed and head into her room where she's managed to pass back out cold in the twenty-five minutes I've been gone. For all this effort, the coffee isn't even going to make it to her though because the way she's sleeping, her entire back is exposed to me. Every vertebra all the way down to the little dimples at her tailbone, the perfect place for my thumbs to rest as I fuck her from behind. My dick stands at attention the moment I see her subconsciously arch her back slightly in her slumber.

I set the steaming mug down and crawl in beside her, running my hand over her curvy hip and down around her front as I plant kisses on her back and shoulders. She stirs and moans as my fingers find her nipple under the sheets.

"Hey, it's the next day," she whispers, but it sounds like the last thing she's going to do is stop me.

I marvel that I've had sex with this woman three times already in twelve hours, and I still feel like I haven't got enough of her. Not even close.

"No, I think you misunderstood me. I meant a full day. Twenty-four hours. We still have until ten o'clock tonight."

"Mmhmm. And I am busy tonight," she murmurs, still half asleep.

"I would feel like we weren't doing ourselves justice if we didn't use this time to the fullest," I say as she rocks her ass into my cock, just as hungry for me as I am for her. I smirk into her shoulder.

"That makes sense," she moans as her legs part and my fingers slide into her already soaking pussy—the pussy that feels like it was made to wrap around me. The fervor I feel for her builds low in my hips and in my spine.

CeCe turns over to face me and begins to press her palm to my cock. Swiping pre-cum off the head, she licks it off her thumb as she climbs on top of me and starts to kiss me. Her hot wet pussy presses up against me, just her skin on mine as she rocks over me.

I let my hands roam her lower back and her hair falls over her nipples as she sits up. Her head tips back as I press my thumb against her clit. The curve of her waist to her full hips over me is hypnotizing. The way she looks right now is enough to break any man, even me.

A flurry of want rushes through me and before I can stop it, I blurt out exactly what I'm thinking. "I want to feel you, Rae, just you and me," I tell her.

She looks at me, understanding exactly what I mean. If this is my last shot with her, I want to feel it all. She said she's on the pill and I know she's clean. I know I'm clean, not only have I never had sex with a woman without a condom, but like I told her, it's been almost two years for me and I don't fuck around with that sort of thing, I was always on top of getting checked when I was in the NHL. But when I expect her to verify, she doesn't; she just looks at me with total trust in her eyes, fucking me up even more than I already am. Then she rises up enough to let the head of my cock grace the slice of paradise between her legs.

"I trust you," CeCe says as she sinks down onto me an inch at a time, panting with every attempt to get lower. She's so fucking tight, there's a moment I'm not sure if she can actually take all of me like this. She moans the cutest fucking sounds I've ever heard as she continues, until she's finally fully seated on my cock. We both breathe out as she meets my depth.

"Nash," she murmurs my name as her head falls back and she begins to move.

"Goddamn, Rae, you feel so fucking good," I breathe out as my eyes remain focused on where we connect.

I can no longer tell where one of us begins and the other one ends and I never fucking care to find out. I want to stay suspended in this alternate reality of her and I. One where we have nothing to lose. One where I could keep her and not wake up every day, afraid it could all just disappear. One where I don't care that I have no control over any of it. One where I'm not broken to start with.

Her tiny hands press against my chest like hot branding irons, marking her place as she rocks her hips over me. Every cell in my body is alive and buzzing with the feel of her pussy wrapped around my cock and nothing between us. I move my hips up to meet her, thrusting as deeply into her as I can, holding myself there for a beat as she shudders above me, moaning and whimpering when I pull back again then fuck my body up to meet her.

"That's it, open up for me like a good girl, this pussy was made to take all of me."

Moving my hands to her breasts I rub and pinch her nipples until she's a whimpering mess above me. I sit up and take each one into my mouth as she continues to move over me, losing her rhythm inside her desire, letting go. Her warm chest crashes to mine as I grip her neck and move up to her lips, kissing her, taking over for her, sliding my hand into her long thick hair, and crushing her to me. I kiss with everything I have, like it's the last kiss I'll ever have with her as the heat and pressure dances up my spine. For the first time in my life, I'm speechless as I just savor every single second of her, of this, of us.

I feel her start to quiver around me, clenching me as I keep the continuous rhythm that's inching her closer to her high.

"Eyes on me, Rae. I want to see that fire while you fall apart around my cock."

"Oh God, *Nash*," she moans.

I grip her shoulders as she rides me, holding her tightly, her nails cutting into my flesh. She loses it, and I push myself to make it one more second. One more second of this to last my memory a lifetime.

Just as I feel her pussy tighten, her walls gripping me, she grabs my face and kisses me, then stares into my eyes as she starts to come undone.

"Nash... come inside me, baby," she whimpers and I fall apart with her, spilling into her with a force that attempts to tear me apart.

"Holy *fuck*," I mutter into her neck as my cock still jerks inside her.

Moments pass like this; I have no idea how many, the only sound is our breath.

CeCe kisses me on my lips as she comes down and I feel it. It's a kiss that says she wants me and goodbye all at the same time.

We stay like this for a few moments and just breathe each other in.

I lift CeCe off of me and lie her down on the bed. We both huff out a breath as I pull myself from her.

I'm not sure what to do now. That's it. I know it. She said one night. She's just coming out of something heavy with Andrew. Not to mention, her brothers will probably try to beat the shit out of me like a WWE tag team for this. I get up and put my boxers on, heading to the bathroom in silence to grab a warm cloth to clean CeCe with.

"Your coffee is cold," I say awkwardly when she's clean. "I'll make a new one."

She smiles at me and nods as I venture out to the kitchen with the lukewarm brew that I set down earlier.

I figure out the coffee maker a lot quicker this time and I'm waiting for the coffee to finish as CeCe ventures out into the small kitchen in the morning light.

"Your back, your arms," she gasps. "I'm so sorry."

I look at my shoulders and run a hand over my back. I grin. She scratched the shit out of me. It looks like I've been attacked by a mountain lion. I smile wide and look at her with one eyebrow raised. Is she joking?

"Darlin', this is the proof of how hard I made you come. I'll take the scars. They're worth it," I say while I pour our coffees.

CeCe blushes as she takes a mug from me.

She is wearing her little silk pajama shorts and a worn, oversized Dallas Stars hoodie.

"Nice," I say, chuckling at the choice.

"I felt it was only fitting, and you haven't seen the best part." She smiles and takes her coffee to the table, hiking a thumb to her back. CARTER 10.

I drop to the chair across from her to absorb the way she looks with my name and number on her back. Damn, she looks like *mine*.

I clear my throat. "When... uh... did you buy that? Were you a secret fan and I never knew?" I joke to keep it light as my heart beats rapidly in my chest.

"I bought it just after you got drafted," she says. "It's actually my age old favorite hoodie, if you must know. And yes, I've always been your fan, Nash. I've watched as many of your games as I could."

I sip my coffee in silence and stare at her across the table.

"This isn't going to be weird now is it?" CeCe asks. "This is really good by the way." She holds her coffee up.

"I almost felt like I needed to go back to university to learn how to make coffee with that thing."

She laughs a clear, full laugh. It's fucking beautiful. I reach across the table and touch her hand. The electricity between us is still fiercely undeniable.

"It's not going to be weird. Not on my part. I promise. You're the same CeCe and I'm the same Nash."

"We're both adults. We've been spending a lot of time together. Maybe it was inevitable. A phase we had to go through." She's not looking at me as she rambles, and I'm not sure if she's asking me if this is how I feel or if she's convincing herself.

I speak to try to make her feel better. "I don't want to take anything from you that you don't have to give. This is complicated. Your brothers trust me to look out for you and protect you—"

"Not ruin me for life with mind blowing sex?" She laughs. "I get it."

I nod. My ego loves that I've ruined her for anyone else—and her words are my sentiments exactly. I can't imagine any other woman comparing to last night or this morning.

"I do have one question now that all this has happened and I think we're at the point where we shouldn't have to hide anything from each other," she says.

I eye her curiously, wondering what she could possibly think I've hidden from her.

"My mom, our ranch, are you helping us? Financially?"

I rub my jaw as I contemplate her question, Jo didn't want anyone to know. She told Wade only because there is no way to hide it from him.

I scrub my face with my hand and huff out a breath. I'm not about to lie to CeCe if she's figured it out. But I owe her the whole story.

CHAPTER TWENTY-SEVEN
Nash

"When I was nineteen, I came home on the anniversary of my parents' death. It was after the last derby—I didn't have enough to keep myself busy and U of K hockey was over for the season. I couldn't get the demons out of my head. I just needed to numb it. I brought a bottle of bourbon into the north pasture. You found me there. Do you remember that night?"

CeCe nods. "Yes, I was twelve? You told me to go away but I didn't, I sat with you. I was worried. You said you were a mess sometimes and I wouldn't understand. I was too young. It was a grown up problem."

I blink and say nothing because I can't believe she remembered word for word what I said to her.

"You sat there with me for a while and we listened to Kenny Chesney on my iPod. You prattled on about Shania and your friends at school, and it made me forget what I was going through for a little while. I was grateful for your pre-teen rambling that night."

"I knew I couldn't help you but I didn't want to leave you

alone. You felt almost like my big brother back then," she says, lost in the memory.

"Cole came and sat with us, then after a bit, he sent you back to the house. He tried to get me to stay but I wouldn't listen to him, so I left. You guys went home."

I sigh, because this part is the hardest to admit.

"I drove, I shouldn't have. I knew it when I turned the key. Of all things to try and do after how *they* died? I live with that idiotic decision every day. I didn't make it far. I thought I saw something in the road. I swerved to avoid the ditch but not before I took out two county signs and hit Mr. Saulito's fence. I took part of it out and ended up on his lawn. Your mom and dad came flying up behind me, Cole had told them I left. Your dad took one look at what happened and forced me to get in the car with your mom. She brought me back here and your dad took the wrap for all of it. Said it was him driving my dad's old truck to the store in town because it was blocking his and that a deer ran into the road. He paid the damages to Mr. Saulito, met with the cops and took responsibility for the signs. If he would've left me to deal with it on my own, I would've been charged with an underage DUI and property damage. It would've ruined me and my upcoming hockey career. We came back to the ranch and they stayed up with me into the night. They told me it was my one get out of jail free card, but that it was time to grow up and get help."

"I remember waking up the next morning and dad telling me he was in an accident." She looks shocked and a giant tear spills over her cheek. She's realizing all over again what kind of man her father was.

"The rest is history you know, until two years ago when your mom called me. Your dad's medical bills were out of this world, just his surgery alone was almost two-hundred-thousand dollars. They needed help but she didn't ask, she was just venting. I just contacted the medical unit and paid the bill myself and every bill after that."

"I had no idea," she says as she wipes her tears away and sniffs. "The experimental treatment?

"Yes."

"The doctors said that gave us two more months with him. That was you?"

"Yes. I've also been helping her stay on her feet for the last year. It's been hard as you know since your dad..."

She buries her face in her hands.

"I don't know as much as you did, apparently. I should've been here."

"Don't do that. She knew I could afford it, CeCe, and she never wanted to burden you. She didn't want you to know she was struggling. You were in Seattle, you had a life there. She knew that if she said she needed you, you would put her first."

"I know you and my dad were close, but I didn't realize how close."

"He got me into more therapy after the night of the accident, to try to deal with everything. Because even though I was living under their roof, he didn't realize how much I was still suffering. He gave me more work here. They came to every single one of my games and brought you, Cole, and Wade. He told me everything in life is a choice. I could either let it pull me or I could take the reins and hold them tight," I repeat his words. "Your future is yours and you can direct that horse any way you choose."

"I miss him so much," CeCe says, her tears now dry, she pushes her hair off her shoulder.

"So do I."

We sit for a beat in silence, sipping our respective coffees.

"My life could've gone down a completely different path if it hadn't been for him. I'll never, ever forget that."

"Do you know, the only two times I've sat at a table with you in the last month in the morning, you've had me crying?" CeCe's eyes are still glassy but she's laughing now.

"Next time no tears," I say. "Promise."

"I think I'm just extra sappy because maybe you've fucked all my sense out of me." She smirks.

"Well, I'm definitely taking advantage of that today at the office then. I'll be giving you a whole list of things to do that you'd normally give me a hard time for."

"Don't push your luck, Nash. It rebuilds, you know—the sass. By noon, I'll be full force again." She wags a finger at me, and my infatuated cock is already craving her again, as I imagine pulling that finger into my mouth.

I chuckle and sip my coffee—which *is* actually really good. Her fancy-ass coffee maker is worth the mental suffering I went through.

The sun fully engulfs the mountain side behind her perfect face and the beauty of it across the table stuns me. I never thought I'd find a view I've loved more than riding horseback through Silver Pines, watching the sun rise over Sugarland Mountain, until I sat across from Cecilia Ashby, freshly fucked with a coffee in the morning.

We finish the rest of our coffee in silence. I get up and tidy her kitchen as she heads to the shower. I'm starting to spiral. I think about joining her but I don't try. Maybe it makes me a sick fuck, but I want the scent of her on my skin a little bit longer.

I get dressed in my clothes from last night and make her bed, folding her throws carefully and placing her fifty pillows in perfect order. I stand in front of it and start remembering every face she made while I was inside her as my phone buzzes on the table interrupting my fresh memories.

I turn it over and I see it's Wade, so I answer.

"You at CeCe's? I just noticed your truck on my way to the barn."

Shit. I realize that we're lucky it's Thursday. The only day of the week that Wade sleeps in and Cole comes to work through the morning chores. Cole would've gone straight to the barn at five.

"Yeah, we had an issue with our accounts last night. I just got here, we've been going over some things since seven-thirty."

I'm sweating. Why am I sweating? I'm a thirty-three-year-old man. It was one night.

"Cool, I need to show you the package we put together for your festival. I'll pop by in a minute."

I go through the scenario of Wade arriving and CeCe being in the shower, plus it has to still smell like sex in here.

"No, I'm just leaving. I'll come to you," I say quickly, searching for my keys and wallet.

"Okay, I'm at the north barn, but meet me at the big house."

"There in five."

I text CeCe as I go.

> Had to leave. Wade was going to come to your place, he saw my truck so I went to him instead.

I huff out a breath when the fresh air hits me and I run a hand through my hair. I grab a t-shirt from my truck because I always have spare ones—habit from my younger years. I toss it on and throw my dress shirt in the back and snatch my cowboy hat off the back seat and head to the big house.

CHAPTER TWENTY-EIGHT
CeCe

I stay in the shower longer than I should. I just need a few minutes away from his face to think clearly.

This was supposed to just be sex but I can't get Nash out of my head, and not just the sex—which has now officially ruined me for all future sex—but him. His eyes, the selfless way he is helping my family, my parents. The way he looked in my kitchen in his boxers, moving around seamlessly. How the space seems too small for him but he *just fits* here. Watching him use my fancy, dainty European coffee maker with confidence might just be the manliest thing I've ever seen.

I let the hot water run out and then feel like a jerk because I'm sure Nash will want a shower before he leaves.

I walk out of the bathroom and wander my house, but he's gone. I don't even know where my phone is. Last night, from the time Nash got here until I opened my eyes this morning is a total blur and it's like I'm being plunged back into reality now.

I find my phone on the coffee table in the living room and pick it up. One message from Nash telling me he left to avoid Wade from stopping by, and several from my girls. I skim through our group chat because there's so many messages.

GINGER

Your mom told my mom who told me that
Andrew was in town tonight.

LIV

And you didn't tell us?

GINGER

She also said a certain hot boss gave him a
beat down outside the coffee shop.

LIV

Damn.

GINGER

Yep. He was huffing his chest like a caveman
or so I heard, and punched Andrew right in
the face, more than once. God what I
would've done to see that.

LIV

Why do I find that extremely hot?

GINGER

Right? It's been a long time since I've seen
the Ashby boys give someone a good ass-
whooping.

LIV

CeCe, tell me he took his shirt off for ease of
mobility?

GINGER

I'm sure he was just being nice. It's probably
because he just thinks of her as any other
employee. Nothing more, nothing less. 😊

LIV

Totally. I'm sure it has nothing to do with the
way he looks at her like she's his next meal
and he's been fasting for months.

GINGER

OR how he conveniently shows up at our table every time a man approaches CeCe every damn Sunday.

LIV

Or how he always plays all of CeCe's favorite songs, brings in a cover artist of her girl crush and always saves us the booth where he can keep an eye on her from the bar.

Enlighten us, CeCe. If you don't answer in thirty minutes we're going to assume you are in fact saving a horse.

GINGER

She isn't answering. It's been an hour. Could it be that her caveman boss actually took her home and gave her a proper evaluation?

LIV

If by evaluation you mean he's evaluating how well she takes his dick than I say I sure fucking hope so. God, you deserve a night like that, babe.

GINGER

If you are doing your hot boss we need the details. He definitely has big dick energy.

LIV

Hell yes, oh God I may never look at Nashby the same. LOL.

GINGER

Good morning, CeCe. Are you dead? Has your hot cowboy boss fucked you to death?

You guys are impossible.

Of course they assume this. There's no way on earth they wouldn't. I love Ginger but she definitely has a gossipy side. I trust her completely but would she be able to deny Cole if he asked her? She's been in a love-hate relationship with him since we were fourteen. They have a weird kind of vibe between them where I'll catch them bickering as he's pouring her a drink in my kitchen. Sometimes I wonder if it's partly why she's my friend.

I don't have to see the girls until tomorrow night for Avery's birthday dinner so I can avoid their questions and give myself a day to even figure out what to say. I decide that is best.

LIV

I didn't hear that we were wrong though.

You're wrong. I'm alive. He didn't fuck me to death.

GINGER

To death.

She rode a cowboy.

LIV

Holy shit I must concur.

I never said that. I'm going to work now. Love you both.

GINGER

She said she loves us. She definitely got laid.

Fine. I hate you both. Gossipy bitches.

GINGER

Too late the cowboy's out of the bag.

I laugh as I pull my blouse out of the closet. I definitely did ride a cowboy—a part-time one, at least—and there's no sense in trying to hide it, my girls clearly already know.

CHAPTER TWENTY-NINE
Nash

I manage to keep it together around Wade, but just barely. The world has shifted on its axis and yet everything here seems the same. The familiar panic creeps up my neck as I sit in the kitchen I've sat in for twenty years eating a muffin like any other Thursday morning.

"Heard you knocked Drew the Dick around a little last night."

"Heard that already?"

"I knew last night." Wade smirks. "Mama looked like she was about to go after him with the town and pitchforks."

"Fuck," I chuckle as I pull my hat off and rub my forehead. I wouldn't want to be on Jo's bad side.

"I'm not complaining. Good to know you still have CeCe Rae's back."

Yeah, her soft, silky, naked back...

"Sometimes she smiles and nods, but she's a mess of emotion on the inside. I wouldn't put it past her to go back to him."

That sentence sobers me up in one second flat. "You think?" I wonder if the horror on my face is apparent.

"You never know. She spent a lot of time with him and she's always wanted to get married and have kids."

I nod and wonder if he realizes the full extent of how Andrew treated CeCe.

"She should find someone that... wants that too and treats her right, then." I clear my throat. Over my dead fucking body will she spend one minute alone with Andrew *ever again*.

"I sure as fuck hope she wouldn't, but stranger things have happened, and CeCe is loyal to a fault. It's one of the reasons I'm so glad she started working with you right away. She sees things through to the end. You've given her a place, something to stay invested in, and this festival as a project. It's good for her, and I guess... well I'm just grateful, bud." Wade claps me on the shoulder.

I hate acting like the saint who's watching out for CeCe when I'm really the mother fucker who can't stop thinking about devouring her with no future plans other than that. One thing is certain—I would never let her go back to Andrew and his fucked-up house of horrors. But would she want to go back just because she wants it all and he would promise to offer it to her? I swallow down the last of my blueberry muffin and refocus.

This is why it's best if we stick to the plan. Stick to the plan. Stay friends, don't let anything get awkward. I repeat this mantra over and over.

When we're finished with our coffee break, I leave Wade, toting the auction package so I can bring it to the office to show CeCe and start to head home. Just as I settle for sticking to the plan, her name pops up on my phone and like the budding addict I am, I pull over to give her my attention.

RAE

It's a good thing you left when you did. I saved you no hot water and my friends were about to send out a search party for me.

It's a good thing they didn't come looking for you an hour ago.

RAE

Ginger has been telling me to save a horse, ride a cowboy for years, She'd probably be proud.

I'm not a cowboy.

RAE

I think a part-time cowboy counts.

I start typing several different things before deleting them.
I had fun last night.
Lame.
That was the most incredible sex I've ever had.
Even more lame.
You look so beautiful in the morning.
Sappy, rom-com actor lame.

What's an appropriate response for my hot accountant slash best friend's little sister who I can't get out of my head and want to bury myself inside every minute I'm awake. I think for a minute and decide to keep it light.

I'm stopping at Spicer's, did you eat after I left? I can bring you breakfast.

RAE

I think it's the least you can do after abusing my vagina then leaving without a trace into the morning fog.

I chuckle and scrub my face with my hand in my parked

truck. If she only knew the things that were running through my mind, she'd know I'd have stayed. And not just for the morning. I'm starting to think I'd stay with CeCe as long as she let me.

> Apologies to your pussy. I will grovel before her with Danishes and croissants.

RAE

> She says thank you, that's a start, and hurry up, I'm hungry. I'll be at the office by nine.

> I'll meet you there.

I turn onto my driveway ten miles from the ranch and breathe a heavy breath of relief. This is my safe space. My haven. The gravel drive is lined with white fencing and it is almost a half mile long. Maple trees hide the small cabin house until it is right in front of you. I have eight acres here and I love every inch. Some of my friends from my NHL days have massive homes that showcase their millions. I just need this. My simple cabin and some land.

I climb the steps to the wide, wrap around front porch, my four a.m. coffee spot, the space I seek after 3:13 comes and I can't fall back asleep, where I watch the sun wake and listen to the birds.

The house is simple but has every modern amenity. It worked out perfectly that it was for sale when I was making my plan to come home. I viewed it the day before Wyatt died and I know he would've loved it. The owner was going into a nursing home and had lived here since the fifties. He had cared for it but never updated it. So I had it renovated before I retired at the same time I renovated the arena. The cabin walls remain but the kitchen is updated now with new walnut cabinets, stainless steel appliances and a large butcher block kitchen island. My favorite room in the house is a cozy family room off the kitchen with a floor to ceiling original cobblestone fireplace that still burns real wood. The massive tinted windows in that room look out over the fresh water creek that runs behind it. It is deep enough to hold my twenty-five-foot dock and my little skiff fishing boat and clean enough to swim in in the summer. The whole house is crisp creams, wood and wrought iron—rustic and calming. It's all I ever need or want. I hop in the shower quickly, breathing in CeCe's strawberry scent that still clings to my skin one last time, and change into jeans and a clean, white Henley before heading right back out the door to Spicer's. I barely get out of my driveway before Shania Twain's "Whose Bed Have Your Boots Been Under?" begins to play through my sound system. I drive along and sing every damn word with the world's dopiest grin on my face remembering CeCe dancing to this at the pub on Sunday night.

I am absolutely fucked.

I get to the office at nine, drop Sonny's coffee and powdered donut on her desk, and grab the documents she's left for me to look over.

"You're whistling," she says, eyeing me suspiciously.

I look up. *I am?*

"Main street boxing has you feeling happy this morning, boss?" She leans back and folds her arms over her chest.

"Jesus Christ, the gossip spreads so fast," I say as I turn to exit her office. "Is CeCe here yet? I didn't see her car."

"I'm right here," she says breezing into Sonny's office.

"Got something for me, *boss*?" she asks.

Fuck. Why does she have to look like sex itself? Her normally wavy hair is hanging thick and straight down her back, and she's wearing a deep green dress the exact color of her eyes. The top has a high neck and is a loose fit, but it's cinching at her tiny waist, just like the sleeves, loose and billowy then cuffing tightly around her wrists. The bottom is the show stopper. It hugs her entire lower half like a second skin to her knees showing every bit of her perfect curves.

I pick my jaw up off the floor and hand her a box filled with every pastry Spicer's has. Visions of her plump ass in my hands last night fill my mind. I avert my eyes from her to avoid a mid-morning woody.

"Thanks." CeCe smirks and then heads out of the office, tossing her hair over her shoulder.

I turn to follow her, shooting Sonny a wave over my shoulder to notice her shaking her head at me like a disapproving mother.

"Couldn't do it, could ya, boss?"

"Boundaries, Sonny. Enjoy your donut," I chirp back as I steal out of her office.

"Mmhmm." I hear from behind me.

CHAPTER THIRTY
CeCe

After a long list of phone calls I had to return, I finally get a chance to eat. I'm pretty sure I look like a fourteen-year-old school girl with a crush as I pull open my box of goodies from Spicer's. He bought *everything*. Every single pastry they offer.

On the inside of the box, he's done an absolutely terrible sketch of a little cat and wrote "peace offering" beside it. *This man.*

I start laughing as I pull out a maple pecan Danish and start happily munching. My phone buzzes on my desk.

> GINGER
>
> Avery says a certain part-time cowboy/hot boss was just in the equipment room this morning humming Shania Twain. I wonder why that could be?

I blush and lean back in my chair.

> Who wouldn't sing Shania?

LIV

There are only two reasons men hum. When they have just gotten laid or when they think they're going to get laid.

GINGER

So babe, on a scale of banana to eggplant what are we talking here?

Don't you have young minds to mold this morning?

Ginger ignores my question.

GINGER

Change of plans tonight, forget hot yoga, I'm coming to your little party. Tell Mabel I'd like a mani and pedi please. Cherry red.

LIV

I'm not missing out either. I'll be there at seven. I'll bring chocolate and wine.

You two need to find a hobby and don't forget to wear pink, it's a pink party.

GINGER

I do not own anything pink.

I trust you can be creative. See you at seven.

LIV

I say eggplant.

Goodbye y'all.

I put my head in my hands. So much for having a day to myself to think.

Is Mabes still excited for our sleepover tonight?

COLE

> She hasn't stopped talking about it for two days.

Ok, I'll see you at six, I've got dinner for her.

COLE

> You ok? Heard Andrew was here last night.

Yes. I'm starting to think the whole town is connected through cans and string.

COLE

> Mama called me last night and filled me in. Said he got put in his place by Nash. Glad he was there.

I sigh and dig into another Danish—cherry this time. Running on four hours of sleep, confusing new or old? Feelings for my hot boss and a plan to spend my night with an excited seven year old means I will need this extra sugar today. Summer break is almost over and she's been begging me for this for two weeks.

By the middle of my second Danish I can't help myself. I cave and send Nash a message.

Thank you for breakfast. My vagina almost forgives you.

I expect him to respond but I don't hear from Nash or see him for the rest of the day. Avoiding overthinking, I turn my playlist up and get a ton of work done in my office. By three, I realize Nash hasn't even opened my message. I don't want to seem like a needy woman the morning after, so I just pack up and get ready to leave at four. *I'm* the one that told him one night only after all, and we sure pushed that definition to its limit.

I check my phone again when I get to my car like the needy

woman I actually am, but there's nothing. I stop at the grocery store for fixings so Mama and I can make Mabel dinner and to load up on the standard s'mores items and junk food.

By the time I get home at five, I'm kicking myself in the ass for sleeping with him. I must have been crazy to think that I could have just sex with Nash Carter and then just forget about it like it never happened.

I'm still berating myself when my phone finally buzzes.

MR. CARTER

> Long day. Two trainers called in sick and had meetings with potential sponsors from Lexington for the festival. Can't wait to fill you in. Glad to hear I'm almost forgiven... I was ready to start groveling.

I smile at his newly appointed contact name flashing over my lock screen. *Mr. Carter.* Yes, he is. I sigh, and realize I'm over-thinking everything as usual. The man was busy, CeCe. That is all.

> Good thing it was only one night. I don't think I could take any more.

Why did I say that? I'm the definition of facepalm in this moment. He mercifully ignores my comment and changes the subject.

MR. CARTER

> So why are you busy tonight?

> How do you know I'm busy?

MR. CARTER

> You told me this morning.

I did?

I did?

MR. CARTER

Yes, pre morning sex.

I remember telling him when I read his response, I had completely forgotten until now. Proof my brain doesn't work properly when he's kissing me or touching me.

MR. CARTER

In your defense, I was distracting you at the time.

That I remember.

Yes, I'll take that defense. Too much sex = temporary amnesia.

MR. CARTER

I'm ok with that, it makes me look good.

If you must know, I am having a sleepover with Mabel. We'll be roasting mellows.

MR. CARTER

I'll be slinging whiskeys and keeping the drunkards of this town in order. Have a good night with Mabes.

Have a good night slinging drinks.

Why does this seem so awkward? The reality that this is it actually hits me as I start Mabel's pizza. It's too late for me. I've gone and done it. I've let Nash Carter in where he doesn't belong.

CHAPTER THIRTY-ONE
CeCe

"I knew it," Ginger squeals as I wrap the flannel blanket around my body tighter. It's cool tonight and we've been out here for hours. Mabel finally went to bed with Mama Jo after we wore her out with manis and pedis all around, way too much sugar and song after song on Just Dance.

"I really feel like I've made a mistake now. It was just fine this morning but I don't know... felt a little awkward this afternoon," I say. "Ugh, why does he have to be so fucking incredible?" I bury my head in my hands.

"Was it good, is the real question," Olivia asks.

I look at her like 'are you fucking kidding me?'

"It was, wasn't it?" She covers her mouth with her hand. "Oh my God. How good?"

"So fucking good. The best ever," I give.

"Why only one night? He doesn't look at you like *only one night*," Ginger says, thinking carefully.

"He told me when I got home that he doesn't want a relationship. Forever the playboy, I guess. Besides, he's got his hands in everything. When would he have time for something more? I'm also pretty sure he thinks Wade and Cole will kill him."

"Kill who?" Cole asks, coming out the back door onto the deck. All three of us girls turn to face him as the last of the daylight sinks down behind the house.

"Andrew," I improvise. "Y'all done burning brush?" I ask quickly, trying to change the subject.

"Yeah, I'd like to have a go at him but it sounds like Nash did the job for me." He looks at the three of us and frowns "How long have the *Not Angels* been influencing my daughter?" His brow furrows.

"We're just teaching her how to have fun, Cole. No need to get your panties in a twist," Ginger quips instantly.

Cole grunts.

"We only drank half a bottle of vodka while she was with us. We know our limits and stayed within them," Ginger snickers.

"God dammit," Cole mutters.

"Seriously, it was a perfectly innocent night. You should be thanking us, deputy. We only let her have five s'mores and a bag of candy while we watched *Saw*. Oh, and we made sure all the gangster rap we listened to limited the fucks to five a song. Best behavior. Promise." Ginger taps her heart like scouts honor.

We all laugh but Cole doesn't even crack a grin.

"These are the friends you choose?" he asks me.

Olivia scoffs. "I have nothing to do with this. It was all her." She points to Ginger.

"Oh, trust me, I know it is," Cole says as Olivia and Ginger double over. He turns to head inside, then stops and faces us again.

"If my daughter utters one inappropriate word tomorrow, you're banned from seeing her." Cole gestures at Ginger.

"I heard you're looking for a nanny, Cole? I could give you a family discount."

"Like fuck. Night, CeCe. I'll be back in the morning," is all he mutters before heading back through the house.

"Why do you insist on pushing him?" I ask Ginger.

"Because I love to see him all hot and bothered. He never looks better."

"Eww." I shudder which makes her laugh even harder.

In truth, Mabel loves Ginger and watching them together reminds me why she's a teacher. Kids flock to her and her larger than life, happy persona. She's a natural.

"Okay, so back to my problem at hand," I say as I pop a marshmallow onto a poker.

"I don't see your problem. He can say whatever he wants, he has it bad for you. I watch him at the bar. How do you not notice it?"

I stare at her clueless. The last few times we've gone to Sangria Sundays, I've barely seen Nash.

"It's true, he hides in the shadows and intercepts any man that heads our way," Olivia giggles.

"Maybe it's not that he doesn't want a relationship," Ginger says in all of her wisdom, watching my marshmallow turn a perfect shade of burnt. "Maybe he hasn't met the right person yet. Ooh, I have an idea."

"Oh fuck," I say indistinctly.

Ginger's ideas usually mean I'm about to get into trouble.

"No... listen, it's good and easy. Tomorrow night, just watch him. Really take notice. It's Friday. The busiest night of the week, live music, Avery's birthday dinner. There will be plenty of available men there. See how he reacts when one of them talks to you."

"Or even looks at you," Olivia pipes up, still giggling at the two of us as she pops her own marshmallow into her mouth.

"I have to let it go, I can't dwell on Nash Carter. I'm just going to go and have fun. It was one night. One *incredible* night, but I have to put it behind me. He's too close to all of us and I've only been out of my relationship with Andrew for a month."

"Please, you were done with him months ago, and fate has a way of showing up when you least expect it," Olivia says, her eyes full of every whimsical romance she's ever read.

"I don't know about you but he isn't family if he's fucking you ten ways from Sunday until the wee hours of the morning," Ginger says confidently. "You'll see."

"I just don't want to get hurt. If I let myself have any kind of feelings for him, I'm *going* to get hurt. I have to keep things platonic. Nash doesn't want anything else and I'm not the hit-it-and-quit-it type."

Olivia snorts back laughter. "I hate to tell you, but after last night I'd say you are—at least with him."

I groan and pop my burnt mellow into my mouth. Damn Nash Carter and his perfect body, endearing personality and mind-blowing sexual tactics. Tomorrow, things will be just like before. I am good at faking it, I did it with Andrew for months. I can do this.

CHAPTER THIRTY-TWO
Nash

The bar is quiet for a Thursday, and I'm actually so fucking tired. Staying up with CeCe all night has taken its toll on me. I've almost texted her 15 times but I stop because I know she's having a night with Mabel and I don't want to suffocate her. I just can't stop thinking about her and I have no idea how to handle this. This doesn't happen to me. Women text *me*. Women chase *me*. I thought if I let this happen, I would get all these feelings out of my system but the exact opposite has happened—now that I've had CeCe, I only want her more.

"You know if you just text her, she'll answer. Mabel's in bed." I look up from staring at my phone to see Ginger Danforth standing in my office doorway in a bubble gum pink t-shirt that says, 'That's a terrible idea, what time?'

"What do you want, Ginger? Is CeCe here?" My hope fizzles out when she shakes her head no.

"Nope, she's at home, I just left her. I came just to see you, Nashby."

Oh fuck.

"Don't look so shocked, she didn't tell me, I figured it out all on my own, and your secret is safe with me. I'm okay if Wade and Cole don't know as long as when they find out, I have a front row seat to them handing you a beat down." She giggles.

I take my hat off and rub my forehead. I've been going over any scenario in my mind where Wade and Cole would be okay with this and I come up dry every time.

"God dammit, Ginger. It was one night."

"Yeah I know, that's why I'm here."

I look at her confused. Is she here to threaten me? I grin at her. I definitely get a small kick out of this. Ginger is a tiny little thing but she's feisty as fuck and probably oddly strong.

I sit back in my chair and fold my arms across my chest.

"This where you tell me not to hurt your friend and all that?" I ask.

"No," she scoffs and surprises me.

"I know you wouldn't hurt, CeCe. This is where I tell you to get your head out of your ass and tell her how you *so obviously* feel about her."

She's too confident with that, so I deny it. Naturally.

"I like CeCe, respect her and care about her so much, but her brothers are my brothers. Her family is my family."

"Bullshit," Ginger says with a laugh like she sees right through me.

"You're using them as an excuse. They're grown ass men and CeCe is a grown woman. They'd get over it. You aren't the traveling playboy you used to be. You've been home for months, and I see the difference in you. What you are is afraid, Nash. And not afraid that you'll hurt her, you're afraid she'll hurt *you*, or you'll lose her or some form of the two."

I grunt in response but somewhere in my head, I know she's right. We both know it.

"She just got out of a long toxic relationship," I say, grasping.

"She's been separated from Andrew in her heart for months. Since Wyatt died really, maybe even before that."

She saunters over to me and points. "You need to stop making excuses and admit how you feel to yourself. Maybe it's gonna take you some time, but you need to figure it out. A girl like CeCe doesn't stay single for long. You should know that by the hordes of men you have to practically beat away with a stick every time we come into this bar."

The thought of CeCe with any other man sends fire through my veins.

"What CeCe tells you and what she might want are different ends of the spectrum. I can tell by looking at you right now that you care about her. Don't waste your chance. Let the universe take control for once. Just because you lost them doesn't mean you'll lose her too. God offers joy and pain. *She* isn't that cruel." She winks, and I gulp because Ginger's words are way too close to home for my comfort.

"Okay, that's it, Dr. Phil." I get up and motion for the door.

"Think about it, and for what it's worth, I've never seen her look the way she does when she mentions your name. Oh, and get that bar stocked with Pina Colada fixins. See ya tomorrow night if the creek don't rise." She ducks through my door and disappears into the crowd.

I shut the door, sitting at my desk, running a hand through my hair. What do I want? I have no fucking idea. I lean back and close my eyes, images of CeCe running through my mind.

What I want is to hear her voice. I grab my keys and nod to Asher on my way out. I pull my phone out of my pocket when I get into my truck and without thinking, I call her. She picks up on the second ring with a sexy little "Mr. Carter."

Her voice floods my ears and I let out a breath I didn't even know I was holding.

CHAPTER THIRTY-THREE
CeCe

My alarm wakes me after very little sleep, and I groan, realizing I have a very full day and a night out with the girls ahead of me. Nash calling last night surprised me, but I answered because my first instinct was maybe something was wrong, and I'll admit I really wanted to hear his voice.

Turns out all he wanted was the contact for the municipality because only he would be working at ten thirty at night. We ended up working on the proposal over the phone until almost midnight and then talked until way too late about nothing in particular, and everything all at once—work, my dad, our favorite music, stories from the road in the NHL, places I visited in Seattle, TV shows, food, sports, you name it. It was the kind of call I haven't had since high school, if ever, which was heightened by the fact I was sleeping in my old room at the big house, whispering like a teenager so I wouldn't wake my mom. It was the kind of phone call that by the end of it, he was saying "are you tired?" and I was saying "no," even though I was but didn't want it to end.

Finally, after almost falling asleep somewhere between two

and three, I vaguely remember him saying, "Go to sleep, CeCe, I'll see you tomorrow."

And I hung up, then dreamt about his hands on me all night long, like a lovesick teenager.

Mabel's voice echoes down the hallway before she comes busting into my room and bounces on my bed. "Nana Jo made us chocolate chip pancakes."

I pretend I'm asleep then grab her and tickle her into fits of laughter before allowing her to escape back down stairs. I yawn and look out the window, feeling odd and almost giddy. I decide five more minutes is warranted.

I flop backwards on the bed, my arms in a makeshift U. One-night flings don't talk on the phone until three in the morning debating whether Green Day or The White Stripes were more influential, do they? I close my eyes and picture him hovering over me with his strong, inked arms and navy eyes or better yet, looking up at me with his face buried between my legs, my fingers winding in his wavy hair. Heat floods my veins at the sight in my mind's eye.

My eyes fly open. I need to get up or I'm going to resort to getting myself off in my childhood bedroom. I pull my cotton robe on over my standard tank and shorts, grab my phone and pad down to the kitchen and the smell of coffee and pancakes.

I skim through a barrage of texts from Ginger, Avery and Olivia about tonight and what they're all going to wear and eat at Dolcettos for Avery's birthday.

"Morning, CeCe."

I lift my gaze to see devastating part-time cowboy Nash. Wranglers, white t-shirt, cowboy hat on his knee, dusty and dirty from his morning with Wade in the barns, sitting at my kitchen table with a coffee in one hand and my heart in the other.

CHAPTER THIRTY-FOUR
Nash

Up and at the ranch at seven in the morning after three hours of sleep is gonna mean a little power nap between the Center and tonight's rowdy, Friday night bar crowd.

I completely fucking chickened out and made the phone call about work last night but it did the trick. It kept that sweet, husky voice in my ear for four hours, talking in a whisper on her end so she wouldn't wake anyone. You'd think she was telling me the most interesting story I'd ever heard the way I was grinning into that phone.

My cheeks literally hurt from smiling so much this morning. After a three-hour snooze, I was up and running through the trails on my property, all because I talked on the phone with a woman and didn't want to hang up. I wanted the opposite, to do anything in my power to keep her talking.

I ran through all the scenarios in my mind about CeCe as I jogged through my woods. I pictured odd things I've never thought about in my life. Random things like grocery shopping together, dancing with her, taking her on a date. I've given up on myself completely at this point because the truth is, I'm not strong enough to fight whatever this is with her. So here I sit, in her kitchen for no reason other than to see CeCe's beautiful face when she first wakes up and it doesn't disappoint.

She comes down that big oak staircase in those fucking silk pajamas and I'm a total goner.

"Morning." She smiles looking between me and her Mama.

"Morning, baby. Nash is here to meet Wade and have some of my famous pancakes, aren't ya, baby?

"Wouldn't miss 'em," I say, keeping my eyes on CeCe and the way her hair falls around her shoulders.

She grabs a coffee while I check out how goddamn perfect her ass is in those shorts as Wade comes into the kitchen and nearly busts me.

"I hate when people waste my time. I have shit to do, and waiting around just pisses me off."

"Two dollars," Mabel says while she chows down water-melon at the table.

Wade grunts and stuffs some money in the boot.

"Morning, Sarge," CeCe snickers as she sips her coffee.

"No luck with hiring a trainer yet?" I ask.

"Two under qualified interviews so far this week and now this next one is six minutes late. I only have one other interview set up for later today. Pickings are slim."

CeCe and I look at each other across the table and a grin breaks out across her gorgeous face. It's contagious so I smile back and then we're laughing.

"Not six minutes," CeCe says, feigning shock and still giggling.

Wade doesn't find it funny.

"Time means something, there's no reason for—"

The front door bell rings. We're still laughing at his grumpy ass as he storms over to it, coffee in hand like he's ready to lose it. He swings it open and a very pretty young woman with long raven colored hair is standing in front of him, disheveled and speaking quickly.

"I'm so sorry I'm late, I got lost coming in here. Y'all are really hidden. I took country road seventy-four but there was construction so I had to take the detour."

Wade grunts as he lets her in. Her accent isn't Kentucky, it's more Tennessee.

"Leaving early to account for unpredictable instances is always a thing," he growls at her, and her face shows her shock at his rude tone.

"I-I'm sorry."

Mama Jo flops the last of the pancakes onto a plate and heads out to the entryway to calm Wade down and make a better impression.

"A few minutes ain't a big deal, darlin', welcome. I'm Jolene Ashby, this grumpy bugger is my son, Wade. That there's my daughter, CeCe Rae and my almost son, Nash."

"Good morning, y'all. Sorry to interrupt your breakfast, and I'm sorry I'm late. It's really not like me at all," she says, and I believe her. "I'm Ivy Spencer, I'm here to interview for your trainer position."

"Where's that drawl from, darlin'?" Jo asks.

"The smallest little town you've probably never heard of on the border, Jellico, Tennessee." Ivy grins.

CeCe gets up and wraps her robe tightly around her.

"We're pretty casual around here, we're just about to eat, would you like to join us?" She shakes her hand.

I follow suit. "Nice to meet you," I say as I take my turn shaking her hand.

"I have a busy day, so let's just get to it, we can go to my office in the Silos," Wade grunts out.

Ivy looks at us, then back to Wade, probably trying to figure out how we're all so nice and he's such a horse's ass.

"Maybe another time then. I'm super pleased to meet you all. I read about your family online. Your father's horse River Rising, came in third in the Kentucky Derby in '06. Impressive."

CeCe nods and winces like she always does behind her smile at the mention of Wyatt.

"And your ranch is so beautiful, whatta view of Sugarland."

Wade clears his throat and I almost feel sorry for the nice girl. She seems young, not much older than CeCe.

"Well, have a nice day y'all, it smells delicious."

"Nice to meet you!" CeCe calls.

We turn to each other and laugh as Ivy heads out the front door and Mama Jo whisper-yells at Wade before he follows her. "Be nice. Jesus, Wade, she's had a good career with the American Quarter Association and she trained for Bellingham Ranch for the last three years. Don't be such an old jackoff," she says, as I snicker at Mama Jo saying jackoff. She almost pulled the words from my head.

Wade doesn't answer, he just grunts again and heads out the door.

CeCe and I move back to the table with Jo and Mabel stacking pancakes onto our plates as we go.

"He seems extra crabby this morning," CeCe comments.

"He signed his divorce papers yesterday," Jo says.

I knew it but I didn't know if he wanted the whole family knowing.

"Janelle finally agreed?" CeCe asks.

"Agreed is an overstatement. They settled. She's keeping the house." Jo grimaces.

"Shit." CeCe bites her lip in thought and my dick stirs at the sight. "Maybe a pretty girl like that is just what he needs to have around to distract him from her. I feel for him."

I sit and look from Mabel to CeCe and wait. Nothing.

"I'm sorry, hold up a minute. Auntie can say shit and doesn't have to put a dollar in?" I ask Mabel.

She and CeCe share a grin.

CeCe pats me on the chest as she breezes by me on her way to the other side of the table. "Put my dollar in when you put yours in, cowboy."

She and Mabel start to laugh. I shake my head and lean over to pop the two dollars in the boot.

Mama Jo and Mabel start into a deep discussion about school starting in a week and what she still needs supplies wise. I feel my phone buzz in my pocket.

> RAE
>
> Do you ever sleep?

I look up and meet her eyes across the table then answer her under the table text.

> Not really, no.

> RAE
>
> Are you even human?

> Human enough to notice how pretty you look in the morning.

I've officially hit rom-com actor lame, and I don't even give a fuck.

> RAE
>
> What I look is tired. Some hockey player/part-time cowboy kept me up all night long talking.

> Good thing your boss gave you the day off then.

> RAE
>
> I'm surprised. He's such a hard ass.

206

> He's not that bad, I hear he can be fun in the sack.

RAE

> Yeah, but he has a cardinal rule, like I said, hard-ass.

> Someone should tell him rules are meant to be broken.

Her eyes meet mine again across the table and hold me there for a beat as she grins.

"Baby, can you come with me?" Mama Jo interrupts our under the table banter. She's looking at CeCe. "To take Mabel shopping for school clothes next week?"

"Of course." CeCe smiles at Mabel then looks back to her mom. Mama Jo looks at me, then CeCe before turning her attention back to Mabel who's happily shoveling pancakes into her mouth.

I clear my throat and stand. "Gotta go make sure Wade isn't putting this poor girl through the wringer," I say. I don't want to leave but I can only hang around for so long before it will get weird.

"See ya, Mama Jo," I say, giving her a squeeze. "Thanks for breakfast." I give Mabel a high five. "Abel Mabel, be good."

I turn to CeCe and resist the urge to physically crush myself to her. It takes a lot to resist. It's been two days but the thought of her lips on mine have me over a fucking barrel.

"See ya later."

"Bye bye, Nash," she says in that fucking sexy singsong voice.

I hate that I won't see her today, she's off because she worked Monday. Suddenly, waiting until she saunters her perfect little ass into the bar tonight with her crew seems like way too long of a wait.

CHAPTER THIRTY-FIVE
CeCe

"Let's go, girls," Ginger chants in her best Shania impression as Asher shows up at our table with the first round of butter ripple shots. I'm already tipsy from our dinner for Avery's birthday at Dolcettos. Risotto and the best Italian Pinot Grigio in town are making me feel all kinds of warm and fuzzy as I take a shot off the tray.

Asher locks eyes with Olivia for a split second as she takes the shot from him. I can't say if it's my buzzed brain or if I'm just seeing things, but his dark eyes seem to feast on her, like she's his next meal.

He backs away as she croaks out, "Thank you."

He nods and disappears into the crowd.

"Goddamn, that man could've incinerated you with those deep gray eyes." Ginger giggles.

Olivia looks over at him fleetingly.

"He scares me a little."

I turn to see what she sees, and a little scary? Yeah, I can see that.

"It's like his eyes stare right through me," Olivia says, using her hair to curtain between his watchful eye, as if he could hear her from the other side of the bar.

"He's the fire chief, right?" I ask. "Maybe we're judging a book by its cover. He has to have a good soul to save people from fire, right?"

Olivia's eyes flit back to him. "I suppose," she mutters, but she doesn't seem entirely convinced.

"Moving on from sexy, scary fire chief, to Avery," Ginger says.

We all follow suit and clink shots like it's the biggest deal on earth that Avery is turning twenty-four.

My nerves have me frazzled. I actually did it. I wore the dress. The red Max Mara I reserve for only when I want to look *hot*. I want Nash to want me when he looks at me. The late-night phone call, the glances, the coffee on my rail again this morning, all while knowing how fucking hot we are together. It's too much to fight. I want another shot with him even if it's only once more.

After I've been seated for about fifteen minutes and the hard realization hits me that when whatever this is with Nash Carter ends, it's gonna hurt like hell, I see him, and he steals my breath. No man has ever looked that good in a pair of jeans, a long-sleeved flannel over a t-shirt and that goddamn backwards baseball hat. His eyes meet mine from across the room and he grins at me. I physically melt where I sit.

"Oh yeah, totally just a one-night hook up," Ginger whispers then snorts from beside me. I nudge her elbow with mine and Avery turns to see what we're both whispering about.

"Wait, are you the reason he's been singing Shania around the Center the last two days? And Sonny said he was whistling the other day." Avery looks at me with the most incredulous face and then deadpans. "*Whistling.*"

Olivia keels over laughing as I shake my head.

"We're old friends," I say.

"Friends with benefits friends? Or *just* friends?"

"Nash has enough friends with benefits," I say to shut Avery down.

I trust my girls, and she's sweet but I don't know Avery well enough to trust her fully just yet.

Avery shrugs. "If it helps, I've never seen him with anyone in the five months I've worked with him. So if it is you giving him the happy vibes, I say go for it. The man is hot." She looks him over as she says it and it bothers me, even though I know she doesn't mean anything sinister by it.

"To hot men!" Olivia says as she raises another shot and we all follow suit. The sugary sweet liquid burns down my throat. It tastes like caramel.

I focus on Nash at the bar from the corner of my eye. He's talking to a blonde and a brunette. I eye their outfits. The blonde is wearing jeans that hug her every curve and a frilly peasant blouse that hangs off her tanned shoulders. I can only see her profile but she seems familiar. Whatever they're talking about, they're deep in conversation. I raise my hand to Asher who comes over to us quickly.

"Three strawberry margaritas please." I smile at him, my fear from earlier subsiding with my buzz.

I usually stop after four or five drinks, even on a night out like this. I know my limits but tonight I feel wild, I just want to dance and forget that Nash Carter is invading my head for even five minutes. I watch him as he writes something down and hands it to the blonde. Heat floods me as I come to the conclusion that it's got to be his phone number. What else would it be? She says something and laughs tipping her head back, then shoves the paper into her tight jean pocket. When she turns and I see her full face, I realize who she is. She's Flirty McShows-Her-Ass from the Sage and Salt. And Nash just gave her his number?

Two hours and Lord knows how many strawberry margaritas later, the girls and I are up on the dance floor shaking our asses to the incredible country band that Nash has playing tonight. They're pushing out all the crowd favorites and my feet would be killing me in these heels if alcohol wasn't numbing the pain.

I'm pretending Nash Carter doesn't exist as I dance. I need my dignity. In fact, I'm fucking desperate for it. I was so dumb to think maybe, possibly something real was happening between us. Something beyond just great sex. Miss Flirty stayed at the bar for another twenty minutes before finding a table with her friend and Nash talked to her the whole time. Just Nash being Nash, planting the seed for his next conquest.

The band starts playing Luke Bryan's "Country Girl" and everyone goes wild. The dance floor is packed with people, and Ginger, Olivia and I move right smack to the center. We know every word, of course, so we're singing along as we move to the music. We're the best dancers in this place, I'm sure of it— maybe even in the world. Or is that the margaritas talking? Either way, I don't particularly care.

We give it our all for three more songs, I can feel hands on me, no clue who's they are but I don't care as Ginger and I dance our hearts out to Sweet Home Alabama. Someone grips my hips from behind me again and is swaying to the music before Olivia grabs me.

"Let's go get a drink. Your boss looks all hot and bothered."

I turn around to see whose hands are on me, a moment of

clarity coming to me. I don't recognize the tall, blonde football player type in a cowboy hat holding my body.

Olivia pulls me away, and the man nods at me

"See you when you get back, gorgeous," he says over the music.

I smile because sure, I'll see him—he's cute and I bet he doesn't flirt with blonde waitresses.

I turn my fuzzy gaze back to the bar Olivia pulls me toward and my eyes meet Nash's glare from across the room.

The look he's wearing could set fire to the bar and burn it down around us.

CHAPTER THIRTY-SIX
Nash

If Brent Wilson puts his hands on her one more time, I'm going to snap his neck right in the middle of the bar. I've never really liked him anyway, he's always hitting on women in here and he seems to think he's something special because he's the newest member of the Laurel Creek's police force.

I have been doing nothing other than watch CeCe for the last hour and a half because for some reason tonight, she's out of control, and the men in this bar are all over her and that slip of a dress she walked in wearing. Short and tight with long sleeves, a low-cut back and fire engine red. She's showing more cleavage than I've ever seen, and all I want to do is tear it off her and push my face into those perfect tits.

"No more alcohol to CeCe," I say to Asher as he heads off to a table.

He nods and continues on.

Just as I see that mother fucker touch her again, I lock eyes with Olivia and she knows I'm fucking pissed. I start to walk over but I see Olivia pull CeCe away from handsy so I stop and let them come to me. Logically, I know I have no claim on

CeCe. I have no right to be mad but I am fucking mad, and right now, I don't give a fuck who knows it.

Olivia pulls CeCe to the bar just as a mini fight breaks out on the other side of it. I grab one of the guys involved as Victor grabs hold of the other and we take their drunk asses outside and kick them to the curb.

When I get back in, CeCe is still at the bar with Olivia. Just as I approach, Margaret, my newest bartender, passes CeCe a shot of something. Handsy spots her and starts to walk toward her.

That is fucking it. The straw just broke the camel's back. I grab CeCe's elbow and I'm pulling her through the crowd. She stumbles as I drag her ass through the hallway, shoving her into the office, and I slam the door behind her.

"What the hell, part-time cowboy?" She's drunk, but still fucking sexy as all hell.

"You're cut off and I'm taking you home."

"Oh... right, it's bar Nash tonight. Is the big bad bartender angry? Am I here for you to punish me with expensive drinks and cheap wings?" CeCe laughs. *This fucking woman.* "You have no right to take me home, Nash Carter," she slurs.

"Like hell I don't."

"Why don't you take Flirty McShows-Her-Ass home? You know you're gonna eventually." She laughs as she says it, and I'm fucking baffled as to what she is even talking about.

She's still laughing as she goes to raise her shot in the air that is miraculously still in her hand and hasn't spilled all over the floor.

"To hot men and flirty blondes with great asses!" CeCe calls in a drunken toast.

I try to grab it from her so she won't drink it but she is a quick little thing.

"Give me the shot, Rae, you *really* don't need it."

"You want this shot, Nash?" she asks, her voice hits a lower octave, sending rage to my chest and heat to my dick all at the same time.

"You're gonna have to take it from me," she says as she stuffs the shot glass between her full breasts.

I move toward her until I'm standing right in front of her. I place my hand on the wall beside her head, staring down at her. She gulps. The only sound in the room is our breathing in sync and the thumping of the music beyond my office door. She's testing me. Testing everything in me. How can I be so angry but yet so fucking feral for this woman at the same time? I'll never understand it.

I slide my hand down the wall and wrap both of them around her tiny waist, pulling her closer to me, her breath hitches as I do.

I keep my voice calm and even because hiding rage is something I am really fucking good at when I need to be. "Cecilia Rae, I *never* want to see another man's hands on your body again," I say as I lean in and allow myself to kiss her once on the neck.

Goosebumps cover her flesh instantly and images of the other night flash through my mind in real-time.

"Do I make myself clear?" I ask, lowering my voice so she knows I'm fucking serious as I kiss her again on her collarbone and she moans.

I add a third kiss to her just above her breasts, my lips are steady just above the shot glass. I'm so fucking hungry for her, the restraint I'm using should win me a goddamn award.

"Do you understand?" I repeat, louder this time.

"Yes, *sir*," she whispers. There's a sass in her tone that makes me grit my molars to stop myself from ruining her, her chest is heaving as she waits for me to do something, anything. So naturally, I give it right back to her.

"Good girl. Don't ever make me tell you again."

My dick is so fucking hard against my zipper. The sheer fucking torture of knowing that tight, sweet cunt is definitely soaking wet beneath that skirt is almost too much to bear.

I slide my hands up the sides of her waist under her breasts, pushing them up so the shot glass rises up just enough for me to wrap my lips around it. Another tiny moan escapes her lips. I pull the shot glass out with my mouth and knock it back with one fell swoop. The burn of the tequila down my throat doesn't compare to the ache in my jeans but I fight it with everything in me.

I won't take her. Not like this, not after she's been drinking this much. But two things are certain. I'm not leaving her alone for even one more second tonight and two, she's going to fucking pay for this torture she's putting me through.

I set the glass down on my desk and lean down, tequila still fresh on my tongue. I lick a slow, hot trail across her bottom lip, pulling it into my mouth for only a few seconds. I normally hate tequila, but mix it with CeCe's sweet lips and I'd drink it every damn day. I'd drink it for survival. "That's the only taste of that shot you're getting."

Her tongue darts out to wet her plump, cherry red lips and I almost lose control. I grit my teeth and look away from her.

"And if you think for one second that you're in here in this fucking dress, and I'm looking at anyone else, you've lost your damn mind." I look back at her and my gaze meets her wide eyes. "There is nothing I want to do more right now than fuck you so hard, for so long that you'll know, without a doubt, that the only woman I'm looking at is *you*."

Her lips are an inch from mine and I can smell the sweetness of her breath.

"I hate how much I want you right now," she says and I smirk at her.

"The feeling is mutual. Now get your purse, we're leaving."

She follows me out of the office and into the crowd, finding Ginger and Olivia, I tell them I'm taking her home. I make sure Asher is good, he has enough staff tonight. I call Cole on my way out the door and tell him to come get the other girls, that CeCe is sick and I'm taking her home.

He agrees because Mabel is at Jo's again tonight. And it won't be the first time Cole's had to pick Ginger's drunk ass up and take her home. He's on duty but there is no harm in driving the girls home on a slow night in Laurel Creek.

I get CeCe to the safety of my truck and she stumbles as I lift her in the door. I move to my side and climb in.

"I wish you weren't so hot, it would make my attempt at not wanting you a lot easier," she mumbles as I start the truck, leaning her head on the cool glass.

"Again, feeling's mutual," I bite out.

I start down the highway and realize I could take her to her house. I have the key to Stardust and every other door on the ranch. But if I do that, I have to leave my truck there and that just won't do. The last thing she's going to need in the morning is questions about me sleeping there because I'm not leaving her like this.

I make the snap decision to continue on past the cut-off to the ranch and head to my own house. She can stay with me tonight.

"You weren't looking at Flirty McShowHerWhatever? I saw you give her your number," she mumbles out in a slur.

"Are you jealous, CeCe Ashby?" I chuckle at this realization as I cruise through the dark countryside.

"No," she answers quickly.

"Just because I wanted to pull her cowboy hat back and strangle her with the stampede strings doesn't mean I'm jeal-

217

ous. I'm not the jealous type. I'm actually the unjealous type," she rambles.

I feel my anger subsiding as she talks. Even this drunk she's so fucking adorable.

"Well, not that you'll remember this tomorrow but I didn't give her my number."

"Sure," she scoffs.

CHAPTER THIRTY-SEVEN
Nash

I pull into my driveway and start down the long stretch of it.

"Where are we?"

"My house. You're staying with me tonight. I figured you didn't want me to sleep on your couch and have the whole damn family questioning that in the morning."

"You don't have to stay with me. I can take care of myself," she whispers.

I chuckle from my spot beside her. "I just like your company, CeCe."

I grin at her and she flips me the bird.

"Fine. I'd kind of like to see where Nash Carter, the Stanley Cup winning right-winger *doesn't* sleep every night anyway."

She opens the door on her side and I barely make it there in time to catch her as she stumbles out of the truck.

"Shit," she mumbles. "My heel is stuck; this dirt is so soft."

There isn't a sound in the air save for the insects as I shut the truck door around her. She tries to take a step but sinks right into the gravel in her four inch heels.

"I just gotta take my shoes off, one second," she mumbles, tipping to the right and holding one finger in the air as she struggles to remove her heel.

I roll my eyes and scoop her up into my arms. She weighs nothing and I'm not surprised that she fits right in like she was made for me to hold her; her warm naked back is like silk against my forearm.

"I can walk, Nash. Put me down," CeCe protests.

"Shh, you'll wake the crickets," I scold her.

She gasps. "Look at all the fireflies."

I grin down at her in response.

It's so dark on my property, it's like its own little world. The fireflies are still out, even though it's August. People say they run in cycles but here in this heat, they thrive, especially around midnight. I've sat on my porch many nights when I couldn't sleep and just let them entertain me. No matter how dark it is, their little spark of light always breaks through.

The creek shimmers behind us and the only light guiding me to the house is the moon and the porch lantern.

Somewhere in CeCe's drunken headspace, she's taking in the beauty of my land and looking around at her surroundings.

"This is stunning, Nash. It's like a little private oasis," she breathes out.

"You think this is special? Look up," I say.

She does and gasps as a million stars come into her view. I stand in front of my porch and let her take it in for a second, just holding her in my arms.

"Amazing," she whispers. She stares up at the sky in awe and I just stand there and let her. I look down at her in my arms in this light, and feel that twisting feeling in my chest again. Fuck the stars, there's nothing more beautiful than her.

Her eyes come down from the sky looking glassy and spent.

"You gonna carry me inside, Mr. Carter?"

I nod and do just that, again fighting the urge to crush myself against her. I gently set her down in my entryway. She removes her shoes and stands in my hallway in her bare feet. The strangest look crosses her face.

"Room. Spinning," she says as she reaches up to hold her head.

"Shit," I mutter as I pick her back up and carry her to the bathroom attached to my bedroom.

My room is dark and moody as I flick on the lamp on my dresser. Deep grays and creams against the dark cabin walls set an earthy vibe. My bed is a massive California King with the best sheets money can buy. I may not be showy but there are certain things I don't skimp on and my bed is one of them. What little sleep I do get, I want to be comfortable.

I grab her a t-shirt out of my drawer and hand it to her. It will be like a nightgown on her tiny frame. It's odd having a woman here. I've been alone for so long, but I don't hate seeing her standing in my bedroom—not one bit.

CeCe stands in the doorway like a squirrel afraid to move. I pass by her into the bathroom. It's much like my bedroom. Gray with white heated travertine tile floor and shower tile as well as the world's largest seven-foot bathtub because there are days after coaching all day that I just need an Epsom salt bath and I don't fit into a regular sized tub well. I reach into the walnut vanity and grab her a new toothbrush and a clean face cloth, turning on the heated floor for her feet.

"I'll... give you some privacy."

She nods.

"I'm right out here if you need me." I close the door and pace my bedroom while I hear her turn on the faucet.

I pull the heavy duvet back on my bed and reveal my deep gray 1200-thread count sheets. I grab a Gatorade from my kitchen, pour it over ice and place it on a coaster on my bedside table with some Tylenol because something tells me she's going to need that in the morning. Then I sit and wait, tapping my foot on my bedroom floor.

Fifteen minutes pass by, but she doesn't come out. I internally argue with myself about knocking. The water is off and I don't hear anything.

"CeCe," I call

No answer comes so I knock.

"I feel... sick. Stay out." I hear through the door.

"Not a fucking chance," I mutter as I unlock the door and go in. She's in her dress, still sitting on the bathroom floor with her head over the toilet. Mascara under her glassy eyes. The realization that she's probably been sitting like this since I left her tugs at my heart.

"Fuck baby..." I go right to her and hunch down on the floor beside her.

"You don't need to see this. I... brushed my teeth but then I felt sick. The toothpaste. Too many margaritas. I might throw up," she says.

"I'm not going anywhere until you're ready to leave this bathroom," I whisper.

I pull her hair from her clasped hand and carefully crouch behind her, smoothing it off her face and braiding it down her back. A trick I've learned from watching Cole braid Mabel's hair all the time. I don't have any girly hair elastics or anything that even resembles one. I improvise. I reach over and pull dental floss out of the bathroom drawer and break a piece off tying it around the bottom of her braid in a bow. It does the trick nicely. Another fifteen minutes pass as we sit on the floor while I rub her back.

"I feel better now. I'm just so thirsty," she says, leaning against the bathtub.

I grab the Gatorade from my room and bring it to her. I

don't say anything as she drinks some down. She looks better now, the color is back in her cheeks

"What do you want, Rae?" I ask her as I push a strand of hair off her face and tuck it behind her ear.

CeCe looks around. "This is a nice bathroom."

"Only you would notice the décor," I say as I stand up and run a facecloth under hot water.

"I'm never drinking again," she mumbles, and I chuckle.

I use the hot cloth to wash her face and hold it on the back of her neck. She sighs at the simple feeling and closes her eyes. The obsessive beast in me realizes how close my hand is to her inner thighs and how far up her dress is hiked as she's crumpled on my bathroom floor. Am I wrong for thinking about burying myself in her while she's drunk and vulnerable? Probably.

Do I want to anyway? Fuck yes.

"Come on, let's get you to bed," I say, instead of acting on my thoughts. I stand and lift her with me. "I'm gonna take your dress off and put my t-shirt on, okay?"

She nuzzles into my arms like I'm her home.

"Okay, Nash," she sighs.

The feeling of her needing me sends intense warmth right through my chest. I set her down on my bed and move behind her, unzipping her dress under her arm quickly, sliding it down over her shoulders. Her silky skin under my fingertips sends all the blood in my body straight to my cock. Goosebumps break out over her flesh with my touch and the urge to reach around and feel those pink pebbled nipples under my fingers makes my knees weak. If I wasn't sitting right now, I would need to.

I slide her dress down and it lands on my floor.

I close my eyes. *Fuck.*

"Jesus Christ, CeCe, you might be the death of me."

She giggles and grabs the shirt from beside her, tossing it

on. Her glistening bare pussy mercifully disappears from my view.

I speak slowly and refrained. "You came into the bar tonight in that dress, and you've been beside me all this time tonight and you *aren't wearing any panties?*" My voice is a different octave as I try to control myself.

"I didn't want panty lines." She shrugs, sounding as innocent as ever and then she lies down. On *my* side of the bed.

"Oh my God, these sheets are incredible," she hums the throaty sound I'm becoming desperate to hear.

I don't move her. I just use all my will to cover her as she closes her eyes. I refill her drink, grab a pillow, and make my way out to the couch.

I don't know why they made me rake all those leaves when I should've been training. Now I'm rushing to get out the door to my game and I don't feel prepared. If I'm going to get a scholarship to the University of Kentucky, I should be training three hours a day. At least that's what Harry says, and he'll know if I'm not.

"There's no reason the leaves couldn't have waited until tomorrow," I grunt to my mother as she comes out the door.

"Can you pop the trunk?" I bite out. I'm annoyed and she knows it, her face is in a frown as she pops the trunk and I throw my hockey bag in.

"Where's Dad?" I look at my iPod, it's already three.

"He's coming, Nash, and the leaves had to be done today, we're having an appraisal tomorrow."

Right, the bank is coming so we can extend our mortgage

because we are strapped. Because of me, and how much competitive hockey has cost them over the last two years.

I soften because as annoyed as I am, I'm grateful for them always doing everything they can for me to play. I work when I can at the arena emptying garbage and cleaning the change rooms, but training takes up so much time, it's hard to fit it in.

My dad hobbles down the step, his knee has been messed up for a while. His job at the only factory in town is labor intensive and he definitely should be filing an OSHA complaint but we need the money so he goes every day, popping two Aleve for breakfast.

He comes around to me at the back of the car and pats me on the shoulder. "There's such a thing as too much, son. You need to have a little down time. An hour of raking leaves won't make you any less of a winger, and it's a work out. You've got this."

This game is important, there are going to be scouts in the stands and I could be drafted right out of the minors. I need to be ready.

I shake the rain off my hoodie and we get on our way.

"I'll get us there on time, don't worry." My dad rubs his knee in the front seat and my mom grabs his hand. It's pouring rain and the sky is a deep dark gray. The fall has a way of feeling gloomy all the time. Everyone I know will be there tonight. All my friends from school, the Ashby's, it will even be on local TV. My mind is flooded with nothing but nerves and plays.

I pop my headphones in and check the time on my cell phone, 3:13, we have fifteen minutes to get there. I turn up Jay-Z on my iPod to try to calm myself down and stare out the window at the countryside.

Lights, swerving, screaming, glass shattering, cracking. It all happens in an instant and it's all around me. We're moving, spinning—we hit something with a thud. I think I black out, and when I pull my head back, I feel my mom's hair in my face. I instantly know that's not right. My mom is in the front seat; I shouldn't feel her hair in my face. I try to move but I can't, something is pinning my legs, and glass is broken all around me. Pain. Everywhere. My leg is broken. I'm going to throw up. I do, I think. Blood trickles into my mouth but I don't know where it's coming from.

"Mom," I call but I hear nothing.

"Dad." Again, nothing.

I focus, or try to, but my head is buzzing. I open my eyes and narrow them to see my parents' shadows in front of me. Where are we? The front of the car is almost part of me and my parents are part of it. I'm shaking my mom's shoulders, calling to her but she doesn't move. I wrap my hand around the front seat to feel her with a shaky hand, trying to pull my leg out from under her seat but the pain is too much. My hand is over her chest. She isn't breathing or barely. I can't tell.

"Mom. Breathe, Mama..." I call, but there's no answer from her.

I hear whimpering. Crying. Is it me?

"No! Fuck, Dad?" I call to him but then I see his eyes, focused on me, my head pounds.

His arm dangles behind the seat. His eyes are open and empty.

They're dead.

I hear the sound of sirens and everything fades to black.

CHAPTER THIRTY-EIGHT
CeCe

"*No! Fuck, No!*"

My eyes fly open and I look around. Dark everywhere except for the orange glow of a clock. 3:14 am.

"Noo!"

I'm up and I'm running, despite the fact that my head is pounding. The layout of his house is fuzzy because I was definitely still drunk when I went to sleep. I see Nash's figure on the living room couch, lit by the moonlight and I am to him in seconds.

"Nash." I reach for his arm at the same time he sits up and grips me so hard I fear he'll leave my skin bruised. His eyes fly open but he's staring right through me.

"Nash!" I yell louder, placing my palm on his face.

He blinks and grabs my face on either side with his large hands.

"Rae?" he says, loosening his grip on my face.

He's visibly shaking and sweating. I've never seen this kind of night terror before so I have no idea what to do. I just kneel down beside him, swiping his damp hair off his forehead and pull his shaking body to me. His arms wrap around me and he holds me. So tightly I can barely breathe, but I don't protest. I let him.

"I was so selfish," he says. "All I cared about was myself, I was rushing them and we had plenty of time to get there," he almost whines.

"Shh. It's okay. I'm right here," I say, not sure what else to offer him. So I start to hum—Shania, of course—as I hold him.

I never understood how Nash ever survived the trauma of that day. A drunk driver drove down county 23 in the middle of the afternoon, and within seconds he witnessed both his parents die in front of him, in a gruesome way. I remember my mom saying they had to remove his mother from the dash of the car. She was part of it. I can't imagine what he saw.

Afterwards, he had nothing, no other family. He was still a minor, so he couldn't even stay in the house, nor could he afford it. The estate lawyer sold it and he ended up with a little money from it, but my parents stepped up and immediately took him in when the sale closed. He moved into Wade's room the week after their funeral. He missed his draft chance with a broken leg and some broken ribs but still managed to go to the U of K and get drafted to the NHL—it just took until his senior year to get there.

The blink of an eye. That's what my father said when Nash lost his mom and dad. One moment they were here, and the next moment they weren't, and Nash was at the center of it.

"It was my fault. I couldn't save them. I couldn't move."

I grip him tighter and continue to hum quietly, I feel his breathing start to return to normal.

"It wasn't your fault, Nash. It wasn't," I coo in his ear, stroking his hair as my heart breaks for him.

He grips my waist tighter and lifts his head so his eyes meet mine. They're hollow, vulnerable like I've never seen them and

I wonder how often he dreams like this. How often he re-lives this nightmare. I kiss his forehead.

"Come," I say, detaching his arms from my waist and I stand. He follows me as I lead him by the hand through his bedroom door.

I lay down in his bed and without saying a word, he gets in beside me. I lay on my back and I pull him and the covers up over us gesturing for him to come close. He does, his head is resting at my collarbone. I feel his strong arms wrap around me, molding me to fit his body. I kiss the top of his head and stroke my fingers through his hair as he breathes out a relaxed sigh.

"Don't let go, Rae," he whispers, and I feel tears sting my eyes.

"I won't," I reply as I lean my head back into the pillows and continue to hum until sleep takes us.

CHAPTER THIRTY-NINE
CeCe

So hot. Too hot. I open one eye and I'm blinded by the sunlight streaming through the crack in the dark drapes just enough to hit my eyes. I squeeze them shut. I'm on fire and pinned to the bed by Nash's large naked torso. We're laying in the exact position that we fell asleep in, his arms still wrapped around me.

"Nash," I croak. "Can't breathe."

He stirs and my hand slides down his smooth, strong arm, He presses his morning erection into my hip unknowingly, stirring something in me, even though I feel awful. I need water or death whichever I can get first.

Nash sits up in bed and stretches like he's had the best sleep of his life. My pounding eyes still register how insanely beautiful he is. His wavy hair is falling over his forehead and his inked muscular body is a clash against the soft creams of his duvet and dark gray sheets. These sheets. I move my legs for the first time and realize I feel like I'm engulfed in silk.

"Gatorade and Tylenol beside you," he grunts out, still half asleep himself, rubbing his eyes.

I turn and focus on the lifeline he thought to leave me last night. I chug the Gatorade and swallow down two extra-strength Tylenol.

He chuckles from beside me. "Feeling rough, darlin'?"

"Ugh," I groan. "Not a word."

He stands and closes the drapes tightly so the sun disappears, and I could cry from relief. My poor head.

"I'll be back, you sleep."

I glance at the clock to see it's not even eight o'clock yet and I have nowhere to be.

It's Saturday. Thank the fucking Lord.

The smell of bacon and coffee wakes me over an hour later and my stomach growls. I starfish in Nash's massive bed, stretching to each corner and realize my head no longer feels like it's in a vice and my stomach is no longer nauseous. I actually feel semi-human, until the memory of accusing Nash of flirting with that waitress comes back to me, and then I want to crawl out his window, sink into the creek and die.

Why did I drink like that? What the hell is the matter with me?

Flashes register from last night. The cowboy on the dance floor, the fury in Nash's eyes when I approached him at the bar, the way he pulled me out of there like a child.

Oh my God, the bathroom floor when I almost got sick. I groan and reach for my hair, which I find is braided and tied with *dental floss*? I didn't dream that?

I get out of bed and head for his bathroom. I'm wearing his t-shirt and remember him pulling my dress off. I remember his words, it's all coming back to me.

I use the toothbrush that is still on the counter from last night, then I find a fresh face cloth and wash myself up. Sliding his vanity drawers open, I find a hair brush, undo my French braided hair and pull it through my waves. His drawers are impeccable. Organized. Spotlessly clean. In fact, this whole house is beautiful.

I move to the bathroom window, look out into the backyard to take in my surroundings and gasp. The wide creek fills my view along with a dock, covered by a gazebo, with a little boat, birds, and other wildlife. Massive red oaks line the space offering shade from the hot August sun. There's a deck off Nash's bedroom with a pergola over it and cozy wicker and cushioned patio furniture adorns it, with a fire pit just beyond that. It's truly beautiful and peaceful, and suddenly I understand why he lives here. After witnessing his nightmare last night, my guess is he takes any peace he can get and my heart goes out to him as I finish up in the bathroom.

Realizing I have no pants or even underwear, I wander back into his bedroom and get back into his bed.

"I thought I heard you." Nash appears in his doorway, wearing nothing but a pair of perfectly fitted gray Nike sweatpants that hang low on his hips, his hair is damp like he had a shower recently and he's holding a tray with steaming coffee and food.

I stare at him for a moment, dumbfounded because he's so gorgeous it makes me ache.

"You're staring." He grins as he sits down beside me on the bed.

I blink and then blush knowing I'm totally busted.

"You look damn good in the morning too, Rae, especially in my shirt," he says, handing me a coffee.

"I have no other clothes here," I blurt out.

"Yes, you do. I went and got you some before I made breakfast, can't have you leaving here in the dress you wore last night."

"What?"

"I have a key to Stardust, I got you clothes," he enunciates and cocks his head to the side. "And panties... since you have none of those." He passes me a coffee and sets the tray down beside me.

"I... thank you," I say, because I don't even protest that he was in my house alone. In fact, I kind of like it.

"What did you bring me?" I ask, amused and extremely curious. God this coffee is good.

Nash disappears for all of five seconds before reappearing with a bag.

I take it from him and set my coffee down to skim the contents.

Jean shorts, white cropped, off-the-shoulder vintage Shania tour t-shirt, the laciest black panties I own, flip flops, hair ties, lip gloss, deodorant, sunglasses.

I hold the black panties up with one finger.

"Nice," I say, one eyebrow raised.

He holds his hands up in defense. "They were the first pair in your drawer, I'm not in the habit of going through a woman's things. Was just being practical."

I laugh and set the bag down, reclaiming my coffee.

"Are you hungry? I made bacon and waffles."

"Starving." I nod and smile at him.

Of all the hats I've seen him wear, making me breakfast in bed Nash is too adorable for words and might be my favorite. He sets the plate in front of me and heads out to grab his own.

Getting into bed beside me and pulling the blankets up under his plate, he starts to eat and I follow suit. We eat in comfortable silence, as I struggle with this feeling. Like having breakfast with him in bed is the most natural thing on earth.

Nash finishes before me and watches me as I swallow the last of my really delicious cinnamon waffles, then takes my plate when I'm done.

"You can cook?" I ask, already knowing the answer from this feast.

"I try."

"Thank you," I say.

"For what?"

"For taking care of me and not rubbing last night in my face this morning. I'm embarrassed I acted like that. It's not my business who you give your number to. I'm sorry."

"Rae—" he says, but I keep talking.

"She's pretty, she obviously likes you. You should take her out."

"Rae," he says a little louder this time, more annoyed. "I'm not taking Chantel out, but it's pretty cute that you're jealous."

Chantel, ugh even her name is pretty. I hate it.

"I'm not jealous."

He smirks, ignoring my lie.

"Her husband passed away suddenly three months ago. They have a son, Luke, he's six, all he loved to do with his dad was play hockey in their driveway. Anyway, after he died, she had to take on another job, at the Sage and Salt to make ends meet. She was talking to me about getting Luke into my skating programs. The number I gave her was Sonny's. I told her Olympia would cover the cost for him. That's all."

"Oh God," I say, pulling the blankets up over my head.

He chuckles, pulling at the blankets.

"I'm never coming out."

He starts really laughing and smacks me on the backside through the blankets. "Yes, you are. Go have a shower. You're spending the day with me."

I pull the blankets off my face and look at him. "I am?"

"Yes, you are." He grins.

"Why?" I ask, trying to understand why he wants to spend the day with me after I acted like a stage-five clinger.

Nash moves closer to me, sliding me down the bed until his face is right over mine and he hovers here.

"Because instead of pretending nothing is going on here, I think we should try something different. Let's just hang out," he says, and I'm speechless.

"Hang out?" I repeat.

"Yes. On Saturday mornings I go fishing, then I go to the bar to get everything ready for the busiest night of the week. You can come with me and work off your asshole-ish behavior, you still have to pay for that." He stands and nods as I ignore the tone of warning in his voice. "Now go get ready, we're fishing in thirty minutes."

"But I don't know how to fish—"

"Thirty minutes," he says from the living room, and I smile wide because there's nothing I'd rather do today than spend the whole day with Nash.

CHAPTER FORTY
Nash

Like I said, I'm done pretending. The fact of the matter is that something *is* going on. I can pretend it's just sex, but I'm not going to pretend for one more second that I don't want Cecilia Ashby with every fiber of my being in more ways than I've ever wanted a woman.

So, I made my mind up. She's with me today and she's going to like it.

I hear the shower shut off and fifteen minutes later, the bathroom door opens. I already took a shower in the other bathroom before I cooked her breakfast this morning, leaving her to her own private quarters in my bedroom, and she looks good there. In my bed, on my side of the bed.

I strive to hold it together as CeCe emerges in the outfit I chose for her, her blonde hair damp and freshly brushed down her back. She's looking hotter than a two-dollar pistol. Just knowing she has those black panties on under those shorts makes my dick twitch but I *will* be patient.

As badly as I want to rip her clothes off, I have plans for her. She's going to pay for what she put me through last night. I've never had to restrain myself like that in my life. I've never wanted someone more that I couldn't have, but I'd never sleep with a woman that drunk.

Today, she's going to want *me*. In fact, she'll be begging for me and I can hardly fucking wait.

"Did you braid my hair last night and tie it with dental floss? Or did I dream that?"

"Nah, you definitely dreamed that." I wink as I grab my tackle box. "Let's go, darlin', we're burning daylight."

She laughs and follows me out the door.

I look over from my end of Cave Run Lake to see CeCe casting just the way I showed her this morning from the water's edge. She's laughing with Rocco Pressley, technically my boss, and my fishing buddy. We fish almost every Saturday together and talk about business and life. He was downright smitten to see CeCe with me this morning. Since then, he's barely talked to me and has spent every second with her, showing her what lures to use, how to reel and telling her all sorts of bullshit stories about how he always catches bigger fish than I do.

Laughter ring's from the other side of the river and I just stare at CeCe in a complete fucking trance of her beauty. Her hair is wind dried now and high on her head in a ponytail, not a stitch of makeup and she's the prettiest thing I've ever seen.

"Oh my God!" CeCe yells. "Rocco!" She's reeling and her pole is bent in a nice curve that says she's got a good sized fish on the other end.

"Just like I showed you, dear, reel it in smooth and steady."

She does as he says, concentration lines her face as I make my way over to her and grab the net on the way by.

"Not too fast, he could snap the line and take your lure, just go slow," Rocco tells her, excitement etched all over his face for her victory.

"She's got one on," he calls as I approach, clearly smitten. "She's a natural."

We both stand and watch with bated breath as she works the reel until finally, a good sized, small mouth bass is flopping on the shore at her feet.

"I did it!" she yells. The giant smile she's wearing is taking up her whole face as my chest twists into knots.

"Atta girl," I praise her. "Now you gotta do three things. First, we take the lure out, then you get the picture for proof, then we let him go.

"We don't keep him and like, eat him?" she asks, her face puzzled.

"No, darlin', we let them go."

"Wait, you want me to touch its *mouth*?" The thought dawns on her and she's already shaking her head. "Nope, I'm not doing that."

Rocco chuckles at her.

"I assure you, you are," I say matter-of-factly. "And hurry, we don't have a lot of time." I see CeCe panic but I move closer and look her in the eyes, settling her and speaking low. "You've got this, babe."

She nods, a little fire returning to her eyes with determination. "I've got this," she tells herself.

We bend down and I show her how to remove the lure so it doesn't hurt the fish and she does it.

"His teeth are prickly but he won't cut you. Grip him hard, it won't hurt him," I say

We get the lure out and the fish is calm now.

"Okay, grip that bottom of his mouth and hold him up tight."

"His teeth are poking my thumb." She laughs as she says it but she holds him up anyway like the little fearless firefly she is. She smiles as I snap the photo on my phone and then Rocco shows her how to release him. It takes the fish a minute but he takes off under the water and she yelps.

"That was intense. I always thought fishing was boring!" She giggles.

"It's boring if you're this fella," Rocco says as he claps me on the shoulder. "He never catches anything."

"Keep living in your dream world, old man." I chuckle, and so goes the rest of our morning, Rocco and I shit talking each other while CeCe shows us both up again and catches another good sized bass.

"I just have one question. What am I doing *right* this fine morning, that y'all are doing *wrong*?" she asks, the most innocent grin on her face as she lets the second fish go all on her own.

Rocco roars with laughter.

"This one's a keeper, Nash, she can shit talk with the best of us."

CeCe's still giggling but I don't argue, I just watch her, beaming with pride for my girl. Of two things, I'm absolutely certain. 1. Whatever is happening between us, we haven't just crossed the boundary of "one night, just sex," we've obliterated it. There may as well have not even been a line in the sand to begin with. 2. Right here on the shore with CeCe in this simple moment, I know I want more moments like this with her. I want to be there for more firsts and I want her—not just for one night, and not in secret. I think I want her for as long as she'll have me. The thought causes my heart to beat faster and fucking terrifies me all at the same time.

CHAPTER FORTY-ONE
CeCe

I'm super hungry by one o'clock when we pack up our fishing gear.

"Pleasure, darlin'," Rocco says, patting my hand.

"Will I see you next week?" he asks.

"We'll see," I say nervously, looking from him to Nash because I have no idea. I don't know what this is but I know it's more than one night of getting it out of our system. This easy morning might be the best morning I've ever had.

"Well I hope I do," he says as he gets in his truck and starts it up.

And then, Nash and I are alone. He rubs my shoulder.

"You did good this morning darlin'. You won Rocco over. He'll be talking about you for weeks."

"How did you start that up? Fishing with him I mean?"

Nash grins. "I came down here the first weekend I was home and he was at the shore. We got to talking and he told me how much he was struggling to keep up at the bar. I offered to give him a hand. We've just showed up here almost every Saturday since. He doesn't have anyone here, his wife died and his son lives in Virginia."

I narrow my eyes at him. Nash is definitely not who I

thought he was when I came home, or even who I remember, and standing here in front of me, a little sweaty, a little sun-kissed, wearing that damn backwards Stars hat, he's never looked so extraordinary.

"You're just full of surprises aren't you, Nash Carter?"

"I'm tryin'," he says, staring into my eyes. Butterflies flitter about in my stomach as he holds my gaze for a beat too long.

"Now, food," he says, pinching my t-shirt. "Let's go."

"Yes, fishing is a workout. I'm starving already. Who knew?" I marvel.

"Who knew?" Nash repeats as he loads everything and we get into his truck and head back to town.

When we're almost back I get the nerve to finally ask him. "Does that happen a lot? The dreams?"

I haven't stopped thinking about it since I woke up this morning and I need to know how often he suffers like that. The way he held me was like I was his life vest.

"Almost every night. Some form of it anyway."

"I'm so sorry that happened to you, Nash." I put my hand on his in the center console.

"You know it's not your fault."

His jaw tenses and he stares straight ahead.

"In my mind, I know that, but it doesn't make me feel any less guilty. The thought of losing someone I love like that ever again..." He shakes his head as he trails off in thought. "I was rushing them. Years of therapy after they died tell me that's not why it happened, but I guess I've always felt a little responsible. It's just something I live with... it will never go away but some days are easier than others. Your dad told me I have two choices, let it consume me or keep holding the reins. So, I keep holding the reins and wait for the next day to come."

I nod. Not wanting to pry, just wanting to help, but hearing my dad's words through him sucker punches me right in the heart.

"On nights you don't have the dreams, what do you do differently? Maybe make a routine out of it?"

He smirks from the seat beside me and I don't understand the look he's wearing as he sighs and pulls into the parking lot of Sage and Salt. Gripping my thigh, he looks into my eyes and takes a second before speaking.

"Well, if I'm being honest, the only nights I've slept long stretches without dreaming, you've been in the bed beside me." My mouth falls open at his admission but he just smiles. "Care to make a habit out of that? As a science experiment?"

I laugh and shrug. "Well, if it's for science..."

"Come on let's get some lunch," he says as he lets go of my thigh.

∞

"They're staring at us," I tell Nash, as we're eating at a patio table outside the Sage and Salt.

"Let them, we're allowed to have lunch together," he says as he grins.

"We're the town gossip. Maybe they've heard about you beating up my ex-fiancé in the street?" I giggle as I bite into my salad.

"Or maybe, they've heard the gossip about your vibrator and are wondering if I've used it on you yet."

My eyes go wide and I swat at him.

"No, scratch that, they'd know, you're loud."

I laugh but I don't deny it. I never was loud... before Nash.

"Maybe they're all drooling over you and that damn backward baseball hat," I blurt out.

He looks up at me, one eyebrow raised as he shoves in a bite, keeping his eyes on mine looking like the Cheshire cat.

"The backward hat?" He analyzes my face. "That's what does it for CeCe Ashby?"

"Hell yes," I say honestly. "Among other things."

"Noted." We chew in silence for a moment.

"What about you? What does it for Nash Carter?"

He's thinking but keeps his eyes on me. "I can't think of a single thing you do that doesn't do it for me, Rae." He leans in so his face is only a couple inches from mine. "Even coming into the bar with no fucking panties and placing that shot glass between your perfect tits just to torture me. It drove me crazy to think about you dancing with fucking Brent Wilson like that but I still wanted you."

I let out a breath I didn't know I was holding. Leaning back in my chair, I sober myself up from his gaze.

"You have no filter, has anyone ever told you that?" I ask

"It's worth it to see the look you're wearing right now."

"Oh yeah, and what look is that?"

"The look that says you're shocked I said that out loud, but that you still want to fuck me."

I scoff, "Says you," I retort, averting my eyes from his.

"If I reached under this table right now and pushed those lacy black panties aside, you would already be wet for me. So yeah, says me." Nash manspreads, leaning back in his chair and takes a drink of his sweet tea, totally collected, his arms folded over his chest. Then he grins at me across the table because he knows he's right. Forward dirty talking Nash makes me sweat, and it has nothing to do with the August heat.

My phone buzzes again in my purse for the hundredth time this morning breaking the never ending current between us.

"Does that thing ever stop?" he asks with a smirk.

"It's just the girls talking shit about me and you, I'm sure." I laugh.

"Fuck." He grimaces.

I giggle as I reach into my purse.

A well of messages go back and forth between Ginger and Olivia about last night as I start to read through them.

"They're about to send out a manhunt. They think you've kidnapped me," I say as I keep scrolling.

> **LIV**
>
> She's definitely with her hot boss. I'm sure they're working on a special project.
>
> **GINGER**
>
> How hungover does one have to be to not answer all morning long?
>
> **LIV**
>
> Maybe the project had to be worked on in bed.
>
> **GINGER**
>
> Ok I went by her house, she's not there, Mama Jo isn't there.
>
> > Cheese and crackers you guys are relentless. I'm at Sage and Salt.
>
> **LIV**
>
> Was I right?
>
> > No you were not right. Not really.
>
> **GINGER**
>
> What the hell does that mean? You're not fucking now, but you were?
>
> > No fucking at all sadly, but I am with who you think I am.

LIV

Say less and get back to it.

GINGER

Did you stay with him last night??? Gah. Your bed was still made.

Yes, nosey old ladies club, I did stay with him.

LIV

What have you been doing all morning if you weren't fucking?

We went fishing.

GINGER

Come again? Is that some weird sex term I'm unfamiliar with?

I laugh at her response.

No, actual fishing. You know, the pole, sun, water?

LIV

Ok, so a date? With your one-night stand. Gotcha. 👌

No, not a date. We're just hanging out.

GINGER

So, a hang-out date?

Nash reaches over. "May I?" he asks as he snatches the phone from my hand and skims through the last ten messages as I laugh at his facial expressions reacting to my girls' dirty minds.

Then he begins typing and I internally panic. He hands me back the phone when he's satisfied and I read what he wrote, burying my head in my hands.

> Hello Not Angels. This is Nash Carter. This definitely is a date. CeCe's in denial about the whole thing, and I'll give her back when I'm done with her. PS If we fuck I'm sure you'll be the first to know. Have a good day, Not Angels, stop being so goddamn nosy.

"Oh my God." I'm laughing so hard and shove my phone back into my purse. "You know you're just fueling their gossip with that?"

"That's the point. Now come on, we have one more job to do, let's get moving so they can't track us," he says as he drops money on the table.

This is the best first hang-out-not-date I've ever been on.

The Horse and Barrel is dark when we enter.

"So this is what you do every Saturday?"

"Pretty much." Nash takes his hat off and throws it on the barstool then looks at me.

"I took it off so you can keep yourself under control while we work," he says, grinning.

He pulls his UV fishing shirt off over his t-shirt and it creeps up just enough so I get a view of those abs. I hate that he's right, I would do just about anything to feel his fingers push my panties to the side right about now.

"Stop thinking about it," he calls as he wanders behind the bar.

I shake my head to rid my mind of my daydreams of his body.

"I should've never told you that." I laugh.

"It's all good, baby, I'll have enough willpower for both of us, I'm well practiced after last night. We have a lot to get through. You can start by wiping down all the countertops, stool seats and tabletops."

He tosses an opening and closing checklist on the bar top for me to view, and I skim over it and nod as he hands me gloves and a cloth, grinning the whole time.

"I'll work on the inventory while you take care of this. I'll be between here and the back, if you need me," Nash says nothing else but turns on his Zach Bryan playlist through the sound system as we get to work.

I go through the list over the next hour as Nash flows between the stock room and where I am.

1. *Polish the glassware*
2. *Polish any silverware and barware*
3. *Clean faucets and taps*
4. *Dust alcohol bottles on display*

I check each one off my list and start on cleaning off the liquor bottles that are on shelves above the bar. All bazillion of them. The amount of work that goes into this simply amazes me. This man is a machine for both his businesses and this community. After staying with him last night and realizing he doesn't get a lot of peace, I see why. It's easier to keep busy, it's easier not to get too close to people, to do everything on your own. That way, you have nothing to lose.

We work together in silence as we balance on this tipping point.

I never want to see another man's hands on your body again.

I remember Nash's words and his lips on my skin as he took the shot from me last night, his breath on my ear when he asked me to tell him I understood, not once but twice.

I feel him moving in and out of the room as I stand on the step stool shining the bottles. He doesn't speak and the music doesn't really allow me to hear him, but I sense when he's in the room and when he's gone, and I can't help but watch him when he's here. The way his biceps flex as he lifts the barstools, his strong back and shoulders as he sweeps the floor, even the way his brows furrow as he's going over the employee list for the night. The simplest, non-sexy actions are way too sexy when Nash executes them. He is driving me crazy.

The song changes and the opening strings of "Something in the Orange" plays through the sound system. As I clean the last bottle, I hear Nash lock the front door.

Before I can start to climb down the stool I feel hands roam up the backs of my thighs stopping just under the rim of my shorts. Nash slides his thumbs under them tracing the lace of my panties at the curve of my bum. I turn to face him, dropping my dusting cloth as he slides his hands up over my shorts and grips my waist, lifting me off the step stool and placing me down on the back counter in front of him. He towers over me as he comes closer, standing between my open legs.

I keep my eyes on him but say nothing because I have no words. I reach my hand up and trace the inky vines running up his neck, and place my palm on his jaw.

My breathing slows as his eyes trace my face, then move to my mouth. I wait for his lips on mine, already feeling heat rushing to my core in anticipation.

"Are you planning on making me beg, Mr. Carter?" I ask, my lips almost on his.

Nash smirks at me and runs one finger over my collarbone slowly as I turn to fiery ash beneath it. He leans in and kisses me just below my ear, and I whimper because I'm so goddamn turned on by everything about him that I can barely stand it.

"You're fucking right I'm going to make you beg, little firefly," he whispers.

"*Oh God.*" Only Nash could call me his little firefly and make it sound sexy as hell. His hand grips my throat and I internally ignite as his lips follow down to my collarbone. His free hand roams my thigh and slides under my shorts while he brings his mouth so painfully close to mine.

"I really am sick of pretending I don't want you every second of fucking every day, CeCe."

Pleasure rolls through my center like match fired gasoline and he's barely even touched me yet. His lips brush my cheek then move to mine, kissing me deeply, meshing our bodies together. I let myself just breathe him and this moment in. He pulls my shirt off over my head and traces a finger down the valley between my breasts while he kisses my cheek and pulls his own shirt from his body, then unbuckles his jeans and kicks them off.

I try to touch him, but he stops me and slides my hand back into my lap.

"No, baby," he says, a dark tone lining his whisper. "You are going to understand what it feels like to want something so fucking badly it almost kills you." He pulls his boxers down and frees his cock. It's so hard and pointing straight at me, rigid and rippled with veins. Pre-cum leaks from the tip. Again, I try to touch him but he denies me.

"Spit," Nash commands as he holds his open palm under my lips.

I blink in shock but I'm a goner for him already so I do as he says then watch as he wraps his large hand around his shaft and begins to stroke himself, watching my reaction. His hand isn't even a match for his mammoth cock, only covering half. The phantom feeling of being so very full of him washes over me and I quiver.

"Take your shorts off. Leave those fucking black panties," he commands, and I do, unbuttoning them and wriggling out of them as I stay seated on the bar counter.

One finger ghosts my hardened nipple through the lace of my bra. Just once.

"That's my girl," he says as his tongue traces my bottom lip.

"You're going to watch me fuck my hand until I come all over your perfect tits while you play with your sweet, tight cunt." He leans in and kisses my lips too gently. I almost lose it. "But you won't come, CeCe. You won't come until I decide it's time."

"Please," I beg, although I'm not really sure what I'm begging for exactly, I just want everything.

Nash grins at me, something dark in his eyes as he fists himself and I die a slow death at the sight.

It's so fucking hot. If this is my punishment, fucking *punish me*.

"Please isn't enough, Rae." He trails his middle finger downwards, grazing the lace over my sensitive, hardened clit. I moan in response as my head falls forward into his muscled chest. "Do you know how hard it was for me not to touch you last night when I realized you came into the bar with no panties like the greedy girl you are for me? How hard it was for me not to take you in my own bed with your bare pussy between my sheets? That of all things, alcohol is what stopped me from taking what I wanted?"

Nash reaches into the freezer below me and grabs a large piece of ice out of it. Slowly popping it into his mouth, he begins to trail it down my neck. The chill of the ice surrounded by his hot lips makes a quick pool of my black lace panties as I pant.

"Nash," I moan.

My entire body goes rigid with the feeling. He pulls my bra

down and exposes my breasts then pulls each of my nipples into his mouth, swirling the ice around them in perfect harmony with his tongue, sending me into a tailspin. I moan as my pussy throbs to the point of pain, I need something, anything. The ice is so cold it almost hurts. My nipples begin to numb just as he releases them and slides his mouth down my stomach, then finally, through the lace of my panties, circling the ice and his tongue there. My will is melting faster than the ice against my hot pussy. Nash continues to suck at my clit through the thin lace, never enough to send me over the edge, just enough to drive me wild. The sounds I'm making would be embarrassing if I actually cared. Nash sucks in a breath through his teeth as the last of the ice melts and he stands and touches me between my legs, I'm dripping through my panties from his freezing assault.

"You feel that? How badly you want me right now?" he rasps in my ear.

"Yes," I manage to breathe out.

"How badly you *need* me?"

"Yes, God, yes."

"Last night, I wanted you a thousand times more," he rasps at my neck and I mewl into him.

All of my senses are overstimulated and out of control, I start grinding into his hand. I'm searching for any friction he will offer me. Just as I'm about to beg again, he pulls one nipple into his hot mouth and I'm ready to come from the feeling of that alone.

"Nash," I beg. "Please."

"Please what, CeCe?" He pulls my other nipple into his mouth and the whole incinerating feeling starts again as his hot tongue soothes the freezing. "Please let you come? No. You can wait a little longer. But you can put one finger into that tight little cunt for me."

I do as he commands and push my middle finger into my pussy.

"Show me how you fuck yourself when you're alone, CeCe, because I know you do," he says as he increases his pace on his cock. He nods his head once.

"Now, another," he commands and I do just as he says. I push two fingers into my soaking pussy and moan as my head falls backward.

"Do you think about me while you make yourself come?"

"Yes, all the time," I reply shakily.

"Fuck, yeah you do," he groans.

It's too much, the sight of him, where we are, his words, all of it. I'm going to explode. Nash pulls my hand away from my pussy and sucks my fingers clean of my arousal, his tongue making languid strokes over them so he doesn't miss one drop. "So fucking sweet."

I whimper as he begins to pump himself faster.

"Now, get on your knees, baby. Push those perfect tits together and stick out your tongue for me. Show me where you want my cum."

I slide off the bar and drop to my knees before him. From this angle, he's so big in every way, I feel so small compared to him and I've never wanted him more. He's fucking glorious smirking down at me as he drags his thumb over my bottom lip.

"Atta girl, such a good little slut, begging for my cum. You're desperate for it, aren't you?"

"Yes," I breathe out, and I am.

"This perfect pussy is mine whenever I want it. Isn't it, CeCe?"

"Yes. It's yours," I cry out.

"Fucking right it is," he growls.

I'm about to start grinding into my heel in search of friction as his legs tense and hot ropes of cum jut out fiercely all over my chest, my tongue, my neck, my chin as he groans, "Cecilia," drawing my name out as he pumps himself to the point of empty.

He uses his thumb to drag cum from my chin as his breathing slows and shoves it into my mouth. I suck it off dutifully and he groans again.

"That's my girl," Nash whispers, kissing me softly on the lips. "Now we're even. Just a little longer for you."

CHAPTER FORTY-TWO
CeCe

After Nash pulls his jeans back on and cleans me off with a warm towel, he proceeds to start cleaning the bar top.

Watching every muscle under his skin contract as he cleans it makes me squeeze my thighs together while I dress. I'm still so sensitive and dying for his touch.

He acts like he has nothing but time.

When he's satisfied with the counter and floor, he tosses his t-shirt over his head.

"Let's go now," he says as he kisses my cheek. I sulk, a little too openly. He chuckles and tilts my chin up so my gaze lands on his.

"Don't worry Rae, I'll let you come soon enough." I humph as he grins wide and leads me out of the bar.

We move toward the front door, and just as Nash unlocks it, Asher comes towards us up the sidewalk.

"Nash," he greets in his very deep tenor before turning to me with a smirk. "CeCe."

It's the first time I've seen him smile. Boyish dimples

appear in his cheeks and they seem like they don't belong with his massive, inked and almost scary, brooding appearance.

"Remind me not to play any drinking games with you anytime soon."

"Ha-ha," I say back. "I won't be drinking like that again for a long time."

"I'm going to take CeCe home, and to be honest, I'm wrecked. I'm going to take the night off," Nash says, and Asher looks at Nash like these are words he's never heard from him before.

"The night off? Uh... yeah, sounds good."

"You have lots of servers in tonight?"

"Yep, eight. Sandy Elliot's 58th birthday."

Nash nods, and I make a mental note that my mother will, in fact, be here tonight with her gang of lady friends. She and Sandy have been friends since high school.

"I've got my cell if you need me. The bar is fully prepped," he says to Asher as he gestures me away and follows behind.

We drive in silence, and as Nash turns down the driveway to the ranch, I realize that he may, in fact, be bringing me home. Anger builds inside me at the idea of him getting off like that and then just taking me home like some sort of piece of ass.

He pulls up to Stardust and I start to speak sarcastically because when I'm nervous as shit, that's what I do. "Thanks for the day today. It was fun having you jack off all over me, I guess I'll... see you around." I grin and then go to open the door.

Nash huffs out a breath as he puts his truck in park, and grabs my arm to stop me.

"Jesus Christ, Rae. I'm not dropping you off. You think I'd just use you like that to get off and then leave you on your doorstep?" He looks amused as fuck as I shrug.

"I don't know what to think, Nash. I don't know what... this is," I say quietly, gesturing between us, suddenly feeling silly for my overreaction.

His eyes soften and he grips my face. I turn my face into his palm. I love the warmth and safety of it too much.

"I'm not done with you yet. I brought you here so you could go get everything you need to last you the weekend. I want you to stay with me."

Nash leans into me and kisses my lips, slow at first, but deliciously calculated, tracing his tongue over my bottom lip and restarting the ever-burning fire between my legs for him.

His voice is low and deep as he pulls his lips away from mine. "Now, let's get your things. I'm going to make you dinner."

I register what we're doing here, what he's saying. Whatever this is, I realize that he's fighting it as much as I am because it's *us*, and there is no doubt that we're crossing that line here now. Once we do, is there any way to go back?

I just nod and get out of the truck as he asked, like the good girl I am.

CHAPTER FORTY-THREE
Nash

I set the plate in front of CeCe and she looks up at me.

"This is too pretty to eat."

"I could say the same thing about you," I retort and she smiles at me with the coy little smile that goes straight to my dick.

"Touché." Cece takes a bite of the chicken marsala I made us and moans, "Oh my God."

Yeah, it's fucking delicious.

"You really can cook," she mumbles between bites.

I shrug and shovel in a bite, smiling at her as I do.

We're sitting at my dining room table. The sun is sinking behind the trees over the creek.

"Well, my house is yours for the next twenty-four hours, do you think we can keep your girl clan and family from calling Cole to search for you?"

"My girl clan knows I'm here." She grins at me. "Ginger secretly likes you."

"Lucky me," I chirp.

"Mama Jo is at Sandra's party, and I don't think Wade would think anything of me being out." She takes in the view beside her and sighs. "I love it here. It's so secluded. Is that why you like it?" she asks, dipping her bread into her marsala and taking the daintiest little bites.

She almost seems nervous and that makes me want to bury myself in her even more, I love bringing out the wild side she has under that sweet façade. She's fucking adorable. Bringing her here was the best idea I've ever had.

I nod. "I need the peace of this place, as soon as I looked at it, I knew. After... they died, I couldn't find any. The only thing that gave me any sense of calm was hockey. It was like I had to prove they didn't die for nothing. If I made it somehow, they'd know. Seems crazy I know."

She smiles at me but says nothing.

"I've never said that out loud before," I offer.

"I think they know," she whispers and reaches for my hand across the table. "I think they'd be proud of you."

I clear my throat and pull my hand away. Emotions like this have always been a no for me, and having her care so much, seeing it in her eyes reminds me that by inviting her here, I'm letting her in. Panic momentarily cripples me.

Her face falls flat when I pull my hand away quickly.

"You know you can talk to me. I just think it's good to say how you feel."

I stand and take our plates to the sink.

"Yeah we can talk... I just—I don't do emotions very well." I have my back to her while I say the words and internally kick myself for shutting her out.

Why can't I just function as a normal human being? I want this woman so fucking badly but any time I think of her and anything real, I'm back in that car losing everything I have.

I'm still lost in my thoughts, drying the dishes when I feel CeCe's hands on me. She's sliding them down my sides and then wrapping them around me as she leans her head on my back.

"It's terrible what happened. Unthinkable. Remember that just because it happened doesn't mean it will happen again," she whispers and my chest twitches.

I turn around and stare down at her, just taking in her perfect face. I'm struggling. I strive to say something, anything. I *should* say something.

Before I can figure out what that something is, CeCe smiles and gives me the most incredible gift. She doesn't *make* me speak. She just lets it go.

"I believe you owe me an orgasm, Mr. Carter, and I'd rather not wait any longer," she says in her sexy voice, one eyebrow raised as she reaches up on her tiptoes and I bend to meet her lips.

Without even trying, CeCe gives me exactly what I need, just like inviting me to bed with her last night and wrapping her arms around me without a word. Just being there. Humming softly until the time on the clock didn't matter anymore. No matter what I try to tell myself, or how much I try to talk myself out of this, all of it is making her something I'm having trouble living without.

Dishes long forgotten, I move my hands to her face and kiss her. I let my hands roam her body, memorizing every curve, every line. I knead the thick cascades of her hair as I plunder her mouth with mine. I want to claim her, own her, be everything for her. I want to have no clue what the future holds and be okay with it. A rush of emotions runs through my being as I kiss her like I've never kissed a woman before, with feelings that go way beyond sex.

CeCe's hands move to my waist, under my shirt, as she fists and tugs, desperately. I use one hand to peel it off and toss it to the floor then pick her up, sliding my hands down her perfect plump ass, gripping her thighs.

She eases up around me like she just belongs, wrapping her legs around my waist and losing her fingers to my hair as I move us toward my bedroom. I pull her down on top of me in the center of my bed, my hands roaming every part of her. I try to get my fill of her. I could wear CeCe like a second skin and still not feel close enough to her. I sit up and tear her shirt over her head, I'm fervent, desperate for her skin on mine.

She moans when my mouth finds each of her nipples through the lace of her bra, I stay here and torture the fuck out of her just because I can. My tongue flicks her pebbled little buds as she whimpers and moans.

"Fire... I'm on fire," she breathes out, and I smile into her lips.

"What do you need, little firefly?" I ask her

"Touch me... everywhere," she begs.

I lift her off me and lay her on her back, shimmying her out of her shorts as she whines for me, skimming her fingers over her clit before I can even get those black lace panties off.

"You want to touch yourself, baby? You can."

She moans and whispers something like, "I need to."

I prop myself beside her and take in the show before me. Her hair is fanned out around her as her fingers slide into her panties and she moans. I pull her hand up and find the fingers glistening with her arousal. I suck the sweet nectar into my mouth and my dick throbs, begging to be freed. I pull her panties off and spit just above her already dripping pussy as she whines my name in response. I slide her finger back down, adding pressure with my own digit just to drive her even more crazy.

"Rub that in and fuck yourself with those sweet little

fingers. Get yourself good and ready for my cock. I want to hear you scream my name when I let you come."

"Nash..." CeCe whines. "I need—please."

I tilt her chin to fix her gaze on me. "I know, little one."

She nods then whimpers, continuing to fuck herself—one finger, then two—shamelessly wild, natural and fucking incredible.

"You're doing such a good job," I say as I hear how wet she is while her fingers work. After only a few moments, I've seen enough. I need to taste her. "I'll let you come now. Is that what you want?"

"Fuck, yes... please," she begs.

I swipe her hand to the side, replacing her tiny fingers with my own. I give her no gentle ease, pushing my first two fingers into her tight wet heat and sucking her clit into my mouth, groaning over her because she's the fucking sweetest thing I've ever tasted. I pull them out then thrust back into her as deep as I can, and crook them to massage her favorite spot, keeping my tongue and lips on her clit as she goes fucking ballistic above me. Not even one minute passes as she writhes above me, completely out of control.

"Nash, oh God..." CeCe screams as she comes undone, soaking the bed and me.

"That's it, my messy girl," I murmur as her whole body spasms around me, but I don't stop. I keep sucking and licking and fucking her with my fingers until she's a whimpering pool for me, and then stand, removing the rest of my clothes and grace her tight heat with the head of my cock.

I slide over her, taking in the sight of her, desperate for me. I don't even think about a condom, I'll never wear one with her ever again, not after feeling her without one.

"I'm not above begging," she breathes out.

"So fucking beg," I say as I give her an inch of my cock. *Fuck, even that is enough to cripple me.*

She moans and whines, "Fuck, Nash. I'm begging you to fuck me."

"Ask nicely, Cecilia. Say please." I grin wickedly.

The fire returns to her eyes, I recognize it now and I fucking love it.

"Please, please fuck me, Mr. Carter, *sir*." She bats her lashes at me like a sweet, southern belle and I instantly cave.

I didn't even stand a fucking chance. She wins.

Driving into *my* beautiful cunt, CeCe screams my name as I take ownership, just like I wanted.

"Too full... so full," she pants.

Her body lets me in and squeezes me out all at the same time and it's fucking miraculous.

"No, baby..." I huff out. "Just full *enough*. Your body was made for me. You take my cock so fucking well."

I drive into her over and over, kissing her lips, slowing my pace, savoring her, worshipping her, offering her gentle, caressing movements with my hands and lips to counter the force in which I fuck her with.

I anchor myself between her legs and just look down at her, her eyes are closed as she moans and readies herself to come for the second time. My greedy fucking girl. CeCe's hands move though my hair and pull just enough on the strands to turn me primal. I search her mouth with mine as the heat and pressure licks up my hips and spine.

Her rhythm matches mine beneath me effortlessly and it's fucking magic. It's the fireworks and violins you hear about. It's fucking otherworldly. Her eyes meet mine, time stops and she smiles at me, breaking me, reducing me to nothing more than hers.

"Come with me, baby," she coos, and then I'm free falling.

Her pussy clenches around me, begging to siphon my release. Her eyes fall closed again and I do something I've never done.

I close mine too.

I let it happen, for the first time in my life, I just let go. There is only her as I spill into her with her name repeatedly on my lips. She forces every last drop from me as I try to steady myself over her and kiss her, holding her like she's the anchor inked onto my chest.

This has gone way beyond fucking.

I settle into the reality that I just made love to Cecilia Ashby and I've never felt more whole than I do right now.

CHAPTER FORTY-FOUR
CeCe

"So if you have two more, we can actually hold a game. We have so many volunteers to play you guys. You have to take it easy on them, let them get some goals. Maybe we can have Damien Smith take the net for the Townies just to give you guys more of a challenge," I say, mentioning the Chicago Blackhawks retired goalie volunteering to play in our festival game. "And we'll toss Dan McKully from the hardware store in net for the Pros."

"I like it," Nash says from behind me into my ear as he pulls the lobe into his mouth.

My head is resting on his chest and his large powerful arms encompass me in the bubbly water. The moment his lips connect, my nipples go rigid and he notices immediately, pinching one as I yelp. We're in his swimming pool of a bathtub talking strategy for the fast approaching Sunset Festival. Nash just got an email from another ex-teammate confirming he can make the festival and that means we almost have what we need numbers-wise for a charity game.

"We can run it at night. Say seven o'clock, when the day is done. We still have lots of time. If we get it out on the social media blitz right away, and to local radio stations, we can sell it out. Oh, and get all the guys to post it to their socials," I say.

He wraps his arms around me from behind and kisses my cheek.

"If anyone can come up with a winning marketing strategy for this, it's you. I have no doubt. I'll do whatever you need," he says as he traces hearts into bubbles over my skin.

"Stop buttering me up just to use my body for your pleasure," I giggle as he dots my shoulders with kisses.

"Are you going to come and watch me play?" he asks. "Like old times?"

"Sure, should I get an official Nash Carter jersey?"

He groans in my ear. "Fuck, yes."

"You just got me clean," I say as I feel his cock harden against me.

"Yeah, but then you said you were going to put on my number, and I can't think of anything fucking sexier than that."

I move away from him and slide over to the other side of the tub. It truly is a tub made for two.

"That's all it takes? Just pop the number ten on my back and you're good to go?"

He comes at me like he's hunting me and perches over me. Water laps around us in tiny little waves.

"Nah Rae, you just have to exist and I just have to be conscious. It's just the way it is. I've come to terms with it."

I giggle again as he kisses me, slow and deep on the mouth, and our whole cycle of pleasure starts again.

MAMA

I can't help but notice your car has been
parked beside Stardust since Friday but I
haven't seen you.

I hope that means your piss poor excuse of
hanging out with Ginger is a lie and you're
with a nice man. Also, I'm coming to Sangria
Sunday with you girls tonight. Save a spot at
your table for me and Sandy.

Mama, I was with Ginger on Friday. I'm with
Nash right now working on the festival. See
you soon.

MAMA

Seems normal, working on a Sunday. See you
soon.

I roll over and face Nash in his bed. It's noon on Sunday and
we've yet to get up, other than to make pancakes and coffee.
I've decided trading between sex and food is pretty much a
perfect existence. I've been naked essentially since last night
and so has he. I flip through Netflix searching for another rom-
com to torture him with as my phone buzzes again.

"She doesn't believe you." Nash smirks

"It's not a lie, we have been working," I say.

"I suppose, among other things." His nose trails my
shoulder and covers me in goosebumps as both our phones buzz
simultaneously. Nash groans and rolls over as do I.

WADE

Everyone should come to the big house in an
hour. I have an announcement. It won't take
long.

Thanks for the summons, Sarge.

MAMA

She and Nash are working.

266

COLE

On a Sunday?

MR. CARTER

These festivals don't plan themselves. We have shit to do. You boys should be practicing… we have enough for a game. Only three weeks to go before I whoop your asses. Like old times.

COLE

A: I taught you everything you know and B: Mabel is beside me she says you owe her two dollars.

WADE

What's this guy gonna do when we break his ankles? Embarrassing.

I laugh at Wade's age old saying for skating circles around someone.

MR. CARTER

Wade: Bring it and Mabel, you're a cheater.

WADE

Come in an hour.

We'll be there.

MAMA

I'll make lunch, glad you two could pull yourselves away from work for an hour.

I flip over and eye the scrumptious man beside me. "Guess our weekend is over."

"Game face, darlin'," Nash says as he pulls me by my wrists and I groan.

CHAPTER FORTY-FIVE
Nash

The drive from my house to the ranch is short but that doesn't stop me from wishing I could pull over and take CeCe in the backseat of my truck at least five times. It's been three hours since I've been buried inside her and I'm already desperate for her again. Every time I take her, I tell myself it will be the last, and every time we finish, I know I'm lying to myself. I can't bring myself to stop, nor can I bring myself to admit that I've lost control of this entire situation.

"Drop me off at Stardust and go to the big house. I want to shower and change then I'll be down," CeCe says. She doesn't look at me; she's looking out the window at nothing. There's something about seeing her overnight bag in the backseat that I hate.

I pull up to Stardust and all the words I want to say are stuck in my throat.

CeCe turns to me. "See ya there." She smiles that earth shattering smile and gets out of my truck before I can say anything.

"Fuck," I say, resting my head on the steering wheel. I knew what this was when it started but some way, somehow, it's me who is breaking the rules, not only her no feelings rule, but all my own rules.

I can feel her pulling down the walls around me that I've spent years building. I'm on a freight train going warp speed to breaking every fucking rule I've ever had with CeCe and there's not a damn thing I can do to stop it. I huff out a breath and get my shit together, readying myself to face the family for Wade's announcement.

"Nash?" Cole pulls me from my daydream of CeCe bouncing on my cock in the black strapless sundress she's wearing at the opposite end of the table.

"Sorry, what?" I ask.

"Did you like Ivy when you met her?"

"Yeah, she seemed great," I say trying to focus on the family discussion of bringing Ivy Spencer on staff.

"She sure is pretty," CeCe adds.

"That's something I worry about. Haden, Brent, and Dusty were at the barn when I took her through, and every single one them behaved like a perfect gentleman around her," Wade says, mentioning a few of the caretaker cowboys.

"So?" CeCe says, confused.

"So... none of them are gentlemen," Wade deadpans. "A pretty new face is exactly the kind of distraction we don't need around here."

CeCe giggles.

"It would have to be on a trial basis," Wade continues. "Her resume is real good but I'm still not convinced she's got what it takes. She's got all sorts of ideas on how to change things 'round here, but I firmly told her we do things a certain way and that way ain't for changing."

"Oh hell, baby, have some faith. I, for one, liked her straight away," Jo says, refreshing the sandwiches on the table.

"You like everyone," Wade bites out.

"That's not true. Depending on the day, she doesn't like you." Cole chuckles.

"Hmmph," Wade grunts.

"Well, she stayed long enough to interview after your grumpy ass greeted her, so I'd say she's a winner." CeCe grins and I can't help but grin back because she's so fucking cute. *How does no one else realize how fucking cute she is?*

"Okay, then it's settled. She'll start in late September and stay on until March with a preemptive thirty-day trial. Mama, you can draw up and ready the contract," Wade orders as he takes a big sip of his steaming mug of coffee.

"There's the sergeant we know and love," CeCe giggles.

"He just don't like change," Jo fires. "A little change might just be exactly what we need around here. No thirty-day trial, she'll do just fine and the contract is for the full year."

Even Wade doesn't argue with Jo, he just sets his jaw and nods.

"To the new hire and hopefully another derby run." Cole raises his mug of coffee. We follow suit.

"We should celebrate tonight, is she still in town? At the Motorside?" Jo asks, and Wade pulls his hat off and rubs his forehead

"Jesus, Ma. Can't we be professional for once?"

"Oh hell, let's show her a good time, Ashby style," Jo says, winking.

I grin at CeCe across the table.

This should be interesting.

CHAPTER FORTY-SIX
Nash

I've been waiting for my chance all night and haven't found my window yet. After coming to the bar early and helping Asher ready everything for ladies' night, I waited in mental anguish over how much I was missing CeCe after just four hours until she entered at seven thirty with her entourage of *Not Angels*: Mama Jo, Sandra, and the newly hired Ivy Spencer.

An hour of drinking, gabbing and dancing ensued before the impossible happens. Fucking Cole and Wade saunter into the bar. I wouldn't be more surprised if I woke up tomorrow naked at the top of Sugarland Mountain. These boys *never* come out to the bar. They're both casual, complete with cowboy hats and grimaces that tell the world they should be living in the wild west. They join the ladies at their giant corner booth. I tap Asher on the shoulder to tell him I'm taking a few minutes and I head over, sliding in with the fam.

"Well, well, well, has hell frozen over? The Ashby boys are out? At a *bar?*" I hear Ginger say to them as I approach.

Cole bites immediately. "Some of us left high school thirteen years ago and some of us didn't," he retorts as I chuckle.

I stare at CeCe across the table. Flush in her cheeks from one or two sangrias, wearing that black, structured sundress from earlier, a high ponytail, big hoop earrings and plump cherry red fucking lips.

"You're just jealous we don't invite you out with us." Ginger grins at Cole as he scoffs and rolls his eyes.

"What are you boys doing here anyway?" Olivia asks.

"Making sure you girls don't corrupt our newest employee," Wade bites out, staring straight at Ivy who is fitting right in with the girls in a sundress of her own, wild black hair and red cowboy boots.

"So are you boys all ready to play each other in this hockey game like old times," Olivia asks us.

"All us girls at the arena watching like we're right back in tenth grade," Ginger adds and chuckles.

Cole smacks me on the shoulder. "Ready to kick this old retiree and his fellow old retirees' asses."

I roll my eyes at him.

"Shit, that's right, all these tasty men in town. I love hockey players, so how old are we talking, Nashby? Too old for me?" Ginger asks.

"Maybe not too old, but not crazy enough to get involved with you, if they know what's good for them," Cole chirps.

"Don't be jealous, baby, and go get mama another drink." Ginger grabs Cole's face across the table and wiggles it back and forth as she says it, drawing out her accent like a southern belle.

"Jesus, woman," he says. "I'm not jealous, it would be good if some poor, sad, unsuspecting soul settled your ass down." He stands then adds, "What are you drinking?"

You'd almost think he was actually annoyed with her, but I'm starting to think he isn't quite as annoyed with her as he lets on.

"Sangria, of course." She winks a long-lashed eye at him.

"All around?" The other girls at the table nod and Cole saunters off to get them another drink.

"To clear things up, hockey players retire sometime between thirty and forty. We're not old men," I say to Ginger.

"Good to know, got any coming that you recommend?" Ginger quips.

"Fuck no," I retort instantly.

"Well, on that sweet note..." Ivy drains her sangria in one big gulp as Wade shakes his head, and she notices right away. "My new boss clearly already disapproves of me, so dancing to this fine song can't make it any worse." She smiles at all the girls around the table, flashing Wade a grin. "Come on ladies, let's show them how it's done."

"Hell yes." Ginger laughs. "I like this one," she says, pointing after Ivy.

"Fucking Christ," Wade barks as all the girls slide out of the table leaving Wade and I alone just as the opening strings of "Redneck Woman" start coming through the sound system.

"Loosen up a little, yeah?" I nudge Wade beside me.

"The last thing that girl needs to think is that working here is some kind of a party." Wade shakes his head as the girls move to the music and I can't help but notice his eyes lingering on Ivy a little longer than they should.

Midway through the torture of CeCe swaying her full and perfect hips to "Boots Jeans, & Jesus," I see her tap Ginger on the shoulder and dart out of the crowd heading for the bar. I sit like a nervous teenager for all of five minutes. Too soon and I'll be noticeable, too long and she'll be back on the dance floor.

Wade and Cole are in deep discussion now about the upcoming Titans season so I take the opportunity.

"I'll be back... you guys want another?" I gesture to their near empty beer bottles and they both nod.

I search through the massive crowd that showed up tonight and find her at the back of the room, waiting at the bar, reapplying her lipstick and I get the overwhelming urge to smear it across her pretty little face.

I breeze by her without slowing down.

"Stock room now," I command.

I head into it and wait. Thirty seconds goes by before she's in front of me, already breathing shallow and I haven't even touched her yet, still holding a shot of bourbon in her hand from the bar. I fucking love the effect I have on her. I reach around her and lock the stock room door behind her, grateful. I brought her here because there are no windows in this room. CeCe sets her shot down on the stock table beside a pile of Horse and Barrel t-shirts and smiles at me, that sexy fucking smile that says, *"please fuck me, Mr. Carter,"* with one hand on her hip, challenging me.

"You have less than ten minutes, if you're lucky, before they come looking for me," she says before I crush my lips to hers.

They feel like coming home after an afternoon apart. Her clean, strawberry scent overwhelms me and mixes with her sweet wine soaked breath. My hands are everywhere and so are hers—under my shirt, over my back, into my hair as my dick hardens to the point of pain in my Wranglers.

My hands move to cup her perfect tits and I pull her dress down, letting my mouth find her rigid nipples before spinning her around and bending her right over the wooden table like I've wanted to do for the last two hours.

CeCe yelps as I lift her dress up over her hips and groan.

"No fucking panties."

She turns over her shoulder and blows me a kiss.

I give her a tight slap to her ass in response to her sassy little attitude and she whimpers.

"Stop pretending when we both know the truth." I trail a finger over her already soaking slit. "You came into *my* space with

274

no panties. *My* cunt on full display for one reason and one reason only."

CeCe moans, "Pretty full of yourself, aren't you? Maybe I just don't like panties." She smirks. I smack her ass again, and she yelps.

Fuck, my hand print looks good on her.

"Stop fucking around and tell me just how badly you want me to fill this little slice of paradise with my cock so I can take you right here over my desk. You'll be screaming my name before your friends even notice you're gone." I spread her arousal over her and rub it into her clit.

Her eyes flutter closed.

Not so sassy now, are you, baby?

"I want it s-so badly," she stutters. "I've been thinking about it all fucking day. It's really frustrating. I can't think about anything else," she confesses, and I grin as I move my hands over her bare lower back and her hips, gripping her tight.

I fight the urge to just take her right this second. I love that she's just as desperate for me as I am for her. The desire to drop to my knees and push my face into her sweet pussy overtakes me, but not before I grab the shot of bourbon and pour it slowly just above the cleft of her ass, she jumps but doesn't stop me. It trickles down her crevices over her tight pink rosebud and slides down between her two perfect, bare lips. I'm already there, on my knees, catching the bourbon in my mouth before it has a chance to hit the floor. I swirl it in my mouth and lick a clean trail up her center as her breathing grows frantic.

The mixture of our finest bourbon and her pussy is a fucking delicacy. I lose myself in her, eating CeCe's sweet pussy from behind, spreading her pert little ass wide to let me in fully as she grinds against me, riding my face, seeking her high.

I push two fingers into her and she moans my name. My

fucking name on her lips is a shot straight to my dick that I'll never tire of and I can't take it anymore, my need to fuck her is carnal as I free myself from my clothes in record time and sheath myself in her with one deep, vicious thrust.

"Holy shit," she moans as I almost black out from the feel of her pussy around me like this. This angle...

"Fucking Christ, CeCe," I grit out, staying fully rooted in her. I give her a few seconds to adjust to my size while I knead her hips in a bruising hold.

"I—you're too big, I can't get used to it," CeCe whines.

"No, baby, just enough, remember? All you have to do is breathe." I reach around and slide my middle finger over her clit, waiting for her to relax.

I'm desperate to move. Desperate to fuck her into next week. I slide a hand up the center curve of her back and just let my eyes absorb this view of her, every muscle, every vertebra in her spine, the shape of her tiny waist and back under my fingers. I want to touch her everywhere. All that velvety skin just begging for my lips and my teeth.

I pull out slightly and thrust back into her, forcing that last inch or so of me in and she shudders around me.

"Nash," she moans my name as I wrap a hand in her ponytail and drive us both up.

She grips the table, her knuckles whiten as I take her, raising herself up on her tip toes so I can get even deeper, giving in to my primal need to fuck her like the crazed animal I am for her.

"Harder," she whimpers, knowing just what I want, and I oblige. Driving into her over and over as I feel her tighten around me.

"Deeper, more..." she moans.

This fucking woman.

I slow myself and give her what she wants. I fuck as deeply

and slowly into her as I can take without losing control and she eats it up.

"You better be ready to come because I'm going to," she says in tiny little breaths, knowing that the moment she does, I'm a goner. It's impossible to fight.

Flyers and t-shirts that once lived on the corner of the table hit the floor as I bottom out inside her again and again, nudging the table across the floor with every thrust. I reach my hand around and cover her mouth, smearing the cherry red tint of her lips with my fingers as her eyes water and her pussy clenches. I just know she's going to scream.

"Nash..." Her voice is muffled in my hand.

The churning in my balls responds to her and her tightening pussy instantly. My release fires up my shaft and explodes into her. Static lines my vision as I fill her, each wave that crests pulls us both deeper, each of us desperate for one more second of this euphoria.

"Fuck, you're the most beautiful sight when you come," I say as I kiss her back.

She's the most beautiful sight anytime. She's fucking perfect. She's everything I never knew I wanted.

"So... *that* was the last time then?" she asks breathlessly, and I grin at the sass I love as I lean into her golden hair, deciding I'll worry about all these feelings overwhelming the fuck out of me later.

CHAPTER FORTY-SEVEN
CeCe

I've had more sex in the last three weeks than the entire eight years I spent with Andrew. There isn't a moment any day where I don't want Nash, and we've fallen into a pattern of work, the ranch and being alone, mostly at his house because it's just easier.

He cooks for me, makes sure he has my tea in his pantry, and even bought a monthly subscription to my favorite streaming service so I can get my dose of 'girly movies' as he calls them. It's bliss. It's what I always wanted with Andrew but never had, and it's bittersweet because I know somewhere deep down, it's temporary.

We don't talk about the future because I know the man he is. I know the trauma he's suffered, what he can give me and what he can't. I've decided a few months of happiness is better than nothing at all, and when the time is right, we'll both know and things will hopefully just go back to the way they were before.

I know with the way he's infused with my family that I'll have no choice but to get over him, and I'm dreading that day. But today is not that day as he makes his way down between my legs before breakfast in my bed and makes me come before my coffee maker even has a chance to finish brewing.

"I love hearing you scream my name before breakfast," he says as he peppers kisses up my arms to my shoulders and my breathing returns to normal.

"You go back to sleep; I'm going to work with Wade."

"I'm always willing to do the things you love, you know," I say back as he leaves the room chuckling.

"I bet."

An hour later I'm willing myself to get out of bed so I can drink said coffee and start to finalize the details of the Sunset Festival. It's less than a week away. I flip my phone over.

MAMA

> I see you stayed home last night, come on down to the house for brunch this morning.

I'm pretty sure my mother knows something is going on because I'm never home. She never asks who I'm with, only tells me that she hopes I'm happy because she is truly the best mother on the planet and just doesn't meddle. Wade and Cole notice nothing; Wade is in the field by the earliest of hours and Cole only comes to the ranch in the evenings. Only Ginger and Olivia are privy to all the torrid details of this predicament I've gotten myself into—the one where I admit that I am pretty sure I'm falling madly, desperately in love with Nash Carter.

It's not the kind of love I had with Andrew, if that was even love at all. No, this kind of love feels all encompassing. It's a need I have from the depths of my soul to be near him. It's practice scribbling my name with his last name kind of love, or fantasizing about growing old with him, chasing grandkids around the yard kind of love.

As I blow dry my hair, I picture what it would be like to live with Nash in another life, to have him come home to me every night. The pang of 'never gonna happen, CeCe, he doesn't do relationships' hits me in the gut. But this feels damn near like a relationship. I push the worries I have aside and focus on the here and now.

We have for tonight—Nash is taking the night off, something he's done three times in the last three weeks, much to Asher's surprise. And he's informed me it's Naked Friday. No clothes until tomorrow, which I'm happy to agree to if it means he's going to ravish me with everything his incredible body has to offer. I've even bought a sexy little dress I plan to wear with no panties, just the way he likes it.

I finish my coffee and read through my work emails, making notes. Everything for the festival seems to be going off without a hitch. The Pros vs Townies game is a hit, we have almost sold out, all 4500 tickets. The NHL even commissioned that two of their current players, Cory Kane and Chris Bell will play in our charity game with all the retirees. We're on track to well surpass our goal of $25,000, but we won't share that with Harry until after we know for sure.

I hear the door click. Nash comes through it as I'm on the phone with the party games company about the bouncy castle and carnival games arrival for the Center's parking lot. He motions to me asking if I want another coffee as I take in the sight of Cowboy Nash and consider hanging up and scaling him like a tree. The choice is taken from me because I'm still on the phone with Parties To Go when he finishes his coffee and protein bar ten minutes later.

I scroll through my email as I wait on hold for her to confirm a time and see one pop up in my personal folder from Andrew.

I haven't heard from him in a month, which is unusual, so I check it.

Cecilia,

I have an all cash buyer that came out of nowhere for our condo. 1.3 million and we'd split the profits fifty-fifty. You should walk away with approximately $425,000 after the mortgage and lawyer are paid out. Looks like buying in a dip and selling high worked in our favor. I have taken the liberty since you've been gone for six weeks now and packed all your belongings up into boxes. They are available for pick up, for you to go through them, donate things, whatever you chose to do. You'll need to come back here for closing. You need to get your things anyway. Let me know what day works well for you and I'll make an appointment with Gary. I can scan the contract Gary has drawn up and send it over so you can read it. You can stay at the condo when you come. I'll vacate it for the two or three days you're here and I'll take a hotel.

Sincerely,

Andrew Waterfield

Just like that, as if we didn't spend almost eight years together, he signs the email like it's being sent to any colleague or business contact.

Andrew also never even informed me that he was planning to put the condo on the market. He's also being way too nice. Something is up. My palms start sweating as I read it and think about going to Seattle.

I know he's right. Gary Beckman is our lawyer. He's been Andrew's family lawyer for thirty-five years and Andrew won't use anyone else. He's also sixty-five and refuses to do anything digitally. I tell myself to pick my battles. One or two days in Seattle, go through my things, sign some papers and I'm almost half a million richer and I can close this chapter of my life for good.

My mama and this ranch could use some of that money and maybe I could buy myself a little house of my own.

"You're quiet this morning. You alright?" Nash pulls me

from my anxiety, he watches me nervously biting my bottom lip from my kitchen island.

"Am I that obvious?"

He nods and comes to me.

"I'm fine," I say. "Just going over all the final details for next Friday."

For some reason, I don't bring myself to tell him about the sale or Seattle. We're not a couple. My problems aren't really his. I compartmentalize this for later as Nash circles behind me, sweeping my hair to the side and kissing the back of my neck.

"We don't have time for that this morning, Mr. Carter," I quip.

"Then you better not call me Mr. Carter again," he rasps in my ear.

"Aren't you taking on the youth riders for Molly this morning?" I whisper as I start to lose my inhibitions while his tongue trails my neck.

"God dammit, yes, and I have to go," he groans.

"I'm going to have brunch with my mama," I say, leaning my head back on his chest sobering myself from his touch.

Nash smells so fucking good. There are moments when I go through my day that I just get his scent in my nose from my clothes or my skin and that alone sends heat to my core. He smells so masculine and fresh, it's mouthwatering.

The dinging of my email stops Nash from kissing my neck further as Andrew's name pops up again on my laptop screen.

"What's *Drew the dick* want?" he asks casually as he makes his way to the counter to fill his reusable bottle of water.

I take all of five seconds to debate keeping this to myself but I don't, because I'm nothing if not honest.

"He sold our condo." The news is enough to make him stop drinking and turn to face me.

"He had it for sale?"

"I'm not sure how but he has a cash buyer."

"Well, that's great, CeCe. You can have a clean slate then. Can we have the rest of your things shipped?"

I chew my bottom lip. "I have to go there next week."

"To Seattle?" he asks, surprise lines his perfect features.

"Yes. Andrew's lawyer is old school, he doesn't do digital signings, and I should go anyway. There's probably a lot of stuff I don't even want anymore and I can donate it and ship the rest myself. I'll only be gone two or three—".

"I'm going with you."

"What?

"I am going with you."

"No," I say quietly.

The silence is deafening.

"I'm going to do this myself. Andrew is going to stay at a hotel while I'm there and I'll have the condo to myself. I don't want anything. None of our décor or furniture, it won't take me long. I need to do this on my own, Nash."

"Not a fucking chance are you going there to sleep in his bed by yourself."

I huff out a breath at him and start laughing. He's behaving like a Neanderthal.

"The apartment has three bedrooms. He won't be there and I certainly won't be sleeping in his bed, I'll take a guest room. And I don't need you to tell me what to do, by the way." I shouldn't say that, but I'm frustrated with Andrew and I've had enough of men telling me what to do to last me a lifetime. I'm a grown woman; I can sign these papers and get my things on my own.

"Besides, bringing you would just escalate Andrew's behavior. I'd like to do this peacefully and get it over with and to be straight forward, it's not exactly your concern," I add.

Nash grits his teeth, his jaw is so tight he looks like he might burst a tendon.

"Everything you do is my concern, CeCe. I can't keep you safe if I'm not there."

"I'm sorry, but this isn't your choice. It's not negotiable. Andrew is an asshole but he'd never physically hurt me. In fact, he's actually being nice. Weirdly nice." I'm rambling. *Get to the point, CeCe.* "I'm going alone. I will handle it, and I'll be back before you know it."

His nostrils flare and I see it—the moment he emotionally shuts down. The icy wall goes back up and the energy in the room shifts.

"I'm late, so I'll see ya later," he says.

I nod because if there's one thing I won't do, it's chase Nash Carter. The way he's fired up right now, I know he cares about me, he just can't or won't say it. This is long past 'just sex.' We both know it, but he's been adamant about his stance on dating and relationships since the beginning and I'm not going to be the one to try to change him.

If Nash wants to have a say in what I do, he can tell me what he wants from me and how he feels about me.

I spent eight years chasing a man. And I won't ever do that again.

CHAPTER FORTY-EIGHT
Nash

I'm mentally cursing the whole way to the barn. For the first time since this 'just one night' thing began, I'm fucking pissed at CeCe. I want to go with her, no... a better way to put it would be I *need* to go with her.

The thought of Andrew anywhere near her without me there makes me fucking crazy.

None of this makes sense. He doesn't tell her about the sale until it's over, gives her no say in the sale price and tells her she has to come all the way to Seattle? Hello? DocuSign?

I grit my teeth. This is why I don't do relationships. This bullshit is the last thing I need. What if something happens to her while she's gone? I also can't stop thinking about Wade's words from weeks ago, that maybe she'd go back to Andrew because he wants to offer her what she thinks I wouldn't. Marriage, babies, family life. The happily ever after.

I ask myself every second of every day what I'm doing with CeCe. I've gone over this in my head a thousand times, as I bury myself inside her every night and feel like it's the second coming of Christ. As I watch her sleep soundly beside me or when I cook with her in my kitchen and her hair on her head in a big messy bun, tasting sauce off the spoon. Or when she's arguing with me over sports or music, the look in her eyes when she's passionate about something and she lights right up like those little fireflies on my land. Even when I sit and watch baseball and she works at my dining room table, looking adorable as fuck in her pajamas and glasses. I find myself wondering shit I never thought I would, like what it would be like if her birth control failed and I got to be the lucky bastard that watched her belly swell with my growing child.

And then, I picture losing it all, and it fucking terrifies me. There's no doubt that CeCe Ashby has broken every rule I've ever put in place. She's tearing down every bit of my defensive wall, brick by brick, and I am a fucking mess trying to hold it up.

"You look like you're chewing fire, not readying yourself to teach a bunch of seven year olds," Wade comments as I enter the barn.

I look up and straighten myself out. "Yeah, I'm fine, just a busy morning."

"Thanks for doing this. Molly really isn't feeling well. You're only on the hook till noon. I gotta ride the adult trails class, so I'll see ya after and we'll grab some food?"

I nod and clap Wade on the back, and for the first time in weeks I feel like shit for going behind his back with CeCe. And for an insane moment, I almost tell him, but I don't. I just put on a fake grin and say, "Sounds good, brother." Then I head out to meet the rowdy group waiting to ride in the barn.

CHAPTER FORTY-NINE
CeCe

> Tell me this is where I get my senses back?

LIV

> Depends, how long has it been since you've
> seen his dick?

> I'm serious.

LIV

> So am I. This is just sex, right? You keep
> saying it, I wonder when you're gonna realize
> that's all a pile of bullshit.

I don't answer because I know she's right.

LIV

> He doesn't have any real feelings for you?
> Which is why you two spend your days
> playing house? Because of sex, CeCe? You
> have to have the talk with him.

GINGER

I think there's more to Nash than meets the eye. I want to remind you that his family was killed in front of him. That fucks a person up. You're not dealing with someone able to spell out his emotions so easily. You need to come to the realization you either have to accept things the way they are, which seem pretty fucking great, or be strong enough for the both of you to admit what we already know.

Which is? And that was the longest text you've ever sent by the way.

GINGER

One handed, baby, while I eat.

We all know that Nash has never let anyone inside his thorny fortress, until you waltzed your ass back into town. You don't see the way he looks at you, CeCe. He doesn't look at you like you're a fling. He looks at you like you're his endgame. Also, people who are just having sex don't have arguments, just saying.

I put my head in my hands and blow out a raspberry as my phone dings again. When the hell did Ginger get so philosophical?

ANDREW

I haven't heard back from you, and Gary would like to set a date and time. Can you confirm?

I flip my laptop open and start searching for flights, coordinating with my schedule for next week because it's busy with it being the last week before the Sunset Festival. I make some quick selections just to get it over with. I take a deep breath and type.

> Set the meeting for Wednesday, I am booking a flight for tomorrow morning. I'll leave after we sign.

ANDREW

> Will do. You should see a scanned copy of the contract in your email soon, have a look over it and let me know what you think, they're ready to sign as soon as we do.

> You know, Andrew, I would've appreciated you telling me you were offering showings of the condo.

ANDREW

> I haven't listed it, obviously. You would've needed to sign for that, this is a friend of a friend. Just so happens they're looking for something downtown. Figured it would be easier than readying the house and waiting weeks for it to sell. I don't have time for that, I'm in court for the foreseeable future. I'm ready to move on now. I just want to put this all behind me too.

Something about his words still sting and I hate that they do. If this is what it feels like after ending things with Andrew, Nash is going to absolutely ruin me.

By the time I get to the big house, Mabel and Cole are at the table. Mabel is shoveling eggs and bacon into her cute little mouth and Cole is reading the newspaper, his booted ankle resting on his other knee.

"You off today?" I ask him.

"Yeah, first Saturday in months."

"Nice." I smile at him. I wish he'd find someone to make him happy. He's gruff, but he has a heart in there, one that was crushed but I'm sure he doesn't want to be alone forever. In a lot of ways, he's like Nash—afraid to get his heart broken again. Afraid of losing that control.

"I'm riding when I'm done eating. Nana Jo is walking me back. Will you watch me ride, Auntie? I'm jogging today," Mabel says.

"Of course, baby." I ruffle her hair and grab a plate to start piling eggs and toast onto it, as Mama comes into the kitchen in her trademark yoga pants and a t-shirt.

"Hey, baby, glad to see you home this morning."

"Aren't you home every morning?" Cole snickers.

I freeze. "Most," I say quietly.

Cole looks at me with one eyebrow raised. "You got someone on the sly, CeCe Rae?"

"Hush your mouth, it's not what you think," I say back.

"Mmhmm," Cole muses. "Hope you made a better choice this time than Andrew, such a d-bag," he says, shaking his head.

"Thanks for the reminder," I say sarcastically,

"It's not like you could've known, he fooled us all at first." Cole says as he makes a face at me like he's ten years old.

"Speaking of Andrew... y'all, I have to go to Seattle," I say, changing the awkward subject of my love life.

Everyone stops what they're doing and looks at me.

"It's not a crisis. Andrew just sold our condo and I have to go back and sign and I really need to face the rest of my things."

"You're not staying with him?" Cole asks, horrified.

These men.

"No, I'm not, he's going to a hotel and I'll stay at the condo. He's actually being very accommodating."

Cole snorts. "That's when I'd worry the most."

"I'll be going tomorrow and coming back Wednesday night," I say, as Nash comes through the front door.

"You hear this? CeCe is going back to face this ass—butt-hole of the century," he says, trying not to lose a dollar.

Nash grunts as he hastily pours himself a coffee and glances at me. "Uh-huh," he says, setting his jaw again.

"Take one of your girl cronies with you, at least. Ginger might be the most irritating woman I know, but I wouldn't put it past her to kick some ass for you if she needed to," Cole says as he stuffs a dollar in the boot in the middle of the table before Mabel can even tell him to.

Mabel notices and smiles, which makes me smile, then she goes back to eating without uttering a word.

"I'll tell you the same thing I told... my friends," I say, looking between Cole and Nash.

"I'm not some helpless young girl anymore. I can go to Seattle and handle Andrew. I'm doing it on my own. I need this closure. I want it to go smoothly so I can put it behind me."

Nash swallows the rest of his coffee and sets his mug in the sink hard enough that Mama and Cole both look up at him.

"See you out there, Mabes," he bites out before exiting.

"What's got his knickers in a twist?" Cole asks.

"Lord only knows," Mama says, her eyes on me while she sips the last of her coffee.

We spend fifteen minutes cleaning up in silence after Cole leaves.

"Thank you for the French toast, Mama."

"Anytime, darlin'," she says, her palm to my cheek. "Walk with me." She turns to the den. "Come on, Mabes, get your boots."

I hear Mabel scramble and we head out the door.

The late August sun is steamy as we walk the short distance to the largest of our pens near the barn. Mabel happily skips

291

twenty feet ahead, stopping every so often to pick up a bug or a flower. The breeze blows around my dress. It's a soft and gauzy linen in white with tank sleeves and hangs to my knees in the front and trails lower in the back almost to the ground. It's loose and billowy in the stifling Kentucky heat. Gravel crunches under my tried and true cowboy boots as the horse pen starts to come into view.

"Nash sure doesn't seem to like the idea of you going to Seattle alone," Mama says as we walk.

I keep my eyes ahead. Focused. Mama is my best friend, and if I look at her, I'm definitely going to spill the tea.

"He's no better than Cole or Wade, doesn't think I can handle anything by myself."

"Mmhmm. That must be it," Mama says slowly.

As if speaking about him would manifest him out of thin air, Nash comes out of the barn on his favorite thoroughbred riding horse, Dad's old Rising River, and just the sight of it almost chokes me up.

Nash rides like a natural, always has, his Wranglers hug him in all the right places down to his worn in cowboy boots, and his gray t-shirt grips his upper arms as he holds the reins tight. His cowboy hat shields his face from the sun and he's smiling at two of the kids in tow as they jog behind him for the first time on their respective horses in our massive two-hundred-foot arena.

"If you're relaxed, your horse is relaxed, Sasha." I hear Nash say to one of the kids.

"Do y'all know horses feel every emotion we feel?" he asks.

"He's great with those kids..." Mama says as we stand to the side of the barn and watch him when he doesn't see us.

"Mabel loves him," I offer, trying not to get too personal.

"CeCe Rae Ashby," Mama says. "Look at me."

"What, Mama?" I ask, turning to her.

She gives me her smug all-knowing grin. "The boys may not notice it, but I do. You're with him every moment you aren't here, aren't you?"

I can't lie to most people but I especially can't lie to my observant Mama, plus I need her advice.

I sigh and go right to the heart of it. "God dammit, I think I love him, Mama. And I have no fucking clue what to do about it."

"I know, baby." She pats my hand gently.

"Do you just know everything?"

"Mostly, yes." Mama grins and her eyes crinkle in the corners. "Well what do you think you *should* do about it?" she asks

"Nothing."

"The hell you mean nothin'?" she asks, her big eyes somehow even bigger.

"He doesn't do relationships. I was just so attracted to him, it was supposed to just be a fling, which is why we've been sneaking around here like ninjas in the night. I didn't expect to feel... whatever this is."

I watch him joke around with the kids, and although I'm still kind of mad for acting the way he did this morning, there's no doubt in my mind that I still want him with everything in me.

Mama sighs and watches Nash. "Well, the handsome ones always are the easiest to fall in love with, and you'd have to be dead to not notice that boy. He's a looker."

"Yeah, it's really irritating," I bark out, and she laughs.

A few minutes pass before she asks, "Has he told you he doesn't want a future with you?"

"In no uncertain terms, yes. When I got home—"

"That was almost two months ago. I mean... have you asked him now?"

"Well, no."

Even I know it's crazy that we've been going on like this for this long without talking about it but I'm just so afraid that any talk about commitment of something real will end it and I don't want this to end, I'm not ready.

She's quiet for a moment. "He's one to tread carefully with. We're all he has, we're all he's had for a long time. You *always* have us to fall back on. Imagine the fear in his mind, whether he admits it or not, at the possibility of things going wrong with you, like Wade or Cole's relationships. He probably thinks he'd lose everything. All of us."

"You guys would never abandon him, no matter what happens with us."

"We know that, but maybe *he* doesn't." Mama turns to me, matter-of-factly. "Go to Seattle, time has a way of working these things out, baby. You know I waited four months for your daddy to admit his feelings for me? He knew it after our first date, I'm sure. But I had to wait patiently for him to come to terms with it. It took me going to Nana Dot's in Tennessee for two weeks the summer of my senior year for him to admit he missed me and didn't want to live without me. Absence makes the heart grow fonder. If he's worth it, your patience is all you can give him."

"Well, I won't chase another man, I spent too long chasing after Andrew's affection and that got me nowhere."

She wraps her arm around me and gives me a big squeeze. "Something tells me you won't have to chase anyone, darlin'. You'll see."

"Auntie! I'm jogging," Mabel calls out to me from the arena as she bounds steadily on her horse Cosmic.

"I see you, baby. I'm so proud of you!" I call back, as Nash turns and registers that I'm standing here.

CHAPTER FIFTY
Nash

I can be frustrated with CeCe and still notice how incredible she looks standing there in the breeze in that pretty little white dress and fucking turquoise cowboy boots.

I put my head down and get back to work, doing my best to pretend she isn't invading my headspace. I get through the two classes I have and then I do something different than I have in five weeks. I get in my truck and drive home. Alone. I just need the time to sort this out. I'm so fucked up over her.

I keep busy all day—I head over to the bar, I work my ass off there, and I meet Rocco for an evening fishing session. This was my life before her, and when this all goes to shit with her, it's what I'll go back to.

By seven-thirty, I'm fed, I'm showered, everything is clean, and CeCe hasn't texted me all day. I'm already regretting my decision and going out of my fucking mind. Everywhere I look, she's here—my bed, my sofa, my goddamn kitchen counter. Not to mention her strawberry scent is everywhere.

I've behaved like an ass. I know that, but this is what I do. Decades of fear and panic simmer to the surface and I go into protection mode. It's the age-old, *you can't hurt me if I hurt you first* and I fucking hate myself for it.

I do something I never do and pour myself a bourbon and knock it back in one shot.

Why hasn't she texted me or called me yet?

By eight, I can't stop myself from testing the waters.

> Still hell bent on going to Seattle alone?

Ten minutes later.

> I just think you should consider the possibility that this is all a ploy to get you alone and try to pressure you into coming back to him.

> I just don't trust him, especially with you.

Another ten minutes later.

> I only say these things to you because I care about you, Rae.

Three minutes later.

> Not answering me is really immature.

Another ten minutes go by, and I grab my keys and mutter, "Fuck sakes," as I blast out the front door to my truck.

I'm driving seventy down the highway asking myself how the fuck I got here, how a woman I've known my whole life has got me so fucking twisted up in knots I can't seem to figure my way out.

I pull into the ranch, gravel spewing from under my tires. I go over what I'm going to say, how calm and logical I'm going to be. I'm the older one, the experienced, level-headed one with more wisdom. I toss my truck in park, not giving a fuck if anyone sees me. I pound on her door.

You can't go to Seattle alone because...

I can't lose you too...

I don't want to live this life without you any longer...

I want you... all of you... all of us... but I'm fucking terrified.

I love you...

The door swings open and CeCe stands before me, her hair loose, and wearing that white linen dress in bare feet.

Fuck me, every thought I have leaves my mind. She's the sun, I just live within her orbit.

"Nash, I'm too tired to argue with you," she says, folding her arms across her chest, pushing her perfect tits up, fire in her eyes.

"Well... fuck... you're so fucking irritating," I blurt out.

Not what you planned, dumbass.

CeCe sighs. "Please, won't you come in?" She waves her hand into her tiny hallway and I bound in like she might change her mind at any second because I fucking would if I was her.

"You just... anything could happen while you're gone. He's up to something, CeCe. Call it a sixth sense, I don't know... but I'm going with you and that's it. I'm putting my foot down." I run my hand through my hair and look down at her.

If fire could shoot out from a woman's eyes, I would, in fact, be a pile of smoking ash right now. Her voice is soft and calm when she speaks. "And just where exactly are you dropping that heavy boot, Nash? Right in the middle of 'we're just fucking?' Or wait, how about smack in the center of 'I don't do relationships,'" she mocks me using air quotes and I want to half punch a wall and half crush myself to her.

"CeCe..." I warn.

She keeps going, hands on her hips, attitude permeating from her. Kentucky fire rising up before me.

"No, really, I'd like to know... what does this situation look like to you? What do I look like to you? Some dutiful little woman who is going to do everything you say? Just because you come into my life like a tornado and fuck me like a caveman doesn't mean you can behave like one outside the bedroom."

Something about the way she's standing, her spicy tone and her need to be in charge turns me instantly desperate for her. All my frustration, all my anger towards myself, her and my past evaporates into thin air and my hands are around her tiny waist before she can say anything more, my lips crashing down on hers.

I'm mad with claiming her, with silencing her debate on my feelings, on us. I can't speak, I just want her and I'm fucking taking.

She kisses me back, parting her lips to let me in, my tongue takes her mouth. I nip at her lips, her jaw, her ear; the heat between us could burn down the whole god damn house but it wouldn't stop me. I'd keep going and fuck her right in the middle of the flames.

"I'm sorry I was upset with you..." I breathe into her neck.

"You mean you're sorry for having a temper tantrum?" she asks. I did have a temper tantrum. Fuck, she's always right and it makes me want her even more if that's possible. "I need to hear those words, Nash."

I grunt, partly out of frustration and partly out of the need I have for her. "I'm sorry I had a temper tantrum. But to answer your question, what you look like, little firefly, is fucking *mine*. And I protect what's mine," I rasp in her ear.

She moans as she tips her head back, offering me a view of that slender, silky, biteable neck. And I'm a crazed man, my hands slide under her dress and squeeze her plump ass, letting my fingers slide under the lace of her almost nonexistent thong. Our bodies mold together instantly like two pieces of a puzzle.

"Goddamn you, why do you have to feel so good?" she asks and I chuckle.

I pull her across the room and sit down on the sofa before her, waiting for her to come to me, unbuckling my jeans as I go.

I can see the debate in her eyes, her want to come to me and her fight. She wants me just as badly as I want her and she doesn't understand it any better than I do.

I pull my cock out and start stroking it in front of her, enticing her. Her emerald eyes turn to saucers and she bites her lower lip.

That's right, baby, you want it, you know you fucking do.

"Fuck you, Nash, thinking I can't resist you," CeCe says, her chest rising heavy with her want.

I smirk back at her.

"That's exactly what I intend to do." I continue stroking myself. "Now, I'm gonna need you to be a good girl, Rae. Come here, lift that flimsy little dress up and seat yourself on my cock. Right where you know you belong."

Breathy pants escape her full pink lips as she stands staring at me for all of one second before lifting her dress up and sliding her thong down over her hips, it slinks to the floor and she kicks it away as my dick throbs in my own hand, pre-cum leaks at the sight of her.

"You don't own me, Nash," she says in the sexiest fucking voice as she moves toward me then straddles me, searching for friction for the aching bud of nerves between her sweet, silky thighs.

I reach down and run my middle finger along her already dripping slit and groan with pleasure.

"No, baby, I don't own you. You own *me*. Now, fuck me like you do."

"Okay but—" She loses her words and moans as I press the crown of my girth against her entrance.

The fire returns to her eyes as her lips meet mine and she sinks the pussy that was made for me down onto my cock in one continuous movement until she's fully seated on me to the hilt.

My girl is a fucking champ and she takes all of me just as she was born to do.

"We're not done talking about this," she breathes out as she rises up.

Static lines my vision. *So fucking tight.*

My head falls back and I grip her fleshy hips in a bruising hold, moving her back down over me. We both breathe out our respective sounds of desire at the same time. There's no fighting how this feels. I don't know who the fuck we think we're kidding.

"I wouldn't have it any other way, baby," I say as I continue to fuck her, lifting her slowly off me and sliding her back down, and she lets me.

CeCe gives me all the control as she lets go, the tiniest act of submission that shows me she feels the same way about me as I do her.

Don't tell her you love her while she's riding your cock.

Don't tell her you love her while she's riding your cock.

I yank her dress down so her breasts bounce in my face as she rides me, it's fucking perfection. Her nipples are pebbled and begging for attention as I pull them each carefully into my mouth and suck. Jesus Christ, I'm fucking high, there is nothing I could ever want more than this. More than her.

"Fuck," she whines as I bottom out inside her. She's never been so full.

"You're incredible, Rae," I whisper. "I want to bury myself inside you every second of every fucking day."

It's so effortless like this. When it's just us in these moments I can believe that she is completely mine. My one and only. That I can convince her back into my arms over and over again and never lose her. Somehow move her into my home, my body, my heart, never let her go until death takes me.

CeCe wraps her arms around my neck, her fingers twisting into my hair, gripping hard as she increases her pace over me. She's close, I can feel her legs begin to shake and her moans grow louder in my ear.

"Nash... please," she begs me.

"You're so fucking pretty riding my cock. Look at you, baby. Now, come. Come all over my cock, little firefly, and take me down with you. You own it."

"Yes..." CeCe moans as she pulls her lips away from mine and smiles at me, and my fucking world ignites at the site.

"And don't you fucking forget it, baby," she breathes out, and then I'm coming.

My release fires through me, from every cell in my soul as I grip her shoulders and hold her down, keeping her rooted to me while I thrust into her and come, every wave more incredible than the last as I keep coming, her name on my lips and mine on hers.

I don't stop, I can't, the waves continue as she falls apart again over me. *Am I still coming or coming again?*

Her sounds echo in the tiny cabin like surround sound and it's music to my ears, a fucking symphony.

I love this woman.

I love this woman like I've never loved anyone or anything. I love her more than the sun on my face rising over the mountain, the feel of fresh ice under my skates, or hoisting that cup over my head. I love my little firefly like I have no other option, and the truth is maybe I never have.

CHAPTER FIFTY-ONE
CeCe

"You didn't answer me tonight, it drove me crazy." Nash is still inside me when he speaks into my shoulder, my dress pools around my waist, and we're both covered in a thin layer of sweat.

"Answer you?"

"I texted you, ridiculous texts I shouldn't have, but in my defense, I was going out of my mind without you."

I grin into his neck.

"If that's part of your apology, I accept it. I didn't check my phone. I didn't want to argue and I was... packing."

His body stiffens below me. "I still hate that you're going there alone."

I brace myself for an argument but Nash's next words surprise me.

"Have me on speed dial. I'll be on the next plane out to murder him if that fucker tries anything even remotely sketchy."

My heart swells in my chest, knowing how much he worries, how much he admitted his feelings for me tonight just by coming here. Maybe Mama is right, time will sort this out, and being in Seattle will give him a few days to think. When I get back, I'm going to have a long, overdue talk with him. I can't keep playing this game with my heart. if he isn't where I am, even though it may kill me, I will have to end this with him.

I savor this moment as much as I can. I kiss his jaw, then his neck, stubble scratching my lips in the best way and his clean, spicy scent fills my senses.

"If I didn't know any better"—I kiss another spot—"I'd say you might care for me a little more than you let on, and I'm okay with you keeping that to yourself." I climb off him, fix my dress, then pull my thong back on. "As long as you get around to telling me sooner rather than later."

Nash is wearing a perfect, lopsided grin as he stands and clothes his lower half. He moves toward me and places his hands on my hips, pulling me close.

"Of course I... care for you, CeCe. So fucking much... I— the thought of anything going wrong while you're across the country alone with that fucker makes me crazy." He tucks a piece of errant hair behind my ear, tips my chin to him and kisses me on the lips, softly, gently.

"I'm really fucking hung up on you, in case you haven't noticed. I'm having a hard time living without you, which is why I stalked here like a beast when you didn't answer me."

I sigh and grin, his honest words surprising me, but I know just how he feels because I've been going out of my mind all damn day.

"Good thing you came to your senses. In case you haven't noticed, I'm hanging right there beside you," I say while Nash lines my neck with kisses and I press myself to him, wrapping my arms up around his neck.

"What the fuck am I seeing?" A loud, deep voice booms across the open space, and Nash and I both jump. We turn to see a pissed off and confused as hell Wade standing ten feet from us.

In my fog of desire, I didn't lock the door and I have no idea how neither of us heard him come in. There's no mistaking what this is, the way we are entangled with each other and Nash's still shirtless body spells it out real clear.

"What the fuck, Nash?" Wade takes his hat off and runs a hand through his hair. "You and *my sister*?"

"Wade—" I start to say.

"She's practically *your family*. What the fuck?"

Nash tosses his shirt over his head. "This isn't what it looks like, man," he says, his voice calm and smooth.

I turn to Nash with wide eyes. *It isn't?*

"It looks like you're in here having your way here with CeCe Rae."

"He's not just having his way with me," I plead.

"Sure as fuck looks like it, how long has this been going on?" Wade looks back and forth between us both. "She's vulnerable. She just got out of a long-term relationship, and you! You're never going to settle down so what the fuck are you doing here? Using her?" Wade is yelling now but Nash, Nash is frozen, his eyes give nothing away.

"It's more than that Wade, we... care about each other," I say, turning to Nash to back me up, but he doesn't, he's a deer in headlights.

"Is that true, Nash? You care about her? What? Do you *love* her? You ready to take care of her and settle down?" Wade puts both his hands on his hips and waits expectantly, looking way too 1950s fatherly and way too southern.

Nash opens his mouth to speak and turns to me, but too much time passes. Wade reaches for Nash's t-shirt and Nash doesn't stop him, he surrenders to Wade's tight grip on his collar.

"It just...we didn't plan this, it just fucking happened," Nash says.

Wade lets go and pushes him back.

"That's what I fucking thought. I trusted you. I *do* fucking trust you like a brother, some things are supposed to be fucking sacred." Then Wade turns to me with a look of disapproval that is the epitome of my father and says, "I came to see if you were alright with going to Seattle on your own, but I see here, you're just fine."

"Wade—" Nash finally speaks up but Wade isn't having it.

"Don't come here in the morning, I need a few days to absorb this bullshit," he says to Nash, and stalks out the door, slamming it behind him.

Tears fill my eyes. There we have it; how could I have been so incredibly stupid? I let myself fall in love with this man, I opened my heart to him but it's my own fault. I should've known—Nash has told me since the beginning where I stand. He couldn't even admit his feelings to himself and have my back when I needed him.

"Go home," I say

"CeCe," Nash whispers. "I froze, I—"

"I don't care. I needed you to back me up, Nash. You know what? It's my fault. I know we're just a phase, and every phase has to end." I start to turn away and then change my mind.

"No, you know what? I'll be the first to say it, I broke the rules. I fell in love with you, like an idiot." I'm yelling now. "I love you so much it consumes me. But I want it *all*. I want you, in every way, and if you don't want me like that, then we're done. I didn't mean to fall in love with you but I did and I'm not afraid to admit it, and that's all there is to it."

He reaches for my arm but still says nothing. My heart shatters into a million pieces while I wait for the words that never come. I pull away from him.

"CeCe... this is happening so fast. I—I don't know how to deal with these emotions. The way I feel about you, I never—"

I sigh and look up at him, tears spilling over my cheeks with my broken heart pooling in my chest.

"Go home, Nash. I guess I want what you can't give me and I'll never chase you."

He wipes a tear from my cheek. "Please don't cry...fuck. I just need—"

"Don't worry, baby, I'll never expect you to be someone you're just not," I say, a sugary sweet and evil tone coats my words.

I want him to want me but I won't try to force him. This fires him up, his blue eyes are intense and bottomless.

"What if I do love you? What if I am so fucking in love with you there are moments I can't see straight? But what if one day, it's just over? If it just disappears? I'll lose everything, not just you, CeCe. I'll lose my family. All fucking over again."

I smile through my tears and start laughing.

"That's the thing about love, Nash. There are no guarantees, it can be here one day and the next, it can all go up in smoke. You can't control it. You can't foresee it, you just have to decide if you can have enough faith to trust it, if the life we could have in between is worth the fear of losing it. I'm going to Seattle, maybe you should take the next few days to figure out what you want, and when I get home you can tell me what this is."

He looks at me pleading, and I see the love in his eyes but I also see how fucking terrified he is to give into it, which just isn't good enough for me.

"Now, you need to go. I have to finish packing."

I turn around and put my hands on the kitchen island, wishing Nash would come to me, wishing he would wrap his strong arms around me and tell me he loves me back, wishing he would hold me close and whisper our future in my ear, telling me everything would be okay.

But he doesn't.

My first mistake was falling for him. My second was expecting him to be something he's not.

I hear the sound of the front door click behind him and I break.

CHAPTER FIFTY-TWO
CeCe

GINGER

Say the word and I'll go kick his ass, babe.

LIV

I'm in.

No, he's gotta make his own choice. I'm not going to pressure him either way. I swore to myself and my dad that the next time I commit to a man he's gonna want me with his whole heart.

GINGER

He loves you, CeCe. I'm sure of it. See what happens when you come back and if Andrew gives you any shit this week… kick him in the balls. Hard.

I laugh in my seat on the plane, the old woman beside me looks at me with a kind smile.

Hold down the fort tonight, girls. Break hearts not the law. Wish me luck.

LIV

You don't need luck, baby girl, you've got this.

GINGER

MR. CARTER

I know you're upset with me, I'm sorry, CeCe. I hope everything goes well. Be safe.

I'm going out of my mind thinking about you there alone. Please don't hesitate to call me if you need me.

I toss my phone on airplane mode and put my headphones over my ears as we prepare for take-off.

ANDREW

I'm here to pick you up.

Andrew, I told you that you didn't have to do that. I could've taken an Uber.

ANDREW

I'm at the outside the terminal.

I put my phone back in my purse and sigh. I haven't seen Andrew in over a month, not since Nash hit him in the middle of main street, so I brace myself. The familiar anxiety creeps up my spine.

The air is cooler in Seattle, it can't be more than sixty-five degrees and I see Andrew before he sees me, his blonde hair perfectly styled, designer pants and a Burberry jacket.

I shiver, suddenly feeling underdressed as Andrew turns and lets his eyes rake over my cut off jean shorts, black Ramones t-shirt, and Birkenstocks.

"Well, Cecilia, I see you've kept it casual," he quips as he leans down and kisses my cheek.

I stiffen under his hold.

"Shall we?"

I nod.

"I have cleared out of the condo for you. There's food there for you, if you'd like. We will meet Gary on Wednesday, but you have the next two days at your disposal to deal with your belongings. For what it's worth, I want to apologize for speaking to you so out of turn when I saw you last."

"Thanks," I say, offering him a tight smile.

The whole vibe between us is weird and forced. Andrew isn't a nice man—he's pompous and he doesn't think about anyone but himself so all this syrupy sweet care is unnerving me. I am just desperate to get away from him.

We pull up to the Crystal Terrace condominium complex as I fidget with my purse strap. I didn't expect coming back here to hit me this way.

My chest tightens and all the memories with Andrew hit me at once. The constant worry, the constant pressure to never ask questions and just accept things the way they were. I realize, staring up at this polished, pristine structure, that after two months of being back home in Kentucky, this feels completely foreign and fake. And right now, all I can think of is Nash and how much he would hate everything about this stuffy, upscale building.

The regret I feel for giving him an ultimatum hits me as I look out the window. I didn't even give him a chance to answer me, I just threw all my feelings at him and expected him to be able to do the same, but Nash isn't me and I have no idea how difficult letting go of the control might be for him.

Andrew clears his throat. I turn to him as he gets out of the car and goes for my bag in the back seat.

"I've got it, Andrew. Thanks."

"I'll bring it upstairs for you."

"No, Andrew. I've got it."

"It's no trouble, really. You shouldn't carry it all the way up —"

"Andrew, please. This will be easier if we don't spend time together. I'm here to get my things and sign the papers, and that's it." I grab the handle of my suitcase from him and pull it towards me. "I'll see you Wednesday," I say firmly.

He takes the hint finally and backs towards his car, nodding at me as he goes,

"Okay, CeCe. If you need anything, I'm just a phone call away."

"Thank you."

He mercifully bows out and gets back into his car, and I venture into the building already regretting I'm here and praying this time goes quickly.

I spend the next forty-eight hours trading between sorting through eight years of my life here, eating, drinking Andrew's most expensive bottles of wine and crying. The women's shelter I used to work with was happy to come when I called this morning and pick up everything I didn't want—piles of clothes, shoes and accessories I'll never wear in Kentucky. After packing up all the things I actually want to keep, I lean back on the couch and take a deep breath.

It's only Tuesday.

ANDREW

The new buyers would like to go through the condo one more time before we sign tomorrow. How are you doing? Would this be possible?

Yes, that's fine, what time?

ANDREW

Six-thirty tonight.

Ok, I'll stay out of their way.

ANDREW

Actually, they'd like to have the place to themselves. I was thinking we could grab a quick bite to eat? Go over everything and be prepared for tomorrow.

I chew my bottom lip. The last thing I want to do is share a meal with Andrew.

ANDREW

I know you're sitting there over analyzing this. It's just a meal, CeCe. We shared eight years together. I'm hoping when this is all said and done, we can be friends. We can go to El Fonzo, and besides, what else are you going to do? It's raining and you'll need to be out for at least an hour.

Ok. I'll meet you there. Tell them they can have an hour.

I text Ginger to tell her what I'm doing so someone knows where I'll be.

I put my phone down and look around the space. Our appointment is scheduled for noon tomorrow and my flight out is scheduled for three fifteen. It hits me all of a sudden that this will be the last time I'll ever see this place. I wipe a tear from my cheek.

I'm not sad for Andrew and I, not sad to see this place go, I'm just sad.

A whole era down the drain, years of my life I'll never get back. I think of Nash's eyes the other night, the fear I saw in them and I wonder if he has it right. Relationships can really suck.

Aside from me taking a break and not answering Nash, he's messaged me every day since I left Kentucky, telling me we need to talk, telling me he froze, how sorry he is. I just have to separate these two sides of my life until I get back, like Church and State. I'll deal with Andrew first, then head home and face Nash. He'll either be able to move forward and we could have a real go at a relationship or he won't. I'm prepared for either.

Texts have come from both my Mama and Cole which means Wade has filled them in. Mama's were sweet and encouraging, telling me to be patient like she said. Cole's weren't angry, but gruff, asking me how I could let this happen with someone who is practically family but then adding in that he's here if I want to talk. He's usually the calmer one of my two brothers.

I wash over every moment with Nash in the last two months. I knew who he was, I just didn't see him coming. And if I'm being completely honest, I would never have been able to stop this even if I had.

I push the door open to El Fonzos and nostalgia hits me. I spent many fun nights here with my friends in college—all of whom I have since lost touch with. The wide, yet still intimate, space is brick on both sides with sprawling glass windows at the front facing out onto Stewart Street. Edison lights twinkle overhead and moody Italian instrumentals play over the sound system.

Andrew is already seated in the busy restaurant but I spot him through the crowd in the dark space.

He raises a hand and I head toward him, wondering what I ever saw in him. He looks worn and tired, as if these last few months haven't been easy on him. I feel sorry for him. He'll never know the feeling of what I have with Nash. Andrew doesn't even know how to love someone, he doesn't even love himself, and because of that, he'll probably always live an empty life.

"Andrew," I say as he stands and squeezes my hand.

We sit, and awkward silence overtakes us.

"Did you get everything sorted out while you were here?" he asks as he peruses the menu.

"Yes, the shipping company is coming in the morning to take the belongings I want back to Kentucky."

The server comes to our table and Andrew orders red wine while I order an iced tea. I've had enough wine in the last two days to meet my quota.

We talk awkwardly about the technical side of the condo sale and the weather, new items on the menu. I start to wonder how I'll ever make it through this meal. Were things this forced before?

Errant chattering beside us draws my attention away from Andrew as familiar faces come through the front door. David and Rachel Thompson and Bradley and Lenora Stanton—Andrew's best friends and colleagues—approach our table.

I look from them to Andrew and then back to them.

"Sorry we're late, traffic was a nightmare," Rachel says as she reaches out to me for a hug.

I'm stunned where I sit before her, and I turn to look at Andrew again.

Rachel's Chanel No. 5 perfume washes over me and her silky red hair presses against my cheek as she hugs me but I don't take my eyes off of Andrew.

"They wanted to see you, I thought we could all have dinner together like old times," he says, a smug look on his face.

CHAPTER FIFTY-THREE
Nash

I pull my hood over my head. Seattle is cold, busy as fuck and rainy. Sure, it's cultured and lively, but I don't see any comparison to the rolling hills and sweeping valleys of Kentucky.

The air is thick with fog as I stalk into the restaurant I saw CeCe head into a few minutes ago. I've been tracking her whereabouts, thanks to none other than Ginger, who came in clutch and is also worried about CeCe spending part of this week alone with her dickhead ex.

I'm giving her space but if she thought for one second I was letting her do this alone with Andrew, she's fucking crazier than I am. If he doesn't touch her or try anything, then I'll stay in the shadows and meet her at the airport tomorrow. I booked a flight on the same one she's taking home.

But, if he even gestures to her the wrong way, I'll rearrange his face and revel in every second of it. Everything in me tells me he's just waiting for his opportunity, and I'm never wrong when it comes to my gut feelings about people. I've had his number pegged since the moment I laid eyes on him in the middle of Main Street.

I sit at a table in the dark corner where I can keep an eye on CeCe through the sea of people as the waitress drops a menu in front of me. I smile and order a coke. I'm fucking exhausted and some caffeine is just what I need.

After I took the night off from the bar Sunday night, I drank a half a bottle of bourbon and scrolled through photos of CeCe's beautiful face on my phone while I blared every song Shania Twain ever made.

I woke up Monday at 3:13 a.m. in a cold sweat, sick to my stomach with the nightmares I haven't had in weeks since CeCe started sleeping beside me. In fact, there were many nights I woke up well past 3:13 with her hot little body beside me and felt comfort. Peace, for the first time in my life, and I'm the fucking bastard that didn't tell her how I felt that before she left.

The only difference in my dream this time was that in the front seat of that car, it was CeCe and Wyatt, not my parents. The look in Wyatt's eyes in my dream haunted me, before he looked back at me from the front seat and said, *"Be there for them, especially the girls."*

The sheer weight of what an asshole I had been hits me like a Mack truck. I had one fucking shot to prove I was worthy of CeCe and I let her down—my fear and panic crippled me. Not fighting for her when I had the chance and telling her she's become my whole fucking world was the biggest mistake I've ever made.

Her words replayed through my mind like a reel. *Love can be here one day and the next it can all go up in smoke.* Those words, along with a hot shower and some Gatorade sobered me right the fuck up. I got my shit together, called my family and headed to the ranch, ready to risk everything and lay it all on the table.

It was just like any other Monday when I walked through the front door, only I had Jo invite Ginger and Olivia. I owed them all, every one of them, and I intended to speak my piece.

Wade grunted at me when he saw me come through but Cole looked indifferent. He poured me a glass of bourbon and slid it across the island. Although the last thing I felt like doing while still hungover was drink, I took it and knocked it on the table before clinking glasses with him—for Wyatt.

"Mabel is with Gemma tonight, so if you want to talk, you've got the floor. I didn't like this one bit when Wade told me, but now, if you can prove to me you're serious, I actually think you might be good for CeCe," Cole said to me, under his breath. I nod, grateful for his small vote of confidence.

I looked around to the people I loved like my family, all of them, even the fucking pain-in-the-ass Ginger Danforth and laid it bare. I told them everything.

"Gimme one good reason not to smack you upside the head, Nash," Ginger started.

"Take it easy, slugger," Cole muttered to her as she cuffed him in the shoulder beside her.

I cleared my throat and took total command of the room, all eyes on me. I knew I had to start off with a bang.

"I deserve that, I should've told you all this before but I really fucking love her, I didn't expect to love anyone, ever. This isn't a fling. CeCe is it for me. She's my future." I looked directly at Wade.

"She's everything to me, and now I'm afraid I may have lost her by not saying so when you came in the other night."

"You haven't lost her," Ginger piped up across the table.

"She's miserable in Seattle. I could hear it in her voice this morning when I talked to her. She's hoping you come to your damn senses when she comes home Wednesday."

"I thought the same thing," Olivia added. "Like she's just biding her time until she can come home. She said she wasn't prepared for how uncomfortable she feels in that apartment."

My chest tightened up immediately at the thought of CeCe being uncomfortable in any way.

"I'm sorry we didn't tell you all when this began, but neither of us could've predicted it. I love you all, you're my family, and fuck, I love that beautiful, spark of a woman who lights me up like a firefly in the night more than anyone or anything. It's important to me you understand my intentions. I'm going to Seattle. I'm done leaving CeCe on her own. She'll never face anything on her own ever again. I don't trust that Andrew fucker for one second. I can't explain it, but my gut is telling me something is off about this whole trip."

Mama Jo's hand came across the table to mine and covered it as best she could with a weathered palm.

"I love you like my own son, Nash. There isn't a man on this earth I would feel more comfortable with loving my baby, and I know Wyatt would say the same thing if he were here. You have our blessing."

I covered her hand with mine and looked at Wade.

"I'm sorry, brother. I'm sorry you had to find out the way you did, and most of all, I'm sorry I didn't speak up the other night."

Wade leaned in to me across the table. "You better fucking be the stand-up man she needs. Just because I've known you my whole life doesn't mean I won't hesitate to kick your ass if I have to." He grimaced across the table at me.

"If I fuck this up, I'll welcome it." I grinned back.

"And no PDA. I want to keep my food in my stomach when

I see you together," Cole added with a shudder, earning another smack from Ginger.

"Just because you're incapable of anything other than fuckboy emotion doesn't mean everyone else should keep their love under wraps. I think it's beautiful." She smiled at me and I almost found myself liking her for a second.

"Yeah, just hush your mouth, boy. It's adorable," Mama Jo noted to Cole and then whispered to me, "You have her heart, boy. Do good by it."

I nodded and ignored the stinging at the bridge of my nose for the woman that was for, all intents and purposes, my mother for half my life.

"Fuck me." Wade surprised us all as his grumpy-ass grimace broke into a wide grin.

I only see Wade smile like that once, maybe twice, a year.

"Don't expect me to actually settle down."

I smiled back, remembering our conversation in the barn at the beginning of the summer. *He'd settle down when I do.*

"Better get on that, bud," I laughed, as he punched me on the shoulder.

"To Wy. And to Nash and CeCe." Jo raised her glass of bourbon and the rest of us followed with a table tap and a swallow.

"Let's eat," Jo added as I sat with my family for the rest of our typical Monday night dinner.

After a quick flight yesterday from Cincinnati, a check-in at the Four Seasons across town from her condo—far enough that I can keep myself from going to her when she doesn't need me,

I'm cold and I'm wet. And I'm ten seconds—or one of Andrew's hands touching CeCe again, whichever happens to come first—away from knocking him to his ass one final time, taking my girl home and telling her how fucking desperately in love with her I am as I beg for her forgiveness for acting like a total asshole on Saturday. Then I'll be rightly burying myself in her every second I can until a natural disaster or death forces us from my house.

I order some alfredo, realizing I haven't really eaten anything but a protein bar today, and watch CeCe's face from across the room. She looks stiff and uncomfortable as she browses the menu and I fucking love it. I revel in it.

It definitely would've gutted me if she looked happy and relaxed around the douchebag. I see her tap her high-heeled clad foot and absorb her beauty as I watch her order. She's casual but perfect in black tights and open heels with a long loose button down silk blouse.

The two of them seem to be chatting quietly as I wolf down my food. I'm half-finished as a loud, obnoxious foursome comes into the restaurant, they look way too expensive to be eating here and they head directly over to CeCe's table. The copper haired one—who looks like she's had more plastic surgery than her twenty-something-face warrants—throws herself into CeCe's tense arms. I can see CeCe's face over Fancy's shoulder and she's hating every second of this. It appears like a little group date and I'm getting the vibe CeCe had no idea these people were coming.

From what Ginger said, CeCe and Andrew were supposed to be meeting to discuss the deal while buyers went through the condo. Doesn't seem like any deals are going to be talked about. It seems like an ambush, and CeCe's at the center of it.

My knuckles turn white as I grip the table. I'm giving her all of five minutes to get out of this on her own.

CHAPTER FIFTY-FOUR
CeCe

"Andrew said you were coming back into town, we're all so glad to hear it, he's just been lost without you," Rachel whispers as the three men talk work stuff across the table.

"I'm not, I'm here to pack up my things."

My mind is reeling, and more than once I'm asking myself why I'm still sitting here. Why don't I just stand up and throw something at Andrew across the table? I already know the answer. Doing that would fuel him. It would give him a reason to say I'm crazy, and then it would be poor Andrew. He'd be the victim and I'm not giving him the satisfaction. I'm going to eat this meal, get the fuck out of his condo and go home after tomorrow's meeting.

"We were hoping you two had worked things out when he invited us. We really miss you."

Yeah, right.

They really miss gossiping about me the same way they do everyone in our social circle. These girls are the Real Housewives of Seattle types and they don't have much below the surface. Drama is their cornerstone.

"That's not happening. I have a life in Kentucky now. A job I'm proud of." *Hopefully, I still do.*

"We just think maybe you're being a little overdramatic," Lenora says, her glossy pink lips turn into a pitying smile.

"We don't have powerful men without putting up with a little indiscretion every once and a while. It's just something you have to accept. Every man ventures out at some point. At least when these ones do, we have a luxury condo and a black Amex to soften the blow." Lenora chuckles a regal laugh, and I stare at her incredulously.

Did Andrew bring these women here to try to convince me to go back to him?

Suddenly, my stomach is churning. Everything I hated about this life comes flooding back to me and I need out. I look at Andrew across the table.

"Excuse me," I say to the table, grabbing my purse as I beeline for the ladies' room.

I can feel Andrew on my heels as I round the corner for the rest room.

"Cecilia," Andrew calls

I spin around in the dark hallway. Red neon glow of the rest room signs light it.

"I can't believe you brought them here!" I whisper-yell. "Did you put them up to that ridiculous little speech too?"

"Someone needs to talk some sense into you, CeCe. The reason I sold the condo is to give you what you've always wanted. I'm buying a house in Lawrenceville." He mentions a nearby town in the suburbs. "Where you've always wanted. I want to settle down, raise a family together. I know now how wrong I was, how I was even wrong to come to Laurel Creek when I wasn't ready to give you everything you wanted then."

Am I having a stroke?

"Andrew, we're *over*. I'm not coming back here. I have a

life, a job, my friends, I'm closer to my mom than I have been in years and I'll never trust you. Not to mention—I don't love you."

Andrew steps forward, his signature Burberry scent fills my nostrils. I used to love it, now it makes me queasy. He places his hands on either side of me against the wall.

"Yes, you do. You don't mean that. I miss you, doll, and I'm done being nice. You're coming back to me whether you want to or not. I always get my way, tell me what you want and I'll make it happen," he whispers.

I shudder. I should've known by that nickname. That's all I was—his trophy, his doll.

I panic. My mind reels as I come to terms with the reality that he did all of this to get me here, and I wonder briefly if signing in person with Gary was even a necessity.

Andrew has lost his fucking mind if he thinks he's going to touch me. I quickly run through my plan of kneeing him in the balls like Ginger said and escaping out the front door before he can follow me. I'd have to go to a hotel—

"Not one more fucking step." I'm having an out of body experience as I hear Nash's voice from behind Andrew.

I turn to meet Nash's eyes and my mouth falls open. He's dressed in all black, his dark hair hangs over his forehead and the vines inked on his neck creep out from under his hoodie. He looks sinister and he looks like he's about to *kill* Andrew.

Andrew turns and registers the shock of seeing him there, but then he grins. Cocky on his own turf. "Of course he is here." He says to me then turns back to face Nash.

"This is between me and my fiancée," His hand reaches down to touch my face but I manage to duck out of the way and dart out of his grasp, hiding behind the safety of Nash.

I don't care why he's here or how he knew where to find me, only that I'm glad he is.

He was right all along. Andrew lied to me to get me here so he could try to pressure me into coming back to him. I'm convinced he doesn't even care about me. He just cares about *winning.*

Nash wastes no time. He moves toward Andrew and wraps a large hand around his throat, pinning him against the wall, and lifting him with one hand until his toes graze the floor.

Andrew claws meekly at him and grunts.

"I don't think you quite understand all the ways I'd be happy to hurt you. I've been fucking dreaming of them."

"Lawsuit..." Andrew bites out

Nash chuckles evilly. "You're such a fucking pussy. I told you that you would never see CeCe again without me. Now I'm telling you that this is the last time you'll ever see her." He uses his spare hand to clap Andrew twice on the face. Hard. "You're going to meet her truck tomorrow to send her things to Kentucky, 9:30, got it, *Drew?* And if you ever call her your fiancée again, I'll rip your fucking tongue out with my bare hand."

Andrew struggles for breath, his red face quickly darkening. A moment passes and I fear Nash may not let him go, but just as I open my mouth to say something he drops a gasping, purple Andrew to the ground and turns around, grabbing my hand, and pulls me toward the door, tossing a hundred-dollar bill on a table on the other side of the restaurant from where Andrew and I were sitting. I look back at it over my shoulder and register that he's been here the whole time.

Nash walks quickly, I scamper behind him, the anger radiating off of him. He speaks quietly and calmly to me in the rain. "The first thing you're going to do is call that fucking lawyer in the morning and tell him you want a separate appointment from Andrew to sign and I'll go with you."

"Nash—"

"And you're not staying one more night in that fucking condo."

"Nash—"

"You'll stay with me at the Four Seasons."

"Nash!" I yell

I stop dead in my tracks and drop my hand from his.

He follows suit, spinning around to face me as I finally get through to him.

"What are you doing here?" I whisper. "How did you know where I was? Were you following me?"

"Yes," he says it confidently, moving toward me in the rain and gripping both of my shoulders. "There is nothing I wouldn't do to keep you safe and I knew he was up to something."

"Nash, I don't want you to give me what you can't. I don't want to ask you to be someone you're not, because you're fucking great the way you are. It's okay that we were just a phase. You didn't have to follow me across the country. With time, I think we can be—"

"Just stop talking, Rae." He grips my face with both of his large palms and tilts my head just enough to meet my lips with his in one soft, searing kiss.

"We're not a phase. We're the exact opposite of a phase. You're my always. I fucking love you more than I've ever loved anything in this life and I came here to make sure you knew it. Following you across the country is nothing. I'm going to follow you everywhere you go for the rest of this life. And then, I'm going to follow you into the next."

Nash's lips come back down on mine in the middle of 6th Ave, and my heart beats rapidly in my chest as I kiss him back with all the passion I feel for him, knowing how hard that would be for him, knowing what he's doing. He's letting go. Trusting me. Trusting us.

"I love you so much," I whisper as he pulls his lips back from mine. It feels so good to say it.

"I'm so fucking sorry, CeCe. I should've spoken up when Wade walked in on us. I should've been what you needed and I wasn't. I'll spend every second of every day making that up to you, if you'll let me."

"I'm sorry, too. I knew what you could offer me, Nash, and I want you with all my heart. We'll take everything else one step at a time."

Nash shakes his head, his lips braise mine, the taste of him and the rain sends heat to my core as he smiles into my lips.

"I don't need any time, little firefly. I want it *all*. I want the birthdays, the babies, the holidays, the lazy Sunday mornings making pancakes for our kids. I want to be their hockey coach, fish with them in the creek, and I want to complain when you ask me to clean out the garage and fix the leaky faucet. I want to sit on the porch with you and drink coffee every fucking morning. CeCe, I want a life with you. One I'm fucking terrified to lose."

Tears spring to my eyes as I reach my hand up to his stubble covered jaw.

"Get me out of this rain, Mr. Carter," I whisper into his lips as he grins.

"I love you, my little firefly, my little ray of sun." His thumb traces my cheek as I kiss him, picturing all the beautiful things he just filled my head with as tears roll down my cheeks.

CHAPTER FIFTY-FIVE
Nash

CeCe is with me and that's all that matters. I turn to look over at her beside me in the back of the cab just to make sure she's real and she's really here. CeCe didn't get angry that I stalked her across the country to Seattle —she seemed grateful, she didn't second guess my apology, she just kissed me back and let me in like I've always belonged in her arms and it made me fall even more in love with her. She's perfect, she's the sunlight in the corners of my dark and other-wise doomed soul.

She's my little firefly, my Rae and I'll never stop proving to her that I mean the words I spoke. Never.

We made it back to her condo in record time, packed up the last of her personal items and got the fuck out of there. CeCe didn't even look back as she dropped the key on the counter and let the door click behind her.

Her eyes meet mine in the dark of the cab now and the need to touch her takes over my body, it's primal. I slide a hand between her thighs, over her silky tights and find the heat already waiting for me at the apex. Fuck, it's only been three days but I missed her so fucking much, it hurts. Her hand covers mine as my fingers squeeze the fleshy goodness of her thighs.

I look out the window, gathering my bearings about where we are and how far across the city we still have to go. The cab driver in the front seat is wearing AirPods and I can hear his podcast through them from here. I use my thumb to find the sweet little berry between her legs, I press lightly and she pants out a weathered breath in the dark. I circle her clit as her breath increases with my every touch.

"You're gonna have to be quiet, baby," I whisper to her, and she nods.

CeCe leans her head back on the seat and I slide my hand into her tights, shielding her with her tote bag so there's no chance the driver or a passerby sees what's mine. All the blood in my body rushes to my cock as I slide a finger over her center. I use her arousal to circle her clit.

I can't wait to put my mouth on her. So soon... fifteen minutes until we get to the hotel. Fifteen minutes to paradise.

"I still haven't completely forgiven you," she whispers with a grin, but she isn't protesting.

"That's okay, baby, I just want to make you come. You can forgive me later."

I feel CeCe squeeze her thighs together around my hand and grind into my palm that presses against her pussy. Her breathing is shallow and uneven but she stays as quiet as a mouse in the backseat of the cab as I fuck my middle finger in and out of her without even moving, only using the muscles of my forearm. I continue fucking into her, adding another finger to her tight, wet heat as Seattle rain pelts against the windows. I whisper into her ear how pretty she looks when she comes and what a good girl she is for staying quiet.

She props an elbow in the window and places a long, graceful finger between her lips and bites down as I feel her pussy clench around my fingers. My cock pulses against my zipper as I feel her legs quiver with her orgasm, her head falls back against the seat and the tiniest little squeaking noise leaves her lips, once, then twice as she falls apart over my digits.

"Nash..." she whispers.

My eyes meet the cab driver's in the front seat. He's oblivious as he pushes out the last five minutes of our drive. I pull my fingers out of her tights and suck them clean, then kiss her while I wait not so patiently to pull up to our hotel so I can ravage her.

The Four Seasons is quiet when we enter.

"You've been here since yesterday?" CeCe asks as we enter the lobby, understanding my need to be near her.

I sling her bag over my shoulder and nod. The only thing I can think about is tearing every strip of clothing off her body.

"I couldn't let you be here alone. I knew there was a good possibility you would need me, but I wanted to let you be unless you did. I hope you understand why I had to come."

"I was just trying to prove I could do it on my own. I'm glad you were there. As soon as I saw you, I knew I was safe."

I squeeze her hand as we get to the elevator and wait to make it to the tenth floor.

The moment the door to my room clicks shut behind us, my mouth is on hers, claiming her.

I've never been so desperate for her in my life as I pull her down on top of me in the overstuffed chair in the sitting room of my suite.

The thought went through my mind more than once over the last few days that I may never get to be with her like this again and that makes this moment even sweeter. A tiny moan escapes her lips as she kisses me back slowly. She settles into the rhythm I offer her and matches me, letting her lips trail down my throat like the little vixen has nothing but time to torture me. I feel her tiny grin into my neck as her plush lips turn up into a smile.

"I'm not letting you off the hook this easily," she whispers as she slips out of my grip and stands.

I move to stand and follow her but one tiny hand pushes me back down to the chair.

"Not yet, baby," CeCe coos as she backs away leaving me in the chair, so desperate for her I can hardly fucking see straight.

CHAPTER FIFTY-SIX
CeCe

"You're feeling regretful, huh baby?" I ask as Nash half growls at me from his place across the small space.

I know my power in this moment, and I know I've got one shot to make him realize that even though I may forgive him, I will never, ever put up with him not standing up for me in a moment where I need him ever again. If he's my ride or die, he's going to goddamn well prove it.

"Rae..." he warns, his voice so deep it hits my core directly but I don't give in.

Instead I tease him, I remove my tights first, sliding them down my thighs until they reach my ankles. I kick them off, leaving my black heels in place which earns another, "CeCe... fuck," from Nash who once again tries to stand.

I shake my head and simply say, "Patience."

Incredibly, he listens and sits back down.

Power surges through my veins and fuels me further with his total and utter submission.

I finger the buttons on my shirt slowly, undoing each one leaving seconds in between. When I reach the last one, I slide the silky blouse off my shoulders and peering down at him, I ask, "Well? just how sorry are you?"

Nash doesn't miss a beat. "The sorriest I've ever fucking been," he grunts with a tense jaw as he instinctively reaches for himself over his jeans.

I drop the blouse from my outstretched hand and stand before him in just my heels, my bra and panties. Quickly unhooking my bra behind my back, I pull it away from my chest one arm at a time, and my nipples instantly harden when the air hits them. Just to torment him, I make sure to squeeze my breasts together enticingly as I let my bra hit the floor. It's the only sound in the room.

Nash groans, a deep rumble from his chest as he watches me.

"I can tell you mean it, baby," I say. "You're mine and I'm yours. We're a team, right?"

Nash nods. "Fuck, yes."

My thumbs hook into my flimsy panties and I slide them down over my hips pulling one leg out at a time so they dangle around my left ankle. I take a wide stance in my heels and cock a hip to the side, naked before him. I pull the pin from my hair so it tumbles down around me and kick the panties off, standing bare in front of him. I've never been so wet and desperate for him with his surrender to my demands.

"Fucking Christ, CeCe."

"Just one more thing, then I'm all yours."

Nash undoes his buckle and slides his jeans off, his boxers barely contain the bulge that I'm sure is desperate for my touch. He grins an almost evil grin. He looks feral and fucking beautiful.

"Cecilia Rae, you have my word. I will never, ever let you down again. Now, let me touch what's mine before I involuntarily blow in my fucking boxers."

I shake my head and smile at him as I slide a hand down my waist and let my middle finger trail over my aching clit.

"*Crawl* to me, baby," I whisper, my voice raspy and sweet.

Nash doesn't even consider what I ask for more than one second. His knees hit the floor with a thud, he discards his shirt and begins moving toward me. My breathing increases as I watch his powerful inked body make his way toward me.

This man is the pinnacle. The basis for which all other men should be compared. He's the alpha and yet he's crawling, *to me*, like this form of worship is the easiest move he could ever make. When he arrives at my feet, his hands grip under my heels and his lips meet the tops of each of my feet, one at a time before he slides his massive hands up the back of my calves to my thighs, trailing kisses along the inside of my legs on the way up.

"You're the queen I crawl to. I'll kneel at your feet for the rest of my fucking life. Now, sit on your throne."

Before I can even register what's happening, Nash pulls me down onto his face, holding my body up with only his arms, gripping the flesh of my lower back as his tongue presses firmly up the slit of my dripping core and I shudder.

I moan and whimper uncontrollably as his tongue begins to make a meal of my pussy. Tight, perfectly pressured flicks swipe my clit as two fingers plunge into me. Some small compartment of my brain comprehends that he's holding me up with only one strong arm wrapped around me and his face.

My legs go weak as he speaks, his voice deep, full of gravel and commanding. The alpha rising from the ashes. "Come, little queen, soak my face. Baptize me... and then, I'll fuck you like the king that owns this pussy."

Nash feasts on me like this may be the last time he ever gets the chance. He is the king—the king of eating pussy.

I lose myself in him and the way he worships me with his

tongue, every movement pulling me deeper into the abyss of pleasure he offers. His fingers coax me in time with his lips, his teeth, and I'm spiraling again as if I have no choice but to come, his fingers violently fuck into me as his tongue stays over my clit and my release consumes me.

I don't hold back, I don't fight it in any way, I can't. I just let my body do what he commands and shatter, soaking him in the process and he revels in it, pushing his face deeper, taking everything I give him and groaning into me as he does.

"That's it, little firefly. Such a good girl. My good girl."

CHAPTER FIFTY-SEVEN
CeCe

I run my fingers through Nash's hair as my cries of pleasure grow silent.

"I—I've never felt anything like that," I whisper. My voice is hoarse.

Three or four seconds is all I get before he lifts me, gripping my thighs tight, his lips find mine in a deep and consuming kiss and I'm moving until my back hits the wall. He somehow frees himself from his boxers, driving his steely cock into me as deeply as he can with one violent thrust.

Murmurs of, "Fucking tight little cunt... my tight little cunt," leave his lips as his mouth finds my nipples, expertly sucking and teasing until the sweet coil of pleasure begins to form low in my belly all over again.

Nash is holding my body against the wall with his own, pinning me here, impaling me with his huge cock. My legs hang by his side and he grunts out a raspy sound as I rock my hips, forcing myself to slide down onto him all the way.

I cry out. I'll never get used to the way he fills me. The way he takes over my entire being the moment he enters me to his full depth.

"Fucking paradise..." Nash mutters as he begins to move. He isn't gentle, his thrusts and kisses are rough. A hand slides up from my breasts to my face and he traces my bottom lip with his thumb before he pulls it between his teeth and bites down hard, then licks over the pain, soothing it as I quiver.

"I dream of these perfect lips every night. *My* lips."

I moan and kiss him back, moving my tongue slowly, savoring him as he bottoms out inside me over and over. The textured grassy hotel wallpaper scratches at my back.

"This beautiful body is all *mine*." Nash pulls himself almost all the way out then drives into me as deep as he can.

"Ah...fuck," he growls as his deep, vicious thrust threatens to break me. He holds me up with one hand under my backside, the other is pressed against my chest, his long fingers trail up my throat, then wrap around it.

"These shoulders are *mine*." *Thrust*.

"These perfect tits are *mine*." *Thrust*.

"This sweet little cunt that was made just for me." *Thrust*.

"It's *mine*."

I'm dangerously close to coming just from his dirty words alone.

"Even your soul is *mine*." *Thrust*.

"All of you is fucking *mine*."

I squeeze my legs around his waist and my pussy clenches around his cock, tightening to a painful grip around him as my orgasm begins to surface.

"Yes, baby, all yours," I say breathlessly, knowing what he needs—to claim me, to convince him that I'm his and I'm never leaving.

Nash's hand grips my throat even tighter, my breathing turns shallow as he squeezes it, but I never once fear. I know I'm safe. I struggle for my breath as he holds me up fucking into me with a violent desperation.

"Fucking Christ, Rae. I love you," he breathes as I begin to come, my vision blackens as my breath turns even more shallow. I let go, I give in as his hand around my throat heightens the pleasure to the most intense level I've ever felt.

"I fucking love you, Nash, and all of you is *mine,* baby," I whisper as my vision goes white and a primal groan erupts from his chest.

I'm pulling every last drop from him as we fall apart together and I swear I can feel it. I can feel his release. Everywhere.

Nash Carter isn't just in my heart; he's taken over my entire being and I'm never, ever letting him go.

CHAPTER FIFTY-EIGHT
CeCe

"Why am I so nervous?" I ask Mama. "This is all in good fun."

"Because, baby, he's your man and you want him to win, even if it is for charity."

I nod. She's right, I do want to see him win. Three minutes to go in the third period of our charity game at the Sunset Festival, and the Pros and Townies are tied.

Nash looks so incredible out there. I've always watched him play, ever since I was young but now, it's different. He's an enigma on the ice. So fast, so much finesse, it's easy to see why he was nicknamed *The Rocket* by his fans. The Pros have really taken it easy on the Townies. They have allowed some real photo-worthy goals in, just to keep the hometown crowd happy, even though it's obvious to everyone that they could wipe the ice with them.

Nash has scored three out of the eight goals for his team on former Chicago Blackhawks goalie, Damien Smith, who's in net for the Townies.

Cole and Wade are reliving their childhood core memories and have had some good hearty races for the puck with Nash.

Everything Nash does on the ice is effortless, even letting the other team score a few and he looks so damn happy doing it, it's contagious.

"I'm just gonna be the one to say it, he's fucking hot," Olivia whispers, so Mabel doesn't hear.

I look at him through her eyes, navy blue jersey and matching equipment, the tiniest bit of his dark hair poking out from his helmet, sweaty and sinister looking out there. Yeah, he's really fucking hot.

Harry didn't even argue when Nash told him he had rush ordered custom jerseys for both teams. And as I sit in the stands in Nash's own jersey from the year he won the cup with the Stars, he looks up at me, winks then taps his heart with his thumb and points as he skates to the corner ice to take the face off. I smile back.

His name and number are on my back, matching his, and it feels damn good. We're a team. Now that Nash has admitted his feelings for me, it's like Pandora's box has opened. I feel lavished upon all day, every day, worshiped the way I now know I deserve, and I've never been happier.

The puck drops and Nash wins the face off passing to his old teammate, Cory Kane. The two of them take off down the ice, Cory sending the puck across to Nash who picks it up immediately, but the whistle blows as the ref calls offside, when it clearly wasn't.

Before I can stop myself, I'm standing and hollering profanities at Roger Booth, my old science teacher, for making a bad call.

Ginger grabs my arm, she's doubled over laughing. "Good thing you weren't with this man when he played in the NHL, you would've been kicked out of the rink," she snorts.

"It was a bad call," I say defensively, while I sit back down as all the women in my life laugh at me.

They faceoff again as the clock continues to wind down. Finally, Nash and his old teammate, Jackson Reynolds, have a two on one against Angus Brewer, a big construction worker from town who plays recreational hockey. Nash passes to Jackson, and I'm sure Jackson is going to take the shot on Damien but at the very last second, he sends it back over to Nash who tips it in right over the shoulder of Damien and the whole arena goes absolutely crazy—including me.

I'm jumping up and down, high fiving Mabel and my mom. I'm a proud puck bunny up in the stands for the man that has my heart and I wouldn't have it any other way.

The day has been incredible, I swear everyone in the surrounding counties came out. The weather has been perfect, and it even felt like a bit of fall was in the air. I've never been so proud to be a part of something in my life, seeing all the smiling faces from our town and surrounding areas, happy vendors, happy local business owners, watching my man in his element.

As I say goodbye to my family and take the time to visit with many of the vendors that showed up, I allow the feeling that this was the first of many things Nash and I will do together that will go this smoothly. My pride to work with him extends well beyond the fact that I am immensely in love with him. It comes from our shared love for this community and the huge heart that he has for it. It's that he wants to give back and really put down his roots in Laurel Creek. Nash says it's his second phase in life, his phase with me. His forever, and as long as he keeps looking at me the way he is now coming towards me, freshly showered from the dressing room, I'm in for whatever he suggests and probably always will be. Because where Nash Carter is concerned, I'm pretty much at his mercy.

"Pants off, leave the jersey," Nash growls as he presses me up against the wall in his front entryway.

"You're not even going to let me get in the door? Take my boots off?"

Nash groans as his hands move swiftly over my body, like I'm his lifeline and he's at rough sea without me. "Oh, I'm going to let you in the door alright. I got the game winning goal today," he rasps into my ear. "I've been so good, baby. I deserve a reward."

"Is that so?" I ask, chuckling at his excuse to have me submit to whatever it is he wants to do to me.

"And what exactly would that be?"

"You on my bed and give me total control, no questions asked, but you have to trust me."

I grin. "You have been *so* good, baby," I breathe out as his hands slide under the jersey I'm wearing and cup my breasts.

"Yeah, I have. It's hard to play hockey and win when you're in the stands wearing my number, looking like a fucking walking wet dream." He pinches my nipple between his thumb and forefinger and my back bows off the wall. He uses this opening to slide his hands down and lift me up around his waist, carrying me toward the bedroom—what feels like our bedroom—at top speed. Nash deposits me on the bed and pulls my jeans off, tossing them to who knows where and then he's on top of me kissing me, his hand meets the apex of my thighs and he groans.

"I'll never get used to how fucking ready you always are for me. Let's see how much more ready we can make you, yeah?"

He gets off the bed and pulls his clothes from his body and

ventures into his bedside drawer, pulling out my beloved teal vibrator.

"Where did you...when did you get that?" I ask, heat coiling between my legs at the idea of him coming anywhere near me with it.

"I brought it from my dirty girl's bedroom today. I've been dying to see you use this since the day I heard you had it. I can't stop imagining how you make yourself feel good with this little fuck toy."

He turns it on and the quiet hum fills the air.

"Tell me, baby"—he slides it down my throat, and I shudder —"who did you think about while you were using this?"

He guides it up over my shoulder, down my arm, then under my breasts and I arch off the bed, hoping he'll keep moving with it.

"You," I say. "Since the day I came home, you."

"Mmhmm," he answers. "That's what I thought."

CHAPTER FIFTY-NINE
Nash

"And just what did you think about?"

"Y-you... touching me," CeCe admits as I run the silky head of the vibrator up her thigh.

I kiss her as I move the wand closer to her already wet core, letting her breathing stiffen as she waits. I grin at her.

"Get up on your knees. Hands on my headboard, baby. And lose the jersey now, I want to see everything," I whisper.

She's panting and nodding and desperate for this hum between her legs.

I run the wand against CeCe's inner thigh and she white knuckles the headboard but her body is pliable and melty in front of me.

I trail it up over her ass onto her spine watching her pant with anticipation. Her thick, golden hair touches the base of her tailbone as her head falls back. I'm the luckiest son-of-a-bitch on the planet.

"Nash..." she whispers, silently begging me to make her feel good.

"Yes, little firefly?"

"I need—"

"I know. Spread your legs, baby."

CeCe does as I ask and widens herself on her knees as I bring the wand around her front and rest it against her nipple. Her head falls backward onto my chest and she pushes her chest out to allow me easier access. Not wanting to leave her other nipple out of the fun, I taunt it too as she moans and whimpers the cutest little sounds I've ever heard.

I'm so fucking hard I can barely stand it. I resist every single urge I have to not just slide into her tight, wet heat from behind. I should win a goddamn medal for withstanding this moment.

She lets out a needy gasp, and begins to move her hips, desperate for relief and I just know that pussy is swollen and desperate for my touch. I bring the wand down over the soft curves of her waist and her hips as she shivers beneath it. I reach around her waist with my free hand and pull her close, sliding the wand between her legs and resting it on her clit.

"Oh...." she lets out an exasperated gasp as the wand buzzes and hums against her.

I love these moments with her where her pleasure surprises even her. Her back presses against my front as she grinds against the toy between her legs for me. I kiss her neck and smile into it, breathing in the fruity scent of her skin.

"That's it, baby...it feels good, doesn't it?"

"Oh God... so good."

CeCe rocks against the wand but her ass is pushing into my cock with every movement and it's about to make me come all over her. I pull back to control myself, wanting this moment to be only about her pleasure.

I slide the wand down so CeCe can control the pressure she rides the vibrator with, holding it in place for her as she finds her rhythm in seconds, while I sit in awe behind her, watching the entire scenario unfold. My cock is past the point of hard. It's an inhuman kind of hard as she moves. Every crevice and line of her back to her waist is torture, sheer torture, as she grinds against the toy with the shamelessness I hoped.

I tell her how beautiful she is as her head falls backward, and her hair tickles the top of her plump ass in front of me. I tell her how much I love her, how stunning she is when she comes, and she moans louder with every bit of praise I offer her.

Waves of ecstasy roll through her body from her toes all the way up as a thin layer of sweat covers her body.

"Good girl, Rae. Come for me, baby," I whisper in her ear as she falls apart, while I glide the wand from the tight rosebud of her asshole back to her clit in a steady sort of movement, back and forth.

My balls are so tight, I fear I may lose it with her. The front row seat I have to the fireworks in front of me is almost too much as she comes, my lips trailing her back and her shoulders.

CeCe calls my name into the silence of the room against the hum of the wand.

"Oh God...Nash," she says as she starts to come down.

I give her no time to catch her breath, I'm beyond desperate for her. I shut the toy off and slide two fingers into her dripping cunt and groan with mad desire for her as she does for me. I crook them into her and fuck her tight, wet paradise as desire rebuilds for her, and then when she begs me, I sheath myself inside her in one smooth deep thrust, calling her name as her body welcomes me home.

"I'd fucking live here forever," I tell her and I would— inside her, as part of her, as hers as she is mine. Always.

CHAPTER SIXTY
Nash

Six Weeks Later

"**E**verything has to be perfect. You got your part done?" I take my hat off and run a hand through my hair.

Wade can see the look of panic on my face.

"You need to relax. Fuck, if a woman ever ties me up in bunches like this, shoot me where I fucking stand," he grunts out as he brushes his horse.

Ivy snorts from the stall next to us. "I don't think you have any fear of that happening, Chief. You'd have to have human emotions for that."

"The girl's got a point." I grin.

She's working out well, after only two weeks on the job. She's got Mama Jo convinced and almost has Wade convinced to make a derby run.

Ivy gets under Wade's skin every chance she gets and I swear some small part of her loves it. On paper, she's a pro. In real life, she's still a pro but she's also a brassy-mouthed free spirit. Playing her worn acoustic guitar under a tree while she eats or reads. Mama Jo calls her a modern flower child. Wade calls her "Trouble."

"Don't you have something better to do than eavesdrop and insult your boss?" he bites out.

Ivy tosses her long black braid over shoulder and pats Wade on the chest as she breezes by him.

"Yeah, but I've only pissed you off twice today, so I figured one more snide comment was warranted."

She turns to me and smiles wide. "You've got this, Nash. Everyone knows how crazy you are about her, don't be nervous. There ain't no need, baby." She pats me on the cheek.

"Thanks, girl," I mutter, blowing out a breath as Ivy leaves the barn.

"Don't forget to meet me at three for Crenshaw's saddle training. And don't be late this time, Trouble," Wade barks at Ivy.

"Can't fuckin wait, Chief," she calls back, waving a hand over her head.

"Fucking Christ, why couldn't I have found a nice polite, silent type?" Wade mutters

I shrug. "She's only like that with you because you do nothing but ride her ass twenty-four-seven. Give the girl a break. She's the best at what she does."

Wade makes a sound like, "Arghh."

"I know. It's really fucking annoying." He rubs his forehead and goes back to brushing his horse.

I chuckle and feel the nerves welling up in my chest. I don't know why I'm such a fucking nervous wreck.

I've been planning this night for almost two months. Ever since I looked up in the stands at the charity game of the Sunset Festival in August and saw CeCe cheering for my game winning goal in her Stars jersey. *My jersey.* It hung almost like a dress on her, but somehow, she managed to make it look fucking adorable paired with tights and boots.

When she turned to high five Mabel and the name Carter flashed before my eyes on her back, I knew. Well, I knew two things. One: I would make her an official Carter as soon as possible, and two: I really wanted to fuck CeCe in nothing *but* that jersey. I've been planning my first thought ever since. Of course, I was a fuck of a lot more confident when it was all just theory.

I call Ginger and Cole and finish my morning tasks before heading home to shower and take CeCe to the office. She's pretty much living with me now, and that's just the way I want it. I want her with me every second of every day and have almost successfully achieved that. We're inseparable.

GINGER

The photographer is arriving early, I'll pick her up and take her to my place. Everything is set. Calm down, I can tell you're sweating just from the way your voice sounded on the phone.

COLE

Stop busting his chops, woman. He's got a right to be nervous, she could say no.

GINGER

God dammit, Cole Emmett Ashby. You don't say that to a man at a time like this. I know your Mama taught you manners. Use 'em.

COLE

Retreat to your corner, Rocky. I'm just messing with him. We know CeCe is saying yes.

GINGER

Now you're just jinxing him.

> I'm starting to think this is a form of weird foreplay between you two.

COLE

Like fuck it is, you gotta actually like someone for that.

GINGER

Feeling is mutual and PS: you couldn't handle me anyway.

> Ok, I want out of this group chat, see you both later.

COLE

You're right, I already can't handle you on the best of days.

Nash has left the chat.
Cole added Nash to the chat.

COLE

We need to be able to talk to each other in two hours, stop being a bitch.

> Fine but if you're gonna foreplay text, do it in private.

GINGER

Fine.

COLE

Fine.

When I get home, CeCe is sitting at the dining room table, her golden hair is piled on top of her head in a big messy bun and she's wearing a black wool turtleneck dress with her glasses. She's on hold on the phone and reading from her beloved Kindle. She almost cried when the damn thing arrived from Seattle with the rest of her belongings.

She looks so mouthwatering that the urge to be scolded by the hot accountant in my kitchen makes my dick twitch. *My* hot accountant.

CeCe shakes her head at me, taking one glimpse at the look I'm wearing raking my eyes over her and taps her wrist.

Thoughts of propping her up on my kitchen table flee my mind when I remember we have a ten a.m. meeting with Harry to distribute the rest of the funds we earned and have finally received after six weeks from the Sunset Festival. The first totals already covered the start of the Lightning's season and watching those kids come in to play nightly provides me more pride than winning the Stanley Cup.

I mouth the word "later" to her as I hike my thumb toward the shower and disappear while she continues her call.

∞

"At least two more years," CeCe beams to Harry as she shows him all the particulars that can be paid for from our festival profits.

It was a massive success; Laurel Creek saw upwards of ten thousand visitors that weekend and the local shops and bed and breakfasts are singing our praises. We already have another planned for next August and even got some big sponsors asking to be a part of the whole day. CeCe is talking about making the event a two-day ordeal, and I just let her creative soul flow when she's brainstorming.

"That's beyond anything we could've ever expected," Harry says, scrubbing his face with his hand.

"We even have provisions to help the kids that can't afford equipment or the entrance fees. All raised by the community, no handouts," CeCe says, showing him the final totals on her laptop.

"The day was just incredible. Exactly what I pictured—family, community, grassroots, teamwork, and you two are a great team. So when do we start planning next year? Maybe we can help out some other organized sports in the surrounding communities too?"

CeCe nods in excitement. Her full lips turning up in the grin I love so fucking much.

"We're already on it, I'm just waiting on the municipality to give me answers on two consecutive dates we can secure. By our next meeting, I'll know more."

"Excellent. I can't thank you two enough. You're a great team," Harry says, standing.

As I watch CeCe, I can't help but picture her face tonight when I ask her to be mine forever.

$$\infty$$

I'm pacing, I need to calm down as I wait for CeCe to finish getting ready.

We're already running late, because she was waiting for confirmation that her condo sale went through, and that her portion of the funds were deposited, finally putting an end to that chapter of her life... only a week after the proposed closing date. The moment she told me the money was deposited, I breathed a heavy sigh of relief. Good fucking riddance, *Drew*.

Now, I can focus on tonight because every detail has been planned, right down to the outfits we are wearing. She doesn't know it, but when I bought the dress for her the other day, I planned it so we would coordinate together perfectly for the photographer who is coming in from Lexington.

When CeCe rounds the corner from our bedroom to where I'm standing in the living room, her beauty overwhelms me. The long black dress almost touches the floor and the slit that reaches her mid-thigh, offers a taunting glimpse of silky skin. The dress hugs every curve her small frame offers, long sleeves and a high neck seem modest and elegant, but I just know.

"Let's see the back, little firefly," I say as she obliges and turns, the expanse of her skin in the wide open back takes my breath away and dips all the way down to her tailbone.

"Beautiful," I whisper as I go to her and kiss the strawberry scented skin of her upper back and neck.

"We're not going to make it to our date if you keep kissing me like that." She giggles.

I sober myself up, there will be plenty of time for that—a lifetime, if she says yes.

"What are we doing?" she asks in anticipation.

"You'll see, I just have to stop by the Horse and Barrel and drop some files off before dinner," I say.

No turning back now... the velvet box is burning a hole in my pocket as I usher her through the door.

CHAPTER SIXTY-ONE
CeCe

Nash has been acting odd all day. He's never concerned with time but he kept checking in on me as I was getting ready, asking me if I needed anything.

It's been three months since the first night he stayed at my house the first time and he's calling it an anniversary dinner. He bought me this beautiful dress, and he's in a three piece suit, stealing my breath and looking so fucking incredible it's making me want to skip dinner.

I look at him as we drive, reaching my hand across to hold his, then running my fingers across the ornate, detailed infinity symbol with a tiny firefly perched in the center that he had tattooed on his wrist a month ago at the base of his ink sleeve— for me, he said, to remind me that he's mine forever. It's an exact replica of the necklace my father gave me and it shows me how much he loves me more than any physical gift he could ever give me.

"You okay?" I ask. "Are you feeling alright?"

Nash nods, staring straight out the window. The town is quiet on a Monday night when we reach it, we pull into the parking lot of the Horse and Barrel. It's empty as it always is on Mondays, and he puts the truck in park.

"Come with me?"

"I'm okay to stay here, I have these heels on." I hold an ankle up.

"Humor me, Rae. I don't want to leave you out here alone."

I roll my eyes. I'm used to Nash being overprotective but this is a little much.

He looks at me expectantly, and I know not to argue. He isn't leaving the truck without me.

I sigh and get out, making the short walk into the bar with him but when I enter, my senses are overtaken with the sight that greets me.

Instead of the usual scene of neon and low-hanging chandeliers, tables, and chairs, I'm greeted with a wide open, empty space. What seems like thousands of twinkling lights suspend from the ceiling like little fireflies in a netting of greenery. The entire space is lined endlessly with flameless candles, fresh roses and Kentucky honeysuckle. I take in so many things at once as my mouth falls open. The scent of all the fresh flowers is heady, beautiful and consuming.

"Nash... what is—"

He's pulling me to the center of the room into a portion of the dance floor that is surrounded by even more candles that are the only light in the room.

The opening strings of "From this Moment" by Shania Twain start to play so softly, almost like background music from an acoustic guitar in the corner, and my eyes turn toward it and meet Ivy in a pretty red gown sitting on an elegant leather stool in the dimly lit corner surrounded by lanterns.

She smiles at me and Nash speaks, "Cecilia, we're not celebrating an anniversary tonight, instead I want to celebrate the first night of the rest of our lives."

"Nash..." I say, because it's all I can get out.

"A wise man once told me to settle down, find a woman to share my life with, to love. That man, of course, was one of the greatest men I've had the pleasure of knowing, your dad. Now, I want you to know I didn't forget him. I went to him, to his grave, and told him my intentions, I told him that I love his only daughter more than I've ever loved anything or anyone in my life, and that if he gave me his blessing, I would love her with my whole heart every day until death took me. And even then, I'd move on to the next life and find her there, because a love like ours isn't limited by space or time. It's eternal."

He cups my face with his hand and tilts my chin. "It's infinite," Nash whispers as he kisses my lips.

I've known Nash in so many different ways over the years. I've always felt an unexplainable familiarity with him, but I'll never forget the look he gave me the night he stood under my porch lights in the summer, with the look that said out of all the people to walk this earth, that I'm the only one he wanted to let in. My Dad always said when you know, you know, and wow, do I know.

Tears prick my eyes as he speaks, and the guitar continues in the background, but I have no strength to talk or I risk a sob escaping from me.

"When I finished my conversation with him, it started to rain and I felt like it was him giving me his blessing. What do you say, little firefly? Will you get lost in the shuffle of this world with me, forever? Will you give me all of your smiles and all your tears? Will you let me make sure you have your coffee every morning and my arms around you every night? Will you let me love you with everything in me for the rest of this life and the next?" Nash pulls a robin egg blue, velvet box from his suit jacket and opens it up, dropping to one knee before me.

"I told you I'd kneel for you forever. It would be my greatest joy to be your husband. Will you marry me, baby?"

I'm nodding and crying, and I somehow manage to get the word "yes" out to him as many things happen simultaneously.

Flashes erupt in the space as someone takes our photos—a photographer? And suddenly, there are people everywhere. As Nash slides the beautiful, perfectly sized, pear-shaped diamond ring onto my finger, I squeal and jump into his arm as our family and friends come from God knows where to surround us in a flurry of activity, all of them dressed to the nines in evening gowns and black tie.

"I love you so much, CeCe Rae Ashby, soon-to-be Carter."

"I love you, Nash," I whisper.

The entire room blurs around us as his lips meet mine and everything I've ever dreamed of becomes my reality.

EPILOGUE
CeCe

Seven Years Later

"Ruby Rae, your daddy is gonna have your behind in a sling if you don't get your shoes on and get out to the truck!" I yell up the stairs to our five-year-old daughter. She's a little mini me, right down to the always running late, and she thinks it's endearing.

"I'm coming, Mama. I couldn't find my lucky charm." My blonde, blue-eyed beauty holds up her dad's Stanley cup ring on a chain in her chubby hand and grins.

I nod because I know she won't play without it tucked safely into her dad's pocket during her game. I usher her out the door, carrying my purse and her baby brother, Rex in his car seat.

Nash shuts the tonneau cover of the truck after dropping Ruby's hockey bag in and comes to me.

I still get butterflies every single time I look at him. Standing right in the same spot on our front lawn that we stood before all our family and friends seven and a half years ago under an arch of wildflowers and said our vows.

The day was perfect and rustic with little firefly-filled lanterns lining the aisle at sunset as Wade gave me away in a simple, elegant sheath dress, my hair wild and wavy, just the way Nash likes it, with flowers woven in. Seeing him standing at the end of that aisle with Cole and Mabel waiting for me in his rustic deep navy three-piece suit that matched his eyes perfectly, and a stark white shirt...I've never seen anything more stunning and I'd never been more certain. Nash Carter was my future and I've never looked back.

"Come on, Little Tendy," he says, ruffling Ruby's hair as he buckles her into her seat.

He smirks at me as I move to buckle in our nine-month-old son on the other side.

"This world revolves around her, little firefly. We're just living in it," he says to me.

"Don't I know it," I mutter.

Life is busy with two kids under five but it's so full of love and light. Of all the roles I've seen him fill, Nash the father and the husband are by far the sexiest and most incredible by a landslide.

He still never stops and runs our business at Olympia daily, but he stepped back from the Horse and Barrel when I got pregnant with Ruby, knowing being a father wasn't going to warrant a nightlife lifestyle. I still get out to the occasional Sangria Sunday with my girls when they aren't tied up with their own busy lives.

This family we've built is blissfully perfect and sometimes that still scares Nash but I remind him all we have is today and that almost always does the trick. But when it doesn't, blow jobs work very well.

We all get settled and start out of the driveway of our property. We moved into Nash's home on the creek when we got married, and when we found out six months later we were pregnant with Ruby, Nash insisted on putting on an addition at the side of the house to incorporate three more bedrooms and a full bathroom, as well as a playroom for the kids.

The winter Ruby was two, he built an ice rink in the backyard and bought her first pair of skates and her obsession was born. Now we're on our way to her first game of the season and her daddy is the proud coach of her team.

"Remember, baby, don't let them sweat you, you're a wall. You got this, they ain't getting nothing by Ruby Rae Carter." Nash looks at her in the review as he delivers his pep talk.

"I know that, Daddy. Easy peasy, lemon squeezy," Ruby quips happily from the backseat as Rex coos his agreement beside her.

When we get into the arena, I take Ruby to the change rooms to meet Nash's assistant coach, Mabel. At almost fifteen, Mabel is happy to help her Uncle Nash with his team, while she scopes out what boys are arriving to suit up for the games after Ruby's.

My family greets me in the stands as I put Rex in my wrap and wear him up to the spot we normally sit. All of them are here to witness Ruby's first game. Even Ginger and Olivia.

"CeCe Rae," Wade greets as I climb the bleachers and hug my Mama.

The twinkle in his eye is happy as he sips his hot chocolate.

"She ready for this?" he asks.

"She seems completely unfazed," I chuckle as Rex pats my face and I smile into his green eyes.

"Almost time to get the next one some skates, ain't it?" Ginger asks, nodding to Rex.

"Bite your tongue. Let him be my baby a little bit longer."

"Have you met your husband? I'm surprised he hasn't already got him trying."

"I've told him Rex has to be two. Gimme these baby years

while I can get 'em." I snuggle and kiss Rex's golden head as I say it.

The teams come through the doors, and the parents and friends in the stands cheer for them. I smile at my gorgeous husband in the box across from us. He's looking like he's coaching the Olympic hockey team, not the house league Laurel Creek Lightning.

He goes over the plays with the team, and sends them out to warm up, with Ruby Rae in net, stretching just like her daddy taught her. I wave at her and she waves back up at me. Seems like just yesterday she was Rex's age.

The game goes off without a hitch and Ruby only lets one goal in. The Lightning win and Nash beams with pride as he hugs his little girl after the game, patting her on the head.

"That's my baby," he says to her as she heads into the change room and I approach him.

"I'm pretty sure Wade looked like he was enjoying himself, like I saw multiple smiles," Nash says to me as he kisses me on the lips.

I look back at my brothers and my family coming toward us, Mama holding Rex and chatting to him like he's just her favorite little man.

"I think they're all happy these days," I say. "Time goes by so fast."

I turn back to Nash and he smirks at me sending heat to my core, just knowing his hands will be on me later sends a thrill through my blood.

"Speaking of which... you think maybe it's time to add to the team, baby?" I ask.

Nash kisses me again and smiles into my lips.

"If I've said it once, I've said it a thousand times. You hold the reins, baby, I'm just here for the ride, and I'll sure have fun trying, but..." He kisses me again, probably a little too eagerly for four o'clock on a Sunday in the community arena but I don't mind. "You might want to ask your boss how he feels about you taking another maternity leave..." He kisses my forehead as I roll my eyes.

"Ugh... he's such a hard-ass." I smirk as he kisses my lips and chuckles.

His bottomless blue eyes remind me one more time that I am, in fact, the luckiest woman in the world to be covered by Nash Carter's safe, warm arms as our perfect existence continues around us.

The End

Acknowledgments

To my amazing husband for accepting his place as number two, delivering me chai lattes and food while I write endlessly because my mind has been filled day in and day out with Nash Carter for months.

To my own amazing Not-Angels Tabitha, Ada, Wren, and Katie. Thank you for being with me through this process. You're stuck with me now through every dirty talking moment from here on out. Thank you for the incredible suggestions, laughs, and ah-ha moments that made this book the absolute best it could be. Cathryn, thank you for making my book into an actual beautiful book and not just a really long, confusing word document.

Caroline, there aren't enough words to write that could show you how grateful I am for your expertise, your patience, and hard work in bringing Nash & CeCe's story to publication. I am forever grateful to you all.

To you, my ARC readers, thank you. I may not do it better than anyone else, but I pour my whole soul into these stories, and every comment, like, share, edit, and mention is noticed and loved wholeheartedly. Finally, to my only Papa, the best grandfather a girl could ask for. Great advice giver, euchre player extraordinaire, Howdy spewing, duct-tape wielding, inappropriate joke telling, hand holding, bear of a man. You are both my Wyatt and my Papa Dean. I love you with my whole heart and miss your mind daily. As long as I can hold your hand, I will. I'll forever tap my bourbon on the table for you and utter your sayings.

IMAGE CREDITS

PLAYLIST

Alexa . . . play Nash & Cece's love story. https://open.spotify.com/playlist/703Yprm7IjtgUVEaHvQ4Yk

1. *Wondering Why*—The Red Clay Strays
2. *Wild Ones*—Jessie Murph, featuring Jellyroll
3. *Hey Driver*—Zach Bryan, featuring The War and Treaty
4. *Cover Me Up*—Morgan Wallen
5. *Any Man of Mine*—Shania Twain (CeCe's anthem)
6. *Takin' Pills*—Pistol Annies
7. *Feeling Whitney*—Post Malone
8. *Holdin' On to You*—Dolly Parton, featuring Elle King
9. *Shake the Frost*—Tyler Childers
10. *Simple Man*—Rhett Walker Band
11. *Jackson*—Johnny Cash and June Carter
12. *Cecilia*—Simon & Garfunkel
13. *Love the Lonely Out of You*—Brothers Osborne
14. *Foolin' Ourselves*—Evan Honer

Read on for an excerpt from the next book in the
Silver Pines Ranch Series

TRAINING THE HEART

by Paisley Hope

PROLOGUE
Wade

July

"In my defense, it was the *longest* slow burn in history. I just lost track of time, and then there was a detour on the way here . . ."

I shuffle down the front steps of the Big House, while this small, animated woman just rambles on beside me, trying to explain in way too much fucking detail the reason why she's late for her interview with me.

I stare out to the field wondering what the fuck she's talking about and what the fuck a *slow burn* is.

She continues laying out the entire damn plot as I breathe in the late morning Kentucky mountain air, knowing somehow that I'm going to regret asking this but fuck, I just need her to get to the goddamn point.

"Explain," I say.

"Explain? A slow burn? Or how the book made me late?" She doesn't even give me room to answer if I wanted to. "Slow burn is . . . you know, the part that leads up to . . . the spicy side of the book . . ."

Spicy?

She waits all of one millisecond for me to speak, and when

I don't, she continues. "Anyway, the main character I liked the best, he had just kissed her, finally . . . because the other man she was with, he had just finished, they were roommates—"

I stop and spin around, startling her as I look down at her with a face that I'm sure asks her what on earth she's talking about.

She blinks and looks up at me, realizing she definitely has gone off the goddamn rails here. But for some reason she *still* keeps talking. "Well, what I mean is, he was about to get his own turn with her and . . ." She trails off for less than one second, looking down at her boots, then starts again. "Any-who . . . I'm here now so I can find out later which one of them—"

Nope.

"Just . . . Jesus Christ . . . Do you understand what it means to be professional? At all?" I ask, stopping her from finishing that sentence because I somehow think that discussing her book—that sounds a hell of a lot like some kind of porn—might be considered sexual harassment, although at this moment, I think I might be the one being violated.

Her mouth pops open but she doesn't speak. I take that as my cue to continue walking.

"I'm sorry for being late and for wasting your time, Mr. Ashby," she says in a much more professional tone, as if I'm giving up on her before the interview even starts. Which, until right this second, I was.

I grit my molars. Something about the way she says my name all defeated like that brings me down a peg. Maybe my family is right. Judging by how nervous this woman sounds right now, maybe I was too abrupt with her when she showed up for her interview all of six minutes late. I just didn't have the patience. All I want is to get through this goddamn day and take a breather after a long as fuck morning with my lawyers and my ex, Janelle.

I stop my long stride again, ready to turn and face this little spitfire, to tell her we'll start the interview over on a much more professional level. Before I can even speak, I realize she's moving too fast and she's not looking up, so she doesn't even notice I've stopped until she plows right into me and stumbles backward in the grass.

"Fuck, shit. Fuck . . . I'm sorry," she offers as I grip her elbows easily in my hands to steady her.

"Look, Miss . . ." I let her elbows go as she regains her balance, trying hard not to notice how pretty her violet blue eyes are when she looks up into mine.

"Spencer." She says it as if it would be beyond rude that I'd forget her name. The one she just repeated when she met my family less than five minutes ago.

Okay, maybe it is, even for me.

"Right. Miss Spencer, I'm gonna cut the bullshit right now." I turn and start to walk again. She keeps up as I approach my office door and plow by two ranch hands who physically stop their work to check the woman out trailing beside me. I shake my head at them as we pass, because they're all a bunch of fucking hornballs on my ranch.

"I'm not looking for somebody inexperienced here," I say. "Even though it's only temporary, I need an experienced trainer to take Sam's place."

I push through my office door and she follows me. As I walk around the back of my desk, she stands on the other side, her worn-in jeans, perfectly fitted black T-shirt, and matching black cowboy boots, arms folded under her perky tits, holding them up like a little shelf. My eyes meet hers and I realize something I said pissed her right off.

"Oh, I get it, you're one of *those?* You think just because I'm young and a woman that I'm inexperienced?"

I take my hat off and toss it on my desk. *Fuck me, I'm the furthest thing from one of those. This bratty little—*

"I can see I'm wasting my time expecting better of you," she challenges.

I lean forward, placing my palms on my desk, speaking low so she realizes I'm done entertaining her attitude, and fuck, I'm the one in charge here—not her.

"It has nothing to do with you being a woman. Some of the most respected trainers in the industry are women. Hell, the trainer you're here to replace now is a woman."

Something in her eyes softens and looks almost sheepish as she drops her arms to her sides.

"Oh, I just assumed with the name Sam . . ."

"Samantha," I cut her off.

"Assumptions most always get you nowhere," I add gruffly.

I rake my hand through my hair and sit down, leaning back in my chair. She's got a feisty attitude, I'll give her that, and she's probably the prettiest woman I've laid eyes on in, hell, a really long time. Alright, she's fucking breathtaking. I'm talking my-dick-stood-at-attention-the moment-she-tossed-her-long-raven-colored-hair-over-her-shoulder-as-her-boots-hit-the-dirt breathtaking.

Ivy Spencer. I look at her now and wonder how I could've forgotten her name.

She follows suit, relaxing a little as she sits down across from me. I take a breath before I continue. I wasn't intending for this interview to start off so intensely. I'm not actually an asshole. I just have so much going on all the damn time that I speak swiftly, and nine times out of ten out of frustration just so I can move on to the next task.

"Look, if we're being honest here, you are young, you can't have more than what? Five years' experience?"

There's that defiant look again, her heart-shaped face gives nothing away, high cheekbones, a slender straight nose, and plump pink lips, those features are all perfectly settled. It's her eyes. Her eyes are stormy and tell me she's fixing to put me in my place and fast. If I wasn't so fucking exhausted today, it might amuse me.

"Almost *fifteen*, actually. If you count all my intern hours, but even without that, I have a degree in equine studies from U of K, on a full scholarship, five years of training thoroughbreds at Bellingham Ranch." She cocks a brow as if to ask, *impressed yet, Mr. Ashby?* "Three years at Nottingham Rehabilitation Center before that as a cooperative. Oh, and four summer internships with the American Quarter Association under Peter Sampson during high school and college." She mentions a well-known trainer who helped to train the 2015 Triple Crown winner.

Well, fuck.

"Hasn't anyone ever told you? Assumptions most always get you nowhere," she says. A coy little grin turns her pretty lips up, and something about it makes me want to do all sorts of things, most of which are highly inappropriate, to wipe that look right off her face.

I grunt and she seems to relax a little.

"Look, I'm good at what I do. I have a modern approach that I'm guessing this ranch doesn't run with—one that might help you—especially if you're hoping to make another derby run at some point," she offers.

I look at her and wonder if she could possibly be the one to take over. Fifteen years? So she's been working with horses since she was . . . a kid? I shake my head, some compartment of my brain asking me why I'm so interested in her life story.

She stands up and motions for the door.

"You want to show me around this place while we talk or is this interview just going to be you sitting there judging me silently?"

My mouth falls slack for a brief moment with her sassy tone, then I get it together and return my hat to my head as I stand.

"Barns are this way," I huff out as I breeze by her.

Twenty minutes later, we're standing outside our large arena watching one of our trainers, Dusty, try to work with a nervous new colt. This colt is skittish and just getting him to keep eyes and not spook has been a task.

Ivy stands watching, learning the horse's ways like she has a telepathic connection with him while I answer questions from three of my ranch hands. For some reason, all of a sudden they've decided they need to be working right where Ivy and I are. As if I don't know it's because she's the attraction of the hour.

One of my leads is chatting Ivy up like they're old friends. They laugh, and I instantly know this woman cannot work here. She's too distracting, too charming. These fuckers will never get anything done if she's here, and I'm all about productivity on my ranch. The last thing I need is one more thing to worry about on the daily.

"How's it going, Sarge?" Nash, my lifelong friend, claps me on the back as he was coming from breakfast at the Big House with my mother and sister.

"Argh," I grunt out.

"That good?" he asks, chuckling. "You think maybe you're being too hard on her? Six minutes late? Really?"

"Maybe. Her résumé is good." I give that much to him, watching as she grabs a training stick down from the tack wall and takes it upon herself to enter the coral.

Nash and I look at each other and then quickly go after her as she swings the gate open, making sure it's safe to enter.

"Mind if I try?" she asks Dusty boldly.

Dusty looks at her like, *who the fuck is this?* And then he smiles wide.

"Have at it, he's a stubborn bugger, won't let me assert any type of dominance with him."

She nods and takes her place in the ring in front of the feisty horse.

"You ever heard of the Parelli Program?" she asks both Dusty and myself.

"Can't say I have," I say as I watch her take the leader rope from Dusty. She's a different person now than she was when she was all fired up in my office. This woman right here is calm, collected, and perfectly at home around this antsy horse. She takes a moment to graze one hand down his nose and whispers something to him none of us can hear.

"It's the idea that horsemanship can be obtained naturally through communication, understanding, and psychology, versus mechanics, fear, and intimidation."

She takes the training stick and lets the string hanging off the bottom come up and rest over the horse's back before sliding it off gently. The horse spooks, but instead of her tightening up on his rope, Ivy simply raises a hand to him and then gives the horse more space.

"That's not the way we do it around here," I say to her as I lean up to the rail and watch her, because, fuck, watching Ivy with this horse is almost mesmerizing.

"Why do you do it the old-fashioned way?" she queries.

To which I lamely reply, "Because that's the way it's always been done."

Ivy keeps moving, trading between trailing the string over the horse's back and swiping it in circles like a lasso in the dirt.

377

Every time the horse spooks, she whispers something to him and then centers him by bringing the string back over his barrel, and fuck, after ten minutes of this continuously, he manages to keep his eyes on her and move with her for a solid thirty seconds, calmly rounding in a circle with her as she leads him.

"See, the way I've been trained is, you want to have a real partnership with your horse. That requires earning his trust and helping him to feel safe. And we can't do that with the old-fashioned, traditional training methods. What they do look for is safety and security. And if they don't find that with us, they will never trust us. They will never become willing partners."

"Sounds like some kind of new age hippy shit to me," I bark out without thinking as Nash nudges me in the ribs with his elbow. Clearly, what she's doing is working. I just don't like being wrong, or out of control. Both of which I am right now.

Ivy takes the horse around the pen a few more times, continuing her method, and when she's satisfied he's had enough, she unhooks the leader and lets him turn out. Walking up to me, she pushes the training stick to my chest, looks up at me with those blue eyes, and says, "Hey, you're the chief around here. I'm just telling you what's worked for me is all. Just like working with people, you gotta build respect, not just expect it. Thanks for the opportunity. I'd love to help your family's ranch while Sam is away." She breezes between Nash and me and turns back over her shoulder, "That is if you don't *assume* I'm not up to the task." She smiles as she says it.

Nash leans into me and whispers "Fuck, Sarge. I think you just met your match."

I cross my arms over my chest and watch her go, knowing full well not only is she going to be trouble but fuck, she pretty much just hired herself.

ONE
Wade

October

"**B**efore my mind is ready, my body is. Chase grabs me by the back of my head, fisting my hair as his mouth devours mine."

"Christ almighty, do you do anything else?" I grunt as I fumble to turn down the volume on the stereo that isn't mine in the truck I don't own.

"I want him on his knees. I want him to drown in my—"

"You need help there, Chief?" Ivy giggles beside me as I finally grasp the right knob to turn down her audiobook so we can avoid listening to the narrator climax us all the way back to the ranch.

"I've got it," I bite out. I push two silky hair ties down on the shifter so I can pop Ivy's Silverado into reverse.

I'm not surprised that I have to fight off these damn things to be able to do something as simple as drive. In the few short weeks Ivy has worked on my ranch, I'm pretty sure she's left one in every crevice of the silos office imaginable. It was day one when she left one on my desk, then came looking for it later, that I learned hair elastics have a specific term when they're all soft and fluffy like this. Scrunchie, and Ivy hoards them. All different shades, all different patterns, as if she may suddenly need thirty-two extra ones at a moment's notice. She has a tower of them on her desk, every color of the rainbow and then some. Bright and happy looking twenty-four-seven—just like her.

In fact, everything about this woman is feminine and sunshiny, including this truck of hers I've been roped into driving tonight. There's a piña colada air freshener hanging from the rearview and a mishmash of lip balms and hand creams in the cup holders. It's a goddamn beauty parlor on wheels.

Her crimson painted lips curl into a devilish grin with my open disdain of her book choice.

"Drive a girl's truck and you have to live with the consequences." Ivy laughs. "You know I like my books." Her wide, almond-shaped eyes dance with mischief as she pulls my blazer tight over her red evening dress, the one I lost to her when she said she was cold and Cole's sleazy cop buddy was about to offer his to her. I'm driving her home. It only makes sense she wears mine.

"Just another way for me to shake your nerves, boss . . . don't you know I do it on purpose?" She giggles as I shake my head at her.

I don't doubt she does. She's been throwing me off and testing my "always in control, always have a plan" mantra since the first day I met her. But she was clearly my best choice as our lead temporary horse trainer. I'll admit she impressed me during her interview, and her mentor with the AQA wouldn't shut up about her when I called him for a reference.

After working with her day in and day out over the last few weeks, I can see what he's raving about. Ivy is brilliant with a knack for calming the horses and connecting with them like no one I've ever seen; she never loses her patience from our feistiest colts to our slow-as-molasses old steeds.

But fuck, she gets under my skin. It's not her fault, it's

mine, because I'm having a hard time ignoring that not only is she gorgeous, but the more I get to know her, the more I realize she's totally oblivious to her looks and her sassy, alluring charm. Which means she thinks nothing of it when every ranch hand I have bends over backwards to get up early and deliver her coffee in the morning or when they offer to take on some of her morning chores for her. These pricks have never shown up early for work a day in their lives, and all of a sudden, they're in the barn before the roosters rise and happy as fuck about it?

Ivy is thrilled they're all "so nice," as she's told me on many occasions, which leads me to believe that for how experienced she presents herself to be, she is a bit naive about the opposite sex.

This has me both keeping an eye out for her constantly and sobering myself up from getting caught staring at her too. I'm holding it together, but it's only been a few weeks and I'm pretty sure the balance of it has aged me ten years already.

I salute my younger brother Cole goodbye out my window as I pull out of our town pub's parking lot. He's standing in the doorway of the Horse and Barrel watching me go, grinning like a fool at me driving Ivy's truck off the lot.

I'm only her chauffeur because my sister CeCe and her girl crew adopted Ivy as one of their own tonight, inviting her to celebrate CeCe's new engagement "Not-Angels" style. Which basically means, drink way too much, and dance all night long on the Horse and Barrel dance floor. So here I am, leaving anyone behind us with a bumper sticker that says COWGIRLS JUST WANNA HAVE FUN.

I look over at her smug grin, and I gather she thinks her book smut has embarrassed me.

"I'm sorry I made you blush at my romance novel," she hums as she pulls her hair down, not sounding sorry in the slightest. I watch in my periphery as it tumbles in waves around her shoulders.

"It takes more than a little *smut* to make me blush," I retort.

Ivy makes a wounded face at my words.

"It's a steamy romance book, not *smut,* and it was just getting to the good part when I got to the bar. I was looking forward to it for on the way home. I didn't expect you'd be driving me." She snickers, still not a hint of embarrassment in her tone.

It's not lost on me that not only does she read it any chance she gets, she also just drives around town listening to full-out porn on any given day and owns it. I'm all about a woman being confident in her own skin and enjoying sex and everything it has to offer, but because I'm my own worst enemy, I scoff at the term she used—*romance*—loud enough for her to swat at me.

She laughs, the cocky laugh of too many "Nash and CeCe are engaged so let's party shots." "Well, we can't all be grumpy prudes; excuse me for enjoying a good love story."

I'm just going to keep my mouth shut here. I'm the furthest thing from a prude she'll ever meet. In fact, I'm a firm believer that there should be no limits when it comes to sex. To hold back would be a waste in the one area of life you can let go, an escape.

So . . . grumpy? Sure. Prude? Not a fucking chance.

"Oh, no, you don't, don't even think you're staying quiet. Inquiring minds want to know, what's making you huff out all those judgy noises at me? Have you got something to say about my choice in literature?" Ivy challenges, then adds, "Cat got your tongue?"

I scrub my face with my free hand. I'm still not completely used to this smug little firecracker and the way she can manage to get under my skin.

"Come on now, spill it," she says, cocking one eyebrow at me. I turn to her for a split second while I drive.

"The plot of this book has fucking nothing to do with love or romance," I deadpan, pointing to the dash.

"Yes, it does," Ivy argues defensively, feigning shock before she adds, "I mean, they both seem to love her in their own way."

They? Jesus fucking Christ.

"Alright, I'll bite. Let's start with this. What's it *called?*" I ask as we pass the Laurel Creek town sign and start cruising through the dark countryside.

"What's it called?" she repeats my question, taking her plush bottom lip between her teeth.

"That's right. This steamy romance you're hell bent on defending, what's the title?" I look over at her, counting the seconds she sits in silence. "What's the matter?" I ask. "Smutty book name got your tongue?"

Ivy grimaces. "No . . . it's just, that's not a fair question because the title doesn't sound romantic."

Now I'm invested.

She looks down to check her nails, in the dark no less, as if they need her attention desperately.

"What's the name, Trouble?" I repeat.

Ivy sighs and stares out the window. "Filthy Lords of Sin," she whispers, barely audible.

I nod. "My mistake. Sounds mighty romantic."

Ivy huffs out a breath but doesn't say one more word on the subject and keeps her eyes out the window.

I rest my fucking case.

I let her off the hook and get the radio working. Colter Wall croons to us as we drive. I settle into it. But the silence only lasts all of three minutes because this woman must talk cheerful chatter at all times.

383

"What a beautiful party for the sweetest couple. I know I've only been here a little while but I really like your family. They're all so nice."

"Yeah, they're all just swell," I say, sounding way more bitter than I intend, before I add, "Never thought I'd see Nash settle down."

My best friend of twenty years and soon to be brother-in-law—officially. It was a surprise to say the least when I found out he was seeing CeCe in secret all summer. But after I had the chance to calm down and realize what his intentions were, I knew without a doubt that they are perfect for each other. Even if their constant kissing and hand holding makes me want to toss up my last meal, I'm glad Nash and my baby sister are happy together; maybe they'll actually break the Ashby curse that has always plagued the three of us when it comes to relationships.

"I just have one question and stop me if it's too personal," Ivy says.

Ah, fuck.

"Don't do personal," I bite out.

"You don't say?" Sarcasm lines her tone. "I promise it won't sting, I'm just curious." She takes my silence as the go ahead. "I just don't get it, what's the real story behind your family then?"

I blink at her, not understanding.

"I mean, they're all so nice and welcoming, and they seem like fairly happy people, so are you like, adopted, maybe grew up in a different household? The long-lost brother that still holds a grudge?"

I turn to look at her. Ivy's blue eyes dance with all the trouble that earned her that nickname. I feel my brow furrow as she laughs at her semi-funny joke for way longer than warranted.

"You know . . . your face does things other than scowl?" she muses as we pull down the driveway of Silver Pines, my family's ranch and training center. My home. My responsibility.

I pass my cabin on the old dirt road to get her home. Ivy has taken Blue Eyes, our fifth cabin, as her humble abode for her time here. It's the one closest to mine. She could have chosen any of the cabins that were empty, but she chose Blue Eyes for two reasons that she prattled on about. One, because she so obviously states, her eyes are blue, which in my opinion is kind of an understatement. They're so blue they're almost violet some days, the color of a cloudless winter sky . . . or whatever.

And her second self-proclaimed reason is because the Blue Eyes deck backs onto the north woods and she says she likes her privacy.

Probably so she can sit out there and read her smutty books in peace.

"Home sweet home," she quips as she turns to me. "Well, thanks for driving me home, Captain Joyful, it was a fun night aside from the last fifteen minutes, of course."

The only response I give her is a huff as I hop out of the truck and walk around to her side. Ivy removes my suit jacket from her curvy frame and hands it to me as she climbs out.

"I'm not cold anymore, thanks," she says as I take it and trade with her, dropping her keys into her palm. Our size difference is a lot more noticeable when we're only a foot apart. She barely reaches past the top of my shoulder even in those shoes she's wearing. I wait, expecting her to go into her house but instead, she mumbles something like, *not waiting one more second,* as she struggles to remove her black heels in the grass.

"Mmm . . . goddamn, that feels good." She groans a throaty sound that makes me swallow, *hard.* "I've been wanting to do that all night." She giggles innocently as the other heel comes off and a few more inches disappear from her height. She turns a smile up to me.

I look away from her to clear my head of the noises she's making while she mumbles how good the grass feels on her bare feet, something about grounding herself to the earth while I gesture to her front door. She looks at it, then back to me with an *are-you-serious?* face.

"I think I'll make it in, boss; you can go home now. I mean, you can see my porch from your porch." She points at my cabin only two hundred feet away.

I shake my head. "I'll go home once you're inside."

She tips her head back and laughs as she saunters up her front steps. "Okay, I'll humor you," Ivy calls over her shoulder. "But only because I've had a few drinks. I'm a big girl though, I can handle myself." She pats her purse and winks. "Bear spray."

Of course she has bear spray in her purse. The little spit-fire probably wouldn't even need it; she'd probably bond with the bear and feed it from her back door.

"Night, Chief, see ya early," she singsongs. Her door closes and I'm left standing there shaking my head at the whirlwind that is Ivy Spencer.

I toss my coat over my forearm and walk the short distance to my own cabin, Bluegrass.

My cabin is the biggest on the property besides the Big House itself. It's the boss's cabin, the only one with two bedrooms and two bathrooms, and I've finally got it the way I want it after being back here since my separation. I've done most of the work myself to update the kitchen with Cole's help.

I walk through the front entryway and flick the light on. I breathe in a sigh of peace. This is my place. Dark log cabin walls and weathered wood floors fill the open space. It still smells faintly like leather and tobacco from previous residents over the years. The little kitchen straight ahead has new walnut cabinets and stainless-steel appliances.

There is a good-size living room to the left, with a floor-to-ceiling cobblestone fireplace and windows that look out to the Big House and barns in the distance. It's the perfect place to sit with a whiskey at the end of the day listening to my favorite vinyl. It's also the only place I don't have to worry about leading everyone, about the ranch, my mom living alone as she gets older, filling my dad's boots, Janelle, the future.

This is my space to just be Wade, whoever the fuck that is these days. No time for self-reflection when you have an entire ranch to run and next year's derby pressure breathing down your back. I loosen my tie and toe my uncomfortable as fuck dress shoes off. I'm mentally going over tomorrow's workday as I feel something light hit my foot while I'm hanging up my suit coat.

I bend down and scoop it up to get a closer look. Ivy was wearing my coat for all of twenty goddam minutes. I bring the soft fabric to my nose and breathe in Ivy's sweet, sugary-like scent. *Fuck me*, it's nice. I pop the black satin scrunchie in the basket on my fridge as I head for the shower.

Finders keepers.

PAISLEY HOPE is an avid lover of romance, a mother, a wife, and a writer. Growing up in Canada, she wrote and dreamed of one day being able to create a place, a world where readers could immerse themselves, a place they wished was real, a place they saw themselves when they envisioned it. She loves her family time, gardening, baking, yoga, and a good cab sav.

Instagram: @authorpaisleyhope